THE WARPATH

BY ZOE SAADIA

THE WARPATH

People of the Longhouse, Book 4

ZOE SAADIA

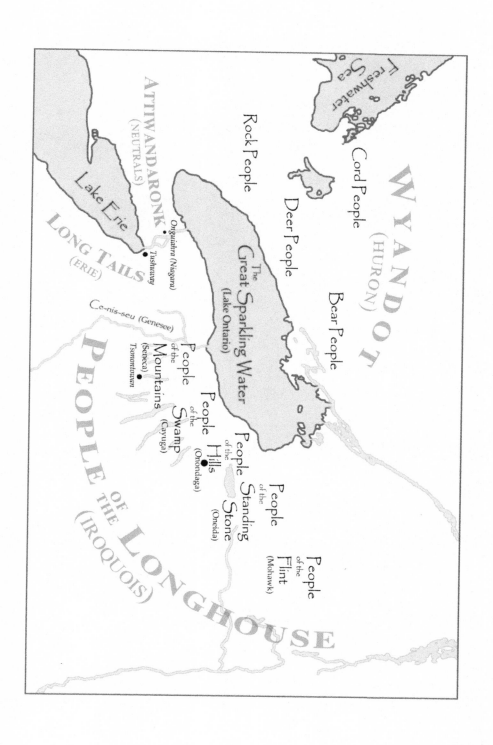

Freshwater Sea

WYANDOT (HURON)

ATTIWANDARONK (NEUTRALS)

Lake Erie

LONG TAILS (ERIE)

Rock People

Cord People

Deer People

Onguiaahra (Niagara)

Tushuway

Bear People

Ce-nis-seu (Genesee)

The Great Sparkling Water (Lake Ontario)

People of the Mountains (Seneca)

Tsonontowan

People of the Swamp (Cayuga)

People of the Hills (Onondaga)

People of the Standing Stone (Oneida)

People of the Flint (Mohawk)

PEOPLE OF THE LONGHOUSE (IROQUOIS)

PROLOGUE

In the lands of the Long Tails,
the eastern edge of Lake Erie

The smoothness of the antler felt slick in her palm, glassy, hard, *reassuring*. It was there to protect her, ever since Grandfather gave it to her and told her to keep it by her side, never to let it slip away.

He had made it especially for her, the knife and the bow, both exceptional tools, works of art. Not the regular hastily prepared weapons, but beautiful instruments. Other people may run around, sporting their simple knives, wooden handles and all. People of this strange, towering settlement for one. They were certainly fond of their weaponry, all those hurried along men, if not women. She didn't make a mistake of letting any of them close, still there was enough time—close to a full moon spent around this place—to make observations.

The man she was watching began talking again, addressing a younger person, a boy about her own age, fifteen summers at the most. Giving instructions, most obviously. His body language was as clear as the sky on a cloudless day. The boy was to run around, deliver a message.

To other gloomy, agitated men, the ones who frequented this man's vicinity? She knew the answer to that. He had received another messenger not long ago, this time a hardened warrior of many summers. They had conversed for a long time, and their body language spoke of agitation mixed with excitement. The news this man received was important. Briefly, she wondered what it was, unable to read their lips, not from such a distance.

The knife cut the air, sticking into the ragged surface of the nearby stump, not too close to where she squatted. Hastily, she rushed to retrieve it. It was not the time for such plays. This man surely didn't notice her following him now, and even though he didn't seem to mind on some other occasions, she didn't want to take any chances. Not this time. These woods weren't her woods, and people were not creatures to be trusted. Grandfather knew what he was talking about.

She fixed her eyes on the man again. Done with his messages, he had turned around, his limp more pronounced than before. Climbing the upward path of the nearby hill must have been difficult with a leg as bad as his. She didn't know what was wrong with it, but it was easy to track his footprints, with one mark being firm, decisive, printed strongly in the muddy earth of the forest, while the other was muffled, tilted strangely, seeming unsure of itself.

Squinting against the glow of the afternoon sun, she tried to see where he was heading. That farther cluster of trees, surely. For a while, she contemplated her next step.

The knife left her palm again, to stick into the bark of the nearest tree, at the spot she planned for it to hit. Even when out of her reach, the glitter of its handle reassured her. Not a simple wooden handle, not on *her* knife. The viciously sharp, curving flint was attached to the perfect smoothness of the antler with special glue, secured with thoroughly tanned pieces of hide, not about to come off, not even when dealing with things that were hard to cut. She had made such a vast use of her knife since she had been given this treasure. Especially since the last snows had melted, since before…

Slipping out of her hiding place and along the moss-covered stones, she sniffed the faint smell of cooking coming out of the town, just up the opposite hill. Oh, but it was terribly hard sometimes to keep away. The aroma of cooking meals was spreading so far. Sometimes it would make her drift close, play with the idea of sneaking in through this or that opening in the fence, against her better judgment. Still, she managed to keep her hunger in check. The woods were safer, offering enough treats to a person who knew where to look and how.

Pitting her face against the softness of the afternoon breeze, such a pleasant feeling in this early summer moon, she contemplated where this man would have held yet another clandestine meeting. Not very far, for certain, not with the evening being imminent. She knew the pattern of those meetings by now. He didn't bother to go too far out, making his gatherings brief, just a quick exchange of information and some fuming around, nothing more.

Unless people of the nearby villages were involved. But even those visitors bothered to come here. With his peculiar way of walking, it took the others half the time to reach their destinations. Must be frustrating.

Another brief moment of contemplation, then she slipped down the hill, in the direction he had disappeared earlier. Sometimes she didn't even bother to conceal her presence. No one seemed to notice her; no one seemed to care.

CHAPTER 1

"The Wyandot leader is dead."

Meeting the gazes that leapt at him from all around, Aingahon lingered at the edge of the clearing, part of his mind calculating, measuring his way to the stump of a tree, taking in possible obstacles. Not many in this case. The clearing was small, even if packed with people, yet his knee protested more vigorously now, sending shafts of sharp pain up and down his leg. It needed to rest, to be wrapped in a supportive band preferably, a treatment that sometimes would help. But not always.

If only there was a way to make that knee right again. He pushed the familiar desperation away. *First, deal with the people you summoned here, then rest.* His news was important, and it couldn't wait.

"Which one?" asked one of the squatting men when no one else ventured a comment.

"The most important one," was Aingahon's laconic response.

Skirting around the remnants of the last night's fire, he put his attention on the attempt not to trip over scattered logs and pinecones, clenching his teeth quite against his will. The pain was still bearable, not the worst of it; just the regular dull throbbing, turning piercing only if he trod on his leg without caution, forgetting the need to watch his step. Not a frequent occurrence these days. After more than two spans of seasons, he had grown used to dealing with his disability, knowing how to move without making his damaged knee work too hard, take much weight or creak in a bad way. If it happened, the pain would explode in a terrible manner, causing his heart to stop and his chest to squeeze in a crushing grip.

Oh, but how careful he was to avoid such happenings. Even if it took him twice as long as it should have to reach whatever was his destination, inside the longhouse or all over the woods, as long as he didn't have to deal with such dislocation, all was well. Or almost well.

The wave of the familiar rage splashed in the outskirts of his mind, to be dominated quickly, in an accustomed way. His willpower was always one of his best qualities, his inner strength and his patience. The people who had done this to him would pay, they would. They were already paying. In small amounts, but they were. The renewed war—not truly a war but a rising amount of skirmishes, raids that grew in frequency—did bother the so-called Keepers of the Western Door and therefore the Great League in general. And it was his doing. He had worked hard to make it happen.

The elders of Tushuway, his hometown and the leading settlement of the entire region, were divided. Some favored the idea of neutrality, of a peaceful arrangement with the Great League of the Longhouse People and the newly concocted Wyandot union alike.

Stuck in the possible path of the two historical foes, the Long Tails People and Attiwandaronk, their neighbors to the north, couldn't do much but keep to their neutrality, could they? They were not strong or numerous enough to oppose either of the unions, unless united themselves, and in this the careful elders didn't believe. Spread too sparsely on too large of a territory, their towns and villages weren't likely to maintain something more complicated than regular trading ties and some peaceful communication. Neutral, unobtrusive.

But how the neutrality hurt! The Mountain People were pushy, a bothersome presence even before their Peacemaker turned them into one political body with their ever aggressive neighbors to the east. The People of the Mountains, the Keepers of the Western Door, were a longtime enemy, but now, backed by the other four nations, they became complacent and pushy.

And yet, after all was said and done, it became apparent that his people's immediate neighbors still warred on their own, claimed more radical, or maybe more sharp-eyed people, Aingahon among them. The Great League did not send warriors' parties to reinforce the frequent skirmishes of the Mountain People. They were *only talking* about their united might, but in fact they were still what they were, five different nations that had stopped fighting among themselves. Nothing more.

They wanted to dominate, to rule, to tell others what to do, but they didn't see the need to invest in it. They weren't one nation. And with the suddenly united Wyandot, the presumptuous union might remain busy elsewhere, leaving their neighbors, such as Long Tails People, to live in peace. Or in war, if they chose to do so; to organize into something more than just scattered villages of different smaller nations. And why not? Even Attiwandaronk People might be willing to cooperate, if approached with care and enough consideration. Not overly popular ideas, not among the majority of the elders, but the younger people of considerable summers—not hotheaded youths who didn't count—were inclined to listen. More and more frequently. One good turn.

"The Bear People's leader, the man who held the gathering at the Cord People's lands last Awakening Season," he repeated, suppressing a sigh of relief while dropping onto the vacant seat a fallen trunk provided. No squatting comfortably like the others did, not for him. His knee wouldn't have it. "He embarked on his Sky Journey at the moon of Many Leafs, not so very long ago. His mourning ceremony was a huge affair, with all four nations sending much representation."

"Did he die of an illness?" One of the men picked up a stick, stirring the blackened remnants of an old fire.

"They say he did. He was old enough."

"Not that old." The man from the nearby village, a fearsome warrior with many scars, frowned. "I was privileged to meet this leader two summers ago. He was not elderly or infirm."

Aingahon just shrugged. "They say he dropped dead in the middle of this or that meeting. He was traveling all over, even after that Great Gathering of theirs. Trying to draw the stubborn Deer into his much-cherished union." To roll his eyes seemed inappropriate, but he couldn't help it. "It happened in their lands, and did these grass-eaters get frightened."

Suppressed chuckles were his answer. They all understood the implications. The Deer People might have wished to have their united neighbors woo them, behaving like a pretty maiden, fluttering their eyelashes, not in a hurry to make up their minds, but they certainly didn't want these same powerful nations to turn their united might against their towns in anger. Important leaders were meant to die in their own lands and among their own people.

"So, will we see the enraged Bears and the Cord crushing the Deer in a spectacular display of their united power?" The man with the scar frowned, not amused. "This is one sight I'm not sure I'll be happy watching."

"Not likely. They are too deep in their process of unification. That same leader, he was set on having the Deer in their union. He even died trying to achieve that. His spirit won't leave in peace if his work is to be unraveled now, and because of his death, of all things."

He listened to the swish of a knife that cut the air before sticking into the muddy ground. Time after time. A glance in that direction confirmed what he assumed would be there without looking. The girl was crouching in the enclosure a pair of trees created, indifferent to her tattered clothes or the way the sodden earth splattered all over it, her undivided attention on her knife and the accuracy of each throw. A strange sight, but nothing out of the ordinary.

"You think it will not affect their union or its ways?"

Returning the gaze of the man who had asked, Aingahon concentrated, shaking off the question of the girl and her strangeness, the mystery of the entire town. A group of hunters had stumbled upon this thing earlier in this moon, an underfed, dirty, neglected little creature out of the wintertime stories, brought into the town quite against her will, or at least with no ardent rejoicing on the part of the rescued child.

Since that time, this had become a familiar picture. The girl and the knife. She wouldn't be separated from her favorite weapon, neither by force nor by persuasion. She wouldn't talk to anyone either, never willing to let people close, or even sleep in one of the longhouses. Small offerings of food and sometimes items of clothing were accepted, until the compassionate people stopped trying and let her be, to wander the woods and sleep on the outskirts of the town. Recently, they stopped speculating on that matter, deciding that the puzzle was better be left alone.

Aingahon shrugged, not interested in any of that. The girl wouldn't be running back into the town, reporting this semi-clandestine meeting of his. She couldn't hear, some said. Or maybe speak. Or both. She might have been simple in the head as well.

"It will affect the Wyandot. It will. For the best, as far as our people may be concerned."

All eyes were upon him again, some narrowed, some inquiring, some sealed, impossible to read. They knew where he was heading, but wished someone would express it aloud. Not them. He didn't care. His views were never a secret.

"The Bear People's leader insisted on peace between the Wyandot and the League of our Longhouse neighbors. He wasn't backed by many, but his influence made people comply." Shrugging, he encircled them with his gaze, challenging. "With this man gone, the fragile relationship, any unspoken agreements between the two unions, will fall apart, won't they?"

Their nods were solemn, reserved. Not ready to commit, not yet. As long as the War Chief remained opposed to the opening of the outright hostilities, they preferred to keep their opinions to themselves.

He suppressed another shrug, feeling the girl's eyes upon him. Another regular occurrence. For the last few days, the strange little thing had developed a habit of shadowing him, him in particular, again with no attempts to communicate, ask questions, or receive permission. She would just be there, keeping a safe distance, not trying to catch his eye. Until now. This was the first time she had stared at him openly. Why? Perturbed, he pretended that he didn't notice.

"Some warriors came to talk to the War Chief on the evening

before," said someone, a noncommittal voice.

That snapped his attention back to his peers. "Who?"

"You know very well who."

He regarded the speaker with a stony glare. "If I asked a question, I want to hear an answer to it."

The man's eyes flashed, but he said nothing, just shrugged.

"What did they want to talk to the warriors' leader about?" asked someone hastily, clearly eager to calm the flaring tempers.

"The retaliation, of course." The first speaker shot Aingahon another dark gaze, to be stared down quickly and firmly. "The Mountain People and their so-called Great League," he added, scowling. "We all know what our warriors want."

"Yes, we do." He wanted to leap to his feet, if for no other reason than to pace back and forth, to face his peers as a worthwhile warrior, a possible leader, to render his words more meaning. "We want to attack their settlements. We want and we *need* to do that! We can't live in the constant fear of their raids, safeguarding our villages and towns while doing nothing in return. Are we helpless women or old men? Don't we have the necessary courage to step onto a warpath? What do our leaders think we are? What are they trying to turn us into?"

Unable to fight the tide of familiar agitation, he did shoot to his feet, careful to make his good leg take most of the weight, if not all of it. His bad knee protested with an ominous creak, but he paid it no attention, determined not to let it interfere. Not this time!

"By forcing us to keep quiet, to do nothing but defend, they mark us as cowards, no warriors, no worthwhile men. But worse than that. They present us as such to the despicable enemy. They rub it into their faces, our worthlessness, our inadequacy, our ineptness." Not succumbing to the temptation of stepping forward, he brought his arms up instead. "It is no wonder that the infamous League doesn't bother to even try talking to us in the way they do attempt to reach their half-hearted agreements with the Wyandot. Not true agreements, with no true meaning—their union wouldn't have anyone on an equal footing—but at least they show their respect, while at us they don't even bother to look. They let our traditional enemy, their current keepers of whatever door of their metaphorical longhouse, raid us as they did from the times immemorial, and they never bother to look in our direction at all!"

Out of breath, he paused, aware that he would do better lowering his tone, not shouting at the top of his voice, because the elders had already been eyeing him with suspicion. His frequent arguments, his speeches, his influence among the more restless elements of the town and the surrounding villages, his impatience with more prudent politics, his inability to keep his mouth shut— there had been no deficiency in men who were spoiling for a fight; they were men and not forest mice, just as he said—all these rendered him odious with the authorities, marked him as a troublesome presence.

And so did his injury, he knew, his inability to do simple tasks, to hunt as efficiently as the others, to travel, to war. Not only a bad influence, but also a man who could not contribute fully to the community, participate in clearing fields, building, or doing any other important work. It now took him so much longer to complete his tasks, to achieve results, he who had been such a doer before. A bitter reality, and what an effort it had taken him to come to grips with any of it. But he did this, came to grips, accepted and didn't let his infirmity influence him into stepping aside, slipping into the shadows. It didn't matter what they thought. Or maybe it did, but what could he do about it? *That monumental failure in the lands of the Onondagas, the shameful downfall two summers ago!*

"The Great League is not a stone giant," he said, holding their gazes, sensing their need to hear more. "They claim they are one and many at the same time. One longhouse, five families, they say. But it is not possible, not on such a large scale. What works for clans and towns, doesn't work for nations." Taking a deep breath, he hurried on, feeling their attention physically. Even the strange girl stopped her knife-throwing exercise and was staring at him through her narrowed, strangely tilted eyes. "We've been warring against the Mountain People for many summers, long before their League was born. And even though the warring slowed down through the last decades, we've still raided an occasional village of theirs, while they raided ours." Another glance at the girl confirmed what he always suspected. Her darkening face and glazing eyes were an indication. Was her entire village destroyed, or only her family, he wondered, then forced his attention back to his audience. "And what happened through all these last summers' warring. Did the Onondagas come to their fellow members of the Great League's aid? Did the Flint People from the far east? No! None of them joined this war, just like these same Mountain People don't travel to join the wars in the lands of the rising sun."

The memory of the cheeky, violent, bubbling-with-life fox from that hilly Onondaga town made his stomach shrink like it always did, every time he remembered. That familiar mix of anger and warmth. She was such a strange-looking thing, a total foreigner, not even pretty or sweet, not feminine, not attractive in the usual sort of way, even though he did fancy her.

Had he wanted to take her away when the chance presented itself? He didn't know, didn't bother to face this question. The following events erased any such thoughts from his mind. The disastrous consequences, the pain of the failure. And she'd had something to do with it. He knew she had. Even without the testimony of his worthless countryman who didn't manage to keep an eye on her, letting her get away, with his bow of all things. How useless could a person be! But even without this solid suspicion... After all, how could a girl, any girl, fierce and violent as she was, interfere in a way that not every man would have managed; guessing his intentions, tracking him down in the darkness of the night, shooting him with surprising accuracy? No, it couldn't have been her. And yet, who else was there to interfere, to foil his plans, and in such a way?

"You say that if we start warring on our neighbors in force their so-called allies would not come to their aid?"

The voice of one of the men cut into his flow of thoughts in time, before his anger turned difficult to control. Her arrow had pierced his shoulder back then, not killing him but interfering, hurting, maiming, ruining his plans. Yet, he had managed to get away, to crawl into the woods and take the lethal shaft out, to stop the bleeding, to wash it thoroughly and cover his tracks.

Oh no, that arrow was not what had made getting away nearly impossible, turning his following journey home into a nightmare, not what had made his life misery ever since. The fall that followed this shot was what rendered him useless, with his leg twisted viciously, its knee dislocated, broken, never to heal properly again. But for his people finding him two days later, he would have died back there, in the Onondaga woods.

He pushed another wave of anger away.

"Yes, I say that, and I say that with a good reason. The Great League would not join our unworthy neighbors in their war, just like these same Mountain People do not go to war in the east." He encircled them with his gaze, glad to put his mind on something he could deal with. "The Flint People, whom they call the Keepers of the Eastern Door, are warring against fierce savages from the lands of the rising sun. The Onondagas are dealing with the Wyandot, their recently ridiculously temporary peace agreements notwithstanding. Those won't last. We all know they won't, and they know it too. So they must be busy watching the shores of their Sparkling Water." He paused, but only for a heartbeat, eyeing them one by one. "No one will join our wars in the west. They will be too busy or too indifferent to do that." Shrugging, he let his smile of contempt show. "Their Great League is nothing but a sham. It helps them avoid the opening of the old squabbling between each other, but it does little else, no matter how they try to make it sound like a great union of one people."

They nodded thoughtfully, offering little in the way of an argument. But of course. They weren't his adversaries, all these hunters and warriors whose pride the current stance of uncertain neutrality hurt. These men were various and many, from all over the region, curbed by the councils, mainly the Town Council of Tushuway, Aingahon's own hometown. Such a major settlement, led by cowards. Only a handful, one or two of the more careful elders, but those were influential people. And very headstrong.

The girl was still watching him, staring with her strangely tilted, disquieting eyes. There was something about her gaze, something ominous. The closeness, he knew. It was unsettling enough before, when she would gaze at nothing in particular, but now, filled with concentration, with an obvious thought process, it made his skin prickle. Like facing an animal, he reflected, a forest creature of unknown quality. Smart, dangerous, dedicated to purpose, some purpose.

"Do you know if the War Council will be meeting any time soon?" inquired one of the men, getting to his feet, as they all did. Their meetings were always a brief affair, lacking in preliminary openings or any form of small talk, just a matter-of-fact exchange of information, of ideas that were not to be sounded around the authorities; a glaring opposite to the traditional gatherings, where the flowery speeches would usually turn into a contest, a battle for the speaker's reputation.

Leaning against the nearby tree, trying to make his pose look natural and not the necessity it was, Aingahon glanced at the man who was reluctant to share the information before. The intensity of his gaze made the rebellious peer drop his.

"Tell us."

"I think yes. As far as I know, the War Chief might be prevailed to call a meeting of other leading warriors." Another study of the moss-covered stones that dotted the forested ground ensued. "He has been pressured into doing this. It is not only we, the regular men, who are anxious to prove our worth."

"When?"

But a shrug was his answer. "It is not decided as yet."

He kept staring at the man, willing his adversary to look up. "When you know more, let us know." Hearing the cutting edge to his own voice, he made an effort to control it. "Your help is appreciated. Very much so." A brief glance at the others, who were watching him, all expectancy. "We will meet again soon. After the Strawberry Moon Ceremonies, at the latest."

They nodded readily, not lingering. Not waiting for him to lead their way back to the town, or anywhere. Knowing better than this.

Pursing his lips, he waited for them to dissolve behind the trees, enjoying the silence that prevailed, the lightness of it, the peaceful buzzing of day insects, the cheerfulness of the birds' chirping. The woods didn't mind people's troubles or petty dilemmas. They neither approved, nor condemned. Alliances or wars were nothing to them.

He let his breath out, gathering his courage in order to leave the support of the tree. To start walking after a long pause was usually a challenge he didn't look forward to. Sometimes it was better not to sit down at all.

"What in the name—"

The familiar swish of the knife flying a short distance, to enter the split bark of the nearby tree, caught him unprepared. He had forgotten all about the girl, and now the sharp movement made him fight for balance, struggling to leave his knee out of it.

"What are you still doing here?" Breathing with relief at the lack of pangs of piercing pain shooting up his leg—only a dull throbbing was there, the regular thing—he glared at her, not amused.

She didn't look up, her knife back in her smeared palms, busy preparing another throw.

"Go away," he growled, angered by her lack of response as opposed to the unsuitability of his own agitation. Even his hands shook. The reaction to his struggle not to trigger an outburst from his bad knee, he knew. Still, it was unseemly to tremble like a leaf in the wind.

Again, no indication that she had heard him, but as he moved away from his cherished support, preparing to brave the walk toward the edge of the clearing, her gaze leapt up, filling with tension, measuring and ready to act. In what way?

Fleeing, most certainly, he decided, putting his attention back to his step, but not all of it, just in case. To turn his back on her did not seem like the wisest of choices. That one knew how to handle her knife. Her ability to throw it in one sharp, unerring movement was indisputable. And impressive. It might burrow its way into his back, not with the same ease it was cutting the earth now, but not with terrible difficulty either. The skill and the distance were on her side.

"Why do you follow me?" he asked, studying her openly, for the first time since she had started trailing after him. For quite a few days, come to think of it. He frowned. "What do you want from me?"

Her scowl was brief, passing over her face like a bright cloud, making it look almost regular. *Almost.* The entangled mass of her hair combined with excessive paleness, with streaks of mud and old and new scratches, all those numerous bruises and badly healed cuts, clearly the signs of her living out there in the woods for only Great Spirits knew how long, didn't mark her as regular human creature. He watched the suspicion, the painful concentration seeping out of her eyes, now fixed on his face, not on his own eyes, but lower, somewhere around his mouth. Some people said she couldn't hear, he remembered.

"You can't hear? Is this your thing?"

He recalled the boy from the nearby village, a cousin of his closest of friends many summers ago, when they all had been nothing but mischievous children. He had spoken funny, this boy, with too high of a pitch, uttering words in a different way, shouting rather than talking. He needed to see people's lips to understand what had been said. Always full of funny ideas, amusing things to say, pulling practical jokes, inventing mischievous larks, the deaf boy didn't get teased as often as he could have been. To play on his infirmity was tempting but unsafe. That one wouldn't get angry or violent, but he was sure to get back at his offender, later rather than sooner, as sure as the thunderstorm in early summer he would land some sort of retribution. Still, it was amusing sometimes to creep up behind him and then make a huge amount of sudden noise. How could one not to notice? But this boy wouldn't.

Turning around with care—not only because of his knee now, but as not to startle the wary creature into immediate fleeing—he held her gaze, taking one step closer, bringing his hands forward, palms up, displaying his harmless intentions.

"Do you understand what I say?"

This time, he spoke slower, pronouncing every word, exaggerating the movement of his lips.

Her gaze was fixed on his eyes now, emanating open suspicion. Its narrowness made him feel silly. Was he wrong in his hasty assumption?

"Can you speak?"

She still didn't move, staring at him like a deer about to break into a headlong run – wary, not terrified, sure of its ability to get away.

He froze where he was. "I won't hurt you," he stated, feeling incredibly silly. Maybe she couldn't talk. There were such people. Or those who could do neither. "You've been following me around for quite a while. You may as well tell me what you want."

More wary staring through the narrow slits for the eyes. Those were quite large, nicely spaced, he noticed. Dominating her face, which was small, heart-shaped, wide in the cheekbones but sliding sharply toward the pointed chin. Not an unpleasant-looking thing, but for all the neglect. How old was she?

"At least nod if you hear me, if you understand what I say. Do you?"

The muted mass of hair moved, not in a nod but in a slight tilt of the head. It was as though she was trying to see him better. He watched the unblinking eyes narrowing into near-disappearance.

"Well, if you don't want to talk, stop following me," he said, beginning to turn away. It was getting silly, and he had better things to do than to try fishing for information with the strange creature out of the woods.

"What do you want me to tell you?" The low creaking voice made his heart jump, catching him unprepared. It was too low, too strident to belong to this tiny thing. Was she a bad *uki* and not a human child after all?

Careful to go easy on his damaged leg, he turned back to see her standing where she was, in this ready-to-flee pose. Not a bad *uki*. Just a girl, a neglected little thing lucky to survive in the woods. How long had she been out there all alone, and why? For the first time, he wondered.

"I want you to tell me who are you and why do you follow me."

A frown made her look older, its concentration painful, strange, out of place. Again, her eyes slipped toward his chin.

"You can't hear, can you?" he asked slowly, moving his lips in a pronounced way.

Her shrug was barely visible, just a twist of one shoulder.

"But you understand what I say?"

No reaction this time. Her eyes clung to him, gauging.

He measured his way back toward the fallen stump. Just a few paces. Oh well.

While making himself comfortable, he didn't look at her, stretching his bad leg in a way that relieved some of the constant throbbing, resting it on the bed of a moss-covered surface. The afternoon sun warmed the air, coloring the ground in a spotted pattern, pleasantly soft, the breeze caressing. It was difficult to cling to his anger in such surroundings, no matter what the Longhouse People or the leaders of his native Tushuway did.

Glancing at his unexpected company at long last, he noticed that his move put the girl back at ease, just like he had expected. The frown cleared, and the tensed shoulders relaxed. She wasn't about to squat comfortably and get back to her regular knife-throwing activities, but she didn't seem ready to break into a run either.

He watched her face taking a strangely childish look. How old *was* she?

"Are you hungry?"

A silly question. He had nothing to offer her, not even a snack, a slice of dried meat or a handful of nuts for cracking. All the usual things men carried in their pouches while setting out on even the shortest of missions or forays.

Not surprisingly, her eyes lit with expectation.

"I'll get you a good meal when we are back in town." Encouraged, he held her gaze, the matter-of-fact expression that had replaced some of the wariness promising. "But first tell me what I want to know. Who are you? Where do you come from?"

Another blank stare was his answer.

He tried not to roll his eyes. "What town? Where did you live before?" He listened to his own words ringing loudly, exaggeratedly slow. "Where is your family? Mother? Father?"

The painful frown was back, banishing the lighter expression.

"Don't you have any family?"

Frustrated, he looked away. It was of no use. This girl might be simple-minded, on top of being deaf. Was this why she lived in the woods? Unwanted, maybe banished. No. No family or clan would throw away an unsatisfactory child. But this one wasn't a child, come to think of it, and she was violent, one could see that. Just witness her handling that knife. Had she done something bad, injured someone, or maybe even killed?

He studied her with new interest. Small yes, skinny, underfed, dirty, but not to a disgusting point. She clearly did take a basic care of herself, washed in rivers and ate enough not to go sick on account of hunger. How? He wouldn't imagine such a thing surviving on her own, but here she was, living alone for quite some time, judging by the worn-out rags she wore, adept in using some weaponry. Well, a knife certainly, but maybe other things too. An accurately thrown stone could kill a small prey, a rabbit or a bird.

"Grandfather."

The short word made him jump, again her strident, jarringly dissonant voice catching him unprepared. "What?"

She regarded him with a frowning look of her own. "Grandfather. Family. You asked about family. My family."

"Oh." He tried to collect his senses and fast. "Where is he? Your grandfather."

A shadow crossed her face, making the previously deep frown deepen some more. "He is gone."

"Where to?" A silly question. He wanted to kick himself. Where could a grandfather go but on a Sky Journey, leaving the young vulnerable girl to fare for herself in the woods? Her pressed mouth confirmed his suspicion, now a thin line, almost invisible.

"What town did you live in?"

The narrowness of her eyes threatened to match her lips.

"Clan? Longhouse?" It was of no use. He felt like cursing.

"No town." Again, the answer came where he last expected it. "Grandfather and I, we live by the spring. We have cabin, field. We..." Suddenly, the pressed lips quivered. "We, we don't live there anymore."

His stomach tightening, he watched her blinking one time, then another. Then only the view of her back remained, the tousled mass of her hair covering the sagging shoulders, concealing their trembling, yet not entirely. Only now did he notice that she had spoken in the way the Attiwandaronk people did. So she was coming from the north if so, the western side of the Sparkling Water.

"How long has it been since he left on his Sky Journey?" he asked, at a loss, his compassion welling.

No answer. Getting up with an effort, he made his way toward her desolated figure, careful not to trip.

She may not have been able to hear his advance, but her instincts were evidently good, her other senses honed surely, enough to enable her survival in the woods. Indeed, she whirled back before he was close enough to reach for her shoulder, to touch it in a comforting manner. What else was there to do?

"Wait, don't run away." His hand still stretched forward, palm up, he tried to make his expression as reassuring as possible. "I will not hurt you. And maybe I'll be able to help. Somehow."

How?

He didn't know that. Yet, one thing was certain. Strangely wild this girl might be, a true survivor judging by her story and her appearances, she could not be left with no word of encouragement, not a pat on her back. She was in a dire need of company, at least a little bit of it, no matter how independent and unfriendly she might have appeared.

"Stay here and tell me your story," he said slowly, not daring to move, despite the protests of his bad knee. "Then we'll go back and you eat. Something tasty. A good meal. The women of our longhouse will be back from their fields soon, to warm morning meals. Something good. Mashed beans with bear meat. Wouldn't you kill to eat some like that now?"

The eyes that stared at him were wide open again, filling with life.

"But first you will tell me what I want to know. Do you understand me?"

A slight twist of the thin shoulder was familiar by now, to be expected. He didn't need to take his eyes off her face to see that.

Nodding toward his previously abandoned seat, he looked at her firmly. "Sit there."

Surprisingly, she complied. A hesitation of a heartbeat, a wary, measuring glance, then she slipped toward the indicated stump, sitting not upon it but next to it, squatting quite comfortably, as though about to stay. Shaking his head, he remained where he was, leaning against the nearest tree for support.

"When did your grandfather embark on his Sky Journey? When did it happen?"

A familiar half-shrug was to be predicted.

"What season was it? What moon?"

She frowned as though trying to remember. Looking like a child confronted with a difficult question, he thought, amused ever so slightly. *Displaying* how hard she was thinking.

"Cold," she said finally. "It was cold." Another quick pondering. "Snow everywhere."

It didn't make sense. The Cold Moons were long behind them now that the summer was near its highest. He studied her, free to do so as she was still busy wandering her memories, now for real, not pretending. Could it be that this thing had survived all alone in the woods for so long? Two seasons at the very least, some of it being the vicious Cold Moons? No, it couldn't be. Even though her appearance testified for her words.

"We were hungry. Because he couldn't hunt. He was coughing all the time, made much noise. The animals were scattering," she was saying, her words rolling lightly now, with no effort, although the quality of her voice didn't improve, the same disharmonious ups and downs. "We put traps, snares. He was trying to prepare for the Cold Moons. Trying to store as much meat as we could. There wasn't much corn, you see? Our field, it was good, but somehow the maize didn't grow well this time, only the squash." Suddenly, her eyes focused, fixed on him, eager to convince. "I hunted rabbits, you see? And other small game. I shoot good. I never miss! But Grandfather wouldn't let me go far, to hunt something serious. He said no. He never let me go to the woods all alone. Only close by." Again, her lips quivered, and her eyes dropped to study the ground.

Aingahon sighed. "So you had a hungry winter, eh?" To predict her half-shrug was easy. He shook his head. "Where did all this happen? How far from here?"

Another lift of the thin shoulder. Poor thing. She didn't want to remember. Had she wandered away from their hut the moment she could after the old man died? Or did she have to wait for the snow to melt? To roam the woods for so many moons, alone, unprotected, unable to hear. No wonder her grandfather wasn't ready to let her—

Suddenly, the thought hit him, and he peered at her, startled. Her eyes were boring holes in the ground. For some time by now, since after she stopped talking, and yet, she had reacted to his words. She most certainly had. Or was this last shrug just an involuntary movement?

"Your grandfather died during the Cold Moons?" he asked loudly, testing her.

No reaction. So maybe it was just a coincidence. He nodded to himself.

"Yes."

Again, it caught him off guard. He narrowed his eyes, although his glare went quite unnoticed, as she was still studying the ground.

"You can hear what I say." He made it a statement.

This time both fragile shoulders lifted in a somewhat challenging manner.

"Why do you talk strangely, then?" His irritation welled, together with his tiredness, and the old frustration. He needed to make his way back to the town—a challenge in itself with the way he walked—to seek an opportunity to talk to the War Chief. The leading warrior wouldn't grant him an interview upon his request. He would know better than that. But he, Aingahon, had promised to talk to the stubborn leader nevertheless. Some of the most impatient of his followers demanded that. A fruitless attempt, but one he knew that needed to be made. They all must know that a peaceful way of solving the matter had been explored.

He glanced at the girl, suddenly anxious to be on his way. Her story was sad, touching, but he had no time for this. She should have been confining with some of the town's womenfolk. They would have known what to say, how to help.

The large eyes were peering at him, studying him openly. "I hear better now, yes." She seemed as though tasting her words before letting them roll out of her mouth, in no breathless rush like before. "When it thunders, I hear it. Or the river. Or falls. Even rain..." Her eyes sparkled with excitement. "I can hear them sometimes." Then a surprisingly mischievous smile flashed. "When you speak, I can hear a little. And the other men. But not when you talk all at once. And not when women speak. Women are difficult."

He felt his own frown spreading. "It doesn't make sense."

She shrugged. "Grandfather said it does. He talked about low sounds. Something about them being easier to hear. Somehow."

Now it was his turn to shrug. "I need to go." Then he remembered his promise. "Come. We'll get you that bean porridge I promised. With plenty of bear meat and some maple syrup, eh?" The way she hesitated, seeming as though about to shrink back to her previous air of wary uncertainty, brought the wave of compassion back. "You have nothing to fear out there in the town. No one will hurt you, or force you into anything you don't want to do." He suppressed a sigh, knowing that he was getting into something he didn't want to. "If you would feel better about it, I'll keep an eye on you while you are there."

Her frown deepened, then cleared all at once, like a stormy cloud blown out of the sky by a gust of strong wind. Not wasting her time on any more talk, she jumped to her feet. "You promise, yes?"

He stifled a sigh. "Yes."

CHAPTER 2

"What in the name of the Sky Spirits are you doing here?"

Staring into the handsome broadness of his brother's face, Ganayeda drew a deep breath, not trying to conceal the depth of his surprise.

It had been very busy around Onondaga Town, with the entire region bubbling, agitating with life, preparing for yet another meeting of the Great Council. Nothing new or out of the ordinary; still, such events drew much attention, requiring a great deal of preparing and organizing. Especially from the people entrusted with the responsibility of making it all work.

The smile of satisfaction was again difficult to hide. Oh, yes, since coming back from the lands of the Crooked Tongues a whole span of seasons ago, he had certainly been noticed, recognized for his abilities and skills. A very pleasing development that kept him busy, working day and night sometimes, yet not feeling like complaining, not at all. Required to report directly to the true leaders, the Head of the Great Council, the War Chief, and other important representatives, he was on his way up now, a sure thing.

"Me? Nothing. Just wandering around." Smirking, Okwaho shifted his shoulders, looking more impressive than ever, his warrior's lock swaying in the breeze, decorated with colorful strings, the freshly shaved parts of his head glistening, chest bared, sporting a new scar, arms encircled by leather bands, an image of the perfect warrior. "Thought to check on you, smug leaders and organizers. To make sure that you do your work properly."

"Look who is talking about doing things properly. The wandering warrior."

Fighting the wideness of his own grin, Ganayeda looked his brother up and down, pleased with what he saw, despite the showiness on the part of the young beast.

Not so young anymore, Okwaho was busy carving his own path, as glaringly different, as unorthodox as one could have expected from the unruly thing. No painful dilemmas or insecurities, not for this one.

Forceful in a good-natured way, unless pushed, expecting to be approved and accepted as a matter of fact, Okwaho was a force of nature, a person living by his own standards and laws, unconcerned with the rest. If people disapproved or argued, he would just go ahead and do what he deemed necessary to do, oblivious of hurdles, complications, or frowns, investing all this bubbling energy and plenty of hard work in everything he undertook. There was no lack of dedication there, and no lack of adherence. Only the ability of listening to others, one's elders and betters, was missing. Giving his name, his tattoos, and the nature of his guiding spirit, Okwaho was either a lonely wolf or a head of the pack. Nothing in between. No one made the mistake of assuming otherwise these days.

Last Awakening Season, just as Ganayeda had headed for the Crooked Tongues' lands, his brother also departed, his destination unclear. Too restless to keep up with the measured way of the town's life, with the warfare in the lands of the rising sun ceasing to be a possibility due to his woman's origins, Okwaho had wandered westward, taking this same woman with him, scandalizing the entire settlement. Father was reported to be the only one to take this escapade with a measure of good humor, and the active backing of the powerful War Chief made a difference. The authorities frowned but left the matter alone.

When Okwaho came back, a moon or so later, he was said to tell interesting stories. The Mountain People, the Keepers of the Western Door, reported unrest among their immediate neighbors, the would-be neutral Long Tails. Occasional raids were nothing to worry about, but the Crooked Tongues' efforts of organizing into a union had done something to those smaller outside nations spread on too wide of a territory, rounding the western side of the Great Sparkling Water.

Something was brewing there, claimed Okwaho, his observations based on nothing but occasional stories, rumors, assumptions, but those made his skin prickle, he had told Father. Something was wrong in the west; something was happening.

Convinced with surprising ease, and not only because his son was involved, as some narrow-minded people claimed, the War Chief consulted with other leading people, even the Head of the Great Council, and shortly thereafter, Ganayeda's brother was reported to disappear in the mists of the east again, officially this time, leading a small band of hand-picked men.

To do what?

Not many knew. To ask questions, some claimed, or maybe offer help, give advice, participate in the warfare. A warrior of Okwaho's experience and skill could always be of a great help in any troubled area. Ganayeda had no doubts about that.

This time, his woman did stay behind. At least that! Given a choice, the wild thing would have taken a bow and joined her unorthodox husband in his unorthodox enterprises. Or so claimed Jideah, amused and indignant at the same time. There was a limit to messing with convention, even where his young hothead of a brother was concerned.

Through all this, Ganayeda has still been away, attending the Crooked Tongues affair, busy with his own dilemmas and troubles. A truly important happening that worried the Great Council to the greater extent than some petty squabbling in the lands of the setting sun. But not according to Okwaho. When the young man came back, moons later, just before the first snow, sporting new scars and more warring experience, he was unduly thoughtful, huddling with Father evening after evening, talking and talking, both men, pondering, reflecting.

Something was happening in the lands of the setting sun. The Onondaga War Chief had felt it in his bones, and so did his son, who had headed back there the moment the snows had melted. Alone this time, with no other warriors, and no eager women, with only Father left to explain. A warrior of Okwaho's skill might be of help, claimed the War Chief. He had enough fighting experience, enough natural talent and organization skill to offer good advice.

In fact, Father would say, looking thoughtful, as though listening to his inner voices, this might be an important new position to develop. The entire Great League might benefit from closer cooperation, not only among the representatives as it happened until now, but among its warriors' forces as well. There could be no harm in mutual help, in sharing experience and advice. They were one longhouse now, after all, even if made of five families.

Ganayeda forced his thoughts back to his brother, sensing the new air of calm authority emanating from the crinkling eyes, sitting well with the weathered, prominent features.

"When did you come back?"

"Some dawns ago." Waving away an insistent fly, Okwaho grinned, noncommittal. "Two or three dawns, to be precise."

"Three dawns and you are already here? But you are restless, Little Brother. Didn't you miss High Springs, your family? Your wife, for all the great and small *ukis'* sake?" From the corner of his eye, he saw people heading in their direction, two separate groups, their paces hurried. No more than a few more heartbeats to spend with his brother before he would be accosted with questions or complaints, consulted or asked to help, engulfed with well-concealed messages to relay. He shook his head. "You do have a duty to your woman, you know that? It's not only about making a hasty love to the pretty maiden and then being off again."

Okwaho made a face that resembled a person who had bitten into a sweet strawberry, only to discover that it had a taste of a wild onion. Amused and indignant at the same time. A funny sight.

"Will you lecture me on what to do with my woman?" he cried out, incredulous. Then the amusement won. "You never change, *Big Brother*. Full of useful advice, asked or unasked for, ready to lecture a person to death, or until he cries for mercy."

"I haven't heard you begging for your life yet." Glancing at the approaching people, Ganayeda sighed. "Don't run away. I want to talk to you, to hear all about your last foray into the lands of the setting sun. You came back sooner than we thought. Why? Father expected you to stay there until at least the end of the Hot Moons."

Okwaho's face closed. "Yes, I want to talk to you about that. To hear what you think." The young man's frown deepened. "Father sent messages. Some of them urgent, some can wait." A shrug. "He would be here by now himself, but for the need to wait for the High Springs' representative. Some dignitaries do take their time to start their travels!"

"What are the urgent among his messages?" Nodding at the men who halted at some distance, waiting politely, their expressions sealed, Ganayeda found himself wishing the High Springs' representative would delay for as long as he could. Father was always the most welcomed presence, reassuring and helpful, full of useful advice. But then this gathering, the smoothness of its running, would not be his, Ganayeda's, achievement anymore, would it?

"The Crooked Tongues leader, the one Father was communicating with, is dead." Okwaho's voice dropped to a near whisper. "Father received this news on the day I returned."

"The Bear People's leader?" Incredulous, he stared into the broadness of his brother's face, hoping to hear more, the explanation that would make it clear that he had misunderstood what had been said, that he had heard it all wrong. "It can't be!"

Okwaho's eyes squinted, openly puzzled. "Yes, the Bear People's leader. I think those were Bears. Mother's people, yes? I keep confusing them, Crooked Tongues that they are."

"Yes, those are our mother's people, and their leader was the one who worked with Father to achieve peace between our people. He was an outstanding man."

Was? He tried to make his mind work. How could it be? That man, he wasn't old, not truly. He was of Father's age, more or less. Tall, powerful, fit, walking everywhere with this forceful stride of his, in the middle of everything, managing meetings, handling troubles, solving them, never asleep. He didn't look sick or infirm. He didn't look as though he could be stopped either. Unless...

"Did he die of illness? Or was it..." He didn't wish to say that aloud, a terrible suspicion. This man, he had enemies, aplenty. Like every great leader. Just witness what could have happened to Father on that ill-fated Harvest Ceremony two spans of seasons ago. "How did he die?"

Okwaho's wide shoulders lifted in a shrug. "I didn't ask. But maybe Father knows. He seemed to be shaken by this news as well. Which makes one wonder." Another scan of the narrowed eyes. "I understand his feelings, but I didn't know you were that fond of this man."

Ganayeda drew a deep breath. "He was a great man, great leader. I was privileged to learn from this man."

"I see." The teasing spark disappeared, replaced by a sincere nod. "I'm sorry, Brother. Sorry to hear about your loss."

"It's not only my loss, or Father's. In this man our people have lost a firm ally, a true partner, a person we could trust to respect the reached agreements."

He caught his breath, realizing the implications. Oh, but this man's death did change things, on a large enough scale to have them all worried. Not many wanted that peace, the fragile, tottering understandings that were achieved. On either side, few were the people of influence who would stop the war from breaking with vengeance. Only two men, to be precise. Father, and that other man, now gone, dead, most untimely.

"The war with the Crooked Tongues is back in the air, isn't it?" Okwaho's eyes were an open study, squinted into slits.

"Maybe." He forced his mind to focus. "What else do you know?"

The full lips twisted in a familiar half-grin. "About the Crooked Tongues? Not much else. Father would have more to tell you, I'm sure." A light nod toward the waiting people related the old mischievous lightness. "Everything else would wait until you are free to talk, oh busy dignitary. I'll be around and on the lookout for that precious moment."

Ganayeda fought the urge to grin back, an inappropriate

expression at such a moment. "Do that. Find Osweda or Iheks and tell them to place you next to our tents. We'll have plenty of time this evening, hopefully just the two of us, at least some of the time. Then you will tell me all your news."

The young man's grin widened, turned more crooked than before. "We'll spend this evening together, Brother. Of course we will. But don't count on me sleeping next to your tents or staying around for more than this much-awaited evening. I'm off with the first light."

Already turning away, Ganayeda halted. "What do you mean? Where will you be going?"

One muscled arm rose, indicating the general direction of the lake, or somewhere around. "Here and there. I will be back to attend the ceremonies of the first opening day, though. Fancy showing Kentika how our people manage their affairs, in a grand style. She has never seen anything even remotely close to it."

"Your woman? Is she here?" Again, he found himself staring.

"Yes, she is. Wild bears wouldn't make her stay behind after I left her in High Springs since the Cold Moons. So here she is, about to see the Great Gathering with her own eyes. But not before we prowl some of the local woods, having a good time until you organize that whole thing for us to witness." The beaming smile was impossible to stare down, even though Ganayeda did try. "She deserves this break before I head back to the Mountain People and their troubles. It will take long again to come back." The smile disappeared, replaced by a direful frown. "Something serious is going on there. The Long Tails aren't quiet or happy, not anymore. They will give our Western Door Keepers trouble, and soon."

"We'll talk about it this evening," said Ganayeda, swallowing a thousand questions that tottered on the tip of his tongue. "Don't run away before that. Stay as you promised."

"I will, of course I will." Okwaho's arms flew up again, in a defensive gesture. "Kentika will wait until tomorrow. She is a reasonable girl." The large eyes sparkled with familiar baiting challenge. "Since she is getting more than just a quick lovemaking, as you were so kindly worried about, she can afford to be patient."

This time, his grin was impossible to control. "I'm glad to know I was worried in vain." Turning away, he shook his head. "Well, find Iheks anyway. He will help you get around, find a quick snack and all that." Then another thought hit. "Tell him to find the Crooked Tongue from Lone Hill. I need to see him as soon as I can. Tell Iheks this."

What Crooked Tongue? asked arching eyebrows, but he turned around without more explanations. The people who needed to see him had grown into quite a large group, containing all gamut of young or older, with some respectable-looking women among them. Clan mothers? Oh, no. Those meant trouble with supplies, accommodations, discipline, or all in between. A bother!

The hum of the valley interfered with the natural sounds of the forest behind his back, the wind from Onondaga Lake swishing strongly, bringing relief in the humidity. It made him think of the Great Lake. Was this man, the Bear People's leader, truly dead?

He remembered the tall, dignified bearing, the firmness of the straight shoulders, the arrogance of the proudly held head, the reserve of the piercing eyes. Distant, cold, but not really. The man was good, wise, genuine, well-meaning; unhappy too, haunted, but above taking his frustrations out on other people. A decent man, most fascinating company, with whom he had enjoyed spending his time for enough dawns after the crisis caused by the wild son of this same leader died away. It was a most pleasant time, during which he had learned so much, heard the history of that other colder side of the Great Lake, the stories of various nations, their side of the conflict, their grievances and complaints, and above it all, the tales about the Great Peacemaker, and even his own family—Father, even Mother. The Crooked Tongues leader and the woman of Ossossane apparently knew them both, closely at that.

When he had left, he felt sorry, not opposed to spending more time in the busy leader's company, knowing that the great man might have been cherishing the same thought. An interesting realization. He had hoped that they would meet again, somehow. If the peace talks progressed into serious agreements, if more delegations were sent and received. It would be a pleasure to greet this man on their side of the Great Sparkling Water, to have him meet Father, and after all these summers...

He suppressed a sigh, concentrating on the people who were approaching him, too many at the same time. Who would have thought that the Crooked Tongues leader would be embarking on his Sky Journey, and so soon. His son—he would have to find the Lone Hill's Crooked Tongue and tell him.

CHAPTER 3

The hoop was glaringly small, made of bark wrapped in rawhide, decorated with shells. Strips of well-tanned material crossed it from the inside, many thongs of leather, creating a spider web. Such an invested thing!

"It's too small," said Ogteah, turning it over for the second time. The shells fastened to the outside parts of the web didn't rustle. They would hold on, at least through some of the throws. "Who competes with such things?"

The owner of the contested item grinned, pleased with himself. "Those who know how to throw a spear, brother," he drawled, his eyes deeply set, narrowed, sparkling with challenge. "Where I come from, even small boys play with just this sort of a hoop. We are not a spoiled, lazy lot like your Sparkling Water's dwellers. We know how to make good warriors."

"Don't get carried away, boasting like this," said Ogteah, not offended.

Since arriving here, in this vast Onondaga Lake's valley, to help with the Great Ceremony's preparations at the request of the High Springs man, he had spent enough time in the company of various people from all over those lands.

The ugly beasts of the other side, he thought to himself, hiding his smirk. One span of seasons later, and here he was, not thinking any of that, not anymore, but still finding it difficult to tell them apart, one nation from another.

The Flint People, he remembered. The man with the hoop was Flint. He had said it quite proudly when introducing himself. But what town he had named Ogteah wouldn't remember. They all sounded alike to him, not helped by the peculiar accent of the speakers. Why did they have to pronounce the same words so differently?

He shrugged. "We can use this hoop, if others would not object. It's child's play to fit one's spear through it. Not an effort at all."

"Not an effort, eh?" The squinted eyes widened back to their natural proportions, together with the climbing up eyebrows. "Let's see you make it fall, hitting even just the outer ring."

The others, two more of their companions and a few onlookers, grinned.

"When we play, I will fit it through that hole in the middle, easily too." He knew he wouldn't. It would be difficult enough to hit the ring itself while rolling, as were the rules of the contest. Unless it was made to roll leisurely, taking its time. Which he knew it wouldn't be. The fierce Flint throwers would be putting it all into making the hoop race over the field. Could they truly be that good?

Inspecting the beautifully decorated item one more time in order to conceal his misgivings mainly, Ogteah side-glanced his adversary, taking in the wideness of the man's frame and the arrogantly swaying warrior's lock. Oh, yes, this one wasn't bluffing. Not a showoff dressed as a warrior for the occasion. He shrugged again.

"If others agree, we play with this thing," he repeated, tossing the ring toward its rightful owner. "It's too pretty not to use. Your warriors' time must be spent mainly on weaving pretty things, the way this one looks."

While the man's companions stiffened with rage, the direct object of his needling roared with laughter.

"You are something else, local. Funny man. Why don't you use your spear now? We'll make sample throws, you and me. See if you Onondagas are any good."

"I'm not an Onondaga, but we can sample your ring. Why not?"

He could fit his spear in, maybe not through the middle of the web, but close enough. He was good in this particular game, his second preferred betting contest, and this man could not be much better than this.

Measuring his opponent once again, this time openly, he made sure his expression reflected lightest of disdain, even though he could not help but actually like this potential adversary of his. Certainly not a showoff, hiding no real malice under the good-natured baiting, harboring no hard feelings, no visible frustrations or grudges. Not an enemy. Did Flint and Onondaga, and the rest of that much-praised alliance of theirs, feel like true brothers, indeed? Somehow he assumed it would be like with his Wyandot People, maybe not intense rivalry, but no brotherly love, either. They were different peoples, after all, five different nations.

"No Onondaga? Then who are you? You do speak strange, come to think of it."

Ogteah rolled his eyes. "I live here, in an Onondaga village. My woman is Onondaga." He grinned. "That's enough storytelling for you, *foreigner*."

"Foreigner?" Another outburst of healthy laughter shook the afternoon air. "Take a good hold of your spear and let us see if you, or your mysterious people, whoever they are, are worthy of something." Businesslike, the Flint guest looked around. "Did you find a proper spot for the competition to be held? This entire valley is all ups and downs. Not a flat piece of land, not as far as I could find." A wave of the muscled arm indicated their surroundings, indeed one hilly ground preceding another. "One grows tired ascending and descending all the time." A broad palm slapped the scarred thigh. "Not everyone here is lazy and as peaceful as little rabbits. Some of us carry reminders of old wars." Indeed, the slapped thigh was visibly disfigured, covered with a vast scar tissue.

"My mother was a Flint woman, but that is not why I'll beat you on that spear throwing thing." Not far away, another group of people was chatting in a loud, lively manner. "There is that flat enough stretch of land, down by the lake. I inspected it today, and to my opinion, it fits. Not too much space to run all over and throw your javelins without care, but teams of five men each can make it without jostling each other. Even with this undersized ring of yours."

"Let us go and see." Limping ever so slightly, the warrior turned away, setting a brisk pace for them all to keep up with.

"Do they want to make it a big thing?" asked another of the Flint visitors, a slight fellow of an average height and thin but pleasant features. "Like a ball game of all Five Nations?"

Pushing himself forward, to lead the way—it was his piece of land they were looking for after all—Ogteah made a face. "All five nations it may be taking it too far. Who could organize everyone in such a way? But we can try to pull it off with, say, fifty or so men, alternate teams."

Warming to the idea, he made quick calculations. And why not? But all five nations? How many men were expected to fill this valley? Hundreds?

Even now, it held too many of the newcomers, with more trickling in every day, already hosting more guests than the gathering of his people back in Ossossane, or so it seemed. But of course! Father had brought together two nations, and some visitors from the third, while here, here they were expecting twice as much, or more. How would they manage?

The thought of Father brought another. He would have to find a way to contact the man, and soon. After this gathering was over. Through the last few moons, he was racking his brain, trying to think of a way to send word, if for no other reason than to make Father aware that he hadn't forgotten, that he was busy working on their mutual secret goal, that he wasn't returning to his old ways.

There was not much progress to report yet, but he was learning, and fast, speaking now as they did, with almost no accent—an achievement that left Gayeri in awe; she couldn't stop commenting on it—making plenty of contacts, having many acquaintances from all over those Onondaga lands, and even a few among their neighbors to the east and to the west. He hadn't worked the exact strategy out as yet, but he was heading there. No empty existence like back among his people, even though it was not that promising in the beginning. But for the War Chief and his son!

He glanced back at the valley they were leaving, hoping to see the High Springs man somewhere among the crowds, the way he always seemed to be, walking all over it, instructing, calming, pacifying, distributing orders. A good man, with enough common sense and authority to make it all work. There would be a need to receive this one's approval for the enterprise of the spear-throwing contest. When done inspecting the field, it would be a good time to do that, should he decide that the place was good enough. His pushy Flint companions could be of help.

But how many guests would be filling this valley when it was all done and ready? *The entire Onondaga Town valley turns into one large bowl of food.* Oh, but he remembered the High Springs man saying that, long ago, but not so long, back in the lands of the Cord People. It sounded like wild exaggeration back then, but now, oh now, he wasn't so sure. Five Nations they were, five powerful, large nations.

"They held this sacred game last time, when the Great Council was meeting. Planting season, wasn't it?" One of his Flint followers turned to his peers, frowning with concentration. "Or was it the summer before that?"

"I wouldn't know." The spectacular spear-thrower was walking beside Ogteah, his limp barely there, just a different sort of a stroll. "Last summer I could travel, but not far. While before that," —rolling his eyes, he slapped his formidable thigh again— "I was grateful if I managed to hobble outside our town's fence. I was in no position to attend Great Council meetings or run around, tossing playing sticks."

"Yes, it was two summers ago," confirmed Tauini, a youth from Onondaga Town, whom Ogteah had been getting along very well with since arriving in this valley a few dawns ago. "There were hundreds of players for each team. One couldn't move along that field, let alone wield a shaft. It was a sight worth seeing. I'm sorry you missed it, brother."

"Well, maybe the organizer of throwing spears will make something spectacular for us to see as yet." The crinkling eyes rested on Ogteah. "You Onondagas can spend your time organizing games and gatherings. You haven't warred since the

times of the Great Peacemaker, nothing like what we have with
our annoying neighbors to the east. You people are growing soft."

"Not too soft to put you in your place, you showy Flint." Less
amused now, Ogteah narrowed his eyes, ridiculously offended on
behalf of the Onondagas all of a sudden. He didn't always feel at
home here, not yet, but these were good people, and fat cowards
they weren't. "There is enough activity here, from raids to politics,
and if they hold another ball game, you better prepare to accept a
glaring defeat even before the contest has started."

Who won on that last grandiose game they were talking about?
he wondered. Not Flint, hopefully.

"There won't be any glaring defeats for anyone," said Tauini,
not offended at all for some reason. "They won't put a team of one
peoples against another."

"Of course they won't." The narrowed eyes of one of the Flint
measured Ogteah, openly wondering. "Where have you been
those few summers ago?"

"Ask around if you want to know." Shooting a quick glance at
the trail they walked, its view blocked by the rustling bushes,
Ogteah shrugged. Everyone in these lands knew where he came
from. Courtesy of the rumors rather than his accent or the way he
behaved. There were no secrets around the Onondaga Town's
valley and along the shores of the Great Lake. Even his connection
to the powerful War Chief was aired to all and sundry.

He wanted to shake his head, now, moons later, amused at the
flow of revelations that continued flooding him since the moment
he had learned of his mother's identity, each less probable than
the previous one. As though what he had been told by Father, and
later on by Gayeri, wasn't enough.

His amusement gone, he remembered his first days on this side
of the Great Lake. A ghastly memory. The sense of triumph at the
smoothness of the last part of their journey, the difficult crossing
that he managed to make as light as a morning sail on a small
lake—but how proud he was of that achievement!—didn't last
beyond their arrival in her village. The moment they had entered,
things changed for the worst.

The commotion they caused was enormous, lasting for days.

But of course it was. She was the daughter of an important dignitary, a generally liked, pretty thing, one whom they had given up on, counted as lost forever. But how happy they were to see her, her family, and the entire village as it seemed, flooding her with questions, hugs, tears, burying her under too much attention.

Through all this, she made a considerable effort of clinging to him on this first day, and the days that followed, to introduce him to everyone as her savior, the man who had rescued her and made her return possible. Not a wild exaggeration, come to think of it, and yet, not many shared her enthusiasm. Of course they didn't. Whatever his claimed deeds and achievements were, he still represented the worst of the enemy, a person from the other side. This village was too close to the Great Sparkling Water, carrying memories of nothing but wars. Not a single family here had not suffered this or that loss, damage, hurt. All of which had been caused by his, Ogteah's, people. Beyond forgivable.

She had made it clear that he was her man, to be accepted or else. In the case of "or else," they didn't know their exact rights. Generally, the Grandmother of her longhouse would have to give her consent, with the proper procedures, with his mother, or the appointed grandmother of his longhouse, either receiving or sending out the marriage cookies.

However, aside from the fact that he had no family on this side of the Great Lake, apparently, Gayeri herself did not belong to her longhouse properly, having lived with her aunt instead, for many summers prior to the kidnapping.

What the headstrong thing had envisioned, apparently, was them both coming to live in her old longhouse, with her aunt and her family. Which left the entire village puzzled, all those clan mothers wondering, furrowing their foreheads, at a loss, shooting direful glances at him. An enemy who couldn't even speak their tongue, but who wasn't above complicating the already-complicated situation. More unforgivable deeds!

He made an effort to be patient, disregarding undeserved glares. Her father was away, attending an important gathering, or so she had told him, unaware of the wonderful surprise that awaited the old man upon his return. She was shining brighter than the high-noon sun when she said that. Oh, how surprised Father would be!

With the identity of her chosen mate as well, he mused bitterly, trying to keep those thoughts off his face. But for the ability to just take off, as he would have done under different circumstances. Was he destined to live like that from now on, surrounded by a wall of suspicion and indifference?

She tried to make it as pleasant as possible for him, but she couldn't stay and keep him company all the time. Two more dawns following their arrival and she was already out there in the fields, surrounded by happy female members of her family and other old friends. Which left him kicking his heels in their temporary longhouse, with absolutely nothing to do and no one to talk to. He didn't dare to wander about, brooding through this first long, tiring day. When she came back, he told her that she must arrange for him to do some work, anything really. Did the men of her village work at all, lazy pieces of meat that they were?

As always, the ability to make her laugh caused him feel better, as did the hurried lovemaking, strangled under the blankets in their corner of the longhouse, delighted and amused at their own effrontery. It was still good to be with her, better now that her fears seemed to be disappearing. If only her entire village would disappear along with them.

True to her word, the next day he had been invited to join a small hunting party. Just a quick foray into the woods, nothing huge or well-organized, not in this bountiful season. A few dawns spent that saw him coming back more frustrated than before. The hunters weren't rude or mean, or violent, or nasty. Unable to converse properly, they made no attempt to communicate with him at all, leaving him to his own devices, not inviting to take any part in their plans of ambushing the herd they had quickly spotted. Which left him to do nothing more than tend to the fire and camp arrangements. Like a youth allowed to trail along!

He managed to hang on to his temper, finding it somewhat difficult not to do something violent, to break things, or yell, or pick a fight. For her sake, only for her, because at this point, he didn't care what would happen to him, not even a little bit.

Upon their return, he said nothing while she was happily fussing around their share of the meat—every participant was entitled, whether actually hunting something or not—but before the next dawn broke, he had slipped away, heading for the woods, to do what, he didn't know. In this time of the late spring it was pleasant out there, and he needed to clear his head, to think about all this, to decide what to do.

Tracing a large group of whitetails helped. By the early afternoon, he had shot a good fat male, spending the rest of the day on carving its meat, keeping all the best parts and as much of the fat as he could carry.

It was already dark when he had staggered in, wavering under his heavy burden, having no bags to carry his spoils in. The hide of the creature helped, but didn't make it more comfortable.

The villagers gaped at him, their eyes wide open, some curious, even amused, some reproachful. Women mostly. The latter was explained as soon as he reached home. She was in tears, all puffy and stammering, having cried for a long time as it seemed.

"I think you go, leave," she had sobbed, trembling in his arms. "I thought you not come back."

The good feeling dispersed.

"You are silly, you know that?" he whispered, stroking her hair, uncomfortable at speaking his tongue in these surroundings, but as always warmed by the mere feel of her. "Why would I leave without telling you?"

"Because you not happy. I know you not." She snuggled close, pressing into him, like in the old times. "I don't know, don't know what to do."

He stifled a sigh. "Yes, you are right. As far as this place goes, I don't feel like staying. But we just arrived here, didn't we? We'll give it some time, see how it goes. Maybe it will get better." He knew it wouldn't, but in her warmth, it felt nice to assume silly things. "I won't be giving up on you that easily, wild girl. You can trust me on that."

"I leave with you," she had breathed into his chest, which still bore witness to his afternoon work but was now smeared with her tears as well. "If you leave, take me along, yes? I not stay, not without you."

Which was the perfect finish to a good day, the first satisfactory day since after the crossing. Reinforced by the firm evidence of her devotion—oh yes, he was more than her means to get back to her people, now he knew it for sure—while showing her fellow villagers that he was not a boy to be treated with indifferent disdain, he proceeded to go out and wash, only to run into a huge commotion upon his return.

Apparently, a large party of visitors descended upon the village in his absence, nightfall and all, many people, important dignitaries among them. Or so he had gathered, his sense of well-being evaporating. Her father, in the company of the War Chief of the entire nation, no more, no less! The fires were lit everywhere, the hectic preparations of food burst out next to quite a few longhouses, with everyone busy or excited, milling around, talking all at once.

He had sneaked away toward the safety of their abandoned longhouse, unsettled, wishing to keep out of the important people's way. Her father, of all things! As though he had not faced enough enmity until now. What would the powerful leader do? Demand her to throw away the unfitting husband she had found? Or worse yet, with no official peace agreements between their people, would the enraged elder make a pretty ceremony while executing the presumptuous foreigner?

His stomach churning, with hunger he hoped, he had pretended to fall asleep, in case someone came, but her footsteps rang uncompromisingly, and her hand shook his shoulder, pulling him with much force.

"You come, come now. They want to see, my father and War Chief, they want to meet. Come!"

"I'm sleeping," he said. "Tell them you didn't find me."

She pulled him yet stronger. "You not. You pretend. I can see. You breathe funny, pretend." Her face shone brighter than a full moon, beaming in the darkness. "Come. They want meet. They not angry. The War Chief, he ask to meet. Not my father. The War Chief ask. Come!" Tossing a pair of fresh leggings at him, she nearly danced around the abandoned compartment, rummaging after more clean garments, he assumed, dazed. "Remember what you say, what your father say about War Chief? Well, maybe he right. It strange, but the War Chief want meet, and the High Springs man, his son, he here too. They all expect you, you see. So hurry, dress nice and come."

And now, descending the incline that led toward that piece of flat ground near Onondaga Lake, he did his best to suppress his smile, the uninhibited quality of it.

The War Chief indeed wished to meet him, apparently, just like Father had promised. The most impressive man, truly a great leader, as straight-backed and as important as Father, with the most arresting pattern of scars covering the noble face like a war paint, the man was not reserved or foreboding, not at all. Warm, welcoming, ready to smile. He had spoken in the Bear People's tongue, easily and with no misgivings, paying no attention to the surprised stares of the villagers all around them.

The other leader, her father most probably, was the only one unsurprised. That man eyed his newly gained son reservedly, with less enthusiasm than the great leader displayed, but it did nothing to dampen Ogteah's spirits. He wasn't alone anymore, he knew, glancing at the rest of the visitors, answering the crooked grin of none other than the High Springs man, the War Chief's son, who had squatted alongside the leaders, calm and at home, confident, a trustworthy presence. This man had proved his worth, his courage, his presence of mind back there in Ossossane, Ogteah remembered. Another impressive person. Like father, like son.

He had mused about it for a while, until the War Chief burst out with more unlikely revelations regarding his, Ogteah's, family and origins. Apparently, the powerful leader's interest was rooted in more than just kindness, the willingness to offer the foreigner a chance, to repay some old debt to his father, maybe. Oh no! Apparently, they had closer ties than this. Again, the mysterious mother. When he had learned that she was not only a Flint People woman but a favorite cousin of this same influential War Chief, the girl the old man had grown up with, whom he knew and loved very well until she had left to follow Ogteah's father, he wanted to laugh aloud and shake his head. It was too wild, more than the wildest storyteller would think of on an especially long winter night, with no other entertainment in sight.

No, no one would think about something like that, but at this point, he didn't care. New life was starting to look promising, a true possibility, with some powerful men ready to accept him, to give him a real chance. The stunned gazes of his fellow villagers told him that, the hesitation of their smiles. No more indifferent treatment, not for him.

"I say this place is not bad at all!"

The exclamation of the man beside him pulled Ogteah out of his reverie, made him realize that they had reached the clearing he had in mind. A spacious, long stretch of land, it broke the straightness of its surface only at its far edge, promising to allow a good path for the rolling ring to follow, even if it was to be pushed viciously, with much strength.

Eyeing his own find with a new appreciation, Ogteah frowned. "We can make it the entire-gathering event, come to think of it. Just like that ball game of yours. Have everyone participate." Small islands of rustling bushes drew his attention. "If we remove these, we have a truly good field."

"Yes, we do." The Flint warrior seemed to be as immersed in the study of their find. "You put teams of fifteen, maybe twenty warriors, but you limit their time to less throws."

Ogteah found himself nodding. "This way, even if a hundred people ended up playing, we have everyone participating, and in an orderly manner." He glanced at his company, amused. "Good thinking, Warrior. Apparently you Flints can do more than just mindless fighting."

A huge grin was his answer. "We are yet to see what would-be Onondagas are capable of. Or is it all you can do, organize and count teams and players, eh? That pretty spear you carry, is it any good? Or is it just for decorative purposes?"

Ogteah narrowed his eyes. "Get busy rolling that hoop of yours. How many tries?"

"Depends on how many of us," said his companion,

impressed. "If just the two of us, no teams, then two, three throws would be enough to determine the winner." The eyes squinted again, slid over Ogteah's javelin. "Pretty spear. I won't mind adding it to my collection."

"Wake up from that dream."

Aware of the growing expectation among his rival's following, Ogteah tried to push the bad feeling away. The man was spoiling for the contest, and it wasn't promising. He might be damn good at this, maybe the best spear-thrower of his town, whatever its name was. Didn't his words indicate a considerable collection of javelins already?

It would be embarrassing to lose his spear now, at the beginning of an important gathering and just as he was aspiring to organize an event that involved this exact sort of weaponry. The rumor was sure to make its way everywhere, and he loved that spear of his, decorations and all. It was light but balanced, easy to use, and Gayeri had spent quite a few winter evenings weaving special adornments around its shaft.

"So?" The man's eyes were taunting, as though aware of his rival's misgivings.

"So nothing. Let me see your spear before we start. I won't be spending my efforts on winning some polished stick. Mine is good, invested."

A movement among the other Flints produced the prettiest spear he had ever seen, its shaft long and slick, garnished with carvings, decorated by feathers colored in different shades.

"Care to bet against this one?"

"Maybe."

Coming closer, he inspected the offered spoil, out of curiosity, but also to gain time. He shouldn't be doing this, he just shouldn't. Hadn't he promised himself not to engage in purposeless games of luck or just this sort of private betting? As a part of ceremonial gaming, yes, but not in the way he used to do. A difficult enough resolution to keep, and one he had broken from time to time through the last span of seasons, when life became boring at times. Still, now was not the occasion and bored he wasn't, was he? Yet, the spear of this man was a work of art, such a valuable item.

"Two throws each, unless we both fit the spear through," the Flint went on, businesslike now, the good-natured needling forgotten. "Then we go on, trying one more time. If one of us puts the spear through the middle hole, he wins with no argument. Same with the one who misses the hoop completely. That would be a declared defeat."

Shrugging, Ogtaeh nodded. These were fair rules and only two, three throws, maximum, promised to put him on the safe side. He wouldn't miss this ring, smaller than usual though it was. He was an accurate thrower. Not enough to fit the spear through the middle opening—who could do that?—but enough to make the ring fall each time he tried.

"It won't take long," he said to Tauini and some other of his people who bothered to trail along, trying not to sound apologetic. "This field needs to be checked, and what better way is there?" He glanced at the conversing Flints again. "When we are through, I'm off to talk to the High Springs man. To see if he approves and will lend us his support in organizing this thing."

They nodded readily, and so did their growing audience, some idling people drifting closer, sensing a source of entertainment. Meeting the gaze of an interesting-looking woman around his own age, standing with her friends, holding a basket, Ogteah grinned at her rather out of custom, his thoughts on the impending competition.

"Are you ready, mysterious non-Onondaga man?" The Flint was back in his good humor, balancing his precious javelin in his hand, playing with it, displaying his skill.

"Who throws first?"

"You. The host has the honor."

"My pleasure." Swinging his spear in his turn, Ogteah strolled toward the nearest spot that had less chances of the sun glowing directly in his eyes. The Flint man, he noticed, skipped quite a few tens of paces away, his limp again barely noticeable. Was he pretending to have this liability?

Ogtaeh pushed a new wave of misgivings away, sensing the eyes of the woman, the lively chatter of her companions distracting.

"Ready?"

The shout came from far enough, making him wish to grind his teeth. From what distance was this man intending to have them aiming? With this smaller hoop, and now from farther than customary, was he planning to have them both missing the target?

"Go on."

Deciding to brazen it out rather than spend his time worrying over something he could not prevent at this point, Ogteah focused, measuring the distance, guessing the possible path of the ring with his eyes. There was no need to concentrate on the starting point. A veteran of many such contests, he knew that a brief glance in the hoop-thrower's direction was more than enough. Those who studied the man, trying to predict his movements, missed half of their chances to hit the target before the ring rolled its course.

The deepening silence of those who watched warned him, heightened his awareness, made his muscles tense, his body tilting, the hand holding the spear only a part of the effort. As did the swish that his ears didn't miss.

The hoop shot forward, like a pouncing predator, pushed with enough force to make it almost fly. At the same moment, Ogteah's entire body came to life, his instincts deciding for him, as they always did.

Another swish, this of his spear, was louder, resonating in his ears. He could feel the force of the throw, the unerring path of the lethal weapon. It wouldn't miss, he knew. It couldn't.

Indeed, the hum of the air released from quite a few chests at once told him that the target was down, before his eyes confirmed that. The women behind his back giggled as one of them shouted too loudly, not quick enough to hide her admiration.

"Not bad." The Flint man didn't bother to retrieve the fallen hoop, letting one of his friends rush along the tramped-on grass. "Impressive, really."

But there was no real appreciation in the warrior's voice. Or maybe there was, but his eyes flickered amusedly, unconcerned. It took the edge off Ogteah's sense of victory.

"No trouble," he said lightly, heading toward the man with the hoop and his own spear. "Show us what the Flint can do from such distance."

"Quite a lot, mysterious local. Quite a lot."

Rolling the ring was never his favorite part of the competition. He did not do it well, not like some others, who could send the hoop practically flying. Like the annoyingly self-assured Flint.

"Ready?"

He just shoved it forward, in no showy manner, not surprised when the colorful spear pushed it violently, made it fall before it reached the middle of its journey, losing no momentum. Worried a little, he rushed forward, to see that the missile did not go through the perfect middle.

"Not bad as well," he called out, relieved. The spear didn't even stick in the web, but was lying quite a distance away, having probably hit the outer ring.

A near miss, he thought, smirking. Why did he let stupid misgivings bother him at all?

His rival didn't lose any of his previous baiting amusement.

"Sometimes one needs to get used to the new field," he commented, grinning good-naturedly. "A different lay of the land." Receiving the ring, he made a face. "But you roll this thing like a beginner. Give it a more spirited push next time. It's boring. I can throw my spear toward an unmoving target just as well."

Ogtaeh rolled his eyes. "Look who is talking. The man who didn't even put his spear through the web. Your push made it barely fall."

But there was no pricking the high-flying confidence of his opponent. "A new field, like I said. But if you insist on making it easy for me, I won't keep complaining."

Shaking his head, Ogtaeh readied for another throw, wishing nothing more than to finish this business with no shameful miss. The dirty skunk would capitalize on it, carrying on and on, for days on end and in the loudest of manners. He could feel the eyes of the onlookers, burning his back. Especially those of the pretty local foxes.

"This field is good, isn't it?" Ohanda, one of his fellow Lone

Hill villagers, a youth of an average built and light disposition, came to stand next to Ogtaeh, watching his preparation for the next throw. They had spent quite a few days tossing spears on one especially boring hunting trip. "Will you truly make a huge contest out of it?"

"Yes, I will. If the High Springs man and the local authorities approve."

"They should. No ball games are rumored to be planned, and people do need to do something with themselves."

"Ready?"

A sharp call made Ogteah's muscles tense. This time, his glance lingered on his rival for a fraction of a heartbeat longer, wishing to make his target fall before it reached the midway mark of its course. The annoying showoff might enjoy being eclipsed even in this.

Satisfied with yet another fallen target—not as close to its starting point as he hoped for, but still close enough—he flexed his shoulders, then turned toward his young supporter, pretending indifference he didn't feel. But it was good to do such exercise and with nice, impressive enough results.

"The moment we are through with this, I'm off to accost the authorities. The idea of such contest is too good to dismiss it."

The youth nodded, his wide-open gaze full of admiration.

"One more time." This time, the Flint man came back carrying the ring and Ogteah's spear, having evidently detoured by the fallen target instead of letting his friends do the dirty work for him. "You missed the web as well this time. Hurried to get that hoop from the beginning, didn't you?" The openly mocking eyes sparkled. "Don't rush into it. I'll enjoy getting your spear, but by besting you with my throws, not by winning when you miss. I like watching your tosses. They are good. Don't spoil it by losing your patience."

"You are lecturing me on how to go about beating you to that spear of yours, aren't you?" Exhaling loudly, Ogtaeh shook his head. "You are something out of the wintertime stories."

"Wait until I win," was the nonchalant reply that made him wish to put the arrogant beast in his place by whatever means.

This time, he pushed the ring so violently it almost faltered, which made his stomach twist with fear. How embarrassing would that be? Luckily, the hoop leapt on its way, a more difficult target than before. Good! When its flight was cut midway, he wanted to curse. The damn skunk *was* good.

"The last round, or do we call it a draw?" he shouted, while picking up the fallen items. This time, the spear had pierced the web, closer to the middle section of it, the crossing of the straps, rather than the harder outer parts.

"The last round of course." His rival hurried toward him, not waiting for the ring to be delivered to him. Oh, yes, that one was well enmeshed in a competitive mood by now, desperate to win. One could see it most clearly. How to use that impatience to his advantage? "Unless you give up."

"No chance of that." To shrug with pretended indifference felt like the best thing to do, sure to annoy the man. He tried to pay no attention to the gauging gaze of the woman who was cheering for him the loudest before. Not a bad-looking fox, temptingly well built and well curved, a trouble. "I would have gone on tossing those spears until Father Sun goes to sleep, but for the lack of time. One of us would have made a mistake eventually. Maybe in the darkness, eh?" He let the grin of contempt show. "Wonder how good you are without help of the light."

"Good enough." The wide back was already upon him, hurrying away, the words tossed out with less taunting spark than before. Oh, yes, that one was losing some of his confidence, definitely. Concentrating back on his spear, Ogteah tried to remember various tricks of tossing the hoop in more challenging ways.

"Would be nice if he missed this last throw completely." Tauini, the Onondaga Town's man, was another one losing his patience. "I didn't know you were so good at that."

"Not good. Just practice here and there." Eyes on his rival, who was reaching that far away spot, about to put it all into his last roll of the hoop, surely, Ogteah shrugged. "I prefer the spear to a bow, when hunting."

"Ready?"

This time, he didn't spend his time on looking at his rival at all, not minding the ring covering as much of the ground as it could. There was no chance to hit that hole in the middle, not from such a distance and in such a small thing, but he could try, couldn't he?

His arm steady, mind calculating, he let the hoop roll until the watching audience seemed to be gulping. When his feathered shaft finally pounced, the hoop was already wavering, changing its course, yet it crashed to the ground faster, pierced by his spear so near its middle that he held his breath. As did the others.

The Flint warrior was running toward the place, his limp more pronounced, though ignored. Was he watching his walk on regular circumstances?

Releasing his breath, Ogteah knew it didn't go through when the man picked up both items, his entire stance relating his relief, even before he turned to face them.

It didn't matter. He tried to pay no attention to the wave of acute disappointment. This contest was good, and he had proved himself. He didn't lose his spear, even if he didn't win the other. What were the chances of this happening? None, not with this man being as good, not about to miss any of his throws any more than he, Ogteah, was.

"That was close!" cried out his opponent, nearing them with a more measured step, again not limping but just walking strangely. "It's stuck right next to the center. See?" Openly appreciative, he offered Ogteah's spear as a spoil, displayed on his spread palms, the hoop still hanging on it, pierced so very near the opening. A fraction of a palm nearer...

Ogteah grinned, trying to look as nonchalant as he could. "Close, but not close enough." Snatching his rightful weapon, he shook the hoop off with little consideration. "Let us get on with your throw and be done with. I'm still expected to run all over the place, pleading with the authorities, trying to convince them."

The smile of the Flint warrior was reserved for a change, just a light twist of the lips. "Yes, let's get it over with."

Turning to go, he saw a group of men descending the trail he and his companions had emerged from before. Their faces looked familiar, the High Springs lot. Good! He could enquire among this crowd where their leader and organizer was, sparing himself some running around.

"Ready?"

Paying little attention to the task of rolling it this time, he watched the hoop spinning leisurely, passing by the cluster of low bushes, not in a hurry to reach the other side.

They would have to get rid of this vegetation, he thought, and maybe some of the surrounding greenery, to make it comfortable for the watching crowds. This space would have to be cleared like a field. Would they find enough volunteers to do this? He didn't manage to suppress his chuckle, knowing how the bulk of men felt about it; all those escorting warriors, happy to get away from their towns and its fields for that particular reason.

The spear swished by, pinning the ring before it left the background of the bushes. Still deep in thought, Ogteah strolled toward it. The High Springs man would help. He was a highly organized person, with enough authority and drive. He would see the benefit of the suggested entertainment, the possibilities it offered. Too many idling men congregating in one place for long days spelt trouble, unless given a way to spill their accumulated energies. Boredom was the root of all trouble. He, Ogteah, knew all about it.

He saw the Flint hurrying toward the fallen ring, again more agitated than before. Hastening his step, Ogteah smirked. Did this one truly hope he would miss any of his throws?

Then the thoughts cleared from his mind all at once. The hoop lay before him, pierced in its middle, in the cleanest of manners, with the leather thongs not cut or damaged, but just pushed aside, to accommodate the spear's wider base. It was as though someone threaded it there leisurely, with much care.

Incredulous, he just stared. As did the man beside him, now unusually quite as opposed to his talkatively provoking self of before.

"Looks like you won this round." It took him time to find his own voice, but he was pleased to hear it ringing steadily, in a respectable way. Others were nearing them, also in a hurry, his and the other man's followers.

"Yes." The Flint nodded thoughtfully. "But it was a good competition. You made me work."

That sounded outright offensive, such open patronizing. "You made me work as well."

"That I did." The man grinned, rendering his previous statement harmless with the wideness of his smile. "You are good, brother. Truly good. The team you will play for in that grand competition of yours will not lose any of its weaponry. I'm prepared to bet something good on that." The wide palms came up, in a surrendering gesture. "It's just that I had a whole span of seasons to do nothing but practice throwing spears and knives. Until I learned to walk again, and even after that, before I could do it well."

"What happened to your leg?" asked Ogteah, mainly to maintain the conversation, to keep his thoughts off this monumental loss of his. His favorite spear! And she decorated it so lovingly, claiming that the patterns she wove were to keep him safe.

The others had reached them by now, staring at the fallen ring, suspiciously solemn. As though no one had ever put a spear through a ring before. He wanted to curse them, even the huddling women, all agog with excitement, the curvy one still stealing glances at him, a silly fox. With such a resounding defeat, she should have transferred her adoration to the winning Flint.

"A long story. I got one nasty wound that decided to start rotting when it saw that it didn't kill me on the spot." The impressive Flint shrugged. "It was a long recovery, and but for one Onondaga boy, the best of friends that I ever had, and one strange local fox, I wouldn't be here, winning your Onondaga spears." Another wide smile, then the man headed toward his javelin. "I'm telling you, unless your notorious Crooked Tongues moved off their fat behinds and start making trouble, you will be boasting one true Onondaga warrior in this entire land, and he is half a Flint at that."

"Crooked Tongues won't be moving off their fat behinds in a hurry," growled Ogteah, caught unprepared. Usually, it was easy to pay no attention to the casual slander his people were rendered here whenever their subject came up, unless someone said something truly ugly. A rare occurrence, as they all knew of his origins, and he was generally well enough liked now not to prompt people into stirring unnecessary trouble. "We have peaceful agreements with their union. Something you arrogant Flint might have paid attention to had you not been so busy with your noses stuck in your own fat behinds."

"What?" The Flint stopped pulling his spear and whirled to stare at Ogteah, eyes wide. "What in the name of all bad forest spirits made you so touchy?" The narrowing eyes accompanied by derisively twisted lips. "Can't lose with dignity, can you?"

"I can lose, or win, in any way you like, but I won't be listening to you badmouthing people we have peaceful agreements with."

A swift movement startled them both as they glared at each other, but it was only Tauini pushing himself between them, just in case. By this time, the newcomers were upon them too, with the broad shoulders of Iheks, one of the High Springs man's closest aides, in the lead, eyeing them with open curiosity.

"Our leader wishes to see you, Crooked Tongue," he said, nodding at Ogteah with open friendliness. They had gotten along well enough through his last stay in High Springs, right after the Cold Moons. "Something urgent." His eyes slid over their Flint company, acknowledging the entire group with an amiable nod. "Greetings."

"Crooked Tongue?" repeated Ogteah's adversary, incredulous. Ohanda and his friends chuckled loudly. "Oh, that explains it. Of all things! But how?"

Ogteah just shrugged.

"Enjoy your new spear," he said, thrusting his favorite weapon into the man's hands as casually as he could, anxious to be on his way before his temper got the better of him again. The Onondaga Town man's interruption could not have come with any better timing. "We'll compete on this field again."

"Throwing spears, eh?" Iheks had evidently already appraised the situation, taking in the sight of the Flint holding Ogteah's and his own javelin, with the hoop still impaled on its shaft.

"He wants to make it a large scale competition," contributed the man who stood next to Ohanda, another local. "Like the sacred ball game we had here last summer."

As matter-of-fact as always, the High Springs newcomer measured the field with his gaze. "It's large enough," he muttered, nodding with appreciation. "But how would you conduct it in an orderly way, with hundreds of players involved?"

"Many teams and a limited amount of throws," said Ogteah, relieved to feel the previous wave of rage receding, fading into the crispness of the afternoon.

"Like we did just now," contributed the Flint, obviously over his brief spell of indignation as well.

"I see." Another nod and the High Springs man began turning away. "You can explain on your way back, enterprising player. Ganayeda wants to talk to you, urgently." He gave the hesitating guests a brief glance. "Would you accompany us back to the valley?"

"We'll wander around some more," said the Flint warrior, typically speaking for his peers as well. His eyes flashed at Ogteah, holding all previous baiting. "Pleasure to meet you, mysterious man. It was a most interesting encounter. I'll make good use of your spear through your competition."

"Prepare to be relieved of this thing as well as your pretty javelin upon our next encounter," Ogteah tossed over his shoulder, now back in control, even if still not happy about his loss. She had spent more than two evenings decorating its shaft, and with what would he play if the competition was indeed held? "Thanks to you, brother, boring my afternoon wasn't. Anything but."

CHAPTER 4

The path was narrow and steep, winding itself precariously among the towering rocks. Careful not to slip, she made her way up, skipping between the hurdles, taking sharp turns, supporting herself with her hands every time it seemed to be required.

The silence enveloped her, deceptive, bad silence. What appeared to be a good, surprisingly kind place to hide all those summers ago was now nothing but a trap.

Back then she had welcomed the opportunity to hide, to dive into the silence and thus escape the nightmare. As soon as she had awakened from the terrible winter fever, to find her mother and brothers gone, her father dying, her favorite cousin nothing but a coughing shadow, and others, so many others, their entire longhouse decimated to barely half of its denizens.

They had expected her to die too, a thin, fragile girl of barely ten summers. How could she survive so many days of fever? But Grandfather didn't give up. With people dying all around, he didn't move from her side, the only surviving member of his immediate family after this terrible moon of illness.

He made her drink water, and various smelly brews; he did ceremonies he wasn't authorized to do; he even brewed medicine, he who was no healer. Grandfather was a warrior, a fearsome person the entire town admired, but he changed upon losing his family. When the fever refused to go away, taking more toll on the shrinking town, he had made a sleigh, and putting her, still feverish and dreaming, upon it, nothing but a bundle of blankets, with barely anything in it, he had left. In the clearness of the woods she would get better, he maintained. With no more people coughing the sickness all around her.

She didn't know any of it back then, having not been around, wandering other worlds and conversing with spirits. But later, he had told her.

She couldn't hear at all in the beginning, so he had taught her to talk with signs, and how to read his lips. How he knew all that she couldn't surmise. But he was Grandfather, the wisest person in the entire world. Of course he knew everything; why wouldn't he?

She blinked, to make the suspicious wetness go away. They never went back to the town, to find out what happened to it. Instead, they settled in a nice little cabin he had built far away in the woods, and he had taught her everything, how to hunt and not only cook, how to trace animals, how to rely on her other senses, as, despite his hopes, her hearing returned, but only a little.

When she began deciphering lower sounds, he was elated. Hopeful, he danced around the fire he had made, performing a long, strange-looking ceremony. He was very grateful to the spirits, but as the moons passed, no other sounds penetrated her wall of silence, and he was downcast. She knew he was, even though he tried to conceal it. One didn't need one's hearing, he would claim, as long as one was prepared to use other senses and never let one's guard down.

So she did her best to learn, not because she thought it that necessary—he was there to care for her and protect her, wasn't he?—but because she didn't want to disappoint him. He believed in her so wholeheartedly!

The tears were streaming now, so she stopped and wiped them resolutely. He would be sad to see her crying, watching from the Sky World, wishing her to be as happy as she was before, through their wonderful summers in the loneliness of their woods. He would wish to see her strong and determined, walking her chosen path.

What path, she didn't know yet, but as sure as Father Sun who comes to lighten their world with every dawn, she would find something good, truly good, something that would make

Grandfather proud.

The split between the rocks she was looking for peeked at her discreetly behind the old tree, not far away from the top of the trail. Holding her breath, she peered into the dank semidarkness, fearing the worst, even though no sight of recent infringement but hers marked the path or its moss-covered surroundings. Still, her heart pounded wildly against her chest. Before reaching out, she listened to her inner senses, making sure there was no one nearby, no men and no animals. One could never be too careful with those things.

To her new surge of relief, the badly tanned hide was still there, lying where she had left it on her previous invasion into this heart of the woods, untouched, even by forest dwellers.

Hands trembling, she felt its contents rather than examined it, as though her eyesight was as nonexistent as her hearing.

Oh, yes, it was there, the most magnificent bow that ever existed, the sturdiest, most accurate of weapons. Grandfather knew how to make those things. He claimed he had been inspired by the Great Spirits themselves when he made it for her.

Reassured by this happy memory as opposed to the previous unhappy ones, she pressed the bundle close to her chest, then whispered hurriedly, thanking the spirits who guarded this place, asking for their permission to use it again should the need arise.

He would appreciate her surprise, she thought, hurrying down the trail, careful not to slip. He wouldn't expect anything of that sort.

Aingahon shifted tiredly. He had been on his feet since the sunrise, running from one meeting to another, speaking to too many people, all of them important, various elders and leaders, not easily persuadable warriors, his regular audience.

Visitors from nearby villages crowded the town, worried and agitated, as did the guests from some farther settlements. Two dead hunters who had been found more than five dawns ago near one of the villages did not belong to this town, but the indignant visitors flooded Tushuway nevertheless, demanding support.

The despicable Mountain People had been the ones to do it, everyone knew, even though there was no concrete evidence to that claim. The location of murdered group pointed in every direction, with wandering Attiwandaronk or even Wyandot as likely to be the culprits, or maybe even enraged, vengeful locals from this or that settlement, seeking to settle a score. There were cases like this in people's history.

Still, everyone tended to blame the notorious Longhouse neighbors for everything these days. Which let Aingahon know that his incessant activities of the past two summers might have borne fruit, after all. But for the stubbornness of the War Chief and one particular member of the Town Council…

"We have heard your words, brothers," one of the leading elders of the town had been heard saying earlier, facing the visitors, the original complainers among them. "Our hearts are bleeding for you. We shall wipe your tears, brothers, we shall…"

The customary words of consoling went on, uninterrupted. People could not be so impolite as to interfere the condolence speech, yet the crowds weren't listening. He knew they weren't. Their stormy, closed faces told him that, the darkness of their eyes.

"It's the lowly skunks from the east," people muttered, just voices in the crowd. "Will we let them get away with this?"

"No, we won't."

Firmly, Aingahon pushed his way through the crowds, to see the orating elders clearly. The members of the Town Council and leading people from the nearby settlements, along with the War Chief of another town stood next to their own warriors' leader, two impressive forms, elaborately decorated, showing no disagreement. But their views were not in accordance, Aingahon knew, having received many reports. He had traveled to that other settlement with the end of the Cold Moons—a difficult journey of more than a few days of sailing—to an arranged meeting with this same another war leader. He had come back encouraged, determined to make their own leaders listen. Only to run into an even more solid wall of resistance, of open disapproval, of barely concealed enmity. The authorities of Tushuway wouldn't listen.

Their own War Chief was speaking now, mounting platitudes, saying little, promising nothing. Some of the elders were eyeing Aingahon suspiciously, not liking his lingering so close to the forefront, anticipating trouble.

And why wouldn't they? he thought bitterly, waiting for the orating warrior to finish. This opportunity was too good to miss. So many people whose opinions were reported to be in agreement with his own, but the visiting leaders were a novelty.

"Will the death of these brave hunters remain unavenged?" He had heard his own voice rolling loudly, filling the open space, reaching everyone with the same ease the words of the War Chief had before. "Will we sit by and do nothing, condole our brothers with words and little else?"

The warriors' leader stiffened so visibly, the vein upon his forehead pulsated, and the elders beside him pursed their mouths in displeasure.

"Our brothers can rest assured that their grievances will not be overlooked, *warrior*." The freezing gaze was clearly meant to make Aingahon fall silent, or better yet, disappear. Something he couldn't do, not anymore.

"We all know who did the despicable deed," he said, disregarding the pause that suddenly ensued, a heavy, foreboding silence. "We all know who feel safe to invade our woods, to roam our hunting grounds, to kill our game and our people. The real enemy!" He didn't dare to pause, because even a heartbeat of silence would give the elders, or most likely the warriors' leader himself, the opportunity to gather their senses and override his words with theirs, having the right and the authority to do so. Also his courage, if not his resolve to say what had to be said aloud and in such a noble assembly, might falter. "Had we had enough courage, enough determination and drive, we would be uniting now, all our towns and villages, no matter how far they are from each other and how disinterested in the affairs of the others. We would be inviting the Attiwandaronk People to join our union as well." For a heartbeat, he paused, having run out of breath. "Our neighbors from both sides showed us that the time for living apart is gone. First the Longhouse People, and now the Wyandot, they have both shown us the way, had we been willing to learn. But what do we do with their examples? Instead of organizing amongst ourselves, uniting our own towns and villages, while turning to talk to our neighbors in the north, we grovel and fawn upon those newly concocted unions, trying to ingratiate ourselves with them as though we were nothing but beggars, unable to stand up for ourselves. We, the Long Tails, called so after the most magnificent predator residing in our woods, the Mountain Lion! People who used to be proud and worthy, but are not anymore. What has become of us?"

Forgetting his misgivings, he stepped forward, then turned to look at the people among whom he had stood until now, eager to have their attention, their interest. The leaders of this town were the lost case, but not the people, not his true countryfolk. Nor were the visitors, those curious guests and their leadership.

"Are we to live like that forever? Trying to keep quiet, to offend neither side, to pacify both unions; struggling to remain neutral, afraid to take a wrong step. Is this the way of the proud, warlike people we used to be? Our fathers and their fathers would be ashamed to learn what we are reduced to. And maybe they are ashamed now, maybe they are! Watching from their place in the star-studded sky, shaking their heads, their hearts heavy."

Bringing his arms up and forward, he wished he were standing on the elevated ground like the leaders did. People needed to see his face and not hear his voice only; and he needed to see what their expressions held. Were they listening?

"Will we go on shaming our forefathers? Will we agree to live in humbleness and fear, bending to every whim of the so-called Great League, or the now-strengthened Wyandot?" Another wide gesture of his spread palms. "We, who are not an insignificant cluster of villages but independent people, people who can stand up for themselves, people who can work together like the brothers that we really are and not just affable neighbors. Because we can help each other to fight off the enemy. We can—"

"Halt your words, young man." Surprisingly, that came from one of the elders and not the War Chief, whose expression Aingahon wanted to see badly but couldn't. To glance back would be to admit his misgivings. "This is neither the time nor the place to make speeches you are not authorized to make." The voice of the older man rose, displaying no anger but only the need to speak louder when addressing the crowds. "We will discuss all that pains us, the complicated matters our leaders are trying to solve in a way that no harm would come to our people. Our guests, all of you who came visiting, arrived here for just that reason." A quick pause, to encircle the crowds with his gaze, assumed Aingahon, still facing the people, their expressions mixed, encouraging, eyes darting from him to the speaking elder and back. "We will have these matters discussed until we have found a clear path to walk, the best road that would suit our people, who are indeed great people, fearless and strong. Take heed of my words, and do not lose your patience." This time, the eyes were burning holes in his back, he could feel it most clearly, while turning to face the orating elder. "Some of you are old enough to behave better than youths of no manners and little restraint."

An open reprimand he found difficult to cope with, to bite his tongue and say nothing in return. His goal was achieved, even if at the price of this humiliating telling off. Someone had to air people's thoughts aloud, show them that the leaders' decisions could be questioned openly and with no fear. They had to know that there was an alternative, a different course of an action, a different path to walk; the visiting leaders as much as the local townsfolk. Too many people agreed with him, and it was time to commit himself, and thus make them commit as well. He hadn't planned for this opportunity, but he couldn't miss it when it presented itself.

Other elders were talking, directing visiting dignitaries to the meeting in the relevant longhouse, the one that hosted the Head of the Town Council.

"The War Council will meet outside, tomorrow at noon, at a place the invited people will be notified about." Not to be outshone by the civil authorities, the War Chief was speaking loudly, striving to be heard. "As for you, warrior," this time the voice dropped to a lower tone, as the wide frame of the man nearly pushed into Aingahon, making him wish to step back. Which he didn't, but with a conscious effort. "Come to the Flat Rock tomorrow with the first light. Bring other discontents with you, if you wish. As many as you wish, all those who are eager to say their piece."

For a heartbeat, Aingahon just stared, taken aback by the strange nature of the invitation. The Flat Rock was tucked far enough in the woods, towering above a cluster of gushing streams, a good place to hold a private meeting, but for what purpose?

"There are no discontents here," he said sternly, standing the cutting glare. "Only people who take to heart the plight of our towns and villages, people who believe that we can, and should, stand up for ourselves."

The older warrior's eyes flickered with cold disapproval. "Like I said, you are allowed to come and share your grievances with the people of our War Council, warrior, those who would find it important to honor you with their presence. And while I'm not certain we would be able to help you with your misgivings and fears, which you made sure to share with everyone who was ready to listen over the course of many moons, I do hope your ears will remain open to the opinions of your elders and betters. You are not a youth, and from a person of so many summers, one might expect more subtlety, a better display of manners and self-control."

This was spoken in a loud enough voice to attracted attention, he knew, feeling his limbs going stiff with anger. He was not a youth indeed, not a person of no importance to be reprimanded so openly.

"There is no custom that prevents people from speaking their minds, from sharing their doubts and misgivings with leaders who were elected to do just that—take care of their countryfolk." He heard his own voice ringing as clearly, as loudly, listened to by their possible audience, of that he was sure. There were more people who shared his views than those who didn't. "To speak one's mind in a general assembly that gathered for this exact purpose, to turn to one's leaders with questions or requests of reassurance, is not a sign of bad manners or lack of self-control. We all have our people's best interests in heart, and we all are entitled to speak our minds."

This came out well. The dangerous flash in his accuser's eyes told him so. He was treading a thin line here, challenging the warriors' leader so openly.

"As I said, you have much to learn, younger brother."

Apparently, the man was in tighter control than his eyes showed, but the sense of relief it brought made Aingahon angry. Was he afraid of a violent confrontation? He could best this man, maybe, if acting quickly and decisively, putting it all into the first blow or thrust. Not a question that would have bothered him two summers ago, before the accursed trip onto Onondaga lands, before the injury. He clenched his teeth.

"Sadly, your impatience clogs your ears, even when your natural arrogance doesn't do that." The warriors' leader lifted his shoulders with exaggerated indifference. "One can understand some of it, given your limitations. It must be a difficult reality to face when one is unable to do the simplest things." The thin grin that stretched the man's lips was openly taunting, gone almost before noticed. *Almost.* "Well, come to Flat Rock tomorrow with dawn, and don't make your elders and betters wait. You will be allowed to state your grievances, to share what is in your heart, as you so eloquently put."

This time, he clung to his temper with such difficulty his hands shook, and his teeth threatened to crack from the force with which he clenched them together. *Given your limitations; don't make your elders wait.* But how low that man could step, how obvious in his hints. Flat Rock was a spot not easily reachable, even for people with no broken limbs. But he would be there, he would! Well before dawn too, and alone. He was not a coward like that man, seeking support of his peers, attacking a person only when he felt safe, backed by the others. No! He, Aingahon, had more courage than that.

What did this man want to tell him in private? Probably nothing, he decided, diving into the freshness of the woods beyond the town's fence, welcoming the opportunity to be alone for a while. The familiar trails beckoned. How did he get here so fast? Or maybe he wasn't fast; maybe he had just lost track of time. A likelier possibility. Had he just turned around and stormed off? He stifled a grunt.

Shrugging he went on, indifferent now. The Flat Rock meeting would serve nothing, bring them nowhere. All the War Chief wanted was to make a show of openness and acceptance, of a great leader bending his ear to the worst of the discontents. Was this how the man had put it? What a belittling way. As though he were a child refused a sweet cake, throwing tantrums about it, deaf to good reasoning.

Discontents! But the people who thought like him were many and not far between, the leading visitors from the nearby settlements among those.

The clearing glimmered emptily, shadowed in this later afternoon light. He looked around, slightly disappointed. Could this day get any worse? The pouch tied to his girdle contained deliciously fresh cakes that he had all but stolen, taking a chance at being caught and looking silly to the women of his longhouse, those who had baked those delicacies, preparing for the feast that was certain to be laid out to honor and impress the visitors. Not fried or boiled but a bread baked in embers, a true treat.

Reaching out with his senses, while casting another glance around, he sighed. The place was empty, and it had been so for two more dawns, because on the day before he was too busy to come out and spend a leisurely afternoon in the woods. The visitors had been expected some time prior to their actual arrival.

Shrugging, he retraced his steps, back toward the open grounds, the shores of the nearby spring and the cliffs surrounding it.

Flat Rock? But he would have a hideous time negotiating its trail. What a filthy rat the War Chief was, stooping so low in order to get back at the man who presented a threat, not above trying to humiliate his rival by all means.

He cursed venomously, for even now, his knee was protesting against the sharpening incline, sending shafts of pain up his thigh, forcing him to slow his step.

Leaning against a wide trunk, he paused, remembering how he had to brave this same trail only two dawns ago, keeping up with the briskness of the girl's step. She had been nearly racing on that day, dancing with happiness, clutching the rabbit she had shot using his bow, waving it like a mighty spoil. She had shot it from a regular distance, still, it was a good hit and he didn't mind her making a big thing out of it. She had been boasting her skill with a bow before, not happy with his freely expressed doubts, so having proven herself, she deserved her moment of triumph and a bit of close-mouthed praise.

Where was she? Why wasn't she waiting, stalking him whenever he came out, as was her custom?

She had begun doing it before that day when he had talked to her and heard her story, bringing her to the town afterwards, as promised, guarding her until she ate her first warm meal in moons, or so he suspected. She had sneaked away shortly thereafter, he remembered, but since that day, he could be certain that she would be around, every time he went out, approaching him if he was alone, settling for a walk or a talk, or both, perfectly at ease, trustful.

Through the half a moon that had passed since, it had become a custom, and several times it happened that he made sure to go out alone, to clear his head, yes, but not in a perfect solitude. It was good to talk to her, to vent his frustrations aloud. Despite her ridiculously young age—she claimed being born fifteen summers ago, but he didn't believe her on that; she looked nothing but a child, skinny, long-limbed, underfed—or her inability to hear properly, she turned out to be a good listener. It was difficult to tell if she heard all of his words or not, because sometimes she would stare at his lips, and he knew she was reading them, but sometimes she would concentrate on a different sight, her knife leaping toward yet another target, her hands busy breaking sticks and branches. And yet, when he would fall silent she would look up and comment, say something surprisingly wise, reflect on what he had been talking about. So could she hear properly or not? Half a moon later and he hadn't arrived at the definite conclusion as yet.

Out of his reverie, he began pushing himself off his temporary support just as a familiar hiss tore the peacefulness of the afternoon air, making his body react on its own. Throwing himself away, he groaned at the tearing pain that shot all the way from his knee and up, clearly unhappy with the unexpected exercise.

Staggering, he forced his way into the bushes, counting on their readily offered coverage, before collapsing into a heap, desperate to contain the pain. Was it dislocated again? Would he manage to twist it with enough force and sharpness to put it back in place all by himself?

He swallowed a groan. It would take him half a day or more to crawl back to the town, to reach a healer who would be able to help? Oh no, he would never manage!

Amidst the colorful outburst of pain and the wild racing of his heart, the thoughts rushed through his mind, chasing one another, with no logic and no pattern, with the main question looming, too complicated to let it near—*who was shooting at him?*

When able to straighten up, he pushed himself into a sitting position, gathering courage to inspect the damage. It was possible to recognize with his eyes sometimes, without pressing his knee into bending. He had learned all about it through the last summer of intensive traveling.

The obvious rustling took his attention away. Someone was running up the trail, in a hurry, not trying to conceal his approach.

Freezing, he listened, his knife out, heart thumping again. Was this the same person who shot at him? Did he think his target was hit?

The footsteps neared, plopping upon the muddy ground, making more noise than a hungry bear in winter. A small, slender bear at that.

When she burst into his view, slowing her step near the tree with the arrow sticking out of it, he already knew who it was, his relief imminent. Still, he said nothing, just stared, safe in his semi-hidden location, trying to understand. When she peered around, clearly unsettled, he shrugged, then waved his hand.

"Are you hurt?" she shouted in her usual strident voice. "It can't be!"

The relief that smoothed her features made a pleasant sight. As she dropped beside him, he could not keep his frown on, not all of it.

"Stop yelling," he said, putting his attention back to the attempt of moving his leg. It was swollen, but only a little, and it did move, with a painful protest, but it did. "Why did you shoot at me?"

She was peering at him, eyes troubled and huge, openly offended. As though he was the one to aim an arrow at her. "What?"

"Why did you shoot at me?" he repeated, this time facing her for enough time to let her see the movement of his lips. "It's your arrow sticking up there, isn't it?"

A light nod in the direction of the tree at fault had her jumping to her feet, rushing toward the forest giant, very eager. Standing on her toes in order to reach it, she tugged at the wooden shaft gently then transferred her grip to the flint tip, loosening its hold on the bark with practiced ease, careful not to dislodge the arrowhead or make it to come off.

Impressed, he returned to tending his knee. But this one knew what she was doing, like in the case of her knife. He had seen her cleaning the impressively massive flint carefully upon the occasion, after shooting that rabbit, tending to her favorite weapon in a way only a careful owner would do.

"I didn't shoot you," she said, this time keeping her voice considerably lower. "My arrow hit it next to your head, yes, but I was aiming that way." Glancing at her briefly, he caught a glimpse of the shyest of smiles. "I wanted to show you what I can do with *my* bow."

Postponing the need to rise to his feet with the readiness he knew was far from being admirable, he squinted. "Show me this thing."

She didn't hesitate. Kneeling beside him with atypical care, she who would usually drop where she stood, with abandon and not a thought spared to her clothes or limbs, she extended both hands reverently, balancing her precious weapon, its large well-polished body glimmering in the little sun that managed to sneak through the bushes. Very sturdy-looking, the shaft itself displayed two colors, its outer side considerably brighter than the inner lining. Yet, it didn't look as though it was made out of two different pieces of wood. How could it? No glue would hold two sticks together unless tied, but then the shooting device would turn clumsy, not comfortable to use.

"Let me see it."

Forgetting his knee and the alarming throb in it, he reached for the perfectly polished shaft, enjoying its touch. Very sturdy, indeed. And yes, made out of a single piece. His fingers told him that, running along the smooth surface, noting no bulges. "Where did you get this bow?"

She kept absolutely still, her eyes following his fingers, full of fascination. Which made her miss his question, he realized, his own concentration returning to the wonderful weapon, exploring the string now, a braided sinew, another very solid, evidently durable thing, not too wide to lose its flexibility, nor too thin to chance a tearing. A perfect weapon.

"Where did you get this thing?" he asked louder, pulling at the braided string lightly, impressed with the readiness the body of the bow was responding with. So sturdy, yet so pliant!

"Grandfather did it for me," she said proudly, face aglow. "He did it when I was younger, but he let me use it only before the last Cold Moons, after I could shoot anything he asked me to with his bow. Only then he let me use mine." Eyes on her obviously most precious of possessions, the girl—by now he had learned that her name was Tsutahi—was practically shining, lips quivering in the widest of smiles, the usually pale cheeks coloring into a darker shade, glowing with life. "I can shoot from great distances with it. No regular bow can reach that far." Suddenly, her gaze changed, turned mischievous, resting on him, glimmering with mirth. "I shot at you from so far away. I sat on that cliff top. See? Over there, behind those trees." The slim arm leapt upward, muddied and covered with old and fresh scratches, its color like that of early maize, yellowish pale. "I could see you walking away from the clearing and up this trail. I could see it most clearly. That high and far I was. And still my arrow got here. Easily at that!"

The unmistakable bragging of her tone made him wish to laugh. Shaking his head, he ensured that only the crooked side of his smile showed. "Don't do this again. You could have missed."

"No!" In her turn, she shook her head forcefully, eyes opened even wider now, sincere, eager to convince. "I told you, I never miss. Grandfather didn't let me touch this bow before I hit everything he asked without missing. He made me not to miss one single shot for a whole moon before he said I was ready."

He watched her animated face, strangely pleased, warmed by the sight of her glowing cheeks. They were always so unhealthily pale. And her eyes. All of a sudden, she looked just the child she was, not a strange forest creature.

"Still, I don't want you to practice on me, not even when you are dead sure. Many things can influence your shooting. A good aim and a firm hand are just a part of it. Wind, for one, can interfere, can make your arrow veer from its intended target. A slight change in course and here you have it, sticking out of my face." He frowned, the lightness of his mood evaporating again. The stupid girl almost shot him, didn't she? "If you ever aim at me again, arrow or knife or anything else, I will never come to speak to you or be with you out here. Never. Even if no harm happens, like today."

The glow dulled. Clasping her lips tight, she dropped her gaze, to stare at the glistening ground, scowling, her mutter barely heard, for a change.

"I know about the wind. I took that into account. Grandfather made me learn all about the wind. A good shooter always checks this, its direction and its strength." The misshapen tip of her moccasin kicked at a pinecone, then kept on digging into the softness of the moss-covered ground. "Also the sun. Grandfather told me all about it, about the play of the light, the way the sun makes things look different from a distance, sometimes. When water, or polished things, reflect it."

Fascinated, he listened, over his brief spell of anger already.

How could she know all this, child that she was? Did the old man truly teach her so many things, training her day and night? But for what purpose? Was he determined to make a warrior out of her? The thought made him chuckle.

"What did he want you to do with all this knowledge?" She was still staring at the ground, so he picked up a small pinecone, throwing it at her with matching accuracy, to bounce against her shoulder and make her gaze leap up. "Why did your grandfather teach you to shoot so well?"

Her scowl was stubborn, like that of an offended cub. The shrug that followed completed the picture.

He rolled his eyes, greatly amused. "Stop making faces and answer my question."

"Grandfather wanted me to know those things," she said with another shrug, as though it explained it all. "He taught me everything, how to hunt game, how to skin it so nothing would be lost, no meat and no fat, and the hide would look as though it has just been taken off the animal, you see?" Again, the mention of the old man made her eyes shine. "We would wander the woods for days, not coming back to our cabin at all. Only when Cold Moons came."

"Why didn't you live in a village or a town, like other people?"

To get to his feet was actually easier with his attention on her words and not the reactions of his knee. It hurt, but no more than expected. No bad twisting, no dislocation, thank all the small and great spirits for that.

Her closed expression told him that he shouldn't have asked.

He suppressed a shrug. "Come. Let us reach the top of this trail, enjoy the view, and spoil ourselves on deliciously fresh cookies. How about that, eh?"

Reaching into the small bag, still attached to his girdle despite all the thrashing in the bushes, he fished one of the crumbling slices of sweetened bread out, waving it before her face.

Her reaction was everything he hoped for. No more gloom or bad thoughts, not for now. If only it was so easy to disperse his own grievances and frustrations.

"Oh, oh, oh, they are still warm!" There was no stopping her now, her effort to snatch his bait crowding with quick success.

He didn't try to take it away anyway, other than the mocking attempt to move it out of her reach. She was too quick, too decisive, unerring in her instincts. Truly a warrior-girl, if there was such a thing.

"The rest of it you get when we reach our destination."

"Why are we going there?" she asked, falling into his step easily, talking again with annoying loudness. He had noticed that the more confident she felt, the louder she talked, as though forgetting to watch her speech. "It's a long walk back to the town."

He knew what she meant, and it angered him. He was not a cripple, was he? He could go out and up difficult trails if he wished to do so. Even if it took him longer to get to his destination.

Well, the trail to the Flat Rock would be harder to climb, and with no light to show his way. Maybe he could take that walking stick he used rarely, when wandering the woods all alone, away from prying eyes. He could hide it when near the designated place, before meeting the War Chief and his cronies. What did this man want from him? Nothing good, that much was obvious.

"I want to enjoy some peace and quiet," he said, shrugging, not sure she would understand him while seeing nothing but his profile, with no help from his moving lips. "That's all."

Indeed, she skipped over a cluster of stones, paying no attention to what he said. Such a strange thing. Though having spent days in her company, he still knew next to nothing about her, still could not predict her reactions to various words or deeds. Fancy shooting at him in order to display her skill! Rigorous training or not, she could have missed, anyone could.

The view of the valley beneath their feet opened with typical suddenness, one moment thick forest, the other nothing but dusky sky and the breeze on their sweaty faces, and the magnificent sight of the river gushing far away, pushing its way through the lake of green.

The cliffs of the Flat Rock were clearly visible, deceptively near, but not really. To reach it, he would have to retrace his way,

circumvent another hill, then push his course up, a difficult climb
for a man who needed a walking stick to cover true distances. Did
the filthy War Chief choose this particular location to get back at
him in one more way? There was no need to answer this question.

She was watching the same direction, shielding her eyes
against the glow of the setting sun.

"See this?" Pointing at the horizontal tops that lined the
twisting snake of the river, she smiled. "If there were a deer out
there right now, or anything else, whitetail or a moose, I could
shoot it for you. Easily!"

"That far?" He watched the swaying trees that adorned the cliff
she pointed at. "I'm not sure the arrow would arrive there with
enough force to kill. It's too far."

The abruptness with which she grabbed his hand startled him,
made him wish to pull it away. "Yes, it will. My bow is better,
remember? Its arrows reach far. See?"

Again, the wondrous weapon was thrust into his hands, with
much force. He rolled his eyes, but the touch of the hard polished
wood gripped, caused his resentment to lessen.

In the better light than the dimness of the grove, it was easy to
see how invested this bow was, how thoroughly prepared. One
piece of wood, definitely now, but of two kinds. Must be a good
combination of the outer trunk's portion as opposed to the inner
parts of it. Different sorts of strength, different flexibility,
complimenting each other while combined. The old man must
have searched for the proper branch or trunk forever. Why did he
do such a thing, and for a girl?

Taking a better position, he aimed at the cliff in question,
marveling at the readiness with which the hard wood bent,
wondering how it would feel to possess such a thing. With no
agility to move around nimbly enough while hunting, he could
use just this sort of an advantage on others.

Scanning imagined targets that might be lining those cliffs, he
turned slightly, catching the outline of the Flat Rock again,
seemingly different when observed through the medium of a
good bow. If only the War Chief were standing there now.

The thought hit him like a punch in his stomach, made his

chest empty of air. But no, he couldn't do that. It would be too obvious, too wrong for plenty of reasons. Was he a coward to shoot people who displeased him, and from a safe distance? No!

He dropped his hand, feeling it trembling, even if lightly.

"It's a good bow, yes."

The forced words barely disturbed the crispness of the air, but she read them all the same, indifferent to the volume of his voice of course.

"It's the best bow in the whole world of the Sky Woman," she declared, not put out with the abruptness with which he shoved it back into her hands. The mere touch of the polished wood burned his skin now. "If something appears there, I'll shoot it now." To his growing uneasiness, she snatched the arrow that was only so recently recovered from the tree trunk, aiming directly at the Flat Rock, poising with her legs wide apart, stable, ready, unerring. *Lethal.* She would be able to hit her target, he knew. She would be —

The new thought made the blood freeze in his veins. No, no, he couldn't do *that*. He couldn't! It would be worse than to do the deed himself, although, of all people, she would never be suspected, never. Anyone but her. And if she happened to sleep somewhere near, coming to greet the sun from this particular spot as it came to lighten the world, the valley, and the cliffs, Flat Rock and those who would be treading it, standing or squatting...

No, it was insane, impossible, unwise. He couldn't possibly ask her to do that, couldn't trust her to stick to such a wild, dishonorable plan, couldn't expect her to manage even if she agreed to try. And what if she missed and got caught? He would have to stick by her, take the blame, turn into a true outcast, if not worse. He had already ruined his life by trying to do just that, by conceiving a plan to get rid of the annoying Onondaga leader and then rushing to do it all by himself, with no one the wiser, no one involved, no one to tell, to incriminate.

Well, even if he had succeeded in that and no one besides one unscrupulous elder of High Springs knew or suspected, he had failed in the implementation so miserably his life had been altered, changed for the worse; not to say ruined. The Great Spirits had showed him what they thought of immoral men. They had punished him harshly for straying from the straight path, and this time they might be more thorough, more unforgiving.

"Can you shoot from such distance without missing?" he asked, not recognizing his own voice, so hoarse and broken it sounded.

She paid his words no heed, her attention on the cliff she was watching and not his lips. Stepping closer, he stood beside her.

"Hit that tree above the cluster of bushes over there, near the edge of the cliff," he said slowly, every word measured, ready to repeat them should she need to watch his lips. "Make your arrow stick in its bark."

CHAPTER 5

Ganayeda watched the Crooked Tongues man nearing in his typical springy stroll, walking beside Iheks, both men talking, laughing lazily, perfectly at ease.

It never ceased to surprise him, the foreigner's ability to blend, to feel at home in every surroundings he reached. He was a stranger, wasn't he? A newly adopted person, with less than a whole span of seasons spent on this side of the Great Lake. The village he resided in hated this man's countryfolk with relish, having suffered from the Crooked Tongues for more time than anyone could remember, the recent tentative peace agreements notwithstanding.

And it's not that the foreigner has been accepted that readily, easy familiarity or not. Not until Father threw his weight behind this village's unexpected and actually unasked-for guest, letting everyone know that this man was his personal protégé, to be accepted and treated well. If it didn't work out in Lone Hill for him, High Springs would be offering better hospitality. Or so the Onondaga War Chief had indicated, for the benefit of the villagers and their visitor alike, and to the wild rejoicing of Gayeri, who apparently had decided to stick to her rescuer, proving that for her the Crooked Tongue was more than her means to return home.

Ganayeda grudged her none of it. Her return to Lone Hill was what mattered. Beyond that, she was nothing to him, a passing fancy from the time when he had briefly lost direction, began doubting the path he had been walking. All of it in the past now, thank all the great and small spirits for that.

"The representative of Tsonontowan wanted to know if the War Chief will be arriving tomorrow as rumored." The man who was hurrying to keep up with him seemed to do that with a certain effort.

Ganayeda slowed his step. "The Mountain People are as impatient as always."

"Yes, they are." His companion grinned lightly. The local of Onondaga Town, he evidently didn't feel offended on behalf of their western neighbors.

"Did they give an indication as to the matter that they wish to bring before the War Chief, or maybe the Great Council, with such urgency?"

Iheks and his Crooked Tongues company reached the flat ground and were looking around, shielding their eyes. Well, Iheks did the searching, while the foreigner seemed to maintain a lively conversation with the rest of their following, Flint People judging by the aggressive spikes that adorned their cleanly shaved topknots. The Keepers of the Eastern Door loved to emphasis their warlike appearances, reflected Ganayeda, grinning to himself.

"No, they didn't. Their people just talked to me, asked about you and then about the War Chief. All reserved and full of mystery. Said it was an important matter that the War Chief might be interested to hear first-hand." Spreading his arms, the man looked away, studying the valley and the vivid activity all around it. So close to the opening ceremonies it was already filling to the brim. "They didn't say it was urgent."

"You think it's something of importance, though." Ganayeda made it a statement, eyes on the same view, following various groups that rushed about, appraising them, trying to see that all was proceeding in orderly manner, with no troubles brewing.

"Maybe."

"If you run into any of them again, find out if they'll settle for a meeting with me, or anyone else of the organizers." He saw Iheks waving at someone, looking enthusiastic. "But don't seek them out specifically. Only if they try to accost you again."

The man just nodded. Not being one of Ganayeda's friends or closest assistants, he muttered something polite and began wandering off in the direction of the towering town. To Ganayeda's certain sense of relief. It was good to be alone, at least for a little while.

Since the brief conversation with his brother when the sun was still high, he had tried to carve a moment of privacy in order to think about Okwaho's news. An attempt that did not meet with much success. People were not about to let him be, but it was actually good to be busy, an important part of important happenings, to be listened to and consulted with, satisfying to be a person people talked to with an open respect and appreciation.

So far, this gathering was progressing well, growing with each day, readying for the grand opening. Which left him with not enough time to sleep or eat, yet he didn't feel like complaining. That is, until his brother appeared. The unsettling news the young hothead brought needed to be thought about, analyzed, understood. Their political implications, as well as the personal angle of it. With a little bit solitude, he might be able to think about it, to come to grips with the worrisome reality, as well as the sadness at the passing of a great man.

Also, there were these same Mountain People again, he knew, turning to descend the trail leading back toward the valley. Okwaho was worried by the developments in their areas, and Father had evidently taken his youngest son's reports to heart.

What was going on in these lands?

Normally it wouldn't have worried an Onondaga man such as himself. There were no mutual war enterprises between the families of the Peacemaker's metaphorical longhouse. There was no need for that. The Great Messenger stopped the fighting between the brothers, and it was more than enough; the inner peace of the Great League was what mattered. Not occasionally troublesome neighbors. The Flint People being the Keepers of the Eastern Door could take care of any problematic presence or advance, and the same went for the Mountain People. They asked for no help, were offered none, sporting the title of the Keepers with much pride, and for a good reason.

Diving into the shade the cluster of nearby trees provided, he hastened his step in order to reach Iheks and the Crooked Tongue before any more people accosted him with comments, or questions, or things to discuss. It was near dusk already, and he was determined to catch Okwaho for a conversation lasting half the night, at the very least, before the young buck scampered off, with his unruly girl in tow. Fancy dragging one's wife all over the woods in order to please the wild thing!

"We were just looking for you, oh Honorable Leader," cried out Iheks, his hands high in the air, palms up, voice trembling with mirth. "What lucky chance sent you crossing our paths?"

Ganayeda grinned. "Oh, yes, you two do look exhausted from all that effort of looking for me. From up there," he pointed toward the hill he descended, "all one could see was the cloud of dust your running feet were raising."

He met the foreigner's twinkling gaze, at ease in the company of this man as always. His name was Ogteah, he remembered, but no one seemed to use it, except maybe his wife. And Father. For everyone else, he was the Crooked Tongue, the one and the only, the true representative of his people. Other adoptees, occasional former captives, were sporting this dubious place of origins as well—even Ganayeda's own mother, when anyone cared to remember such long-forgotten history—but none of these boasted of it, talked about it, or even cared to remember, while this man never tried to make a secret out of it. On the contrary, he had spoken about his former people on every occasion, with the slightest provocation, or even without it, telling about their ways and their newly organized union, stressing the similarities, oblivious to the spells of resentment this particular topic often raised, unafraid, or maybe just indifferent to it. Sometimes Ganayeda suspected that he might be doing it for a purpose.

"What are you up to?" he asked, grinning with a measure of reserve, taking in the rest of their company, the warlike Flint, now unmistakable.

A shrug was his answer. "We were checking the lay of the land near the lake shores. Could be fitting for holding a sort of a contest, to pass time, make people busy. The restless warriors among us, that is." A gaze that was shot at one of the Flint, a broadly built young man with the most perfect warriors' hairdo

Ganayeda had ever seen and two spears balanced in one hand, held enough baiting friendliness.

"What sort of contest?"

"Spear and hoop."

"Like the ball game of the previous gatherings," added Iheks. "It might provide an interesting diversion."

"You can't do it with spear throwing, fit hundreds of people in two teams." Glancing at the men who were congregating near one of the farthest fires, Ganayeda spotted his brother's unmistakable figure. How could one miss the tallness of that bearing and the showily decorated warlock, all colors and beads, as though they were about to plunge into a battle. Only the paint was missing. The showy beast.

"No need to do that." The Crooked Tongue was speaking lively, the shadows that lurked in his eyes before gone. "We divide people into regular teams, then part those in pairs, make each contester go for one single throw. Or maybe two, depends on the amount of willing to participate. Can handle hundreds of people and more, if we have so many volunteers, in this way"

"It would take an entire day to have everyone who would wish to participate get their chance."

"We can make bigger teams," insisted the foreigner, atypically forceful for a change, his usual facade of slightly bored, mischievous indifference gone. "If we conduct it properly, people won't get bored while waiting for their turn, because they will be busy watching, betting on winners, enjoying themselves."

His Flint audience was nodding vigorously, all four of them.

"Like with the large-scale ball game." The lock of the warlike Flint with two spears swayed, as he leaned forward, not bothering to conceal his excitement. "I heard that the last time they held such a competition here, when all our people gathered, they had to finish tossing that ball by the light of fires and torches."

"That was the one before the last," corrected Iheks. "The gathering of two spans of seasons ago." Giving the Flint a look that was not entirely unfriendly, Ganayeda's old friend grinned. "You haven't been introduced to our highly esteemed organizer of this gathering." This time, a wink was directed at him. "Those are our honorable guests from the lands of the rising sun, the Keepers of the Eastern Door. And when I say the keepers, I mean *the* keepers. Their town, Cohoes Falls, is situated on the true edge of our league, keeping it safe from all sorts of savages from beyond their Great River."

"Cohoes Falls?" Ganayeda eyed his unexpected companions with more interest. "I'm honored to meet you. My brother spent quite a few moons there some spans of seasons ago, while joining your warriors' forces." Squinting against the glow of the setting sun, he looked at the congregation around one of the fires, seeking the object of his musings again. "Yes, it was in Cohoes Falls, I remember it now most clearly."

"Was it?" Their guest's interest piqued, leaving only the Crooked Tongue indifferent, eyeing them with politeness, yet obviously lacking in real attention, his thoughts elsewhere, probably on his projected spear contest.

"Oh, yes, it was," confirmed Iheks. "It wasn't your father's Little Falls, and I don't remember any more 'falls' connected to the names of the eastern settlements." He turned to their guests, grin wide, flickering with mischief. "He came back bringing the most exotic-looking fox from those same troublesome neighbors of yours. Our entire town was at a loss, didn't know how to take it."

"That they did." Even though feeling slightly disloyal, Ganayeda couldn't help but burst out laughing, remembering Jideah's tales. His wife had her way with words, knowing how to tell a story, to make the most trivial happening sound saucy and entertaining. And the adventures concerning Okwaho's girl were anything but trivial.

Then his eyes encountered the Flint warrior's stare, the strange, out-of-place gaping that didn't sit well with the man's prominent features.

"You know Okwaho?" breathed the Flint, leaning forward with his entire body, as though afraid to miss a word. "Is he here?"

"Yes, he is," said Ganayeda, puzzled. "And yes, I do know this wild thing."

"Where?" cried out the warrior, his eyes threatening to pop out of their sockets.

"Somewhere there, in the crowd." Noticing Iheks' barely hidden amusement, Ganayeda waved in the general direction of the valley. "I saw him there only a short time ago. Why?"

But his question remained unanswered, because the warrior was already away, rushing down the incline and toward the worst of the clamor, ready to storm it, limping in a strangely visible way. The rest of the Flint exchanged puzzled glances.

"What was that?" chuckled the Crooked Tongue, apparently out of his musings and listening now. "What did this mysterious Okwaho do to him?"

"Only the Great Spirits know," Iheks' glance reflected the puzzle of the remaining Flint. "Should we send your brother word of warning?"

Still amused, Ganayeda shook his head. "Let him deal with it." With most of their company gone, he concentrated back on the Crooked Tongue. "So spear-throwing contest, eh? Did your people do this on such a large scale?"

The man shook his head. "No, of course not. They hold no such large gatherings, as you know. Not yet." The familiar spark held all the needling mischief, gone almost before noticed. "But I thought about it, and it should work, if we make it orderly, organize it well. True that people would have to wait long for their turn to participate, but they would not be waiting in idleness. Watchers enjoy such contests as much as those who are playing. They would be cheering and betting." The large eyes twinkled again. "I predict that the amount of goods to switch hands will be greater than the amount of lost or won spears."

"I predict you, out of all people, know something about it," chuckled Iheks. "About the goods switching hands." Then the older man sobered. "I say it's a good idea, worth giving it a try. People would welcome the diversion. Not only the break in the main activities of the gathering, but also the novelty of something that hasn't been done before."

The foreigner nodded eagerly. "It can be done. I know it can."

"Well…" Shifting his weight from one foot to another, Ganayeda glanced back at the valley that was coming to life with more flickering fires. "You will be responsible for that. Full responsibility."

He let his gaze harden, remembering what Father had said about this visitor to their lands once, when they had dwelled on the subject, just the two of them. Idleness made people restless, some worse than others. There were good, promising people who just didn't know how to keep themselves busy and away from trouble. Laden one such with interesting tasks and he would do well, throw his energies and skills into a good cause and get things done.

The secret was to recognize such men, usually known troublemakers and notorious no-goods by the verdict of their communities, then make them work for you. Take down two targets with one throw—get things done and keep the troublemakers from making trouble. Many such problematic elements were not bad people by nature, Father said, while some pillars of the society, the most approved and accepted, could turn out to be the worst of the evil.

"It will be up to you, all of it. I will have nothing to do with it," he repeated, looking at his foreign company sternly. "Unless you need concrete help, it is your project, your performance, your responsibility, all of it, from organizing to supervising, to making sure that it goes without blunders and embarrassing failures."

"Of course." The twinkle was gone, leaving the large eyes hardened and sealed. "I'll make it work."

"Good." He glanced at Iheks. "Will you help around, Old Friend?"

A knowing grin was his answer. "We'll enlist support of some good, efficient folks, won't we, Crooked Tongue?"

"Certainly." The foreigner was grinning again, the foreboding mood gone, never prone to linger, not in this one. Unless pushed into violence. Ganayeda shook his head, remembering Ossossane.

"Come," he said, indicating a small trail that was twisting to their left, disappearing in the nearby grove. "If people are looking for me, tell them I'll be back shortly," he added, nodding at Iheks, knowing that his friend would understand.

The foreigner asked no questions, falling into Ganayeda's step with his typical lightness of pace.

"Thank you for backing me up on this spear-throwing thing," he said when the dusky grove swallowed them, made the clamor of the valley behind their backs dim. "It would be a good thing if it worked. Even should every visitor of this valley decide to participate, we could just limit the amount of tries to less, or make the teams smaller. Say, ten people instead of the customary fifteen or twenty. That flat land down there by the lake is large enough to have people throwing their spears without killing each other, or their audience, for that matter." The soft chuckle floated in the crispy air. "Can't have your highly praised union breaking apart because of my game."

"You wish!" Ganayeda didn't try to control his own outburst of mirth. "Our highly praised union is built to weather every possible storm, even wild Crooked Tongues bent on organizing unusual contests."

"That's reassuring."

For a few heartbeats they proceeded in silence, but Ganayeda's companion was not the type to keep his peace.

"The Flint People are something else," he related, picking his way between multitude of protruding roots, kicking at pinecones whenever he had a chance. "For obvious reasons, I was curious to meet these people, but now that I have, I'm not so sure I wish to stick to my heritage in that matter."

"You haven't seen any of it yet. Wait till the first day of the gathering. Then you will see sights worth seeing, including plenty of your favorite Flint strolling around as though they own the place." He grinned. "For your information, the Mountain People are as violently tough. Take my word on this. You haven't seen anything yet."

"So I was lucky to land among the tame Onondagas, eh?" The man's eyes twinkled, turning to Ganayeda, measuring him with an open challenge. "What a stroke of good fortune."

"Don't push it, Crooked Tongue," he retaliated, again wondering at the man's ability to talk so freely in the tongue he didn't know a word of a mere span of seasons before. There was no awkwardness in his companion's speech, and barely any accent. Certainly no crooked way of twisting words, so typical of

his countryfolk, even after summers of living on their side of the
Great Lake. Why, even Mother had her peculiar accent, and this
after nearly four decades residing in High Springs, but not this
foreigner, a relatively new arrival.

Another soft chuckle took his thoughts off their course. "You
are not such an impeccable Onondaga yourself. Come to think of
it, you are half Flint and half Crooked Tongue married to an
Onondaga woman. Sounds somewhat familiar, doesn't it?"

"Cheeky grass-eater." Unable to hold his laughter, Ganayeda
traded it for the widest of grins. "You will never be impeccable
anything, Onondaga, Flint, or Crooked Tongue. I wonder how
long will it take until the villagers of Lone Hill chased you out the
way your countryfolk in Ossossane, or that other Cord People's
settlement, did."

A healthy guffawing was his answer. "Don't hold your breath
waiting for that. Lone Hill is full of reasonable people. Well, to a
certain degree." Another well-contented smirk enlivened the
crispy afternoon. "Don't run to its representative with the
Ossossane story, though. Unless you are bent on witnessing that
pretty show of me running a gauntlet on a carpet of glowing
embers and all that."

"Oh, I see. Her father didn't fall under your spell, eh? Give him
time. He is a reasonable person. He'll accept."

The pleasant face of his companion twisted as though he had
bitten a green strawberry. "If it was up to him, he would issue an
order against every Crooked Tongue passing the entrance of his
precious village's fence. Especially the detested foreigners who
dare to look at his pretty daughters. I swear he watches me like a
hawk when Gayeri's sister is around, as though afraid I would try
to charm that underage child of his into taking me in as well."

That had Ganayeda doubling with laughter. "Two wives made
out of two sisters? Not bad, come to think of it. Same longhouse,
same family. You won't even have to hunt twice as much meat
because it'd still be the same longhouse."

"Not that easy, storyteller. They are from different mothers, so
no, not the same longhouse. But yes the same menacing father full
of dark glares and angrily pressed lips. How is that for a pleasant

daydreaming?" The man rolled his eyes. "Also, her sister is too young to think of her in this way. So you can take hold on that wild imagination of yours."

"Oh, so he thinks of you that badly, afraid to let an underage child around you? Then, brother, you *are* in trouble."

"Tell me about it!" The voice of his companion grew warmer. "Gayeri is not the type to let anyone, even her greatly admired father, interfere with her peace of mind. Still, it's good that the old man is busy and away most of the time."

"Women's fathers can be a nuisance sometimes, but not like their mothers and other womenfolk. Never like those. So if it's only her father who gives you dark looks, then you are well set."

Coming upon a small clearing, with the sounds of a nearby brook murmuring faintly, calming in its monotonous trickling, Ganayeda halted, the reason of this stroll entering his mind, dampening the mirthfulness of his previous mood. How to break his terrible news after such a lighthearted beginning? It wasn't appropriate, not after their hearty laughter and silly jokes.

"When will your father be arriving?" As easygoing as ever, the Crooked Tongue perched upon one of the protruding stones, apparently oblivious to his companion's deteriorating mood. "Hope he will be here in time to participate in our spear-throwing." The full lips twisted into a good smile, free of its usual good-natured mockery. "Bet he will participate, make us all look like pitiful beginners."

"Maybe," said Ganayeda absently, thoughts on the matter in hand. How to break his news? Was there a good, proper way to do that?

"What did you want to talk about?" The contemplative eyes rested on Ganayeda calmly, not urging him to proceed. Careful, difficult to read. Oh, but this man knew it was something important. He had probably known all along, while busy making small talk. Again, he remembered his conclusion of long ago, that the unpredictable Crooked Tongue was much deeper than he cared to display.

"Something bad."

The eyes resting upon him clouded some more. "What?"

"Your father. He has embarked on his Sky Journey. On the moon of Many Leaves. Not so very long ago."

The eyes peering at him grew in proportion, turned ridiculously round. "He what?"

Ganayeda drew a deep breath. "I have received this news just now. My father sent the word, so it must be the truth." He brought his arms up. "I wish it wasn't."

The man's gaze was unsettling in its intensity, all sorts of expressions chasing each other across the pleasant-looking face – astonishment, confusion, bewilderment. Pain? It was difficult to tell. Before he could decide, the gaping mouth closed and the wild gaze left his. He watched the man turning away with suspicious abruptness.

"I'm sorry to be the bearer of bad news."

"What happened?" This came out in a strained if a steady voice.

Ganayeda shrugged helplessly. "I don't know. Father might know more. He will be here shortly, in a few dawns probably. He is waiting for the High Springs representative to start the traveling." What an outburst of irrelevant information. Why would this man care about the reasons Father wasn't here yet? "He will be able to tell us more."

Getting to his feet in one forceful movement, the Crooked Tongue nodded. "Thank you for telling me." Another curt, impassive statement.

He watched the mask setting in, hardening the strong features. Did the foreigner love his father? It didn't appear so, judging by both men's behavior back in the Cord People's lands. But then, how could one know something like that?

"We will not let his achievements unravel or fall apart," he said, suddenly anxious to ease this man's pain if only a little. His companion did suffer from that knowledge, this much was obvious. The tight jaw, the tense shoulders, the sealed eyes told him that. A mask, a stone figurine, where before, it was nothing but easily bubbling energy and purpose. "From our side of the Great Lake, we can still try to keep what he managed to achieve with so much struggle and hard work."

A shrug was his answer. Sighing, he didn't follow the wide back as it disappeared behind the trees of the trail they had followed while coming here. Instead, he turned to watch the end of the incline, the breeze bringing pleasant aroma of the lake, disclosing its close proximity.

Too bad the Bear People's leader had to die so soon, leaving so much emptiness and acute grief behind. His work, but also people who loved him. There must be quite a few of them if even he, Ganayeda, who had come to know the man briefly, felt as though he had lost someone close and important, someone he might be offering many valuables to keep alive and safe. And if so, how must it feel to be told of one's father's death, and in such a light, causal manner? There must have been a better way to deliver such news. He had failed, failed miserably, first dumping his information like that, with no preliminaries or preparations, then failing to condole the man with the right words or expressions.

As though it would have helped. He knew it wouldn't; still, such an effort would have served better than meaningless muttering about traveling between here and the town of High Springs. How stupid!

Rubbing his face with his palms to banish he tiredness, he turned back toward the trail. The Crooked Tongue would be all right. There was nothing he could do about any of it. The man would be back, keeping busy with his spear-throwing contest of unheard-of proportions. Which was a good thing. For the originator of the idea as much as for the rest of the visitors. If this one could be trusted to actually implement it. One more worry to add to his pile of organization topics.

CHAPTER 6

The wind was blowing gently, creating ripples upon the surface of the lake. It was still bright enough to see all of it, the wavering surface and the faint outline of the distant shore. No Great Sparkling Water, not this one. Just a lake, and not the largest.

Frustrated, Ogteah shut his eyes, wishing the wind would strike its hardest, would lunge with everything it had, would storm the shore with vengeance and break things. The gentleness of the breeze was annoying, out of place. It was inappropriate. It behaved as though nothing had happened.

His palms, locked around his forehead, pressed tighter, trying to push the headache back in. Or maybe to force it away, somehow. It was such a lousy day! First losing his favorite spear and in the silliest of ways, when it was so easy to avoid the unnecessary betting. Wasn't the annoying Flint's self-assurance, the way he was pushing toward the quick competition, not bothering to conceal his confidence, an indication? Of course it was. Still he, Ogteah, had gone ahead, letting himself get involved, trusting his own expertise, his experience and his skill.

And not that he did badly, shamed himself with bad throws. Not at all. But that other warrior was not just good. He was brilliant, a true expert. How did one manage such accuracy, such unerring throwing? To nearly miss the first try on purpose in order to put one's rival at ease, to make him lower his guard, oh, but that was true expertise, a level of confidence one doesn't encounter often, if ever. He would have to keep an eye on this one when in his contest, would have to make sure the Flint teams didn't send this man to participate in more than one round. How to go about it?

Feeling a little better, he forced his thoughts to stay on spears and hoops. The best of directions. To think of the news from across the Great Lake was to risk a fall into a bad pit, somewhere deep and with no way out.

Father, dead? But how could it be?

The man wasn't especially old or sick. Or was he? They had spent such a brief time together on their last encounter, mainly trying to avoid each other. Or at least he, Ogteah, did this. Father was too busy for that. He had his great gathering to run, to make it work, to protect against disrupting influences, some of which were caused by his criminal of a son.

The old pain was back, squeezing his chest in a stony grip. Father didn't deserve this, yet he had stayed to face the mess his, Ogteah's, brief visit had created. He did everything a good father should, more, much more than he had to—helped to escape, gave direction, a good purpose in life, then stayed to face the troubles the fleeing criminal left behind. Had it hastened the great man's end in some way? Somehow, he suspected it had.

The recollection of Father's face on the shore of that other Great Water, upon his and Gayeri's first arrival, sustained the suspicion. Father did look aged back then, thinner and grayer, not only in hair but in skin coloring. Was he sick and not only tired? Oh, Mighty Spirits, but he needed to know. Yet how? Whom to ask? Whom to approach?

No one—of course there was no one, unless he crossed the Great Lake himself, went to visit his old town, maybe. He could do it, couldn't he?

The wish to hit himself welled. What a stupid thought! When Father was there, it might have been a possibility. He had played with these ideas before the Cold Moons and during the long winter nights. He had almost begun preparing his journey after the snows melted and the trees began budding with new green. A quick dash there and back, just a few dawns, less than half a moon maybe. He would find Father, would tell the man about his progress, his observations, his plans for the future, ideas of how to make the bond between their people and their unions stronger.

There were plenty of things one could do while being in such an unusual position, plenty of changes for both sides. With Father's active help and with the unreserved backing from the powerful Onondaga War Chief, Father's equal in status, he, Ogteah, could render some help, could promote the lifelong work of these great men to progress into a better future.

But now?

Oh, now Father was dead, and there was no way to reach him, to let him know, to ask for reassurance or advice, to report the achievements. Now Father might never even discover if he had tried to do something or not. With no word to the contrary, the Great Man might as well have assumed that his son had plunged into his old way of life, drifting on this side of the Great Lake, breezing through, indifferent to his mission and their mutual goal. Who could blame him for thinking something like that, with his, Ogteah's, history to date being of purposelessness and crimes?

Leaning forward, as though intending to plunge into the shallow water headfirst, he swallowed hard, thinking about the things he wanted to tell Father, all those reports he was gathering through the last winter. All in vain. Who would need any of it now? The High Springs man maintained that they would not let their fathers' work fade into nothing, but those were mere words of condolence, meaningless politeness, an attempt to make him feel better. Nothing more.

He ground his teeth, wishing to close his eyes and drift into oblivion. In Gayeri's arms, preferably. If only she were here, if only... She would know what to do or what to say to make him feel better, to stop the feeling of uselessness, meaninglessness, of being just an empty vessel. Fancy playing at secret missions! Without Father, it was nothing but the fruit of his imagination, like a child amusing himself with a private game originating in his own head, feeling oh so very mysterious and important, bursting with knowledge of something no one else knew.

Stupid, stupid, stupid!

Even to tell her about any of it was out of the question. She was an Onondaga woman through and through. She would not take it kindly, his underlying intent of spying on her people, of learning their ways in order to use this knowledge, even if for the goal of promoting peace and not war.

No, he was alone in this, completely alone now. Like always. The briefly gained sense of belonging and purpose didn't last enough to let the leaves change their colors again. A mere span of seasons and it was back to normal, living an empty life, betting in a reckless fashion, drifting with no purpose. How long would it take her to recognize his true nature and drop him like a scorching kernel of maize fished from a boiling pot, to roll away in the dust, back to his own people probably, if they would be silly enough to accept him back.

"You took that loss somewhat hard, didn't you?" The voice startled him into near jumping, his heart getting off to a wild start.

Turning abruptly, he peered at the blurry figure, her features hard to make out in the deepening dusk, leaning against a tree, a basket tucked on a thrust out hip, supported by a curve of an arm, her skirt long, fluttering in the breeze. He could hear other voices drifting not far away, hidden by the cluster of greens, following the trail leading up toward the town probably, away from the lake.

"Do you always take losing betting so hard?"

She didn't move, standing there easily, as though belonging, a part of the scenery, her vessel full of folded blankets. He let his own eyebrows climb up, the storm in his head calming, welcoming the distraction.

"Do you always follow those who lose bets?" he countered, at ease at this sort of bantering, a veteran of many summers at handling challenging females. This one wasn't a young girl, and he knew what she wanted. Her taunting gaze told him that. Now and through the stupid afternoon contest that he remembered her watching.

"Only the ones who take it hard enough to run away and grind their teeth so loudly the entire forest can hear them."

He measured her with his gaze, not opposed to whatever she might have been offering. If he was to go back to his old ways, this certainly was the most pleasant part of it.

"So what else do you do besides observing people's behavior

after they lose in betting contests?" The breeze from the lake was strengthening, making him cold in the world with no sun.

"Many things, foreigner." Her eyes flickered, partly angry, mostly amused. She was reading him as easily as he was reading her, he knew, but maybe she still counted on some wooing around.

"Foreigner, eh?" he said, heading up the trail and toward her, not offended, in his element, even though the emptiness in his stomach was still there, still pressing. He would have to go back, find the High Springs man, talk to him probably, make amends for leaving so abruptly before. Also, there was the spear-throwing competition to explain in more detail, to start organizing by talking to the right people. Some of his friends from Lone Hill would help, also Iheks, this High Springs man, as he promised, and that Tauini from Onondaga Town.

"Well, you aren't much of a local, one can see that," the woman was saying, pushing herself away from the supportive tree in one smooth, graceful movement. Not especially beautiful, a little too well-endowed, with her features regular but pleasant—no exquisite beauty of Gayeri's face or the delicacy of her movements, thank all the great and small *uki*s for that!—this one displayed an unconscious sensuality that was difficult to ignore. "Did you come with this or that delegation of the Flint?"

"If you like to think so, I did," he said easily, answering her gaze, not trying to conceal what his held. "Do you have a thing for foreign men, the farther they are coming from the better?"

She frowned. "You are insolent, you know that?"

He nodded readily, his grin wide. Oh, yes, it was better than frustration and grief. A somewhat forgotten feeling. With Gayeri and her lovely warmth always around, there was no need to seek for diversions, even if the temptations were there, sometimes. Quite a few, especially through his second stay at High Springs after the last Cold Moons, by the time he had felt already at home in these lands.

Still, it wasn't too hard to ignore the covert, or sometimes quite open flirtation, to keep some urges and old habits in check, to make it all up for later on, when back in Lone Hill and her longhouse and her warmth, her passion still intense, as fresh as in the beginning, but uninhibited now, thanks to the fading bad memories. Unlike his first try at committing to a woman back in his lands, this one commitment was proving easy to keep up with. A relief. And yet now…

He pushed the thoughts of her away, angry with himself. Now that everything was falling apart, there was no point in keeping to any of his resolutions. She would be wise to throw him out of her longhouse some day, and then everything would go back to what it was, a regular life.

"What?" the woman was asking, peering at him with an open surprise. "Did you lose your brazenness all of a sudden?"

He shrugged. "No, I'm good." Incensed with himself even further, he forced his grin to return. "And you? Are you going to talk on and on about my character traits and behavior?"

She answered it with a toss of her head. "Maybe I will."

"Then we better gather as much firewood as we can."

"Firewood?" The briefly puzzled expression softened her frown, made her look more attractive.

"It'll take time to talk it all over, to cover my numerous flaws and faults, and it still gets cold at nights."

He kept his expression as serious as he could, not a difficult feat given his previous mood, which, as expected, made her snicker.

"You are something, foreigner," she said, her giggle dissolving in the gathering darkness, making him feel better. "Hoping to spend a night with me, and so soon!"

He knew the wideness of his grin would hold a measure of exaggerated innocence.

"Well, I can't," she went on, the challenging expression back, flickering out of the provocative eyes. "I have a man, a family to go back to." The wide lips curved in a less pleasant manner. "Does that cool off your fire?"

Of course it did! Or maybe it could have, under different circumstances. He struggled not to let his expression change. "Why should it?"

"I don't know." Again, the taunting stare.

But this day was getting worse with every passing heartbeat! At this point a wise man would turn around and leave, he knew, preferably using politeness to excuse the hasty retreat.

He kept staring back. "Does it cool off *your* fire?"

This time, her gaze sparkled with fury. "You are terribly insolent!"

The staring contest went on. *Go away now*, urged him his instincts, *just turn around and leave.*

Her lips were nothing but a thin line, eyes simmering darkly. Not a pretty sight. Still, he had to fight the urge to grab her and press her against his body, to feel this fire, this furious energy, to tame it maybe, or just to experience. This day was too bad to finish it with one more disappointment. Would nothing go right from now on?

Suddenly, her eyes changed. They didn't grow any softer, but the open hostility gave way to a peculiar spark, to a somewhat triumphant glow. The thinly pressed lips quivered, opened ever so slightly as he reached for her in one forceful movement, pulling her sharply, steadying her as she swayed. Her basket slipped, but neither paid it any attention. Eyes still locked, so very close now, they kept staring, gauging each other's reactions.

He felt her body pressing against him, fitting there nicely, warm, pulsating with life. Her kiss was anything but gentle, but it set his senses on fire.

Parting her lips with his in return, he felt rather than heard people walking somewhere not far away, the same direction where the voices of her fellow women companions drifted before.

She froze, then pushed him away with much force, slipping from his grip and toward her previous support of a tree, staring at him as though he were a beast out of the woods, breathing heavily, eyes wild.

He willed his heart to slow down. "Your things." A nod in the direction of the fallen basket broke the tension, and she dropped to her knees hastily, picking up the fallen blankets, folding them neatly, swift and purposeful.

When she got up, there was no tension in her eyes, and no challenge. They gazed at him levelly, still measuring his reactions, but in the calmest of ways.

He shrugged. "Sorry. It got out of hand."

Her lips stretched in a crooked sort of a grin. "A strange way to apologize."

"Nothing to apologize for. You are not a child."

But this time, she didn't grow angry. "Indeed, I'm not." Straightening up, she bettered her grip on the woven vessel. "So you aren't afraid, are you?" A brief pause was accompanied by a measuring gaze. "If so, meet me here tomorrow, after the time of the morning meal."

He watched her going away in that pointedly sensual walk of hers, swaying her hips, sending his thoughts in directions he would have rather avoided now. Who needed such complications? So close to home too.

The woman assumed he was a Flint People's man, clearly deeming it safe to have a brief affair with someone who would be gone in a short time. But Lone Hill was just a mere day of walk, and Gayeri did not deserve to be betrayed in this way, to find out any of it, not now that they were settled so nicely, ensconced in her village's life, happy, the bad memories safely forgotten, for both of them. Or so he thought. But Father's death changed it all, didn't it? Life had been too good through this last span of seasons. Too good to last forever.

Glancing again at the shore, memorizing its location, he began trailing off, his chest hurting, head empty of thoughts.

"Is it not our spearman wandering about like a bad spirit out of the woods?"

The call made Ogteah nearly jump out of his skin, his thoughts scattering. He hadn't noticed drifting back toward the valley and the people that were crowding it, spreading in groups, loitering near a multitude of fires, at peace, enjoying quieter evening activities.

The smells of the warmed meals must have brought him back,

he reflected, haunting his nostrils, even as far away as the lake's shores, making his stomach rumble. How long had he been drifting out there? he wondered. Not very long, judging by the easy hubbub of the valley. The evening was far from being over.

He shrugged. Roaming deserted shores and trails didn't help. As always, the solitude offered no reassurance. If anything, it made him feel more confused than before, alone, lost, misplaced. What to do now?

The implications of Father's death kept mounting, adding more and more aspects, not only private but political as well. The war between the two unions would break. The old war that had stopped for such a brief period of time. Without Father and his forceful determination, who would stop people from going back to their old ways? Those who wanted a peaceful solution were not many and far between, none with Father's power and clout. And then there was the other side—*now his side of the Great Lake*—oh, but this side would join in with relish, because over here it was quite the same. The majority of his new countryfolk did not believe in peaceful solutions any more than his original people did, and the Onondaga War Chief, Father's equal on this side, was also not a young man with infinite count of summers ahead of him. The day he might be embarking on his Sky Journey could not be that far, and then his influence, his conviction and power would go along with him, leaving them all with nothing but a memory and frustration, and no help. Just like Father.

"Why are you wandering about like a restless forest spirit?"

With an effort, he forced his thoughts back to the nearest fire, the silhouettes around it distinct, all of them young, bubbling with life. No dignitaries among them, thank all the great and small spirits. Light meal, light company, maybe a round of a bowl game. What better way to escape bad thoughts?

"Not wandering. Just looking for good company." He came nearer, taking in their faces, none of them familiar aside from the Flint spear-thrower. Good! Young men, with no interest in politics most likely, surely not aware of the news of Father or the Crooked Tongues in general. "Got something to eat left around that fire of yours?"

"Drop down, and we'll find you something among the leftovers. Where have you been when the clan mothers were forcing everyone into eating or else?"

Ogteah just shrugged. Crouching at the vacant spot near the fire, he counted their faces, five in all, relatively young but hardened, plenty of scars or other ravages of war, no fresh youngsters. Were those Flint taken to war as soon as they knew how to walk?

"That's the man I've been telling you about, brother," the Flint spear-thrower was saying, addressing one of his friends, himself reclining comfortably upon the bare earth, limbs spread, head resting on folded arms, propped against an entanglement of roots. "He is going to make you all work hard, sweating and running around, throwing your spears, making a spectacle of yourselves every time you miss."

The warrior he had spoken to, a fierce-looking type, all muscles and decorated bands, with a sketch of a wolf tattooed along his protruding jaw, leaned forward, pulling himself into a more upright position. Strangely perturbed, Ogteah concentrated on scanning the remnants of the baked bread lining the bottom of a flat bowl.

"In what way?" asked another young man, not bothering to change his position.

"The spear-throwing contest, you know. Remember how to throw your spear?" Raising his head higher, the impressive Flint grinned at Ogteah. "But with our hoops, not one of theirs, eh, foreigner? The real thing."

Snatching the larger of the crumbling rolls, Ogteah grinned back. "We'll see about that."

"What is so special about the spear throwing?"

The Flint gave his fellow warrior a challenging look. "Have you even aimed a spear at a hoop outside your town's vicinity?"

The other man grunted, trying to reach the edible pile without changing his position. "Yes, I did. Don't you remember? When we were staying at Little Falls, they challenged us to that contest." A chuckle. "Made them regret that, too, didn't we?"

"You made us regret nothing," protested another man. "The

fact that Akweks can't miss one single throw doesn't make all of you into the best spear-throwers. The rest of you weren't any better than we were."

"That's what you think."

"Well," the unerring thrower called Akweks continued, not about to be distracted, "how about you pitting your skill against the entire Five Nations, eh? Ever thought to do that?"

Amidst the growing interest of his newfound company, Ogteah felt the stare of the man with the wolf tattoo most acutely. This one was still sitting upright, peering at him across the fire, eyes narrowed, as though trying to see better.

"What?" he asked in the end, answering the prying gaze with one of his own, a steady stare.

"You are the Crooked Tongue, aren't you?"

He pressed his lips tight. "Yes."

"Oh." The man nodded thoughtfully, not surprised. "Interesting. I've heard plenty about you."

Ogteah tore at his bread with forced calmness. "You have?"

Another unperturbed nod. The man's eyes flickered calmly, neither hostile nor friendly. Displaying mild interest. "Yes."

"Oh, I forgot all about that." The voice of the spear-throwing Flint interrupted the developing staring contest. "Is that true? You are really a Crooked Tongue?" A quick glance shot toward Ogtaeh's adversary. "Do you know him?"

"Not personally," said the tattooed man. "I was not around during the last span of seasons, when my brother came back." The gaze was still on Ogtaeh, measuring him calmly. "And I was away again when you came visiting High Springs."

Finding nothing worthwhile to say, Ogteah just nodded, wondering what this particular Flint had to do with High Springs. Nothing good, he decided, not liking the placid yet unconcealed curiosity with which he was studied.

"Well, your brother better approve of the competition this man proposes," the Flint called Akweks insisted, too full of himself to notice the sudden tension. "I'm telling you, it will be a tremendous affair. Like a ball game between all Five Nations. Not you running all over the field of your hometown, but truly a serious competition. Then we will see who the best warriors in our union are."

"Oh, please!" The man with the wolf tattoo laughed, taking his eyes off Ogteah, rolling them as he did so. "Some lazy elks had too much time on their hands, having nothing to do but practice throwing, while others were busy warring for real, you know."

The returned laughter of the Flint was quite a roaring affair. "Warring against whom? Their own townsfolk, ruining ceremonies?"

His companion threw his head backwards, the loudness of his outburst matching his friend's. "One should be careful while telling you things."

The others, noticed Ogteah, watched the two men with puzzled grins, their eyebrows raised high. Regretting his impulse to join this particular fire, he busied himself with another crumbling piece of bread.

"Which brings me back to our previous discussion," said the tattoo owner, sobering. "I promised my brother to spend an evening with him, and who would dare to make the important dignitary wait?"

"Did you talk to him about any of this?" The Flint's spell of previous mirth dimmed as well.

"No, I wanted to talk it over with the four of you first."

Their eyes went to Ogtaeh all at once, as though following a sigh.

He fought the urge to roll his eyes, his irritation welling. "Well, I'll be off now. See if other fires have something better than crumbles of dry bread to offer."

"Actually," said the wolf man, not bothering with even the most basic politeness, "I don't mind you staying. Maybe you can offer advice, given the strangeness of your situation." His shrug was a fleeting affair. "My family thinks favorably of you, so I suppose I can trust you as well."

"Your family?" asked Ogteah, suddenly fearing the worst. The fragments of the previous conversation kept falling into place, comprising too obvious of a picture. The Onondaga War Chief was reported to have two sons, with the High Springs man indeed mentioning the young hothead of a brother, missing on both of Ogteah's visits in the important town. So much for the hope of spending his time in the company of people who didn't know a thing about his father or couldn't care less for politics, or a serious conversation. What happened to the light-hearted Flint concerned with throwing javelins and little else?

He glanced at the young man, taking in the broadness of his face, the wide jaw protruding firmly under the beak of a nose, eyes looking small, but only due to the prominence of the rest of his features. There was no cheerful ease in the man's expression now but only alertness, watchfulness, matter-of-fact inquiry.

"Our family, come to think of it." The wolf man's eyes sparkled with a taunting challenge. "They say your mother was my father's cousin. Same clan, same longhouse." Another amused grin was directed at their companions, all of them listening, wide-eyed. "His mother was from Little Falls, so careful with your tongues when you badmouth that town with either of us around."

The grins of the others were openly reserved.

"I didn't know you boasted such good connections all around, spearman," said the Flint, his gaze holding less easy friendliness than before.

Ogteah just shrugged, not amused any more than his newly found company was.

The wolf man paid the mounting tension no attention. "So, as I was saying, your Flint People can use some help, certain assistance in their struggle against their enemies. They are the Keepers of the Eastern Door, but they cannot be required to keep their side of our mutual longhouse safe all by themselves, with neither aid nor support. Every nation of our union should be ready to offer help, or to ask for one in case of dire need."

Leaning forward, the man fell silent abruptly, as though running out of breath. Which he probably had, speaking with no pause. The rest of his audience kept absolutely still.

"Do you see what I mean?" he resumed, his eyes traveling from face to face, completing their round quickly. "We can't use titles, such as Keepers of Eastern or Western Doors, without backing them up with more than pretty words of encouragement.

We can't expect either you or the People of the Mountains to keep those same doors secured with no help and no reinforcements." He shrugged. "Neither we the Onondagas can be expected to fend for ourselves should our now-united neighbors from across the lake decide on the warpath instead of the currently semi-peaceful course." The concentrated gaze rested on Ogtaeh, not focusing on him but, rather, looking into its owner's thoughts. "With your father's regretful passing, it becomes a real possibility, doesn't it?"

Somehow, such a casual mention of Father's death, with no pity and no words of condolence involved, did not make him wish to run away into the darkness. It didn't even make him wince.

"It could be a possibility, yes," he said carefully, not sure how to proceed. They didn't expect him to tell them all about the disagreements among the Wyandot People, the two, or maybe three or all four nations and their relationship, did they? He didn't even know the current situation himself. Had the Deer People joined Father's union in the end? Or did it even matter now that he was dead? Oh, yes, the wolf man was right. Without Father, the tentative agreements would not hold, no matter how hard the people like the Onondaga War Chief may try to make it work.

"Well, there you have it," the young man went on, apparently set on sharing his opinions and conclusion rather than forcing the same out of the others. "If we each war our own wars, facing our historical enemies unaided, then what did we gain out of our great union besides reducing the amount of enemies to fight?"

The silence that prevailed wasn't deep, interrupted by cracking of many fires and multitudes of voices floating, filling the semi-darkness, familiar calming noises, fragments of conversations, occasional shouts and laughter. But not around their fire.

"What are you trying to say, brother?" asked one of the men, when even the dominant spear-thrower Akweks wouldn't venture a word.

"I think you know that," stated the wolf man, reaching for a nearby log, half-carrying half-dragging it toward the fire. "Don't you?" This came accompanied by a meaningful glance toward the dominant Flint.

The impressive young warrior shrugged, frowning as though trying to wake from a dream.

"I do see where you are leading to, man," he said, after the added tinder began glimmering around its edges. "But how would you go about changing our ways concerning war and warring? We all have our traditional enemies, as you said. We all are busy with defending our towns and woods." A shrug. "You can't expect our Flint warriors to rush and join People of the Mountains or your Onondagas, leaving our towns and villages unprotected, will you?"

The wolf man shrugged in his turn, not put out with the challenging question.

"It depends," he drawled easily, grimacing in a matter-of-fact way. "If you aren't busy warring at the moment, like we the Onondagas now, then why not? I went to join your war two spans of seasons ago—an Onondaga man, with no acute need to defend anything at home—and it did nothing but good for everyone involved. You received your reinforcements, I gained warriors' experience, and my native Onondaga lands suffered not a bit from my absence, because they were not warring with anyone anyway."

"Your native Onondaga lands gained more than everyone, having you out there and not around, judging by the stories I hear," the Flint said with a chuckle, before sobering again. "Well, brother, it's different, I say. You joined because you wanted to become a warrior. One man, and one who was clearly born to do just that. So of course it was a wise decision. But to have now a few hundred young men leaving their towns to join our wars would be highly unwise. What would their settlements do if your neighbors from across the lake decide to visit?"

The wolf man's fleeting glance made Ogteah uncomfortable.

"First of all, we do have peaceful agreements with our neighbors for now. Secondly, I didn't propose that every man who could wield a club should leave and do it whether he wants it or not. Our people wouldn't have it. They would only be right telling someone who proposed that to go and jump off the nearest cliff. But," the weathered palm rose quickly, to prevent less serious

comments as it seemed, "young men are young men. Many want
to be warriors, many want to do something glorious, to come
home with plenty of stories and heroic deeds. If permitted to
spend a few moons elsewhere, fighting, proving their worth, they
would flock after such an offer, ready to follow you before you
finished saying 'Great Sparkling Water.'" Again he leaned
forward, as though trying to convene his message with the sheer
power of his gaze. "I know what I'm talking about, brother.
Young men want to fight, and they need to gain fighting
experience to defend their own towns and villages if the need
arises. So while having peace all around, they can go and learn
and hone their fighting skills doing something useful, namely
helping our brothers who are defending the entrances of our
mutual longhouse. Everyone gains in the long run from what I
propose, everyone. Don't you see it?"

Fascinated, Ogteah watched the man, his strong, well-defined
face animated, eyes large, sparkling, gleaming with conviction.
Despite the relatively young age and the decidedly striking
warring appearances, despite the simple, straightforward way of
talking, the man had spoken with wisdom, with surprisingly deep
understanding. What he said made sense. If these people's great
union was to be more than a simple alliance of nations, a non-
fighting agreements and trading ties, then, indeed, they would
have to take part in the wars of their brothers, the members of
their Great League. The keepers of their doors could not be
expected to do all the work, to pay the price of their inconvenient
locations. As for the Onondagas…

He shivered, thinking of his own people. Should the war
break—now, following Father's death, a true possibility—with the
united Bear and Cord People, probably Deer by now too, and
maybe even Rock People, the fence-sitters, oh Mighty Spirits, but
this war would be vicious, a bad affair, with much bloodshed, the
old relentlessness and hatred combined with the new power of
united peoples from both sides. Yes, it would be bad, and what
should he do then? Keep neutral? Fight for neither side? Try to
make peace? Leave for home?

"Great schemes, brother," one of the men was saying. "But will the elders listen to your proposals? The Great Law of Peace says nothing about such arrangements, such a way of warfare. It talks about peace matters, not the war ones."

"And yet, we do war," insisted the tattoo owner. "We can't get away from it. Our neighbors wouldn't let us." Scowling, he looked at the fire, shaking his head as he did. "The world around us is changing. It is not the same as it was when the Great Peacemaker came to our lands. He altered our lives, made us into what we are now, a powerful union and not just scattered people with puny wars on their hands. We were like children, running around, punching each other. He made us stop this silliness, he saved us from total destruction. But whether he meant to or not, by changing us, he changed the world around us as well. Our neighbors are no silly children either, even if they didn't receive the word of the Messenger. Take his people, for example." A gaze shot at Ogtaeh held no animosity, only a matter-of-fact proclamation, a statement. "They are united now, aren't they? All their four nations, or almost all of them. His father, he knew the Great Peacemaker as well, and even though the Messenger of the Great Spirits didn't deliver his message to the other side of the Great Lake, his father made them unite all the same."

In the ensuing pause, Ogteah found it easy to nod in agreement, not feeling threatened or pressed into admitting truths he didn't want to. A surprising sensation, given the topic of this conversation and their audience, never fond of his own countryfolk.

"And the same is happening in the lands of the setting sun, among the Long Tails and their neighbors in these very moments," their speaker added, not letting the pause last. "They are also not exactly the same people, or so one hears. The Long Tails who live closer to our Keepers of the Western Door might not be the same as the Long Tails who live closer to the other side of our Sparkling Water and the Crooked Tongues of the western side." Another inquiring glance rested on Ogteah. "Who are the people who live closer to the western side of our Great Lake, nearer to the Long Tails?"

"The People of the Rock." He answered the firm gaze with his own, pushing away his misgivings. This man had already known enough as it seemed, so of course he could find out without his, Ogteah's, help which people lived closer to which shores. There was no need to be cagey from the very first question. He had had enough such conversations over the past span of seasons to learn how to deal with those, how to say nothing while appearing as though sharing generously, telling things, but not really. Where did this one get so much information?

"Did you happen to live there, or at least to visit?"

"No." He shrugged. "The Rock People were not a part of the union at the time I left, but maybe they are now."

A thoughtful nod was his answer. "It seems they are the ones who communicate with our Long Tails, or at least those whom we deem to be the Long Tails. Some people that live beyond the western edge of our Sparkling Water."

"How do you know all that?" exclaimed the Flint spear expert, bursting into the conversation at long last, an indignant note to his voice. "And more importantly, why is it important? Why bother to learn any of that?"

The wolf man frowned again. "I spent some time there, remember, you scattered-minded bear? Haven't you listened to a word of what I said?" The grin flashed, to disappear as quickly. "There is trouble brewing there. The Long Tails are up to no good. Since the Wyandot got organized, the Long Tails are boiling, more restless than before. They have kept very quiet since the beginning of the Great League, but now they are boiling worse than before the Peacemaker came, or so the Mountain People claim. They have been raiding each other with ardor through the last few spans of seasons."

"And what of it?" The Flint warrior's eyebrows climbed high. "Can't the lazy western folk keep their own forests safe? Do they have to run around crying on our shoulders? We've been fighting the eastern savages for longer than any of us can remember, and have you heard us complaining?" A pointed glance encircled his listening peers. "Why can't the Mountain People deal with their old enemies? Why do they need us to hold their hands during their battles?"

But the wolf man's eyes flashed with an open irritation. *"The River People* you've been raiding," he said, stressing every word, "do not give you that much trouble. They are not organized, and they barely raid you back, if at all. Savages or not. Which they aren't!" Another pointed glare had the fearsome Flint dropping his gaze, to Ogtaeh's open puzzlement. What was that all about? He watched the wolf man drawing a deep breath, trying to calm himself, the nostrils of his eagle-like nose widening. "But this thing aside, like I said, they do not give you real trouble. Yet, should they do that, should they get organized, grow powerful, more dangerous, then we would join your wars, would come and help you keep your towns and villages safe." Again, he leaned forward, eyes glimmering, the flickering fire enhancing their glow. "This is what I've been trying to say for this entire evening. We should act like a true longhouse, a true union, and not like a loosely tied alliance of wandering clans."

For a few heartbeats a silence prevailed, with everyone present staring at the flames or the darkness around, the neighboring fires flickering soothingly, wind bringing laughter, the gist of conversations.

This man was right, thought Ogteah, welcoming the opportunity to keep his thoughts on matters that had nothing to do with his people, secret missions, or dead fathers.

Oh, yes, there was a logic in what had been said, a good sense. And yet, how to implement such vision, how to make one nation, or four more, for that matter, send its warriors as reinforcements upon request? No, there was no way to do it. People wouldn't have it, neither elders nor the warriors themselves. Everyone preferred to war for his own settlements and forests.

"How do you envision it?" he asked, mainly to break the uncomfortable silence, but also because he didn't wish to appear as someone whose only contribution was to answer when asked direct questions, meekly at that. Those warriors were younger than him, even the forceful man of ideas, with his perfect warriors' hairdo and the spectacular tattoo. "Even if it makes certain sense, you can't expect four other nations to organize warriors' forces on the demand of someone from far away.

Neither can you hope to have it reaching its destination in time, unless the raid is planned well ahead. And in this case, it would not be an emergency, and therefore, it would not warrant the demand to send warriors to save this or that settlement."

The wolf man was frowning again, pondering his answer with unusual care, while his Flint companion, if not his fellow other warriors, smirked.

"The spearman is right, brother. Your attempted subtlety in politics defeated itself."

"No, it didn't," the wolf man cried out hotly, displaying that his temper was not always under control. "None of you were listening, not even you, Wyandot man. I wasn't speaking of emergencies, of attacked villages and burning fences. Those are the troubles that each people should be able to take care of all by themselves, respectable nations of warriors that they are. No need to run and cry on anyone's shoulders for that, to cite the eloquent words of our Akweks. No need to wipe their running noses and hold their trembling hands, either." He drew a deep breath and looked at them, his frown back, not amused by his own attempt at lightening the atmosphere. "The thing is in prevention. As a union and not just scattered five nations, we need to deter our neighbors, *all our neighbors*, from even thinking of approaching our forests and villages, make them fear even playing with such ideas. And here is where our combined power comes in. As a great league, we are a fearsome presence. As just five nations who pat each other on their backs and call each other brothers, but who are not about to do more than that for one another, we are nothing but an easy prey. Don't you see it?" Another intense scan of their faces. "If we don't join each other's wars, we are a powerful union in nothing but name. It is that simple. And in this case, we better pray that none of our enemies have realized that as yet."

Did Father? wondered Ogteah. Had the great man realized the flaw in the enemy union that this young warrior was pointing out? Oh yes, the wolf man was right. If the Great League didn't coordinate its mutual enterprises, if it wasn't ready to back their own declarations up, by warriors' force if necessary, then it was a hollow organization, not a longhouse in the true sense of it—one building, several families, all belonging to one clan, ready to defend it and every dweller in it, ready to come to each other's aid.

"Did you talk to the War Chief about it?" he asked, suddenly remembering whose son this man was.

The intense gaze leapt at him, measuring him with a new appreciation. "Yes, I did. Of course I talked to my father. Not all of these good ideas are mine. Far from it." The suddenly wide, open smile took Ogtaeh by surprise. It held it all, the amused confession, the admission, even a measure of mischief. "I was privileged to learn from the best, Wyandot man. And I'm still enjoying the great leader's guidance and advice." The amusement disappeared as quickly as it came. "I'm sure Father had plenty of talks with you as well. He seems to be fond enough of you, isn't he?" With agility fitting a more catlike creature than the wolf tattooed on his jaw, the man sprang to his feet, one moment sprawling, the other up and ready to pounce. "I'll be off now. Can't have my brother waiting. Are you coming along, Wyandot man? He might wish to see you." A beam at the rest of their sprawling company. "I'll meet you tomorrow at dawn, before I leave, Akweks. Don't wander away before we talk."

The Flint rolled his eyes in reply. "Still can't believe you are scampering off just like that."

"I'll be back for the opening ceremonies. Won't miss your spear-throwing contest, never fear."

"It's not my contests, it's his." The broad palm flipped lazily, indicating Ogteah. "Make this one stop messing in politics, will you, foreigner? The wild warrior keeps forgetting who he is, rubbing shoulders with important family members. That's bad for his type, not natural." The broad features spread in the most innocent of grins, beaming at the wolf man, not bothering to even sit straight. "That is, when he isn't busy dragging after his wild woman, teaching her how to shoot a bow. I'm telling you, this boy—" Twisting in order to avoid the touch of his standing comrade's moccasin, the tip of which was making its way toward his ribs, the man smirked. "See? He isn't ready to listen to his friends' advice."

"Fine advice one gets from such friends." The wolf man's grin matched that of the sprawling Flint. "And she shoots just fine, I'll let you know. No need to teach her that. But she bettered her aim considerably since our first meeting with her." The mirth was spilling out of the glittering eyes. "And with a real bow, too. No more silly toys."

"I want to meet her, before you leave or after you return. Tell her that. Must show her the fruits of her brother's work, mustn't we?" The man shifted his leg, flexed the muscles of the formidable thigh. "She won't believe it when she sees."

"I'll bring her along tomorrow at dawn. She will be overjoyed to hear that you are here and running about on that rotting leg of yours." Another push with the moccasin was blocked as readily. "I can't even start to describe how good it is to see you, brother."

CHAPTER 7

The mosquito was hovering near her cheek, fluttering its tiny wings, buzzing most probably. Searching for a good place to land, to stick its sting and have its afternoon feast. Annoying pest!

If she dared, she would have waited until it has settled for good, then smashed it with no regard to the surface it was sitting on. A vicious slap was worth the death of yet another bothersome pest. Oh, but how she hated flies! Even though she couldn't hear their annoying noises for enough summers by now, she still remembered it well enough. It was only the good sounds that were determined to escape, to fade into nothingness. Grandfather's voice, for one. No matter how hard she clung to the memory of his deep, measured speech, the way he had spoken, slowly and carefully, very deliberately—for her sake too of course, but he had been speaking in an unhurried way before as well—the recollection of his voice was fading, going away, leaving her alone, every day a little more than before. Only the meaning of his words remained. This no one and nothing could take from her, ever.

She shook her head lightly, not daring to move more than this. Which didn't impress the determined fly in the least. But for the opportunity to smash the irritating thing.

Pressing her bow's shaft tighter, she blessed the spirits for not making her palms sweat. It should be as steady as the rocks towering all around her when it was time. For how much longer?

Even though she prided herself on her ability to keep absolutely still for long periods of time, the result of determined practice, she felt the strain of it, her muscles getting cramped, begging to let go. Squinting, she pressed the arrow closer to the bowstring, not pulling it to its fullest, not yet.

The people upon the clearing were busy working, crouching above fallen carcasses, more than a few of which littered the ground. They had been working hard since high noon, dragging the hunted game here, just like she had predicted they would, carving the meat, skinning the animals before they could begin rotting away. Good hunters, these people weren't lazy or spoiled. Still, one of them was destined to die now.

She sought the prominent figure with her eyes, his shirt richly decorated, helpful in this. From such considerable distance, it was easy to confuse the man with one of his peers. Or worse yet, with Aingahon himself. She shuddered at the very thought. Oh Mighty Spirits!

She never missed, yes, she hadn't been boasting in vain when she told him that. Still, to track down people, to hunt them as though they were the game, the true forest dwellers, was a new experience, thrilling with the power it offered, but dangerous. What if she got caught doing this? Or worse yet, what if she missed?

Oh, local forest uki, don't let it happen, she prayed silently, knowing full well that one wasn't supposed to present spirits with such self-serving requests. Ask for guidance, if you must, for advice in making a decision, but not for outright help. Still, she kept praying, apologetic but determined. She couldn't risk missing her target. He would be impressed and appreciative if she succeeded.

Just like he had been ten dawns ago, when she did it for the first time.

She stifled a smile, swelling with pride all over again. Oh, but to see his face like back then, his eyes smiling, not trying to hide the extent of his wonder, his uneasiness obvious, but also the depth of his appreciation. It was easy to see how impressed he was, awed even. That first time, ten, no eleven downs ago, when he had asked her to shoot at another cliff top, to hit a particular target, a tree that had towered there, not a difficult shot at all.

She had stuck her arrow at the exact point he had asked her to, and he had gone silent for a long while, thinking hard. Proud of herself, she had paid it little attention, trailing after him in order to inspect her shot, to retrieve the arrow and get more compliments. Or so she hoped. Yet, what came next had her gaping at him in the same way he had gaped at her shot, startled into mere staring.

Looking around carefully, he led her back to their previous hideaway, and then, making her squat in front of him so she could see his lips and thus read his words most carefully, he had asked her if she had ever shot a man, a person, a human being. Just the way she had aimed her arrow at him when displaying her skill, he explained, but for real.

When she shook her head in denial, he looked disappointed. Ever so slightly, an expression that was quickly replaced by his regular slightly aloof calmness, still it made her feel bad. He had thought highly of her, hadn't he? Highly enough to ask something like that.

When he kept peering at her, studying her openly, as though gauging her reactions, she frowned, then told him that she could shoot someone if she wanted to. It couldn't be much different from shooting a deer, if not a rabbit.

His face brightened, and he said, yes, it was pretty much the same, but more dangerous, unless she was sure to hit her target or to cover her tracks. People were no harmless game. They tended to go after their offenders, them or their family members and friends.

Annoyed by his still openly contemplative gaze, she declared that she wasn't afraid of people, that she could get away as easily as she could shoot a person and not miss. Which made his lips stretch into a semblance of a grin, very thin, very murky. Not a reassuring smile, but she didn't care at this point. She was too incensed at his open disbelief.

"I can do it most easily," she had declared, jumping to her feet. "I'm not afraid."

He caught her arm, pressing it firmly, not painfully but sternly. "Stop shouting. Such things are not to be discussed in loud ways. Never." She fought to escape his grip, but he didn't let her arm go, not immediately. Instead, he straightened up to face her more easily, not about to follow her suit at getting up, not with his bad knee. "If you calm down and listen, I'll tell you more about it. But only if you show me that you can control your temper; that you can just sit and listen and answer in a quiet, unobtrusive way." The mirthless grin was back, more open than before. "After all, I can hear you even when you are whispering. You tend to forget that."

Still struggling to break free, she complied only when he let her arm go. It took one heartbeat of glaring, of facing the impassiveness of his gaze, the unperturbed sternness of it to drop beside him in the way that allowed her to see his lips clearly. The promise not to jump or to shout any more came with more difficulty, but he wasn't prepared to go on before receiving those.

Forcing her thoughts back to the present, she concentrated on the people moving about the clearing, small, blurry forms, not too distanced to make out their differences. The man she was watching was crouching again, shadowed by the branches of a nearby tree, sheltered by it. But not for long, she knew, not perturbed in the least. The day was still young, and until Father Sun made it difficult to see, or until they were finished, her prey would step into a better spot, would occupy a more fitting position.

Like the previous time. Ten, no eleven dawns ago.

Oh, but how afraid she had been back then, how fretful. What if she missed? What if she hit someone else by mistake? There were quite a few people there, upon this other lonely cliff.

It was called Flat Rock, he had told her when explaining what he wanted her to do. The War Chief of their entire region wanted to meet him there, him and other people who did not agree with the War Chief's policies, he elaborated, holding nothing back, or so it seemed. The warriors' leader was not a bad man, but unfit for the position he held, doing the people he was entrusted to care for more harm than good, hating him, Aingahon, for not holding his tongue on the important subjects.

It was like being at war, he explained. It was rare that bad people were killed, those other warriors belonging to the other side. They were as good, as worthy, but nevertheless, they were to be killed unless one wished to offer his own life as a reward. And she was like any worthy warrior, he went on, having a choice to join or to stay behind. It was her choice, and she would do better to think hard on that matter.

What a funny way to put it!

She tried not to shake her head now, as to not let her concentration wander. What was there to think about? Nothing, nothing at all. She had no misgivings, and the only thing she had feared was the possibility of disappointing him with a bad shot, her only regret the fact that he couldn't be up there with her, supporting with his mere presence, giving her of his strength. But there was no chance of that, of course. He had to be down there with the hunters, or like back then, on the other cliff with the War Chief, to attend the meeting the stubborn leader had initiated, to intimidate him, probably, to make him shut up.

Again, a mosquito buzzed near her elbow, another stubborn creature, like the War Chief who has been dead for some time by now, taken down by a mysterious arrow, mourned, already buried after the customary nine dawns of him lying on a platform to let his spirit embark on his Sky Journey easily, with no hurdles, no misgivings.

Did his spirit know?

She didn't spend her time musing on these matters. What she had done was a warriors' deed, therefore it was acceptable. Did the killed warriors grudge their endings to the others who had taken their lives in a fair battle? When asked, he said no, not likely, unless the killing was done in a dishonorable way. Which wasn't the case in this matter, he had added, glancing at her pensively, knowing what preyed on her mind. In wars, people often used to waylay each other in very similar ways. An open hand-to-hand that so many storytellers praised was not such an often occurrence. Not only people but whole warriors' forces were always busy figuring out ways to ambush each other, to trap the enemy in various manners and minimize the damage of an open clash.

Listening to him helped. As much as spending her time in his company. After that first shooting, he had made it his business to meet her more often, every other day if he could. His food offerings were most welcome, but not as much as his conversations were, his mere presence. Even to sit beside him in silence felt good, pleasantly cozy, the somewhat forgotten sensation of being at ease and at home. He would make himself as comfortable as his bad leg allowed him, and would busy himself with carving things, relaxed and at ease, not a common occurrence for him, she suspected, listening to her inner voices. He was troubled more often than not. And very frustrated with his disability. There was no need to be old and wise to recognize that. Yet, not when with her and not in the privacy of their various hideaways.

So, armed with this knowledge of him not hurrying anywhere as well, she would sprawl somewhere around, and would either daydream or play with her knife, or eat more of the fanciful foodstuff he always brought, the deliciously crunchy rolls of cornbread with berries and nuts, or juicy meatballs, things that she had never had, not even with Grandfather.

Still, wonderfully at peace or not, she would always glance at him, careful not to let him out of her sight, at least at the corner of her eye, in case he was talking and she didn't notice. To miss one single word of his was unspeakable. He never said a thing that was trivial or boring.

Again, she forced her thoughts back to the clearing, her senses alerting her to the movement of her target. The man got up and was talking to someone, shouting in an authoritative voice, judging by the movements of his body. From such distance, she could not see his lips, but it didn't matter. All she needed from him was to move away from the protection of a wide-branched tree, into the spot she didn't intend to let him leave.

Come on!

Her arm clutching the bowstring was trembling, not from strain—she hadn't begun pulling it yet—but from impatience. It was itching all over too, as did other parts of her body, those open to the harassment of the accursed flies. The damn insects were having a feast!

She blew the air through the side of her mouth against the tickling sensation on her cheek. It went away, but not for good, she knew. What made the stubborn man huddle in the safety of his tree for so long?

Moving her fingers to prevent them from getting numb, she made sure the second arrow was clutched tightly between her middle and her small finger, just in case.

In case of what?

No, she couldn't miss. She never did.

Oh, but it was tiring, all this waiting. It went on quicker, much quicker, with the Flat Rock and the other cliff. What if she didn't manage this time?

A sudden gust of wind brushed over her sweating back, making her shiver. *Just move your fat carcass...*

The man was standing again, gesturing with his hands. When he finally moved, he headed in the wrong direction. Oh, all the forest spirits! She fought the urge to spring to her feet and do something violent.

Another man took the abandoned place by the partly cut game. She recognized the familiar uneven gait. He was crossing the clearing too, carrying a large leather pouch. He worked as hard as the others, but he had to stay behind and take care of the camp when they did the actual hunting. He couldn't keep up with their pace, not with his bad knee.

The man with the colorful shirt was coming back, walking easily, in great spirits as it seemed. Pausing by his previous place of working but only for a heartbeat, he headed on, straight into the most perfect of spots, about to enter the frame of two trees, outlined clearly against the darkness of the cliff that guarded the clearing.

She hesitated not even for a fraction of a heartbeat. Like with the Flat Rock shooting, her hand tore at the bowstring, pulling it as far as she could, making the sturdy shaft bend and its curved edges almost straighten, enhancing the impact. When the arrow flew off, it was pushed more forcefully due to those arching edges, she knew, peering ahead, not daring to let out a held breath.

Her victim wavered but didn't fall. A bitter taste in her mouth, she watched him raising his arms abruptly, as though about to address the spirits through a ceremony.

Not trying to comprehend any of this, she felt the spare arrow plunging to take the place of the previous one, her hands already in action, fingers of one making sure it fit, the other already pulling, preparing the lethal thrust.

It was over in less than a heartbeat, her second arrow taking the man down, conclusively at that, to sprawl upon the ground and jerk with his limbs, more alive than the shot deer he was carving, but not by much.

Not daring to wait for the commotion to erupt, she leapt to her feet, collecting the rest of her possessions hastily, just in case. A last glance to make sure no marks were left, nothing to lead those who would come to investigate this perfect vantage spot back to her, and she was fleeing down the trail and alongside it, disappearing into the hills of the eastern valley.

He would be coming out to look for her, if not today then on the day after that, and he would know where to find her.

Amidst the outcries and the growing commotion, Aingahon rushed toward the fallen man as fast as his bad knee allowed him.

Some of his fellow hunters were faster, already kneeling beside the gurgling, jerking form, trying to drag the wounded into the safety of the bushes. The others, more prudent or experienced warriors, grabbed their bows and were scanning their surroundings, ready to answer the shooting.

"Place him there, carefully." Seeing the indecision of the men who carried the wounded, Aingahon pushed his way in, willing his heart to stop its mad racing. "Don't crowd around him like that. Let him breathe."

Obediently, they did as they were told. He squatted beside the shot man, using his hands to support him, to make it easy on his bad leg. The wounded was thrashing upon the ground, beating it with his arms, his screams bubbling, strangled, seeping together with the pinkish foam that was spilling from between the torn lips. A hair-raising sight.

"He can't breathe," muttered someone, watching helplessly as Aingahon struggled to take hold of the lurching shoulders. "He won't stay."

"No." It took much of his power to try to hold the man, balancing on one knee, sparing the other an effort. "Help me!"

Several pairs of supportive arms leapt to answer his curt request. The rest, he noticed, were gone, spreading out and into the forest, refusing to act as a hunted prey.

Eyeing the long polished shaft protruding from the dying man's side, he felt his stomach turning, heaving uneasily. Again, she had proven herself, such an accurate shooter, even though this time, her first shot was not that good.

Oh, but he remembered the cold wave of apprehension upon hearing the familiar hiss, expecting it of course for the entire afternoon, anticipating it. She wouldn't disappoint, not her!

Still, it had taken her such a long time and, not knowing where exactly she had been hiding or for how long, he had assumed that maybe she didn't manage to find a good place or wait long enough due to plenty of different reasons. Still, his tension kept growing, and when the first arrow flew by, he was so jumpy he nearly lost his own balance leaping to his feet, forgetting about his own injuries.

While the first arrow nearly pushed its victim off his feet, he had seen, wounding the man but not killing him, he felt rather than saw the next missile descending like a bird of prey, unerring, and just as their target waved his hands in an attempt not to fall.

Oh, but only a hardened, experienced warrior would have had enough skill, attitude, presence of mind to act that swiftly, to release the second arrow even before it was apparent that the first one wasn't lethal. Who *was* that girl?

"Join our men who are scanning the woods," he said, leaning closer, watching the tormented body slowing its struggling, the gurgling sounds coming in weaker waves, the tremors dying away. Such a terrible death, to drown in one's own blood. He tried not to shudder. "The attackers might be still around and waiting. Atuye, Teyada," he glanced at the younger men, taking in their faces, the intensity of their gazes, their open expectation, their barely hidden fear, "start making a platform. We will carry him home, for the faith-keepers of his clan and the rest of our families to help his spirit reach the Sky World through the smoothest of journeys as he deserves."

The two younger men sprang to their feet readily, glad to busy themselves, having received needed directions.

"Who would do such a filthy thing, shoot a person from behind the trees?" muttered one of the hunters, a squat, heavyset man of many summers.

"Our filthy neighbors, for one," someone cried out. "The lowlifes from either side are capable of even worse treachery."

"Not the people from the north," said Aingahon, still holding his charge, mainly due to the others scampering away, following his directions. "They are our natural allies and brothers. They wouldn't do anything as treacherous."

An uneasy silence was his answer.

"And just after the War Chief..." One of the men still lingered nearby, as though not knowing what to do. "Another shooting from behind the trees."

"It didn't come from behind the trees." The tall hunter who came back carrying a bunch of long flexible branches scanned the nearby hill through his squinted eyes. "It came from farther away. Judging by the angle it descended."

"This hill is too far," said Aingahon, his entire attention on the attempt to lower the body to the ground without taking away from its dignity, not an easy feat with his knee creaking in an unpromising manner. "No arrow would go in with such force, unless shot from closer proximity."

"Maybe." Thoughtfully, the man shook his head, then shielded his eyes, not about to leave the suspected hillside without another scan.

Forcing his thoughts off the troublesome path, Aingahon stifled a breath of relief, successfully rid of his burden, even if briefly. The hunted game needed to be taken care of and it angered him that no one seemed to think about it but him, scattering away to follow his instructions. Couldn't they think of anything themselves? What he said wasn't different or especially innovative. Just plain common sense.

Well, he could take care of these matters, he knew, happy to be back on his feet. Just like many other problems that he had been required to solve these days, to organize or coordinate. Since the death of the War Chief, another untimely passing, many had begun treating him with untoward respect. Not because they suspected something, he knew—if they did he would have been treated in quite the opposite manner—but because, with the most adamant opposition to his popular ideas gone, the rest of his countryfolk began looking up to him, just like his fellow followers did, very numerous these days.

"Two, three men would be enough to work on that platform," he said, noting the others drifting in, clutching their bows or spears. "We will have to finish skinning and packing as well. Hopefully before nightfall."

Yet, part of his mind was dwelling on the hunter who was still glancing at the suspected hill, knowing that a close inspection of the shot council member would prove the suspicious man right. The angle both arrows were sticking out told their tale most clearly.

However, it didn't matter. The construction of the platform would keep them busy for long enough, allowing her to cover her tracks and get as far away from there as possible. To the other side of the valley of course, where the brooks and deepest of pools created one of their frequently visited getaways. A difficult walk for him to manage, but he could not disappoint her, not in this. She would be waiting impatiently, pacing in this restless, jumpy stride of hers, hands swaying and never still, face alive with ever-changing expressions. Such an unruly spirit, full of underlying passions. So easy to read, but not to predict.

Oh, but this girl was a puzzle. The easiness with which she had agreed to his dangerous, shady proposal had surprised him, but not as much as her eagerness to carry the dubious mission on, to face the actual deed and succeed so tremendously. He didn't expect her to even attempt it, certain that at the last moment she wouldn't do it, not a small innocent creature of so little summers, however wild or unusual she may be.

Heading for the Flat Rock on that fateful morning, he had prepared to face the War Chief and his cronies alone, expecting the worst, even a treachery, ready for it. He didn't count on her acting according to their hastily concocted plan, his talking and half-hearted persuading notwithstanding, even though she was crouching upon her vantage spot with her lips clasped and her eyes dark with determination when he had left. Still, the arrow that came surprised him almost as much as it had surprised the rest of those present, five more men of the town and a few guests. One arrow, one shot, apparently more than enough.

He shook his head, remembering how his heart picked up tempo, and his blood seemed to burn under his skin. The shot was as accurate as the one she directed at him on the day before, boasting her skill and her marvelous weaponry, but unlike her first display of prowess, this one was intended to kill, with the feathered shaft fluttering in the exact middle of its victim's chest, as though thrust in there from a very close proximity, like a knife.

He remembered fighting his shock, the urge to sneak a glance in the right direction difficult to contain. She did it, actually did it!

However, it had taken him the rest of this day and a night to sneak out of the flustered town undetected, away from the agitated people and the hastily organized ceremonies, and more time to hobble his way to the spot of the shooting, and later on, to the other possible meeting places they had, until he had found her, distraught and near tears, more unstable than ever, erratic.

She had needed his reassurance, he knew, much of it. So he did just that. Encouraged her and cheered her up, comforted her fears, lauded her shooting skills until she was puffed up with pride, forgetting her misgivings. Such an innocent child, and yet dangerous, different, lethal, a strange combination.

Since then he had made it his business to spend as much time with her as he could, at least every other day, to spoil her with delicious foodstuff the townsfolk women prided themselves on preparing and even a good pair of moccasins one of his sister's daughters threw away because of a tear in its sole. The pretty shoes fit almost perfectly, and it made her so happy, he knew he would go as far as stealing to get her a new dress as well. The unreserved glow of her eyes when he promised her another present, refusing to say what it would be, made his resolution to resort to such lawless means harden, turning into a firm decision at the amount of her begging to reveal to her what it was.

"There is no sight of anyone skulking around, watching our clearing." More men were trickling back, their faces grim.

"To shoot at us from one of the surrounding hills would be difficult," he said, shrugging, forcing his thoughts back to the present. "Besides those ridges up there, there is no good view of here from anywhere around."

"A warrior with a large sturdy bow can shoot from these ridges." The man who had had his eye on the suspected hill was already kneeling next to the fallen elder, examining the second arrow. "It is too far indeed, but possible."

"Maybe." It was unseemly to persist on arguing, and she would be sure to be on her way now, heading in the opposite direction to the one they were coming from. He pretended to scan the towering hill for the first time. "It's too far, but who knows? We have to catch those wandering enemies. They can't go around shooting at our people."

A less than satisfactory speech, he knew, but this one would do for now. Until he found her and warned her to keep away until he was back from his journey to the western shores of the Great Sparkling Water. With the War Chief and his obstructive hostility gone, the Town Council had agreed to his proposal of approaching their neighbors and natural allies, Attiwandaronk People from the northern shores of their own lake and the western edge of the Sparkling Water. At long last! A serious delegation, composed of quite a few important dignitaries and warriors, with him in the leading ranks, empowered with the responsibility of talking, of representing. A rare honor, but a deserved one.

Oh, but this girl did turn his life around, didn't she?

He pushed aside the idea of bringing her along once again. It would be unseemly, wouldn't it? No women were allowed on such missions, let alone strange girls with no ability to hear and a fear of people. She wouldn't welcome the opportunity to cram herself in a boat full of strangers.

And yet, to take her along could be a good thing for her, an opportunity to visit her people. Maybe he would be able to find out the whereabouts of her town and even her family, some of the surviving relatives, or at least the members of the same clan.

It was no life for a girl to skulk around the woods, shooting people at his request. A better life should be offered to her, and he didn't intend to kill anymore of his countryfolk, obstructive as some of them might turn out. The position he had been fighting to achieve was close at hand now anyway, with people accepting the wisdom of his proposals, about to follow his way. No need to resort to low means anymore, and it would be good to know that she was well settled and comfortable, about to join normal life. He would make his point to visit no matter how far away her town might be, to keep an eye on her and make sure she is well and thriving.

Heading toward his fellow hunters who had already made half of the platform ready, he nodded to himself, well-satisfied. Oh yes, he would take her along regardless of convention. Her mere presence would help, as it seemed to do since he had started talking to her, while her absence would leave his own townsfolk with nothing to find when they started combing every tree and a shrub of these woods, seeking the mysterious killer.

CHAPTER 8

"Our Elder Brothers, the Keepers of our Western and Eastern Doors are doing a wonderful work of keeping our Longhouse safe and sound." The tall representative from the Swamp People's lands encircled his audience with his gaze, eyes wide open and sincere. "Just like our Keepers of the Central Fire are making certain the Great Council's hearth never becomes cold or dim, and would always be ready to welcome our brothers, the honorable members of the Great Council and their followers, to sit beside it and share their thoughts." Another gaze at the squatting elders, representatives, war chiefs, and some of the others who were allowed to stand nearby and listen, had the man pausing in a natural manner. "The laws of the Great Peacemaker are wise, dividing our responsibilities in the clearest of manners. It puzzles me that some of you feel the need to try and change his dictates already, even though it's been a mere few decades since the Messenger of the Great Spirits bestowed on us the word of his divine patrons."

Knowing where the man was heading, Ganayeda tried not to let his frown show. It was the second day of the gathering, and the matter of either of the doors' keepers and the possible need to send them reinforcements was the talk of the valley, or so it seemed.

People argued and fumed, divided most thoroughly. Some maintained that the keepers were called the keepers for a reason and that there was no need to intervene in their business by sending unasked-for reinforcements. Others claimed that it wasn't right to expect two nations to take care of the entire union's safety, to carry the burden of perpetual wars on behalf of everyone.

Somehow, since Okwaho had brought this matter up only ten dawns ago, the arguments for and against had taken residence in everyone's minds and tongues. Somehow. Was it a coincidence?

Ganayeda had his doubts. Since that first night of his brother's arrival, before the young rascal had scampered off to take his wife on the promised tour of the pretty countryside—so much like the wild thing to do that, stir up trouble, then go away—he couldn't make the nagging questions and dilemmas leave his mind as well.

Like always, listening to what people said made him see the broader picture than the one close at hand, to understand more implications, farther than the immediate conclusions most people would promptly arrive at. It wasn't about the Door Keepers, he knew, two nations that might have felt like complaining, but who didn't do so officially, not yet. Oh no! The matter was broader and deeper. It was about their entire union, the way it was heading, the new paths it was taking or was expected to take. And it touched his own Onondaga People more closely than some short-sighted people wished to admit.

Long stretches of peace made towns and villages grow softer, overlooking basic protection matters, breeding less warriors and more hunters. There was no need to go far to look for examples. What had happened two spans of seasons ago was as glaring a precedence as ever. Two brothers, one unexpected attack, two different reactions. They had both acted bravely back then, both did their best. But while Okwaho did all the right things, responded like the experienced warrior that he was, he, Ganayeda, had reacted like a person who knew nothing about wars and ambushes, about acting on the spur of the moment and without due preparations. And while the self-doubts that followed this miserable autumn were gone, the lesson learned remained.

To have people act like warriors, there was a need to train them, and, if need be, to have them go away and gain this precious battle experience, something his brother managed to acquire in a mere span of seasons spent in the thickest of the fighting. Just a few moons in the lands torn by wars and here he was, ready to fight when needed, to defend his people and settlements, not losing his senses, not acting like a hunter, those being brave, yes, but still useless when faced by an organized human foe. And yet, how many people like Okwaho were at hand here in the peacefulness of the Onondaga lands? A handful.

Well, maybe more than a handful, but their numbers were dwindling with the accumulating peaceful summers, while whole generations of young men grew up with no fighting experience, not knowing what a war was. A good situation in itself, but only if it could be ensured to remain unchanged indefinitely.

Which was what worried him the most now. Out there, the Crooked Tongues were boiling. And what would his people do should their restless, hostile until recently, neighbors decide to pursue a war course, start sending warriors' parties one after another, as they most certainly could do now that they were uniting as well. What would happen in such a case, when the Onondaga towns and villages were full of people who could hunt more effectively than they could war? Would they manage to repel those attacks, or would that be their turn to send frantic requests of help, receiving dubious glances, flowery words of encouragement and little else? And was it not the best way to prevent such an occurrence by actually doing what his brother had done, going out and gaining this same fighting experience while helping their brother-nations in their struggle, killing two birds with one arrow?

He had shared these thoughts with Okwaho after listening to his brother's passionate speeches that advocated immediate help of large parties of warriors being sent to the Mountain People. On that first evening Okwaho was the one who did most of the talking, making quite a lot of sense at that. He found it surprising to see the young man orating with so much skill, a surprise he had seen in his brother's entourage's faces as well on other similar occasions, after the young hothead came back from his sightseeing trip with his wife, taking a whole five dawns to do that. Okwaho's friends seemed to be as taken aback, everyone but the Crooked Tongue, who had listened with keen interest, his eyes reflecting deep understanding, too deep for Ganayeda's peace of mind. Why did his man come here in the first place?

Well, after hearing Ganayeda's musings on the subject on that first evening, Okwaho grew even more passionate. "Talk to Father about all this, when he arrives," were his parting words. "I will be back in just a few dawns, but he might be here even earlier. He is the wisest man of them all, so maybe he already thought about that aspect of our lacking warriors' experience. But all the same, talk to him about it. He has some interesting ideas he might wish us to implement." The large eyes twinkled in a familiar manner. "You are a deep one, Brother. No wonder they trust you with all sorts of responsibilities, the Great Council and all that." The spark intensified, turned unbearably cheeky. "It would be nice to have a representative in the family. Something to boast around, to use when the need arises."

"Shut up." Fighting the urge to push his elbow into his brother's temptingly exposed ribs, knowing it would be deflected halfway, Ganayeda shook his head, pleased but not about to admit that. Somehow, the taunting praise coming from the wild thing made him feel better than ten compliments from the men of his status and above. "Just come back in a hurry. It is not a good time to make your independent trips, especially if you decided to get involved in more than mere fighting and troublemaking all of a sudden." Frowning, he brought his hands up. "I don't understand why you insist on going away now. It's not prudent and is completely unnecessary. Your timing is bad, to say the least."

But the well defined eyes clouded with familiar stubbornness. "It is what it is. Kentika deserves this trip. It has been cut short by our dealings as it is by now." A shrug. "I will be back soon, before all the dignitaries assemble. They always take their time to arrive, don't they?" A winning smile took the edge off Ganayeda's resentment. "Even when you are the one who is organizing it all, trust me to come back before they start."

And now, watching the gathering of the Great Council, allowed to do so for the first time in his life, Ganayeda found his thoughts wandering, not thrilled by the occasion as he expected it to be. They weren't going to accept these new ideas. Not the headstrong elders, concerned with the well-being of the people they represented and little else beyond it.

If only Father was allowed to speak in this grand assembly, but the war chiefs were only to watch, to hear and not to be heard. Their duty consisted of ensuring that the representatives did not forget their obligations to the people they were elected to represent, to report back home. A pity. Father would stir their talks in an appropriate direction, would give them food for thought, would influence their discussions until they paid attention and deigned to listen.

He sought Father's broad, generously wrinkled face with his eyes, aged but still strong, still noble, its scars faded into invisible lines. From the place he was allowed to squat, all he could see was the prominent profile, its expression difficult to make out. The man would talk to these dignitaries afterward, between the discussions, he knew. He had already sounded some of the prominent men out, and not only from their Onondaga lands. The War Chief had connections everywhere, among his native Flint and around the Standing Stone and the Swamp People. Only the distant western dwellers, always a little apart, seemed to be out of the powerful Onondaga leader's net of influence.

Well, to change people's minds on such an innovative subject, one needed more than great clout. To speak at the Great Council was one thing; to travel everywhere and prepare the ground was another—both goals outside of the old war leader's reach.

"I do not see how the suggestion to reinforce some of our warriors' forces goes against the revered laws of the Great Peacemaker," said a heavyset elder whom Ganayeda recognized as one of the Standing Stone People's representatives. "We are five families of one longhouse. Five families, five brothers. Brothers who would and *should* help each other."

The well-presented claim went on, evidently going down favorably with its listeners. If only more elders would rise to speak in such a way. It was all the preliminary discussions, the opening ceremonies, the way to start, to mark the arrival of every representative and people who mattered. The true meeting of the Great Council would begin in a dawn or two, much different procedures, progressing in groups and not in an open assembly. Every problem, law, and suggestion would be discussed separately between the eastern side of the Central Fire, the Flint and the Standing Stone People, and their western brothers, the Swamp and the Mountain dwellers. Only when those two came to an understanding, to an unanimous agreement, only then would the Onondaga, the Keepers of the Central Fire, be let in, with the agreed matter brought before their attention and for their consideration. The laws of the Peacemaker were clear and very, very wise.

Sighing, Ganayeda suppressed the urge to shake his head. It would be a long gathering, this one. Many issues to discuss, to deliberate, to try to solve. The Wyandot strengthening union and its possibly changing policies being a part of it, a serious part; the troublesome reports from the west—just a side issue, to pay little attention to.

However, this wasn't a side issue, not at all. It was all about the Great League and the way it was functioning. It was all a matter of the great union's future. Didn't they see it?

More speeches for and against reinforcements were sounded, with the dignitaries talking, shortly or at length, convincing those who were already convinced, leaving those against as adamant as before. If only Father were allowed to talk to this revered assembly!

Another glance at the older leader's pressed mouth let him know that Father might have been feeling the same. The dignitaries who spoke at his instigation or behalf were not eloquent or passionate enough.

"But it doesn't matter," said the War Chief later, when the gathering had broken and the smells of the cooking meals began filling the valley, with everyone, even the most dignified elders, sniffing the air, not interested in politics, not for the remainder of the tiring day. "It wouldn't have gone well even had I been allowed to talk until Father Sun left our world and Grandmother Moon came to lighten the night." The broad palm came up, relating the familiar calmness, so typical to the man. "They don't deem the troubles in the west important enough to spend their time on deliberating about it. Nine representative of the Mountain People and some of the others that I had time to convince are not enough to force the Great Council into a serious consideration." The wide shoulders lifted in a shrug. "There will be no decision reached, not this time. Maybe through the next meeting, or the one after that, because the trouble will not go away, but only grow and intensify, until even those who don't care won't be able to ignore it."

"So will we sit and wait and do nothing?" Okwaho called out, halting so abruptly his moccasins raised a cloud of dust upon the dry earth of the trail they descended. Arriving back in the valley two dawns ago, after fooling around the countryside for twice of that period of time, the young man's entire being radiated health and contentment, beaming with happiness, even though now the happy glow dimmed, gave way to the knitted eyebrows and stubbornly protruding jaw. "Only because some of our elders refuse to see beyond the tips of their long noses—"

The tirade stopped as abruptly as it burst out, the nature of their company dawning, making Ganayeda struggle to hide his smirk. Father was not an uptight dignitary and he was on their side; still, he wasn't a fellow warrior to address him in such a way.

"Many of our elders do manage to glimpse farther than that, I would say." There was an amused note to Father's voice, but Ganayeda could see his brother licking his lips, searching for something to say. "But to answer your question, oh farsighted warrior, no, we won't sit and wait and do nothing. We haven't done it so far, and there is no reason we should resort to doing it now."

While Okwaho's eyes bore holes in the ground they treaded upon, Ganayeda asked the obvious. "Do we go on speaking to important people, trying to change their minds?"

"That too." Father's nod was thoughtful, strangely contemplative. "But those of us who cannot not sit and wait and do nothing but talk to dignitaries and their following may take upon themselves more lively tasks." The weathered palm landed on Okwaho's back with much affection. "You've already been doing some of it, Son. Didn't you speak to our Flint guests, the warriors among them, about these same issues? Your brother says that he has been forced to face quite an eager fighting force not long ago, with you and your friends from Cohoes Falls accosting him with those same claims and ideas."

In his typical, quick-to-recover way, Okwaho was peering at Father, all eyes. "Well, yes. It happened. I wanted to talk to Ganayeda about it, and the others just trailed along."

"Even Ogteah?"

Okwaho's eyes widened in a silent question.

"The Crooked Tongue," clarified Ganayeda. "Our cousin from the other side."

"Oh, well, yes." This time, the young man nodded readily, his gaze clearing. "He is a good man. An interesting type. It's not easy to make him talk when it comes to useful information, but it's worth the effort. His knowledge is a rare thing, a firsthand eye-witness account. One doesn't run into something like that every day."

Impressed with his brother's assessment of the man in question, Ganayeda nodded again. "Yes, the Crooked Tongue is deeper than he cares to display. A fascinating man."

"Well, leave him out of it." Father's voice rang out conversationally, holding no resentment and no hostility. "He is, indeed, a good man, a worthy person, and I'm glad you two appreciate him for what he is." A brief pause had them both sneaking glances, as the older man halted, not in a hurry to step out of the shadow the forested incline provided. "Yet, in this, I would rather have him uninvolved. It's not that I don't trust him. I'm sure he is one of us now, to be accepted wholeheartedly. Still, he has not spent enough time among our people to be privy to all our affairs." Another brief pause. "Especially those that involve our possible dealings with his former people."

The wind from the lake greeted them, soft and so very welcomed in this part of the early afternoon. Following the old leader's firm footsteps that led them toward the inviting openness of the shore, Ganayeda tried to organize his thoughts. Was it true that with all his warm, open welcoming, Father didn't trust the foreigner as readily as they all assumed he did? Had he also suspected that the Crooked Tongue might have been motivated by more causes than a decision to change an unsuccessful life?

He thought about the man, his pleasant-looking face, the openness of his grin, the flickering gaze that admitted freely to all his flaws and faults, something regular people would try to change, or least to hide. Such a light disposition, combined with the rare ability to make himself liked for what he was. A strange combination that had claimed his, Ganayeda's, affection and goodwill from the very first meeting, even though they weren't supposed to like each other at all, two enemies bumping into one another by mistake.

Why did this man come here? he asked himself again, slightly puzzled. There were reasons, of course there were. Good, solid reasons. First and foremost, there were the wild man's crimes, past wrongdoings. The Crooked Tongues leader wanted his son safely away, and where was a better place for the troubled man to go than truly far, truly away. Especially considering his mother, a native of these lands, and Gayeri, the woman he seemed to love enough to stick by her and stay in her longhouse, become a part of her family. And yet...

He frowned, suddenly not so sure. Those reasons were good, but not good enough for a person to change his surroundings in such a dramatic way, to switch for the enemy nation and out of his own free will. Was there more to it than simple convenience?

"I've been talking to my friends about it, yes." Okwaho was saying, bringing Ganayeda back from his reverie. Apparently, his companions proceeded with their conversation regardless of his wandering state of mind. "And I can run around and talk to anyone you think fit. But what good would it do? What do warriors' opinions matter?"

"Oh, their opinions do matter, trust me on that." The older man's face twisted with a confident, slightly conspiratorial smile. "And so do their numbers. Think about it in this way. You wanted to join the Flint People's war some time ago, didn't you? There was no law to stop you from doing it. You needed to get no permission, nor ask for anyone's consent. It was your personal decision to join whatever war you wanted to, wasn't it?" The pensive eyes lingered on Ganayeda's brother's face, pregnant with meaning. "What is to stop many more youngsters like you were back a few summers ago, young people eager to fight, eager to learn and grow as true warriors, from doing the same? Nothing. And here is where your persuasive presence comes in. If someone went around, stirring younger men into joining this or that war... Say the war of the Mountain People." The generous lips were twisting into the smuggest of grins. "A few hundred eager, talented hotheads like yourself. Would it be difficult to find such an amount among the towns and villages of our Five Nations? A mere moon of traveling, talking about your adventures out there, telling exciting stories, and you will be tailed with more eager hotheads than you can deal with." The satisfied smile widened. "And what can authorities say about it? Nothing. Our young men wish to do something with themselves. That is all. Nothing bad, nothing unlawful. The elders would frown and maybe fume, but in the end, if you are successful in gathering many people to your lawful enterprise concerning warring and war, then those same reluctant elders would be forced to accept what has been done. Won't they now?"

Taken aback, Ganayeda just stared, astounded by the devious simplicity of the solution. Nothing unlawful, indeed. And yet, Father was ready to twist the hand of the Great Council itself, and with little doubt or hesitation. A somewhat unsettling revelation.

"Oh, I see!" cried out Okwaho, bringing his powerful arms up in an open wonder. "It's brilliant, Father! I'll enlist Akweks and some others! Together we can cover most of the towns in just a moon or so, no more than two." His hands went for his hair, running through the spiked ridge, ruining its perfection. "Before the end of the summer, we will reach the Mountain People's main river, heading for those dreadful falls of the enemy everyone out there is talking about. Our timing would be perfect!"

"What about your timing?" asked Ganayeda, mainly to get himself involved in the discussion, feeling left out.

"Oh, the Hot Moons are the best time to war," muttered Okwaho absently, eyes wandering the depths of his inner thoughts, hands still making a mess out of his warriors' lock.

"The leaves," added Father, his smile encouraging, not patronizing in the least. "Through the late Awakening Season and the Hot Moons the leaves on the trees are thick, making the forests perfect for ambushes and traps, allows an unnoticed progress in general."

"Oh." Nodding, Ganayeda busied himself with a thorough scan of the lake, its surface glimmering, covered with ripples. But for Father's quick explanation, he might have said something silly, commented in an inappropriate way. It was irritating, his lack of warfare knowledge. Small things like leaves on the trees, but what a difference they made.

"Which only strengthens my point," he muttered, thoughts straying from his own lacking warring experience to the general lack of it in the others. A worrisome topic that no one but him seemed to notice.

"What point?" asked Father, his eyes narrowing with attention.

Ganayeda just shrugged. "More people gain warring experience, more chances for us to be ready against anything unexpected." A flat stone caught his gaze and he picked it up, leaning to toss it toward the water in a way that made it skip across its rippling surface several times. "Our Onondaga People, for one, young men and the older ones, people of my age, are not always handy when it comes to actual warring. Even small skirmishes can throw a person out of balance when he is not used to facing warriors instead of the regular forest dwellers." A glance at Okwaho reassured him, let him know that his brother was still busy with his private plans and scheming, not listening. The wandering eyes and the deepest of frowns told him that. "There are too many people like me, and too little like him," he added, returning his gaze to Father's, the older man's eyes boring into him, their attention undivided. "And this is the case with our immediate neighbors, the Standing Stone and Swamp People. Only the doorkeepers still have enough warriors at their disposal."

"It's not that our towns and villages are left unprotected, for every enterprising enemy to storm at their will." The War Chief's frown was deep, somewhat defensive. "We still have double rows of fences and every man of our settlements knows what to do with his bow or club."

"Yes, Father." He nodded out of politeness, not wishing to contradict the great leader or call him out on something the War Chief might have overlooked all those long summers since the Great Peace was created.

Father's eyes, as they rested upon him, reflected a somewhat grudging understanding, a grimly amused admittance. As always, nothing escaped this man's attention, neither a word, nor a gesture, not a deep hidden thought. Okwaho was listening now too, all ears.

"Well, there is a truth to your words, Son." Father's nod related more admittance. "Long summers of peace might have harmed our ability to war properly. Indeed, the doorkeepers may be the only ones to remain the experienced warriors that all our people used to be. This is why our young men had to travel that far to learn this particular skill." The man turned away slowly, scanning the lake's surface in his turn. "Our towns and villages are larger now, more numerous, their fields spread far and wide. Indeed, it might be harder to defend those effectively, to be ready and on guard when the people have grown used to prosperity and an easier life." The wide shoulders lifted in a shrug. "Yes, you are right. Our warriors' prowess is declining, and should a well-organized enemy think of a true war…"

"The Crooked Tongues and their union," Okwaho burst in when the silence lasted longer than a few heartbeats, indicating a possible pause in the speech. Still a glaring impoliteness.

"The Crooked Tongues maybe, yes." The great leader's sigh was heard most clearly, even though it barely shook the air. "With our greatest of allies embarking on his Sky Journey, their union presents a serious danger." The pressed lips were nothing but a thin line now, looking like one of the scars, the old faded pattern. "Yes, we should prepare for all sorts of intensified warfare. These people would be difficult to deal with." A shrug. "Difficult but not impossible. Our Great League is more than a match to that hastily concocted union of theirs."

"And this is what I meant by saying that our men need to gain battle experience," said Ganayeda, feeling infinitely better all of a sudden. Father never held a grudge or insisted on something that wasn't practical or called for. "When I saw Okwaho in action those two spans of seasons ago, I knew that this is what our young man should learn. As I see it," he encircled them with his gaze, enjoying this rare opportunity to sound his thoughts freely and with no reservations. What great company his father and brother were! "We need to make every young man do what Okwaho did, to undergo some training with some battle experience thrown in. And what is the better way to do this but by sending them as reinforcements to our doorkeepers, anywhere each aspiring warrior might fancy to go? Do you see what I mean?"

Father's eyes were narrowed into slits by now, his lips twisting in an appreciative smile. Okwaho, who had heard those musings before, had already let his attention wander again, thinking of his own private plans for the war of the Mountain People, most probably.

"You are thinking of taking down two birds with one arrow. Go on."

Pleased, Ganayeda brought his hands up. "The vision of the Great Peacemaker was of one longhouse with five or more hearths, and while we are walking the right path, I believe we are not there as yet. Our leaders do not think of our Great League first and the towns or nations they represent second. And this is what should be changed, I believe." Taking a short breath, he went on, reassured by Father's narrow, attentive gaze. "As I said, we are walking the right path, but we might be required to hasten our steps, because the world around us is changing. In your times, we were facing scattered nations, but this is not the case anymore. Our union made our enemies unite as well, and should they do it better now, should they help each other more readily than we do, our great league would not remain great for much longer. Because we are the People of the Longhouse, but we still think like separate nations. Brother-nations, yes," he hurried to add when both his listeners' frowns indicated upcoming protests, "brothers who do not wish to war on each other, who wish to live in peace and concord. Yet, as brothers in peace, we should be brothers in difficulties as well." He wanted to lick his lips, but didn't, wishing to appear calm and in full control. "The members of the Great Council seem to be concerned with the people they were chosen to represent more than they are concerned with the general matters of the Great League. Which is only natural, of course. The Great Law of Peace instructs us to act in this way." Not daring to pause, he went on, needing to say it aloud, his own thoughts on the matter suddenly formed and crystal-clear. "Still, as the dwellers of our mutual longhouse, we should be ready to offer help to our brothers, or to ask for it in case of a dire need. Our Union is nothing but a name without meaning if we are not ready to protect each other, to help one another in more than distribution of nicely-sounding titles accompanied with flowery speeches and words." The birds fussing in the treetops above their heads took his attention from his companions' eyes that were narrowed in a ridiculously similar way. "If we each war our own wars, facing our historical enemies unaided, then what did we gain out of our great union besides reducing the amount of enemies to fight? If that's all we wanted, then we could have reached peaceful agreements between our nations and been done with it. No need to build our metaphorical longhouse, the Great League, unless we are ready to act as true families, true brothers."

In the brief silence that prevailed, he could hear people's voices not far away, shouting and talking loudly, in no agitated manner. The preparations for tomorrow's spear throwing competition, he knew, were well on their way.

"How would you change our ways, given the power to do that?" asked Father, his brow adorned by what looked like a thousand small wrinkles. "How would you attempt to unite us more than we are now, make us one nation instead of five?"

Detecting no hostility, no challenging critique in the gauging gaze, Ganayeda took a deep breath.

"There might be several ways to unite us and make us feel more like one longhouse and not several. Your and Okwaho's way, for one. Our warriors traveling and fighting in each other's lands can be the spearhead of such a change. Their travels alone would help them develop a sense of commitment to others besides their own people." He shrugged. "Regardless of the immediate benefit of offering help to our brothers in need, our own people would enjoy the fruits of your plan for many summers to come." Another scan of the fluttering water. "Should the same Crooked Tongues union attack us all of a sudden, doing it in any sort of an organized manner, our Onondaga people might have an easier time standing up to them, without the need to send cries for help eastward and westward right away."

"Not bad thinking, Brother," muttered Okwaho, his attention back, eyes narrow, openly appreciative. "Not bad at all." A closemouthed praise that warmed Ganayeda's insides.

Father's gaze was the one to wander now. "Find me this evening, after the hubbub of the meals dies down," he said quietly. Then his eyes cleared, and he turned to Okwaho. "Do this as well. Bring those of your most trusted friends along. The ones you are planning to involve. Your Flint associates and anyone else you trusted with those talks before."

"I will, Father." His impatience bursting, too obvious to the eye, the young man had already begun turning away, preparing to storm the trail back toward the valley. "Got to find Akweks and the others, to let them know. We will head off tomorrow with dawn. Before the first light."

"Before the spear-throwing contest?" They called it out in such unison, it made all three of them laugh.

"Oh my, I forgot all about it." Rubbing his face in a somewhat showy manner, Okwaho sighed. "Wild grizzled bears won't be able to take Akweks from *that* competition. Damn it." Another sigh, as showily loud as before. "I suppose we'll have to delay for one more day. Hope our Crooked Tongue will manage to make it a one-day competition."

"Not sure about that." Remembering the hectic preparations, Ganayeda grinned. "With so many eager participants, it very well may spill into two days, easily at that. The Crooked Tongue didn't know what he was stirring when he came up with this innovative idea. I bet he expected nothing of the sort."

"He is a good man," said Father proudly. "I'm glad to see he is doing so well on our side of the Great Lake."

Not always that well, thought Ganayeda, slightly amused, remembering a loud argument that resulted in a near–fight only two dawns ago, while the foreigner was busy preparing his large-scale competition.

Having not been around, all Ganayeda heard were rumors, from the chuckling Iheks and then many others, claiming that some enraged Onondaga Town's man accused the foreigner of unauthorized dealings with his woman, or something of the sort. Or maybe it was one of the visitors who had maintained that. All the sources agreed that it was something scandalous, nearly ending with violence, but for the intervention of none other than Okwaho's Flint friend, who had been spending much time in the foreigner's company now, indeed excited about the upcoming competition. It was said that the young Flint, not a little hothead in himself, did manage to calm the spirits instead of making the violence worse.

Being a person responsible for the well-being of the entire gathering, in addition to his more than friendly contact with the foreigner, Ganayeda had brought this matter up on the same evening the rumors were circulating, but all he got was an indifferent shrug accompanied with suggestively rolling eyes. Some people were touchy, stupid enough to overreact on quite silly matters, maintained the Crooked Tongue, his grin tired, laced with exaggerated indifference.

Obviously, there was more to this story, surmised Ganayeda, remembering that the troubles of the foreigner in his native lands also involved women and loose behavior. Still, of course he let the matter rest. It was not his place to lecture a man of his own age on proper ways when it came to commitment and women, and Gayeri wasn't even of his family.

"How about we detour through that field on our way back?" Father was saying, his voice breaking into Ganayeda's thoughts, a welcome distraction. "See how the preparations for the big competition are progressing."

Turning to lead their way in his typical, affable but authoritative way, Father didn't bother to glance back to make sure they followed. It must feel good to wield so much authority, reflected Ganayeda, welcoming the proposed delay. He didn't need to see the competition's last preparations. Like the rest of this event's activities, detailed reports were forthcoming. A person responsible for the Great Gathering and all its aspects, he was of course in the midst of it all, the spear-throwing event presenting the least significant, even if the showiest challenge of them all.

Actually, he thought, trailing after his father and brother, not in a hurry to catch up, not for a moment, the Crooked Tongue had done unexpectedly well in his enterprise. Six dawns of hectic activity—picking a proper field, clearing it in a hasty manner, making people around help and on a volunteer basis, spreading the word and trying to determine everything, from the possible amount of active participants to the changes in rules that would be accepted by everyone—the foreigner conducted his innovative undertaking in a surprisingly independent manner, somehow making people and things work. An impressive ability, not to mention resolve and dedication, in a person Ganayeda liked greatly but had little expectations from.

"In what way do you plan to start recruiting your potential warriors?" Father's voice reached him as he hastened his step, the clamor of the site bursting upon them, bringing many people into their view. Strolling next to Okwaho, the old leader looked casual, as though he was talking about unimportant matters.

Okwaho's eyebrows were creating a single line under his furrowed brow. "I suppose it better be a lighter way of talking to people. Probably about battles and thrills in it." The young man's shrug was light, barely visible. "Politics mean nothing to most of the younger hotheads, but the excitement of wars, of the projected expedition toward heroic deeds, of wild fits of courage, of all the glorious stories to bring home and boast about, oh but do those things make the youngsters' blood boil." Another shrug. "When I went to the Flint People's lands I wanted just that, the glory, the chance to prove myself, to show our entire world that I'm as good as anyone, maybe more than some." The smile stretching the generous lips was wide, unapologetic. "I think that is what drives most of our youth to battles, and that is what I will be offering them. The glory and the thrill. No politics, no talks of brotherhood between our Five Nations and their obligations to each other." A different, shyer sort of a smile flashed. "I won't be deceiving anyone. Those wars are important to our Great League, and our young men deserve to grow up into worthwhile warriors. But we all do it for different reasons, and as long as everyone comes out a winner what does it matter what drives whom?"

Not overly impressed because, by now, he had come to expect such spells of deep thinking coming out of his wild bother's mouth, Ganayeda watched the long stretch of flat land, unrecognizable after six days of strenuous work.

With the most of the vegetation gone, the previously sparsely forested area looked like a field before sowing, reminding him that the regular locally-held spear-throwing contests were, indeed, conducted in the spring, after the men had already cleared the fields, but before the women began working on them—a perfect venue. Well, this stretch of land had been cleared up so well, made so flat and clean, the Onondaga Town dwellers would do wisely starting to plant their additional crops upon it.

"Where is our organizer?" he asked one of the men, who was studying the slope, pacing it as though trying to measure its size.

"Oh, over there." The hand clutching a spear waved toward the trees of the opposite hill, where several men were working with hoes, flattening the ground that appeared to already be perfectly flat. "He said we need to get rid of more bushes."

"Do they intend to scrap the entire hill clean?" muttered Ganayeda, impressed. There would be many hundreds of people wishing to watch the competition, not to miss one single throw or dash. The cleaner the incline was, the easier it would be for the betting spectators.

Okwaho already rushed to cross the flat land, nodding appreciatively as he glanced here and there, but Father lingered, falling into his elder son's step.

"What you said was wise and farsighted." The voice of the older man was quiet, barely heard, his face again a study of ease and lack of concern. "I would love to hear more of your thoughts on this matter."

Enormously pleased, he tried to keep his expression as

unperturbed as he could. "Thank you, Father. It honors me to hear you saying that." Answering people's greetings, they proceeded toward the hill. "Since that encounter with the Crooked Tongues near Lone Hill, when Okwaho did all the right things, behaved like a true warrior and leader, while I had been running around like a bear with a bee up its tail, I couldn't help but start thinking. Our people should be ready to do battle if called upon. Hunters react differently."

The older man's gaze was upon him, narrow with attention. "According to what you two, and the people of Lone Hill, were saying, you weren't cowardly or useless." A light pause came accompanied with somewhat mischievous grin. "It's only later, after coming back and before heading for the Crooked Tongues lands, that you began acting as though something was trying to sting you somewhere there up your tail, indeed."

Not unsettled by those particular memories, not anymore, Ganayeda chuckled. "I was acting like that, wasn't I?" Sobering, he shrugged. "I didn't say I behaved cowardly, nor that I didn't do everything in my power to render these people harmless or save both girls." Apparently, this particular memory still hurt, so he took a deep breath. "But what I learned there was a valuable lesson. Most of our young men should do what Okwaho did, go and find themselves a nice little war, gain fighting experience, help our eastern and western families safeguard the doors of our longhouse and keep it safe."

The clamor of working people was very near now, interrupting the privacy of their conversation. The Crooked Tongue appeared out of nowhere, coming forward in his usual hurried step. Face smeared with fresh earth, hair tied carelessly behind his back, its unshaved sides glittering with wetness, the shirtless torso dirtied and scratched, the man presented a picture that reminded Ganayeda of their first meeting. Nothing respectable or even mildly fitting.

"We need to clean those off before nightfall," he explained, as though already challenged for his activities or appearance. "Should have thought about it earlier, I admit that." There was no apology and not a shadow of regret behind the wideness of the grin bestowed on them both.

"Do you expect such a large attendance of onlookers that you cannot count on the space around the field itself to be sufficient?" asked Father, as always matter-of fact and businesslike, not insisting on honorific address like some other dignitaries might have. "Well, it is excusable to assume that most of this gathering would be busy participating."

"I assumed that too, yes." The Crooked Tongue nodded readily, rushing on in his lively manner of speaking, with no pause for breath and, indeed, no honorific titles, somehow natural in his case, not out of place. "But apparently, the entire female population of this town and all the pretty valley's visitors are determined to watch us competing, making fools of ourselves with bad throws," he added with a winning grin. "So here we are, working ourselves into exhaustion instead of conserving our strength for tomorrow."

"Speaking of the prettier side of this gathering..." This time, Father's voice held a smile, an open amusement, but Ganayeda heard the undercurrent. Those words carried a warning or a well-meaning advice. "There are sights one is better off not looking at. Rumors are an unnecessary thing, better to be avoided. They do a person nothing but damage, needlessly so."

The foreigner's face darkened, drained of its pleasant liveliness. For a long moment he said nothing, his eyes sliding over the freshly flattened ground.

"I thank you for your kind advice, Honorable Leader," he muttered finally, back to reserved and proper address, the hoe he held in both hands clutched tightly, his knuckles turning white.

"No need for such high-flown talk," said Father, his voice holding nothing but warmth, reassuring in its lightness. "Save the titles for the opening ceremonies of your competition tomorrow." Putting his arm on the tense shoulders, he began steering his converser back toward the spot the man had been working on before being interrupted. "Show me how you are planning to place those who are going to watch with no participants blocking the view of the midfield. It looks like a true challenge to me." Brisk and perfectly matter-of-fact, he was leading his companion away, followed by many gazes, as always, rendering his protégé support by his brief attention. "How many people in each team would be involved? For how many throws?"

Ganayeda hid his grin, trading a glance with his brother. The foreigner was safe now, safe from complaint or a persecution should some possibly offended Onondaga Town's dwellers decide to turn to the authorities. The powerful War Chief was showing this gathering that unless having a solid case, there was no point in trying to bother or harass this man.

CHAPTER 9

A sharp call made the hoop dart again, racing along the perfectly clean surface, with nothing to stand in its way, to hinder its progress. The currently competing teams fell quiet, and so did the onlookers, hundreds of those, crowding the slope that had been cleaned of some of its vegetation as well.

Oh, but they worked hard to make the field look the way it did, reflected Ogteah, trying not to let a new wave of pride show. Such a large event, involving so many people, hundreds upon hundreds of those, players and watchers alike, judges, organizers, so many important men, the dignitaries as eager to compete as their escorting warriors. It was a wonder the women didn't try to grab their mate's javelins as well.

The thought made him chuckle, despite the ripples of exhaustion creeping up and into his temples. But he had worked so hard to make it happen. Through those last six dawns he had slaved like never before, but happily, with so much pleasure and satisfaction, putting it all into the attempt to make his unheard-of competition happen.

Which was a difficult task, much more difficult than he had assumed it would be. So many people to involve, make them help, put forward their best effort and cooperation; so many details to take into account, so many preparations. The old rules of the traditional spear-throwing were no good for such an all-encompassing event.

The custom would have people playing in teams, throwing their javelins in turns until one of the players would miss and the other got his spear as a reward. Sometimes the throwers would cast their spears all at once, prizing the skill of a person who managed to nick the rolling ring despite the additional distraction of other flying missiles. None of which were good enough where hundreds of contesters were involved. So new rules were to be determined and everyone had to agree or accept them, a true challenge for a person with no special clout, no title, no real importance. But for the open support of the High Spring's man and, later on, the powerful War Chief; but for the active help of so many good people the Flint warrior and his fierce local companion—the High Springs man's brother and the War Chief's other son—had managed to organize, to force into helping, or usually to persuade and cajole.

Not used to giving orders, to expect people's help and cooperation, Ogteah had attempted to do it all by himself, but his newfound companions were of a different opinion. If people wished to enjoy an unusual competition or a spectacular show, then they should help and do it with good spirits, maintained the wolf tattoo owner. No need to let them sit on their fat behinds and expect others to prepare it all and serve them their new entertainment on a prettily carved plate. In the large-scale ballgames, everyone was involved and helping. The elders and clan mothers wouldn't have it in any other way, and the fact that Ogteah was the man to come up with this new idea didn't mean that he was supposed to prepare it all by himself.

The Flint spearman, Akweks, would smirk and shake his head, needling his companion about his leader-like inclinations. Yet, smirking or not, he was always around and helping as well, and so did the rest of his eastern companions, along with many local Onondagas, and even some mysterious Mountain and Swamp People. Apparently, the wolf man had many connections from all around the Great League, having fought in quite a few places, at each of the frontiers, and having traveled through even more lands.

Surprised, Ogteah had found himself enjoying this man's company greatly, looking forward to the quiet evenings by the fire as much as to the busy days. The hectic preparations for his grand innovation turned out to be the sort of activity he genuinely enjoyed, ever busy, with no time to stop and think, or entertain silly ideas. Like fooling around with that insistent fox from Onondaga Town... Oh, but how he regretted the stupid things he had done on the day he had learned of Father's death!

He hadn't come to meet her on the next day of course, but she kept stalking him, challenging, teasing, flaunting her looks and appeal, and but for him being so preoccupied, he knew he might not have managed to avoid doing something even more silly. Enough that she nearly made him pick a fight on the day before the previous one.

He pushed the bad feeling away. It wasn't wise to flare at her in the way he did, telling her off rudely, and in front of other people. She might have been a nuisance in the way she was determined to get him, but his treatment made her mad enough to yell at him and accuse him of crimes he might have committed but only in his mind. An embarrassment, especially when other locals, her fellow women friends and some of the town's men, got involved. Then it developed into a near fight, as of course by this point, he was enraged beyond control, not about to back away or justify any of his actions, existent and non-existent altogether. But for the Flint man and his friends being around and not hesitating to take his side, it might have been bad.

Shaking his head, he made his mind focus on the field, following yet another flying spear, his concentration difficult to summon. He had watched so many of these through this long, tiring day, some painted or carved, some having feathers attached to their shafts, some sporting hooked edges. Professional players seemed to prefer those weapons, made especially for the game, as opposed to the rest that were just weapons, prettily done or not.

The players of Tsonontowan, one of the Mountain People's main towns, roared with approval as their thrower's spear pierced the hoop, if not in the perfect middle, then close enough to it, pinning it to the ground firmly, uncompromisingly.

Impressed, Ogteah exchanged a look with the other judges then strolled forward, to inspect the throw and declare its results.

Nothing to deliberate about, not this time. He breathed with relief. The instances when the spear only pushed the hoop off its

course but didn't pierce it were the ones to present a challenge
sometimes, causing the judges to deliberate in making decisions.
The impaled hoop spoke for itself.

He glanced at the opposing team of the High Springs' players.
Under regular circumstances the contesters would toss their
spears until one of them missed his throw. As it was now, with
the new readjusted rules, the other team's player could do little
more than try not to miss in his turn, beyond the hope of winning
his rival's spear with no more rounds but one.

A pity, thought Ogteah, walking back toward the people who
were crowding the nearest side of the field. The High Springs man
was the next to display his warrior's skill, and Ogteah wished he
could have influenced this one's rival into missing his throw.

Disbarred from taking a part in the competition due to his
unexpectedly elevated position of a judge—not such a welcomed
development, and something he didn't take into account while
agreeing to do this task—he still wished the High Springs'
organizer would win. With a spectacular throw, preferably. He
was a good man.

"That dirty skunk, I hoped he would miss."

He didn't need to turn his head to recognize the voice of the
speaker, even though the words were muttered in a barely audible
voice. The wolf man was chewing his lower lip, his own spear
clutched tightly in his wide palm. Too tightly. The first to
represent his town's team, he'd had his share of disappointment
to deal with already, his own throw being average, pushing the
hoop but not impaling it. His rival didn't do much better than
that, but the ambitious warrior had the face of a thundercloud
ever since.

"I was thinking the same," breathed Ogteah, afraid to be
overheard. As a judge, he could not afford to be thought of as
anything but an impartial stone slab with no feelings.

"That's not that." As always, Akweks was there too, lingering
close to the action, balancing two spears in one hand with a showy
ease, his winning of the day. The Great Spirits kept smiling upon
the eager spear-thrower, giving him an impressive victory, against
a rival whose throw was good, but not the perfect middle, the

regular hit of the showy Flint. "Our friend here got carried away betting."

"Oh." Disregarding a small twinge of irritation, Ogteah nodded sagely. Of all people, he didn't need further explanations. The wolf man cared for his own brother and wished him well, but his motives were burdened by one more aspect, apparently, the aspect he, Ogteah, envied his friends dearly.

As a judge, he was not allowed to bet. Of course he wasn't. However, when agreeing to take this prominent position—not out of ambition or prestige, not at all, but because the proper amount of judges was missing on the day before and he was eager to have it all settled—he didn't take into account that such a move would disbar him from two main pleasures of the much-awaited game. No participating in the team of his own village, and no betting on the other players and their success, either. He had worked hard, went out of his way to organize a competition of unheard-of proportions, and now he could not even enjoy its benefits the way other people did. What irony!

"The thing is, my brother is brilliant when it comes to shooting," the wolf man was saying quietly, eyes on the man of the Mountain People's team who rushed along the field now, carrying the hoop in his outstretched hand. "He can shoot four, five arrows one after another in the matter of a heartbeat or two, take down whatever target there is out there. He is so good with his bow! But," the wide shoulders lifted in a gesture that was lacking in spirit, not reflecting the proud spark the beaded armbands and the jewelry adorning the wide chest radiated, "the thing is, I don't know how good he is with the spear. He must be good, as he is in everything, but..." another listless shrug, "I shouldn't have bet anything of value."

"What did you bet?" asked Ogteah, shielding his eyes against the strength of the early afternoon sun.

The wolf man just grunted in response, but his Flint friend chuckled, unabashed. "The quiver. He bet that prettily decorated quiver of arrows he cherishes so much."

"Against what?"

"A knife with an antler handle," breathed the wolf man

through his pressed lips. "A pretty-looking piece of weapon I wouldn't object to having, but for that skunk not missing the hoop. Even if I don't lose the quiver, I won't be getting that knife now. Oh well." A livelier shrug ended the tirade.

Taking his eyes off the readying hoop-thrower and toward the object of all this musings, Ogteah pushed another wave of irritation away. So many betting possibilities, all lawful and not frowned upon.

From their slightly elevated position, he could see the High Springs man standing proudly, his usual calmly confident self. Not leaning forward, shifting his legs, or moving a muscle for that matter. Just standing there, waiting, sure of himself.

"He won't miss his throw. You can relax about your quiver."

"I know, I know. He is good at everything he does." Evidently shamed, the young man shifted uneasily. "It's just that I thought of his shooting skills when I jumped into this betting."

"And made me bet a bunch of arrows as well," complained the Flint, beaming with happiness. Which only served to irritate Ogteah even more. Everyone was having a good time, throwing spears and betting, everyone but him!

The sharp call made them lean forward, following the pouncing ring with their eyes, their muscles straining against their will, eyes calculating its path, wishing to have their spears now. The usual way of watching, but since the game had went on for so long, beginning near the high morning, after the due ceremony and the War Dance were commenced, Ogteah had stopped being so involved with each throw. Yet, now his interest stirred anew.

The High Springs man barely moved, letting the hoop—this one of a regular size, not the Flint's smaller version of it—roll almost half of its way, causing their nerves to nearly burst with impatience.

"Come on!" The man's brother's hiss had a strangled quality to it.

When the spear finally flew, it did so in a beautiful arch, forcing its way through the crisp air like a bird of prey, pouncing toward its target, unerring. The hoop had no more chances than a mouse running in the open, with nowhere to hide, nowhere to escape.

Could it be? wondered Ogteah numbly, taking in the force with which the ring jerked, stopped in the middle of its flight, pinned with hopeless firmness.

"It looks like not only your quiver might be safe," he tossed toward his companions, rushing forward, forgetting to coordinate his action with the rest of the judges. They all reached the spot nearly at the same time, so maybe no one bothered with formalities in the face of such a spectacular throw.

Staring at the sturdy stick, the rugged flint half buried in the grass-covered ground, Ogteah took a deep breath before reaching for it, pulling carefully, even though its prey was impaled on it thoroughly, not in a danger of slipping off.

The people around him held their breath, mostly his fellow judges, but some of the onlookers who were closer to this side of the field. The ring wasn't the Flint People's smaller device; still, the hit of the perfect middle was a rare thing.

"It's the perfect hit," he shouted, hard put to hold his elation in check. Swinging the contested spear, he held it high, presenting it to the crowds. People's shouts and yells of excitement enveloped him, and their pushing to get closer in their eagerness to see served to heighten his elation.

"All judges should confirm such a thing," commented one of the observers, clearly the Mountain People's supporter. "One can't just—"

"There is nothing to confirm here," tossed Ogteah, not bothering to look at his doubter while bringing the spear higher. "What is there to argue about?"

"Let us take it back to the elders," said one of his fellow judges mildly. "They will make the declaration."

Forcing himself to nod solemnly, as appropriate for the occasion, Ogteah still felt the small wave of irritation returning. There was nothing to confirm here, absolutely nothing, and if the declaration came from someone else, someone perfectly local... Shrugging, he turned to go.

Back on their edge of the field, the excitement was spilling. The High Springs team went wild with screams and hopping around, and the winner seemed to be in danger of being throttled, with too many hands patting his back and yelling unintelligible things.

Not wishing to tread on any more sensitivities, Ogteah yielded the spear to one of the elders and watched the man and his throng of followers pushing their way through the crowds, congratulating the winner.

Since the beginning of the contest, the perfect hit happened a few times, four to be precise, one of them being on behalf of Cohoes Falls of course. He sought his Flint friend with his eyes, finding it easy to make out both broad-shouldered, over-decorated forms of Akweks and his wolf friend, in the thickest of it, congratulating the winner, exchanging inevitable friendly insults, to hide their feelings but not their admiration.

The winners of their private bets as well now, he thought somewhat bitterly, not minding being temporarily forgotten, but still feeling uncomfortably alone. Would this long, tiring enterprise ever end?

Warily, he calculated again, eyes on the incline allocated for the watching crowds, packed with so many people no vegetation of this side of the hill showed. Quite a view! Barely half of the competitors had had their spears thrown, which meant a few more hundreds of men waited for their turn. Briefly, he played with the idea of deserting his post. Would he be allowed to participate in the actual spear-throwing then?

"That was a throw that didn't shame our War Chief and his family." One of Ogteah's numerous helpers and participants in the preparations of the contest drew closer, nodding as he talked. "Our High Springs organizer deserved it, didn't he?"

"Oh, yes, he did. He is good man."

The man nodded again. "A word to the wise. The Onondaga Town team, keep an eye on them. Or rather, keep away, if you can."

"What do you mean?" Forgetting politeness and small talk, he turned to face his companion sharply. "What did you hear?"

"Nothing in particular." The man's eyes slid over the crowded hillside, surveying it idly. "You are not popular in some quarters there, and I hear that one of their players is your most eager non-admirer."

Ogteah felt like groaning aloud. Not *this* again!

"They are stupid skunks with no confidence and no finesse."

The man just shrugged, his grin flickering knowingly. "Just be careful. Maybe let the other judges handle the game when their turn to play comes."

Flickering another knowing smile, his informer began drifting away just as the judges and other dignitaries began trickling back, clearly done making a fuss around an important person who won the game.

There was much less commotion around Akweks when he did the same thing, thought Ogteah resentfully, his stomach knotted at the unexpected warning, mind refusing to deal with the matter, not yet. What was there to do, anyway? He wouldn't be yielding his place to please touchy Onondaga Town skunks with unruly women.

"You look as though you would rather be elsewhere. Cherishing thoughts of running away from your important position, oh honorable innovator and organizer?" This time, it was the Flint's voice breaking the unhappy flow of his thoughts, welcomed in its lightness and friendliness.

"Close enough to it." He forced his shoulders into lifting with as much indifference as he could muster. "I'm tired. Running all over this field, picking up spears while arguing with people about every single hit or miss is not my idea of having a good time."

"You shouldn't have agreed to become a judge."

"I know *that*."

A rough palm landed upon his back with force, encouraging. "Don't take it hard, brother. A few days of too much work, but look where it put you—in a prominent position, a person listened to, noticed, consulted, entrusted with judgment in an important contest. Not as enjoyable as running around, throwing spears and betting on other throws, I grant you that, but just think how many people would wish to change places with you now, freedom to fool around or not. Given your dubious origins,"—a side-glance shot at him held all the mischief—"and no less dubious local activities..."

"Leave my origins and activities alone." Unable to suppress his snicker, Ogteah put his attention back on the field, where another Mountain People's player was readying to put it all into the attempt to redeem his team's reputation. "I just wish they would get on with it. Aren't you tired of running around on that badly patched leg of yours?"

"That leg? Oh, it kills me all right," admitted his companion, displaying no signs of discomfort. "When it's over, I'll be sleeping for the entire night and half a day, snug with my new spears, with yours being still the best of my winnings."

"Go jump off the nearest cliff."

Concentrating on the next thrower, he noticed the High Springs man strolling back toward his place among the observing dignitaries, his newly acquired spear balanced easily in his hand. Formidable, impressive, reliable; unperturbed by the furor his recent success created.

"But Okwaho's brother *is* good." Apparently, his Flint companion was watching the same sights. "What a man! Brilliant in more than talking politics and organizing important events."

"That family," said Ogteah, feeling better by the moment. "They are out of the ordinary, each and every one of them."

"That they are," agreed the Flint, his grin as proud as that of Ogteah. "Like father, like sons. And I heard Okwaho's mother is not only a clan mother but the head of their Clans Council."

"She is." He remembered the woman from his both visits in High Springs, very good-looking, even attractive despite her advanced age, brisk, efficient, busy, her smile reserved but welcoming, warm, with no coldness or pretense. Not the typical clan mother one meets, but according to the rumors that woman wielded much power in her own town and outside of it. A fitting mate for the spectacular War Chief.

"They are out of the ordinary, that family, yes," he repeated. "Not like us, simple human beings."

His smirk was answered with a snort. Oh, but it was good to be near friends again, he reflected, looking for the younger of the brothers with his gaze.

"Where is Okwaho?"

The massive palm waved in the air, non-committal. "Down there. Went to pat the backs of his newfound friends from the west. I bet he is preparing to cheer them the loudest, against the rest of his own townsfolk." A chuckle. "You just can't trust people anymore, can you?"

"No, you can't."

More exchanged smirks joined by another man who was also a part of the stormy or usually cozy evenings around the fire. Another Flint, but from Little Falls.

Ogteah hid his grin, liking these people a great deal since dropping beside their small fire ten dawns ago, on the memorable evening of wandering with no purpose, finding the worst ways of coping with Father's death.

The wolf man turned out to be the most fascinating in the group, young but unexpectedly deep, despite the fierceness and decidedly warrior-like looks. One didn't expect so many interesting thoughts from such a decorated torso and elaborately shaved skull, no encompassing understanding of politics and wars on the larger scale; yet, the young hothead did just that, talked about the Great League and its possible flaws, worrying, coming up with plenty of useful ideas none of the elders seemed to be wishing to hear, other than the powerful War Chief, this same young man's father. But of course fathers tended to be attentive to their offspring, sometimes.

Well, the wolf man was an undeniable leader of this group of younger, whether experienced or aspiring, warriors. Not bored, they would listen to his musings, and so did Ogteah, surprised with himself. Through the few evenings spent in those youths' company, he had learned more about the Great League and how it worked, or how it should have been working but didn't, than he had learned through the whole span of seasons spent on this side of the Great Lake.

The problem of not enough cooperation, not enough readiness to help each other out, worried the wolf man the most. He could speak about it deep into the night. Spending a few seasons fighting with the Flint People had made the young warrior stop and think. This is how he came to have such close ties with his present Flint friends, but later on, through the last span of seasons, he had been staying with the Mountain People, fighting their wars, or more like skirmishes, claimed the wolf man. There was no serious war there, but there would be, and soon. And the Great League better be prepared and ready. This was his favorite topic.

He had saved the brilliant spear-thrower's life while back in the Flint People's lands and fighting, even though the wolf man used to brush this aside. Anyone would do exactly the same, he had claimed, answered by showily rolling eyes of the spectacular Flint and a series of derisive snorts to follow. There was a limit to a person's humbleness, Akweks, the fierce Flint, would maintain, and Okwaho was underplaying this particular performance. Lifesaving was a lifesaving, and there was no way around it. The deed was done.

How? asked Ogteah once, when the wolf man was away, spending his time Great Spirits knew where, enjoying his woman out there in the woods, or so the remaining Flint claimed. A question that prompted a long story of impossibly distant lands, strange savages, lousy leaders, and badly rotting wounds, a hair-raising story of adventure, or rather misadventure, of two warriors struggling to survive, stranded and alone; a story of devoted friendship. The wolf man, indeed, was underplaying his part in his Flint friend's survival and recovery if half of it was true, and judging by the nods of the others, this account was as accurate as a story might be.

Also, the smirking Flints told him, apparently the wolf man had come out of this adventure carrying more than just interesting memories. The most exotic of spoils was a wife of impossibly savage origins.

Warned not to use the word "savages" in the mentioned brave warrior's vicinity, Ogteah found himself racking his brain in an attempt to remember. Had he seen anything strange-looking while paying two visits to the town of High Springs before? The savage woman was living in High Springs, oh, yes, the spear-throwing Flint claimed, and she was around this gathering as well, having made poor Okwaho take her along against custom and tradition. Or so they claimed. Which left him determined to try and spot the exotic-looking fox no matter what, to have a good look.

Shaking the memories off, he squinted against the glow of the early afternoon sun, noticing that his younger companions wandered off, probably bored. So much for the talk of vital work and higher statuses. The spectacular Flint wouldn't switch for Ogteah's important position. Filthy skunk. He tried not to let his grin show.

His eyes stung, unwilling to follow yet another sleek-looking spear, different in length and coloring, pouncing toward its rolling prey, competing against its predecessors. How many more? he asked himself, unwilling to face the answer.

The hoop fell, and to his relief, he saw one of his fellow judges strolling toward it, sparing him and the others the walk. In the beginning they would all rush out, eager to inspect the throw. Now, half a day later, they were doing it in turns by an unspoken agreement.

Amused, even if slightly, he watched the man picking up the spear, bringing it up, confirming. The firmness with which the hoop was impaled on it, pierced quite thoroughly, if not in the exact middle then close enough to it, left no place for an argument. A point for the Onondaga Town's team, who came to replace the previous groups of players. Covertly, Ogteah watched them, remembering the warning.

The man of the opposite team took his rival's place nervously, shifting his weight from one foot to another, the spear dancing in his hand. No promising results for this one. He would have never put a bet on this man.

Still close to the opening call, the hoop was pushed off its course again, not pierced but wavering, fluttering before succumbing to its fate. Not a spectacular throw like the previous one, but still a hit. Trying not to show his impatience—but why did his turn have to fall on such a dismal throw?—Ogteah forced himself to stroll toward it with as much of a purposeful air as he could muster.

The javelin was lying so far away from the ring, he wondered how it made enough contact to make it falter at all. Still, a hit was a hit, so no spears were going to change hands, not this time.

"Who is the next to represent the Onondaga Town?" he shouted, signaling the man from the opposite team to come and fetch his spear.

The players of the Onondaga Town seemed to hesitate, exchanging glances.

"What's the meaning of it? Is it going to be declared a draw?" asked the man whose spear had pierced the hoop so close to the middle.

Ogteah just nodded, turning to head back toward his fellow judges. The tone of the man promised no good, and he had no energy to start an argument over an obvious thing.

"What do you mean by that?" The running footsteps behind his back made him tense, still he was caught unprepared by the hand that grabbed his arm, quite forcefully at that. "You can't claim that this near-miss was an equal to my throw."

"Yes, I can." Turning back sharply, Ogteah tore his arm from the violent grip, surprised with the intensity of his own splash of rage. How dared this man grab him like that, or challenge his authority in such a manner? The leading people of this entire gathering trusted him to do this difficult task, and so far, he had not done that badly. "Get your paws off me!"

The man's eyes burned like a pair of embers. "No, you can't, dirty foreigner! It was a near miss, while my throw pierced the web next to the exact middle. I deserve to have his spear."

For a heartbeat, Ogteah found nothing to say, busy dealing with the fierce wave, desperate not to let it win. Did this man just call him a filthy foreigner? He heard people heading in their direction, other judges and organizers. Oh, but for their sake, he ' had to make an effort.

"The rules of the game are clear and were set and explained in advance," he said as calmly as he could, even though his hands were trembling. Not visibly, or so he hoped. "Only the hit of the exact middle, or the true miss, would gain one of the players an immediate victory."

It came out well, surprisingly eloquent. No matter how easily he could chat with the locals by now, his command of their tongue was not yet well enough to orate and make speeches.

His adversary's eyes narrowed. "These are not the true rules of the game. The throwers keep on tossing their spears until one of them misses. If you weren't a foreigner, you would have known it!"

"The rules of this particular competition were set in advance," said one of the other two judges, nearing them hurriedly, almost at a run. Others seemed to be hot on this man's heels as well, surmised Ogteah, busy dealing with yet another urge to smash the lowlife in front of him into a pulp no matter what now.

"The rules set by the foreigner!" cried out the offended party, so upset he must have missed that he was now addressed by one of the more respectable organizers, a man of influence and perfect origins into the bargain. "I refuse to be told what to do by a filthy Crooked Tongue who cannot even follow the rules of the proper spear-throwing competition."

"It is not your place—" the older man began, but the enraged spear-thrower's eyes were glued to Ogteah, gleaming with hatred.

"A foreigner who cannot even deal with his own filthy urges, harassing women of our town like the cowardly enemy that he is."

This time, he didn't think of prudence and rightful deeds. The field, the players, the watching dignitaries, and the crowding onlookers disappeared, replaced by the familiar wave, this all-consuming urge to crash the face in front of him into pieces, to hit it until it crumbled, to wipe the hateful expression off and push the disgusting accusations back, make them disappear.

His fist shot upwards, acting in perfect accord with his will, his shoulder shoving into the wideness of the man's chest, pushing with viciousness, oblivious of purpose or reason anymore.

His rival, even though slightly surprised by the viciousness of the attack, if not by its suddenness—after all, he must have expected it, with his words heading nowhere but there—wasn't caught completely off guard, spoiling for a fight as badly, apparently. Twisting to escape the worst of the blow, he had his own fist sinking into Ogteah's belly, causing him gasp but not to lose his balance.

Oblivious of the accompanied kick, Ogteah went for another punch, more savage than the first, his knuckles hurting from the crush against something hard, a jaw, or so he hoped. When his rival went down tumbling, it surprised him, as did the man's grip that made him lose his balance, dragging him along and onto the muddy ground.

A veteran of many such brawls, he didn't let this development throw him off balance or cause him stop and reflect on it. Making sure to end up on top of his rival, his fingers claws, he pounced for the momentarily exposed throat, oblivious to the kicks, pressing hard with his fingers, sweat dripping into his eyes, together with pieces of dirt that all those milling around feet raised.

The hands that dragged him off his prey were difficult to ignore, but still he resisted, needing to hurt the filthy, stinking lowlife who dared to declare that he was nothing but dirt.

Breathing heavily, he watched his rival being hauled back to his feet as well, struggling against the hands that held him from behind, coughing and spitting curses.

The sounds were back, and the awareness. He made another effort to break free.

"Let me go." He heard his own voice ringing hoarsely, strident in the ugliest of ways. "I won't... won't fight..."

"Let him go." This time, he recognized the speaker, and it made him feel better. Trust the High Springs man not to lose his senses, to be there, and make it right again. "As for the Onondaga Town team, take your player away and yield your round to the next group of players. When you compete again, you will not have any brawlers among you. Is that understood?" Another thundering pause. "Come." This was directed back at Ogteah.

Shrugging, he didn't bother to wipe his face or smooth his ruffled appearance. Who would be concerned with any of this now? His brief attempt at doing something meaningful lasted a little longer than he expected, all things considered. But it was over for good now, that much he knew.

CHAPTER 10

"Where is the Crooked Tongue?"

Squinting against the glow of the high morning sun, Ganayeda watched his brother shifting his bag, a heavy-looking thing, from one shoulder to another, trying to balance his bow and the quiver of arrows as he did this. Even if old and worn-out, the quiver was comfortable, prettily decorated, made out of such well-tanned leather, it glimmered in the strong sun. He made a face. It still hurt to remember how the cheeky skunk had taken possession of this thing, so easily, tricking him, Ganayeda, into an imprudent bet.

"Gone with Akweks."

That took his thoughts off the quiver, decisively at that. "What do you mean, gone with Akweks? Where to?"

"To his Flint People's towns, and then the Standing Stone folk. Akweks will be covering these areas, remember? I can't be everywhere all at once." A curt nod indicated the valley behind his back and a group of younger warriors, milling around, looking equipped for a journey as well. "We'll be visiting our Onondaga towns and villages, and will spill into the Swamp People's lands if I see it goes quickly and with success. In a moon or so we should be ready, Brother, for you and Father to make it look good and not like an outright revolt."

"I'll do my part, never fear." Hiding his mounting misgivings, he squinted against the gust of fresh wind. "Still, I don't understand how the Crooked Tongue got involved in any of this."

Okwaho's lips twisted into a suggestive grin. "What do you think? After what happened yesterday, naturally he did not feel it wise to stick around." His shrug was a light affair. "You did well by smoothing the matters over. Still, he felt humiliated enough, losing his temper to such an extent and in front of the entire gathering. I don't blame him for wishing to be anywhere but here." The large eyes lost their lightness. "He was about to sneak away, back to his inglorious village, I suppose, or only Great Spirits know where, when we ran into him, I and Akweks. Well, it didn't take long to persuade him to change his plans. He was eager to join our enterprise, and not only because of his private embarrassment. Think about— "

"I understand that." To cut into his brother's speech felt wrong, but he couldn't help it. "Of course this is the sort of an incident that needs to be lived down. I would not stay around as well had it happened to me, and he still may find himself facing this or that accusation from the Onondaga Town folk, as, judging by the screams of that ill-tempered player, it all has to do with his previous indiscretion with some of this town's female dwellers." Shrugging in his turn, Ganayeda shook his head. "The trouble is following this man no matter where he goes, and still, I keep thinking of him as a good man. Strange, if you ask me. But all this aside, why did you bring him into our schemes? Father told you most clearly to avoid doing this, to keep him out of our plans. He did, Okwaho!" he added forcefully, seeing the familiar spark of defiance flashing out of the clouding eyes. Oh, yes, his brother knew he was in the wrong here, but it would only serve to make him argue with more spirit.

"Father said not to get him involved in the general state of affairs. Well, we won't do that. I promise you to discuss no politics with him, no more than he would hear elsewhere." A fleeting grin flashed, gone as quickly. "Right now, he is in no danger of being lectured on the Great League and its possible flaws. Akweks couldn't care less. He doesn't know many of our laws, and even the threat of a painful death wouldn't force him into learning any of it. While the foreigner, well, he can be of help while traveling around, connecting with people. He is good at it. You two said it about him before, and I saw it with my own eyes—witnessed his fast friendship with Akweks and the others. This man is an asset when it comes to making quick contacts, because people feel at ease and talkative in his presence, open to our suggestions. He won't care for what purpose, as long as he doesn't have to go back to his Lone Hill straightaway after what happened. Our purpose won't interest him in the least. Our mission is simply his means to escape a humiliation he got himself into."

"Oh, please!" Exhaling loudly, Ganayeda shook his head. "But you do tend to underestimate people, Brother. Ogteah is very sharp, very deep, even though he likes to present himself as nothing but an easygoing gambler with not a thought in his head. Well, if he fooled you with this appearance of his, then you are naive and need to learn much as yet." Casting another glance toward the valley, he shook his head. "He will know what we are up to, Brother. He will figure it out, and sooner than you think."

As expected, the broad face closed, took the familiar stubborn look. "You exaggerate, take it too far. We need all the help we can get, and the Crooked Tongues man is a perfect person to help us along. There is no need to see an enemy in him only because he wasn't born among us and in one of our towns. For a son of our father, you speak with surprising close-mindedness at times."

He heard his own laughter erupting loudly, attracting the attention of the waiting people. "Oh, but you *are* desperate!" But for the necessity to hurry back to the valley and the gathering that had been progressing since the high morning, he would have stayed to prolong the moment, if for no other reason than to make Okwaho feel silly. "Most childish arguments, Little Brother. I'm not close-minded, and I like that particular foreigner well enough, as you know. He is a good man, and he is doing well on our side of the Great Lake, all things considered. But Father is right. For now, he should be trusted only up to a certain point."

A grunt was his answer. Shielding his eyes, he watched the unmistakably tall, broad-shouldered figure of Okwaho's woman nearing them in her typical long, purposeful stride, not a feminine gait, not for this fox. Clutching a bag in one hand and an impressively long if simple-looking spear in another, clearly Okwaho's possession, she looked very proud carrying it, her excitement unconcealed.

"Is your woman coming along? To recruit our Onondaga and the Swamp People's warriors?" He didn't search for topics to change the subject, but her interruption came in good time. He truly needed to hurry back.

Okwaho's face cleared. "No, not this time. Even though she might be of a great help, Big Preachy Brother. She is shooting so well by now, she could teach people. Young warriors, you know." Clearly satisfied with the scandalizing effect of his statement, the young troublemaker smirked. "She knows everything there is to know about weaponry, and mark my words, she will learn to handle that spear better than you, oh, renowned hunter and warrior."

"Then you should take her along." Deciding to see the funny side of it, Ganayeda still found himself shaking his head. "You won't need to spend your time on enticing these warriors to join. Take her to the Mountain People lands, and the pair of you are sure to make all their enemies crumble."

"Not their enemies, but our enemies." This was clearly a topic that made Okwaho forget any lightness and needling. "Our mutual enemies."

Ganayeda waved his hand in dismissal. "Spare your orating for the Swamp and the rest of our people. Don't start practicing on me; I'm too busy for that."

The girl slowed her step and seemed to be hesitating, not about to burst into the brothers' conversation uninvited. Jideah's evident influence, he knew, remembering the wild thing's first days in High Springs. Two spans of seasons had changed this one, and only for the best. Still outlandish and somewhat strange on the eye, the girl was a pleasant sight to see now, with her smile flashing easily, concealing nothing, and her too-widely-spaced eyes radiating good-natured confidence. Life in High Springs clearly agreed with her, a surprise after such a bad beginning. But then, under Mother's guidance and protection, and with Jideah's active help and support, with Okwaho continuing to indulge the girl's strangely warlike inclinations, oh, yes, there was no reason for this one to feel uncertain or unhappy.

"Greetings," she said in her clear, pleasantly low voice, her accent pronounced and as heavy as in the beginning, even though she wasn't twisting words or putting them together wrongly anymore.

Again, he wondered how Gayeri's Crooked Tongue managed to learn to speak with such clarity and barely any accent after a mere span of seasons spent on their side of the Great Lake. Did he know the Onondaga tongue before and just claimed that he didn't? Oh, yes, this man was deep, deeper than they all thought, and it wasn't wise to get him involved in such delicate matters as forcing the hand of the Great Council into changing some of its usual ways. Okwaho was stupid not to listen to Father's advice in that.

Brushing this musings aside, he smiled at his brother's wife with as much affection as he could summon while being incensed with her husband to such extent. "Greetings, sister. I gather that you are leaving today."

She nodded readily, eyes on Okwaho, expectant, their adoration unconcealed. Did this girl ever bother to hide her feelings? He knew the answer to that.

"Then you should go. High Springs is a long way from here." He pierced Okwaho with his own gaze, his previous displeasure receding. "Send me word every time you can. In half a moon or so, I will be back in High Springs, ready to be of help in any way you can think of."

"Yes, I will." Okwaho nodded thoughtfully, still deep in thought. "It should not take us longer than a moon, two at the most. By then, I'll expect to have word from our Western Door Keepers. The enemy might make a move before then, reveal the size of their forces and their intentions. It would be better if they did." A mirthless half-grin flashed. "The authorities would be less forgiving if I dragged hundreds of warriors into our mountainous west for nothing. They'll demand my blood for that in the very least."

The girl gasped, but was quick to cover her mouth as Okwaho's arm wrapped around her shoulders, squeezed them lightly, with pronounced affection. Not a proper gesture while the eyes of so many people were on them.

"Don't worry. They won't be putting me on the carpet of glowing embers. Unless I caused the death of all those warriors." His outburst of healthy laughter seemed to roll over the valley. "And that won't happen. Not as long as I'm leading them, woman." Another warm squeeze. "Don't you have any faith in your husband? What a shame."

Her giggle suited a younger girl, not sitting well with her warlike appearance, with the way she held her husband's spear, in an expert manner.

"Just be off, the two of you," said Ganayeda, his anger forgotten. "Take care, and come back safely. I may be joining your western adventure, depends on how lawful we manage to make it look before you come back. So keep that in mind, and remember Father's advice." A smile at the girl, a genuine one. "Have a safe journey."

But these two were a fitting pair, he decided, watching their retreating backs, walking side by side, laughing most clearly, shoulders touching, elbows nudging each other already.

Did Okwaho know it would be this way when taking the wild thing along from her faraway savage lands? Or was this just a lucky bet that, surprisingly, paid off, and in the most perfect of manners? His brother wouldn't have found something like that anywhere near the Longhouse People's lands, no chance of that.

Speaking of people who were deeper than they cared to display, the wild buck was certainly one of these. Was he more farsighted in the Crooked Tongue's matter than he, Ganayeda, credited him with? Was he right in keeping the foreigner involved, using his talents and natural inclinations, even against Father's advice?

Shrugging, he turned to go, back toward the valley and the Great Gathering, the first day of their official meetings. An interesting event, yet not like the one his brother was trying to engage their entire union in. Oh, but for this nearest moon to pass faster!

CHAPTER 11

Could it be her home?

She watched it from a safe distance, her breath caught, heart racing, making strange leaps inside her chest.

The palisade was like any other. That other huge town in the south, where Aingahon lived, sported same high stakes, placed as densely, interwoven with long branches. The smells and the feel of it were the same, reminding her of these other villages and towns she had observed so far during their ten-day journey. Quite a few, as their flock of canoes moved along various currents, making their point to reach a settlement every time they stopped for the night. The noise this place generated must be the same too, she assumed, watching it from a safe distance, as always.

He didn't try to confine her movements, to demand that she stayed in the camp or accompanied their other fellow travelers inside the towns and villages when they had been invited to do so. The custom in her former lands was like the one that ruled his people. One didn't presume to near either a double fence of a large town or a simple cabin in the woods without a cordial invitation. The travelers, no matter what their quest or the urgency of it, no matter how their approach might be heralded or expected, would make themselves comfortable out there in the open and wait for the prospective hosts to make a move. Which would be forthcoming, always; another firm custom. Sometimes the invitation would be cordial and quite eager, sometimes it would display barely hidden suspicion in the direfulness frowns, but the guests were always invited in.

Huddling in the safety the thick bushes provided, not wishing to be invited anywhere and for no reason, she hid her smile, thinking about *him* and his drive and conviction. Frowns or not, he wasn't about to be palmed off with mere excuses, and he was an undeniable leader of this delegation, other respectable elders or not. No one dared to be rude to him, neither his fellow travelers nor their sometimes disagreeable hosts.

Like Grandfather, she thought, smiling to herself, straining her eyes in an attempt to recognize the slightly familiar surroundings. No one ever argued with Grandfather, she has been sure of that, even though her memories didn't go much further than their stay in the woods. Before that, it was all vague, shimmering in the cloudy blur, fragments of memories rushing one after another, a whirlpool of dissipating images, not solid enough to get a good grip on.

Unlike Grandfather and their cabin, the peacefulness of their clearing and the neatness of their rectangular field. Those were solid and real. In order to imagine Grandfather's voice again, all she needed to do was close her eyes and think about it. Then his face would appear too, noble, narrowly carved, wrinkled so very generously, like an old drum, with his eyes set so deeply, glimmering with wisdom and understanding.

The Grandfather from the cabin.

The other one from the town and her previous life she couldn't remember, and the realization of that always left her uncomfortable. He must have been there too, in her previous life, in a town that looked exactly like that, towering on the top of a conical hill, overlooking a prettily round lake. There was a trail there, on the other side of the fence, a narrow deer track that led toward the hole in the sky. Oh, yes, this is what they called it – the hole in the sky – that bluest, coldest, clearest pool the children so loved to jump in.

Could it be?

She shut her eyes, the lightness of her mood evaporating, as always, when thinking of the pre-Grandfather days. They must have had a family back then, both of them. They must have! A longhouse to live in, close relatives to share a hearth with. When smaller, she didn't concern herself with such musings, but since

Grandfather departed on his Sky Journey, she couldn't help but think. She had a mother back then, surely. And father, and two elder brothers. Or maybe there was just one. The thin, lanky, thoughtful boy, the mischievous troublemaker. No, there must have been two different boys.

She shut her eyes tighter, desperate. But for the chance to make this strange, murky pool of evasive memories to become as clear as the other ones. Why were they fleeing from her? Were they afraid? Were the spirits of her family offended, hurt? She always avoided this question, but now it nagged, demanding to be faced, urged by that vaguely familiar fence and the heavy scent of the nearby body of water. The round lake, she knew. It was there, cheerful and not as misty as the lake near *his* town, with its sandy shores sloping gently, sliding into the water.

Carefully, she began backing away, out of the bushes and up the incline, knowing the trail and its twists. More evidence? It would wind its way upwards, as though about to lead into the thickest of the grove, but halfway there, it would turn to the south, sharply at that, and take one straightaway toward the prettiest of shores. But for him to be here with her now!

He would have appreciated her knowledge of the local forest, would have enjoyed the view of the sky hole she would show him. He was always so alert, so attentive to details, asking many questions, wishing to know everything there was to know, never sharing his own thoughts. Not like Grandfather at that. Quite the opposite, but she didn't mind. To walk or sit next to him felt good, to tell him things that he wished to know, or sometimes to surprise him with a revelation he didn't expect. Like her bow and the accuracy of her shooting. But was he surprised! Even though also angered, threatening to deprive her of his company if she aimed at him again, still it felt good to remember how he looked at her with wonder, how he asked her to prove her skill, to show him how far she could shoot. He even trusted her with shooting a man, a powerful War Chief, no more and no less. And then the other one. Oh, but she didn't let him down, didn't miss or make any other mistake.

The smile threatened to sneak out, the memory warming her

insides. He was pleased and appreciative, more open than before. He respected her now, she knew, her inner voices convincing, telling her that something had changed, that something was different between them now, and that it was a good change. Would he learn to be good to her like Grandfather was? He certainly trusted her, with that other shooting as well as with the invitation to come along.

When he told her that he was going away, she had been scared, yet before the panic prevailed, he had caught her shoulder gently but firmly, demanding to be heard out. He would be taking her along, he had told her, if she wished to come. Back in her people's lands, they would have a chance to find her former home.

She didn't care about any of that; only the reassurance that he would not be leaving her behind. The woods of his hometown would lose their liveliness without him, she knew, would become empty and dim. Just like the groves in the north had died along with Grandfather. The moment he was gone, the local spirits had left those places as well. Only the bad spirits remained, to mar the previous light and pureness.

Afraid that it would happen again, she let him persuade her to join his expedition, not listening to his arguments, not for real. Whatever his goals were, she didn't care, although he talked about her people, using some funny-sounding name. Attiwandaronk—Those Who Speak Somewhat Differently. Did his people really call hers by such a silly sounding combination of words?

She had laughed and let his other words float over her head, not trying to catch their sound or read it from his lips. Grandfather was her former people, and no one else, and the powerful man certainly spoke just fine. He was the wisest and the strongest, while all the rest didn't even exist. But if Aingahon, now more influential than ever—something that was easy to see watching him interact with people these days—well, if he wanted to visit some towns and villages along the western shores of the Great Sparkling Water, she would come with him, of course she would. Even if it meant that she would have to cram herself in his canoe together with some other people, a few elders and at least twenty other warriors, all tucked in three monstrously long vessels of a kind she had never seen or imagined before, such long, sturdy boats. She didn't believe they would manage to sail at all, but they did, easily at that. Rowed by three or four men at once, they had charged the river's currents most determinedly, with no visible effort.

Curled at the edge of one such vessel, the one that carried him as well—she wouldn't have had it in any other way—she had found herself peeking over the side with more and more frequency, consumed with curiosity, almost enjoying herself. It was interesting to travel in such a way. Grandfather's canoe was narrow and sleek, difficult to maneuver at times, even though he of course made sure she could do so most perfectly on even the vicious rapids that were gushing not far away from their cabin.

Well, ten dawns into their journey she still hadn't come to regret her agreement to come. Of course it would have been better had they been traveling alone, in one of the normal-sized canoes. She would have rowed most of the way, as his bad knee made it difficult for him to use the paddle for long periods of time. She had noticed his discomfort, even though he tried not to let it show. Oh, but how proud he was!

The other people from their monster of a canoe must have seen it as well, but while being a certain nuisance with their covert glances and stares, no one dared to comment, or offer help, just as they didn't dare to bother her with questions and efforts to talk. He had made it clear that she was not to be bothered, and his words were being listened to with the utmost attention, of that she had seen much evidence. Which of course was only natural. Like Grandfather, he was a true leader, so why would anyone argue with what he said?

The lake burst upon her out of nowhere, sooner than she expected. One moment it was the dimness of the grove; the next, brilliant light was pouring in from everywhere, not especially welcome. Not with the view of many shadowy silhouettes lining the nearest shore, filling the narrow strip of land with their unwelcome, loud, overbearing presence. The hum of their voices must have been high, as the shreds of it broke even through her perpetual wall of silence, mere echoes of buzzing voices, annoying in their persistence.

Halting abruptly, she just stared, ready to dive back into the coolness of the woods, into the silent safety they offered. They were so many! Young girls and older matrons dotting the shoreline, their skirts tucked high, the water splashing around their ankles or even thighs in some cases, their baskets held high, swaying under the weight of the wet clothes, dripping water.

Oh, but wasn't it always like that? Mother was coming here to wash their clothes, complaining of boys making her work hard, soiling their garb more often than not. She said it was wiser to birth girls than boys. She would always say that.

Her mind in a daze, she blinked against the glow of the strong sun, searching with her gaze. Mother would usually choose that spot near the cliff, where she could put her basket comfortably. Yes, there. That low cliff that towered in a helpful way, offering the flatness of its top as a shelf.

However, the woman who stood there looked nothing like Mother. Plump and wide-hipped, she was straightening up, waving at a nearby girl, shouting too, probably. Yet, the girl wasn't listening. Wide-eyed, she was busy staring, her gaping mouth matching the roundness of her eyes.

Others were turning to follow her gaze, and then her pointing finger. When the small mask of astonishment crumbled into fearful tears, Tsutahi could feel the loudness of the screams coming out of the gaping mouth. Then the small thing was tucked safely in the skirt of the older woman.

Still dazed, she hesitated, feeling their stares, her instincts telling her that the dead silence that descended upon the shore must have been matching her own wall of soundlessness. Their faces were the replica of the girl's, such intense staring. It was ridiculously funny. She tried not to giggle. They looked like people visited by a bad spirit. Especially the woman by the cliff. Clutching her child with too much force—one could see that even from the distance—the woman seemed to stop breathing, her eyes threatening to pop out of their sockets, her stance hinting at the intention to bolt away, straight into the deepest of the water, in her case.

Well, funny or not, she began feeling like doing the same. Their stares were unsettling, joined with more pointing fingers. Some of the women had evidently regained their ability to speak. Or maybe to scream, judging by their exaggeratedly wide-open mouths. They looked so ridiculous. Yet, when one moved toward her, her paces slow, hands spread, eyes boring into the intruder, concentrated as though gauging her, Tsutahi's, reaction, she knew she had no time for stupid laughter.

Her dread welling, she took a step back, only to be informed by her senses that someone was coming from that direction too, blocking her way of escape. Trying to trap her, or just following the same trail she had walked before? It didn't matter.

Darting aside, her panic rising like a river when the ice of the Cold Moons would break, welling out of proportion, impossible to control, she caught a glimpse of more silhouettes appearing from behind the trees, men or women, it didn't matter. They seemed to be halting, hesitating. Caught by surprise?

Her foot slipped on a cluster of protruding roots, but she regained her balance, not daring to look back. The shore was all screams and clamor. One didn't need the ability to hear properly to know that.

The women from the trail were staring at her in the same manner as those down the lake, taken aback, especially one heavyset matron, her silvery braid fluttering with the wind and her eyes so round they looked like two wooden plates, with a gaping mouth to match.

Not wasting her time on trying to analyze any of that—after all, she was no *uki* to make people that afraid, even if his countryfolk would look at her with suspicion as well—Tsutahi charged straight for the thickest of the grove, jumping above a cluster of bushes, her fear giving more power to her limbs, making her leap impossibly high.

Landing pell-mell, she pushed the ground away with her hands, not bothering to scramble back to her feet, but darting into the protective dimness of the trees with all she had, almost rolling across the damp moss-covered carpet of cones and pine needles.

Anything to get away from the strange people who stared at her as though she were a sickness-stricken coyote out to kill someone.

"As brothers and peers we should unite in more than mere words, should help each other like true family members do."

Holding their gazes, Aingahon eyed his audience sternly, wishing to relay his message. They had been talking for what seemed like a whole day or more, exchanging flowery speeches, meaningless platitudes, empty politeness, *getting nowhere.*

Close to half a moon on the road had him visiting quite a few settlements of their own people, but now that he had made his followers venture northwest and into the lands of Attiwandaronk, their progress had slowed down considerably, becoming less satisfactorily than he had hoped for.

Their neighbors may have been a smaller nation, just scattered towns and villages really, but they were warlike and proud, a bad enemy and a valuable ally, a people worthy of having in an alliance of his vision. Not enough to stand up to the power of either united Wyandot or the Great League, but it was a beginning. The moment he secured their agreement to participate in his first venture against the Great League's Western Door, he would make sure to sail to The Place of the Floating Scum, were yet another smaller nation encroached upon the forests of the Mountain People from the south. Wenro, or Wenrohronon, was what they were called, and their main town stood next to a murky, stagnant pool, with a yellowish-brown substance collecting upon its surface, reported to be used in the local healers' various treatments.

"The Wyandot may resume raiding your lands soon, as they did from the times immemorial," he went on, wishing to gain their attention, to take their minds off meaningless pleasantries and flowery addresses. The people of this town were busy gaining time, not ready to commit, but not willing to anger their more powerful visitors, famous for their skills at war and the shortness of their tempers. "But now they would be coming in force, backed by their united might." Another pause served to let his words sink in. "You cannot stand up to their advances alone, not anymore."

"We can come to an agreement with our neighbors to the north," said a tall, stringy-looking man, who had kept silent until now. "The Wyandot who are calling themselves the People of the Rock, our immediate neighbors, did not join the infamous union, not yet. Maybe they are not willing to take part in it, and if so, they are not presenting a true threat to us, not any more than they did before." A fleeting grin held no mirth and no lightness. "With the man who organized those people dead, I doubt their union will survive as more than just a temporary agreement between two warring nations." The flinty eyes flickered with coldness. "You are the ones who are facing a true union, brother – the Great League of the Longhouse People. You are the ones who need help. Why try to present it as though you are concerned with our well-being? We are not threatened. Not like you."

To keep a hold of his temper was becoming more difficult.

"Your future well-being is threatened as well, unless you chose to turn a blind eye toward it."

The other men stiffened, but he paid them no attention, having spent enough time on the preliminary speeches to his estimation. His style was always direct, and so far, he had been listened to. Well, among the rest of his people, that is. Two other important settlements and four villages promised cooperation, help, reinforcements. But this Attiwandaronk leading town was playing difficult, either unwilling or hoping to get concessions. Well, he was ready to concede, had they indicated what they wanted.

"The death of the Wyandot Leader changed it all, brother," said another among their hosts. "The union of our northern neighbors will not hold."

"Unless they have other able leaders, which I happen to know firsthand that they do have." No harm in embellishing the truth, he thought. The Wyandot leader was sure to leave an impressive following. He had happened to meet this man a few summers ago, before the fateful trip to the Great League's lands, and he had to admit that the man made an impression of a wise leader with deep thinking, not just an able orator successful at making people's spirits boil. "The Bear People's man left a firm legacy. The union of his creation will not fall apart, and it will represent more than two peoples."

Next to the open space, under a wide-branched tree whose shade they had been enjoying in this early afternoon heat, a commotion was developing with no pleasant smells of cooking accompanying it. Oh, but they were truly not welcome here.

Frowning, he listened to the agitated voices pouring into the pleasant shadow of their square. Female high-pitched chattering. Somehow, it made him worry. Did Tsutahi stay in their camp as he instructed her to do? In these foreign woods, it wasn't wise to just wander about. Even though she might have came from these lands.

"Have you met this leader, brother?" one of the men was asking, his eyes blank and cold, if not outright hostile, gaze sealed, giving nothing away. "We've heard that you've been traveling lavishly in your time."

A glance at his awkwardly folded leg was brief but unmistakable. *In your time, indeed.*

Aingahon suppressed a new bout of fury. "I have visited the towns of the Wyandot people, the Cord and the Deer People among them, and I have been greeted by the People of the Longhouse in their capital town of Onondaga lands. I've been raiding our eastern neighbors, the keepers of the Longhouse League's western door for many summers." He let his gaze harden, boring into them, pregnant with meaning. "I have seen our world changing, growing smaller, with its people feeling the need to strengthen their ties, to unite and form larger entities. Just like our families must have united into clans and later on into nations once upon a time. Those who didn't join have perished, while clans and nations survived and thrived. And this is what will happen to those of us who would not greet the changes, would not act upon and readjust their ways."

The renewed shouts cut into his speech, caused him to struggle not to lose his tread of thoughts. Some of the local leaders were frowning, turning their heads.

"Those are gloomy predictions, brother." The thin man shook his head, not impressed. "You presume to recognize the winds of the change, alone among your and our countryfolk, with even our leaders being blind, according to your claim. Or choosing to do so, to turn a blind eye to it. It is a grave accusation, if you ask me. And quite unfounded." The cold eyes were challenging him, the arching eyebrow mocking. "Why do you assume you know better than our leaders? Why come to our town to inform us of that?"

He eyed his adversary closely, narrowing his gaze to see better. A respectable man of enough years, his shirt and leggings richly decorated, his hat sporting matching adornment. A leading person, no doubt. The others were sneaking their glances at the man as well, studying his reactions.

"I do not presume to come to your people in order to force them into an alliance they might not wish to join." His voice rang with clearness that almost surprised him. He expected it to shake in the very least. From rage and impatience of course, nothing else. "However, I do claim that neither yours nor my people should be left struggling all alone, with no support from their brothers. Our people are natural allies, and we do need each other; we cannot protect our towns and villages on our own, not anymore."

Where was his patience coming from? he wondered. Of an old, he would be shooting to his feet by this point, intending to leave in anger and think of violence and revenge.

From the corner of his eye, he saw one of the younger men, who had gotten up earlier clearly to head off toward the commotion, coming back, hesitating behind the sitting men.

"We do not doubt the honorable spirit of your intentions," said one of the elderly warriors who had kept quiet so far. "What we do question is the necessity of the changes you propose. Should the Wyandot unite as you fear they would, we may be inclined to hear you out."

Unless it's too late by then, thought Aingahon, not trusting his temper to engage in any more of these talks. They weren't listening, not to a word of what he said. He and his companions weren't even about to be invited to partake in the locals' meal.

By the edge of the ceremonial grounds that were bordered by tobacco plots, people were crowding, mixing enough population to make the gathering sound louder than it should be. Waving their hands, their laundry baskets still dripping, the women talked with great agitation, overriding each other and some of their male audience. Even the appearance of the unwelcome guests did nothing to quiet their spirits.

"It was a real vision, a real ghost, I'm telling you!" cried out a flustered woman, her braid swinging wildly, wet and seemingly as upset as its owner was, one hand holding a basket, the other pressing a little girl that was clutching the woman's wet skirt. "She appeared out of nowhere, and the way she stared at us, oh, it made our hearts stop."

The murmuring in the crowding females intensified, while the male audience reacted mainly by lifted eyebrows.

"Are you sure, sister?" Some of the female listeners were not as easily convinced, apparently.

"Of course I'm sure," retorted the woman tersely. "There were many of us out there, and we all turned to look."

"Oh no, I don't question your vision, sister." The doubter waved her hands in a defensive gesture. "It's just that it may be some other spirit, or even a real child wandering around. It can't be the girl you recognized. All those people who died back in the bad winter, their spirits could not stay for so long, wandering around. It would be terrible if they did."

"And she didn't even die here," cried out one of the elderly men, waving his hands in the air as though trying to push away an evil presence. "The old leader took her away while she was still alive. I remember it most clearly. Neither of their spirits would be wandering our woods."

"Yes, yes," cried out several voices, while Aingahon busied himself with calculating his way out, determined to skirt the worst of the crowding, his followers close by. "The girl didn't even die here."

"And the rest of them, they couldn't be anywhere around, not after so many summers."

"What happened?" one of the men who were present at the

meeting pushed his way into the heart of the commotion with the determination of a person accustomed to doing so.

"It was Tsutahi, it was," insisted the woman with the basket. "We all saw her." A seeking glance shot out to one of the nearby women. "You, sister, you said you recognized her too."

"Did I now?" The other woman, a beefy matron with a silvery braid shook her head, clearly not opposed to becoming the center of the attention. "She was so close, I could almost touch her. If I dared." The dignified head shook, reinforcing the heaviness of the words. "She didn't look like a person from our world, and yes, she resembled that little girl from the Bear Clan, poor family that they were." Another penetrating gaze encircled the silenced audience. "She stood so close, I'm telling you, I could reach out and touch her if I dared. She was not truly standing there, but hovering. Her feet barely touched the earth, and when she met my gaze..." The pause was heavy, pregnant with meaning.

"What happened then, sister?" someone breathed out, sounding like a ghost himself.

"Oh, when she met my gaze, she rose in the air and flew over the nearby bushes and away from me. But not before she gave me yet another meaningful glance." The noble head shook again. "Oh, but she wanted to tell me something, and but for all your yelling—"

A collective gasp came up, followed by a renewed flood of comments and suggestions, yet Aingahon stopped listening, his heart picking up in tempo.

Tsutahi? Where was she? These people, they were talking about her, but why did they think she was a ghost? She might have looked like such a thing back when he had noticed her first, oh, yes, with her unhealthy pallor and her bones sticking freely from under her almost transparent skin, yet since then, she had gained enough weight and confidence, and her eyes were not as those of a strange forest creature, not anymore. And yet, they were talking about her, weren't they? And she might have been wandering out there, as was her custom, even though he had told her upon their arrival to stay in the camp and wait patiently.

"Where did you see the girl?" he asked without thinking, his voice, accustomed to making speeches by now, ringing clearly, overcoming the commotion.

Their gazes leapt to him, those who stood closest, the men from the meeting and some of the others, seemingly puzzled.

"What do you mean?"

"Tsutahi," he said firmly, not about to let them harm the girl, in case they managed to catch her, somehow. "You were talking about her, weren't you?"

Their eyes grew in proportions.

"What do you know about any of it, foreigner?"

"The girl who had come to live in Tushuway lost her grandfather on the Cold Moons that preceded these warmer times. She had seen close to fifteen summers, and her name is Tsutahi, or so she claims." He narrowed his eyes. "She is a good person and guilty of no crimes, and unless you know her family or what village she came from, you have no business chasing her as though she did something wrong."

Another spell of silence lasted for quite a few heartbeats. Even his companions, who by now had grown accustomed to the girl's questionable presence and his protectiveness of her, were gaping.

"The girl we were talking about, Tushuway man, lived and died in this town, along with many of her townsfolk in the winter of bad disease." The man who had spoken was elderly, his face strong, lined with the ravages of time. "Her entire family is gone, and so is most of her longhouse, if not her entire clan. The girl you might be talking about has nothing to do with any of this, unless you've been visited by an *uki*." The old, heavily lidded eyes narrowed into slits. "If the girl you are talking about is living in Tushuway now, why would she be here, unless having traveled by means none of us can explain?"

Involuntarily, he shivered, the heaviness of the penetrating gaze fraying his nerves, as did the depth of the silence. No one dared to breathe as it seemed. Even the birds in the nearby trees paused their warbling. Were they listening too?

His stomach fluttering in an unpromising manner, he remembered her strange looks, that unhealthy pallor, those haunted eyes, the stridence of her voice, the deafness that would sometimes go away with no pattern or logic, her aversion to people. But she did start shadowing him on her own, didn't she? Drawing a breath, he pushed the unsettling thoughts away.

"Tsutahi is a flesh-and-blood girl," he said firmly, holding their gazes instead of shifting his own. "She is no *uki*, no spirit stuck on its way to the Sky World. For reasons unknown to me, she lived with her grandfather alone in the woods, and maybe it has something to do with sickness, yes. She cannot hear properly, if at all. However," he let his gaze harden, traveling from face to face, willing them into listening, "she is nothing but a girl who went through much. And this is why I have brought her here. Her speech is of your people, and if you cannot find remnants of her immediate family, at least her clan should accept her back with their arms open and their hearts warm, instead of chasing her away like an evil *uki* or a suspicious creature out of the woods."

They were murmuring, mainly the men among them. The women were just gaping, dropping their gazes when confronted by his.

"Why didn't you bring her to the town with you, then?" someone demanded, an accusing voice in the crowd.

"I didn't know what settlement she came from. Only that she belongs to your people." He didn't bother to seek the speaker among their multitude of faces. "Since we entered your lands, she has been staying in our camp, waiting patiently."

"Not so very patiently," murmured someone, to the stifled chuckling from among his own people.

"If it was her, she would recognize her own town and its surroundings, wouldn't she?"

This time, it was the silvery-braided matron speaking, the one who had claimed to see the girl in closer proximity. Flying above the bushes, of all things.

"I don't know why she didn't recognize these surroundings," he said, struggling to push his impatience down. "She might have forgotten."

It was getting quite silly. Why was he arguing with these people, trying to force them into accepting the girl who might not even belong here in the first place? She was acting exactly as expected, wandering away from their camp despite the clear instructions not to do so, but fleeing at the sight of people. Typical behavior. And one that indicated no recognition, indeed. Why did he keep insisting?

"Bring her here, will you?" The woman who said it spoke timidly, her voice barely heard.

He sought her out with his gaze, encouraged by the softness of her well-rounded face and the warm glow her widely open eyes radiated.

"If you promise to treat her well…"

More hesitating nods joined the rustling of their whispers. He began turning away.

"I'll talk to her, and if she is willing I'll send you word. She might not wish to come here, so those of you who care would have to come out and meet her wherever she would indicate her agreement."

The doubt in their eyes and their poses made him regret bringing the matter up at all. Was she better off without this strange encounter? She came from this town, there could be little doubt about it. And yet, he didn't know why she left in the first place, why her grandfather had taken her away? They said something about sickness, but who knew what it truly was? If they thought her to be a ghost, and according to the panic-stricken story, she did bolt away the moment those women spotted her, maybe her memories of this place weren't pleasant or peaceful.

Concentrating on his steps, out of habit as much as out of necessity—it was imperative that he didn't stumble or worse yet, fall flat while walking away, not in front of all those wondering eyes—he suppressed the wish to shake his head. If she was in the camp and waiting, maybe it would be better to load her into his canoe and sail away full speed, before the suspicious locals had their chance to come sniffing around.

She was back in the camp. The faint crackling of fire told him so. Huddled next to it, he knew, hugging her knees in a protective manner, but ready to spring to her feet and dash away with her typical headlong speed, oblivious to any danger other than what the humans might be presenting. Wary, mistrustful. Not of him, but of the others. Confident that he would protect her, but only to a certain limit. Wholeheartedly, she trusted only herself.

Wait here, he gestured to his followers, a huge tail that trailed after him, the entire town, or so it seemed, in addition to his own people, all of them apprehensive, some more than the others, nervous, suspicious, a few openly frightened, wide-eyed.

"I want to talk to her in private first," he repeated, having demanded that before, on their way to the camp. "Do not come out before I give you a sign."

A few of the leading men frowned, but said nothing this time, even though the eyes of the matrons who had followed closely took the color of the darkening sky.

"What makes you think—" began one of them hotly, but he held his hand out, arresting her words in a manner unfitting while addressing an elderly woman.

He didn't care. Neither did her squashing gaze register.

"She can't hear well, but her other senses are sharp," he explained after a heartbeat of thundering silence, his voice no more than a whisper, barely moving his lips. "If you wish to scare her into fleeing, do not respect what I asked or what you promised to do."

He let his cold gaze encircle them, then turned away, heading out and into the clearing, trying to make it look like an easy walk. So many eyes were watching him, not an unusual occurrence by now, but this time, too many wanted him to falter. He straightened his back, then pushed them out of his mind. The conversation with her was more important. How to make her listen? How to convince her to stay?

She deserved a life, a young vulnerable thing that she was. A normal life of a normal person, something that her highly admired if not revered grandfather denied her for some reason; something he, Aingahon, was not offering her, either. And yet...

Indeed, she was curled next to the fire she clearly had bothered to make, or maybe to just bring it back to life, a tiny affair, not likely to draw attention. Typical of her, a wary forest creature that she was.

He hid his smile, then proceeded on, his stomach heavy, eyes taking in her favorite half-squatting, half-kneeling pose, head slightly tilted, listening to her senses if not to her ears, never just deep in thought, never wandering. Another typical trait. A forest dweller, not perfectly human. Were these people right in their assumption?

He shook his head, amused against his will and his mounting uneasiness, this strange sense of foreboding, the spreading emptiness between his stomach and his chest. It was better this way. She deserved a normal life. He didn't try to conceal his progress.

"You made a fire? Good," he said casually, dropping next to her. A futile gesture. He would need to get back up soon enough, putting an unnecessary strain on his already protesting knee. Still, she deserved to have this conversation in the calmest of moods, on his part as much as on hers.

Taking a deep breath, he looked her over, searching for signs of the dramatic encounter with her former townsfolk. Oh, yes, there were quite a few new scratches, and dried mud smeared all over her limbs. Evidently, she didn't stop to wash it off while fleeing back here, into the safety of their camp, into the security of his protection. His stomach shrank a little tighter.

"What have you been up to?" To make his voice sound calm was not necessary, still he heard his words spilling out with exaggerated lightness. Forced. He hoped his face reflected less tension than that.

Her eyes told him that it did, measuring him with an open question. No wariness, no mistrust. Just an inquiry.

"It didn't go well?" she asked, keeping her voice low, in an atypically considerate manner. So unlike her regular near-shouting. "The meeting. They didn't listen?"

He rolled his eyes, having not thought about the general telling-off he had received earlier from these people; nor what it did to his chances of gathering any amount of volunteers from the stubborn Attiwandaronk in general now. This town was too important, too influential not to set the tone for the entire region. After he dealt with her, he would have to rethink his plans. Admit a failure? No, not that. They could still pursue a warring course against their eastern neighbors, but maybe not a full-scale war, considering the risk they were taking. Curse the stubborn Attiwandaronk and their wariness of uniting.

"Tell me," she insisted, talking louder now, shifting closer, moving with her entire body, leaning on her hands, as though afraid to miss a word. "You look bad. Worried. Afraid." Her eyes grew larger under the furrowed wideness of her forehead, making her look unduly anxious, more womanly than ever. Not a forest creature, and not even a little girl. "You look strange. Did they do something bad, these people? Are they dangerous?"

Struggling to compose himself, feeling stranger by the moment, the worried scrutiny of her eyes throwing him off balance, he brought his hand up.

"No, no, they aren't dangerous. It's not that." Another desperate attempt to organize his thoughts. "This is not what happened, little one. What happened was good, not bad. It is good for you, the right thing to do."

Her eyes were glued to his lips, their puzzlement obvious. As was her effort to understand. She knew it was something important, something she needed to hear in its entirety. She, who could never summon enough patience to stay still, or follow more than a few words at the time. His stomach squeezed harder.

"You know this town, don't you? This is where you lived before Grandfather, yes?"

Now her gaze leapt up, fixing on his eyes, openly frightened. He reached out before she could jump to her feet, something the shift of her hips suggested was coming. Wrapping around the delicate wrist, his fingers didn't press, striving to relate nothing but the reassurance of his touch. No pressure, no force. She was so thin and fragile, and yet, if he tried to force her into staying, she would break free, putting everything she had into it, succeeding most probably. The brittleness of her appearance reflected none of her inner strength.

"Don't run away," he said slowly, willing her to listen with the sheer power of his gaze. "Stay and listen until I'm done. Then you can decide. No one will force you into anything. I will make sure of this. You trust me, and I didn't disappoint you until now, did I? I broke no promises to you, and I will continue to do so. You know it, don't you? Tell me you do."

Her eyebrows were threatening to turn into a single line, the painfulness of her frown making his stomach shrink to nothing. But for the chance to shelter her from even this thing. He pushed his welling doubts away.

"Tell me you will let me say it all, and promise you will listen. Just nod if you don't want to talk."

The motion of her head was barely visible, still he knew it was a yes. Her eyes told him that. Trustful again. The stony fist wrapped around his insides tightened some more.

"You recognize this place, don't you? It is your hometown, the place where you lived with your family. Before the illness, before the other life with your grandfather."

Her frown wasn't smoothing, but her gaze sneaked away for a brief moment, giving him his answer. Oh, yes, she understood; and yes, what he said was correct. These people didn't lie or make up strange stories of ghosts and diseases. It *had* happened.

He discarded another splash of worry. To hold her gaze and make her forget her own fears was more important.

"Well, these people, they do remember you. And they remember your family, even your grandfather. They talked good of him, with an utmost respect." To embellish the truth seemed appropriate. He did hear them calling the old man a leader, didn't he? Not a form of address lacking in respect. "They remember you, Tsutahi. They recognized you, and they want you back."

Her gaze was filling with panic again. He let his fingers tighten around her wrist, not as much as to hold her should she try to flee, but to relay some reassurance. She would need it. Much of it. Especially if those people were afraid she was a wandering spirit rather than a child recovered miraculously. And yet, she was better off living a town's life. What he had offered her so far was as bizarre as her grandfather's version of living. Worse so, as her grandfather didn't make her kill people.

"These people, they are your family, Tsutahi. And they didn't forget you. That woman, the one you met out there in the woods, the one who claimed to see you closely," — the stupid fox who maintained to see her flying above the bushes, he thought, but was wiser than to say it aloud — "she remembered you most clearly. She used your name. This is how I knew they were talking about you."

She was struggling to break free now, the thin arm fluttering in his grip, but weakly, with none of her usual forcefulness or drive. He pressed it yet tighter, his heart going out to her.

"Don't be afraid, little one. They are your people, and you need a normal life, a life a girl like you deserves."

She wasn't even listening, her eyes darting everywhere, concentrated on her inner turmoil and not on what his lips were trying to relate. When the struggle to break free turned fiercer, forced him to catch her with both hands, he knew the others were nearing, leaving their coverage of the trees, unable to summon any more patience to wait. Stupid rats.

"Just listen to me." He pressed her shoulders with both hands, almost groaning at the pain as his knee took more of his weight than it could deal with. "Just listen. Look at me!" Somehow, his gaze managed to catch hers, and hold it. "I will not let them harm you. I will come there with you and stay to make sure they receive you well. Do you hear me?" Every word was spoken slowly, well apart from the other, he repeated it again, then again, his hands trembling with tension, with the need to hold her firmly but in no hurtful way.

She was still tottering on the brink, her eyes wild with dread, huge, unblinking, staring at him, panicked but disclosing flickers of recognition. The moment those were gone, she'd be lost, he knew, possibly never to come back. And they weren't even in his lands, where she might try to find her way back to her grandfather's cabin, wherever it was.

"Listen to me," he repeated with as much calm as he could summon, oblivious of his knee and the people around. "Tell me you are listening. Just nod. Give me some sign."

Her head didn't move, but the eyes peering at him changed. Ever so slightly. Just a small difference, an alteration of the gleam. When they shifted toward his lips, he knew he had won.

"I won't let anyone hurt you," he said, calmer himself now, back in control. "I'll come with you, and I will make sure no one bothers you or asks you to do anything you don't want to do."

To get up while holding her was a difficult task, not made easier by so many eyes watching them both. Still afraid she would bolt for the woods, he let his grip loosen, needing his arm to push himself up, at least one of them.

She stayed where she was, but as he propped his fist against the ground, her shoulder slipped under his elbow helpfully, providing support. A flimsy, fragile support, but it was there, an unconscious gesture that he had come to expect, he realized suddenly; through their last moon together, wandering, and this current journey she had become aware of his needs as much as he had became aware of hers.

When upright at last, he faced them, keeping his hold on her shoulders firm, shielding.

"I will accompany her back to the town," he said, the stares of the locals unnerving in their intensity.

"We will be honored to welcome you to our settlement," said one of the elders suddenly, his voice pleasantly cordial, but his face sealed, giving nothing away. "All of you, honorable guests. You have traveled far to talk about an alliance of friendship. Your efforts and goodwill did not go unappreciated." A nod of the grizzled head, and the wide back was upon them, setting a general movement among their hosts. "Please come to our fires and share our meal and a good pipe."

Still a frozen form under the curve of his arm, she was listening to the words of the elder. The way her body relaxed, even if slightly, told him that. Not daring to glance at her, he was ready to bet that her eyes were on the old man's lips, reading them. Good. She was coming around to the idea. She was giving it a chance.

Not to mention that they had been invited in, all of them and not only he, the uncompromising escort of the lost child. And this after being pretty much thrown out of the town, refused even the simplest hospitality, let alone the consideration of the offered ideas. What did that mean?

He didn't dare to let his hope soar. Would he be allowed to state his business again, to elaborate on his idea of mutual help and closer collaboration?

CHAPTER 12

"So we came out, and here it was—the village, the strangest thing you ever saw."

Shifting into a more comfortable position, the spectacular Flint reached out, aiming to get the plate of nuts that somehow managed to escape his attention.

"No longhouses, not even the shortest building with a few hearths, imagine that. Only bizarre-looking huts, popping all around like mushrooms, as though they just grew out there behind the fence." Glancing at the handful of blackish nuts balanced safely in his bowled palm, the young man grinned. "And that fence! So pitifully low it made one wonder why the lazy locals even bothered with this thing. That's how we saw those mushroom-like huts, you see? An easy peek."

Stretching, Ogteah eased his back, straitening the bowl with painted peach pits when it began slipping from its perch upon the folded blanket. With the new round of game temporarily forgotten because of the fascinating storytelling, he didn't mind taking a break from the tiring evening as well.

"So our leader decided that we can take this thing with barely twenty-four warriors, five of whom he was persuaded by this friend of mine to send on another scouting mission." The pause that ensued was loaded, promising a thunderstorm. "Well, apparently he was as wrong as one could get. But, oh Mighty Spirits, how wrong this stupid, hastily organized attack went! The lazy savages who couldn't be bothered with building a decent longhouse happened to fight like wildcats cornered against three walls with no way out. Fighting with everything they had, and even with nothing, when nothing was left."

Another dramatic pause had Akweks' audience ceasing all movement, hanging on his words, breathless.

Ogteah did his best to hide his smirk, himself fascinated. He had heard this story and plenty of others told and retold many times by now, after nearly a moon of traveling all over the Standing Stone People's lands, however their Flint storyteller kept changing his versions, bored with repeating the same tale over and over again, or so it seemed.

Covertly, he glanced at their current audience, a fairly large group of men, from green youths to people way over his own age, crowding around, pushing closer to hear better. Even the players seemed to forget their bowl of painted peach stones, eyes on the spectacular guest as though he was the best storyteller in the entire region.

Which he might very well be, decided Ogteah, satisfied, glancing at the nearest man, noting his fascination. Akweks certainly knew how to tell a story. Close to a moon since they had left Onondaga Town, and here he was, not at all bored by the old tale of the people from beyond the Great River, strange savages with impossible ways. Not to mention the journey itself.

Oh, but this mission turned out to be as promising as it sounded when aired aloud by the fires of the Onondaga Valley, maybe even more so. What the owner of the wolf tattoo envisioned was far more interesting when in reality, and very, very promising indeed.

The young, easily excited men, bored by their everyday lives and eager for glory and freedom to roam were flocking to join the proposed expedition that was presented to them in the right way, full of heroic deeds and feats of daring and courage. No mention of politics, no general needs of the Great League. The young people couldn't care less about it, trusting their leaders to deal with the management of the Great Union, a boring business. What they wanted was glory and a good time, plenty of stories to tell back home, to have girls' heads spinning and their eyes sparkle with adoration reserved for the warriors before anyone else. Girls were girls, always and everywhere.

The wolf man maintained that this way they would gather as many as hundreds of men who were ready to fight, and still no laws would be broken by such unauthorized recruiting, no customs tread upon. An officially organized raid only warriors' leaders could start and only after receiving permission from the clans mothers to do so. But there was no need to receive more than a blessing of one's family should a person, a young warrior, decide to travel to the lands of the neighboring towns and nations independently, joining in an enterprise someone else's leaders managed to obtain the permission to run.

Such things happened all the time, and so what if this time hundreds of young people arrived at the same idea, incidentally ending up in the place they were very much needed? No harm would come out of it and no indignation. Or so they all hoped.

However, in case their activities didn't go unnoticed before they were safely away, sorting out their newly organized warriors' force in the Mountain People's lands, the tattoo owner trusted his brother, an important man the Great Council members recognized and trusted, to take care of any embarrassment the enraged authorities may cause. His brother was one of the initiators of the idea, claimed the young man, firmly behind them in that and watching their backs, just in case.

A promise that left Ogteah greatly relieved. In no position to break local laws and make authorities angry for real, he felt twinges of uneasiness coming and going, despite the great enjoyment of the mission itself. A stranger like him, and after the ugly incident in the spear-throwing contest, no, he was better off breaking no laws, not for a while. The High Springs man showed more tolerance and understanding toward his stupid brawl at the height of the important game than Ogteah would have expected, wishing to kick himself for yet again stupidly lost temper, combined with the results of his other stupid behavior—it was obvious why that Onondaga Town's lowlife sought to make trouble, a relation of the silly fox from the same town, again entirely his fault.

However, the High Springs man made everything proceed as though nothing happened, barring the Onondaga spear-throwing brawler out of the contest, while making it clear that he, Ogteah, while losing his judging position, was invited to participate when his village's turn to cast their spears came. An advantage Ogteah did not take of course. Back then, all he wanted was to crawl somewhere far away and forget all about it, but not before beating himself hard for his own inadequacies, as always.

He pushed the disturbing memories back into the murky depths they belonged. But for the timely interruption of the wolf man and his Flint friend, he would have gone away on the same day, back to Lone Hill, or most probably just to wander about and think of what to do, landing himself in more trouble, maybe. Instead, here he was, in the middle of exciting activities that, even if not perfectly legal, were authorized by important people. Oh, but he did owe much to so many kind people around here. Why were they so good to him?

"Well, at this point, we couldn't do much but wave our clubs and spears, or fight by any means possible."

The Flint's even, pleasantly rolling voice brought Ogteah back from his reverie, in time to see a group of girls pushing their way closer, their eyes sparkling, as did their wet, neatly-woven braids. A welcome addition. The crowding men stirred.

"Don't fall asleep." Smiling easily, he nudged the youth with the peach stones' bowl, adding a friendly wink as an afterthought. "You can play and listen at the same time."

He didn't care for the game or its outcome, not even a little bit. An unfamiliar feeling. Not his favorite game of luck, the pitch stone game served the purpose of gathering as many men around as possible, their main objective. His favorite bean-throwing game was for a limited amount of players, and he was not here to engage in any of it, not for real. His duty was to pack as many adventurous men in one space, to engage them in pleasantly light activity while allowing their Flint spokesmen to burst out with his enticing tales.

After a moon of traveling, they had developed their tactics so well, there was no need to coordinate any of their actions. Near the town, wait for an invitation, then stroll around striking up conversations, making fast friends—Ogteah's job—then an evening or two with a round of this or that betting game, while talking about wars and heroic deeds, and here they were, moving on, with the promise of tens upon tens of young men to present themselves at the lands of the setting sun, in the Mountain People's main town called Tsonontowan near the larger of the Finger Lakes. Two, three days in each settlement, many volunteers, plenty of pleasant pastime—nothing to complain about. Still, he never engaged in the actual betting himself, too busy organizing and conducting this part of their evenings. A surprisingly satisfying pastime.

"One more win and I'm getting his bet." Upon a less successful result of tossing a bowl, the second player grabbed the vessel eagerly, openly beaming. "No wonder he got so busy listening, eh?"

Ogteah grinned absently, motioning for the man to shake his bowl, his ears on his Flint friend's tale. There were new spins to the old story this time, made up, most of them, he suspected, amused but fascinated all the same.

"They were pouring from everywhere, the damn hunters, set on attacking, no matter how many of them we killed or wounded. They just kept spilling in, leaving us with no time to see our, or even their, dead off. As though the shower of fire-arrows we'd been pouring inside their stupid village was nothing but an afternoon rain."

Sure, he thought, trying to imagine the sight all the same. Fire-arrows, yes, his former people talked about those too, but he never stopped to wonder how those things were made to fly without their fire being extinguished on their way. Did the spectacular Flint have the answer? He wasn't sure about it, because knowing the true story, he remembered that their talented storyteller was hurt by the time that village was stormed, loitering on some abandoned shore, trying to survive rotting wounds.

Forcing his thoughts back, he examined the bowl, the peach pits in it gleaming nicely, displaying their painted sides. Five out of six. One more point to the lucky player.

"That was a good round," he said loudly, unwilling to draw

their attention from the story, but doing his duty nevertheless. They had gathered here to play, allegedly, to pass a pleasant afternoon, the hosts and the wandering guests, just an innocent group of people on their way back to the Onondaga lands. The enticing stories were a spontaneous thing. Or so they hoped it appeared.

The first youth gave his opponent a murderous look, but Ogteah was quick, leaning forward to grab the contested items—a necklace of purplish shells and a pair of arrows with prettily colored feathering—patting the loser on his back, while handing the winner his winnings.

"There will be enough time for another round." Holding the youth's gaze, he nodded toward the crowd of people, whose attention was drifting back toward their Flint guest, busy filling his pipe in the meanwhile. "It doesn't look as though they will be in a hurry to disperse."

"There are enough others who didn't play," muttered the youth, refusing to calm down. "I'll grow old before everyone has their turn."

"People are not growing old that fast, man." Tiredly, he rubbed his face, glancing at the crowding townsfolk, selecting the next pair of players with a practiced gaze. "I'll make sure you play again tonight. For now, go and listen to the stories. One can't spend one's life tossing stones and betting. Prove yourself as a warrior, then go on to lose or win your belongings."

The youth nodded gravely, shamed. Arranging the bowl and the painted pits for the next round, Ogteah tried not to grin, feeling people's gazes upon him, expectant, hanging on his words as well. As though he knew what he was talking about. The Flint might be embellishing the truth, might be exaggerating his part in those spectacular battles he was fond of retelling, for the sake of their mission and maybe for his personal glory as well, if the gazes of the listening girls were anything to go by; still, compared to Ogteah's past, it was equal to the most glorious warring deeds. The bulk of his own battle experience came to wild brawls outside longhouses, to furiously spat curses and blows of mindless rage.

"What did the savage women look like?"

This came from one of the girls, a pretty little thing, eating up the spectacular Flint with her eyes, adoring.

Their storyteller didn't seem to mind. "Oh, their women," he drawled, giving the girl an appreciative look, his scrutiny unconcealed. "But you never saw anything like that in your entire life." He shook his head. "Where do I start?"

At the juiciest parts, thought Ogteah, his interest piquing, eyes lingering on the pretty inquirer, taking in the darker glow of her nicely round cheeks. A cute little thing, but not in Gayeri's league of beauty. And probably not in spirit as well.

The longing was back, together with the familiar twinge of guilt. He should have detoured by Lone Hill before embarking on this journey, should have spent an evening with her and told her about his plans. Instead, he had scampered away, eager to flee from another mess he had gotten himself into, and she would learn all about it from rumors and talks, not knowing where he went and why and for how long. Did she deserve such treatment?

"The first savage fox we ran into was shooting like a mad warrior," the Flint continued smugly, assessing the girl with his eyes, evidently pleased. "She discharged all her arrows and, but for the benevolence of the Right-Handed Twin and the quick reaction of my friend, he might have been starting on his Sky Journey and me after him, because by that point, I was sporting this prettily feathered arrow in my thigh, fluttering there like a decoration."

Their audience stopped breathing, spellbound, immersed in the story, even the players. Ogteah tried to imagine the picture, remembering the man's badly scarred thigh, the lightness of his limp, and her, the wolf man's woman he had managed to glimpse back in Onondaga Town's valley but only briefly—a strange-looking fox, indeed, so tall and wide-shouldered, with her eyes large but too widely spaced, and her walk brisk like this of a man, attractive maybe, but in what way, he didn't know. Was it her who had shot that arrow at the Flint man?

As the story progressed, full of mounting exaggerations, even though this aspect of the repeated adventure he hadn't heard in detail before, he noticed that some men didn't like the way the girls were hanging on every word of the speaker. Their frowns were deep, and the glances exchanged between each other meaningful.

Better watch these types, he decided, nudging one of the players into shaking the bowl. They had to finish the game before it grew dark after all.

"Care for a round or two?" asked one of the men later on, when the pool of those wishing to play was exhausted and the bets collected, with the bulk of their party beginning to drift about, milling, and talking, and cracking jokes.

Of their Flint spokesman there was no sight. Neither was the pretty girl with her questions about savage women spotted anywhere around. Ogteah smirked, not envious in the least. A few more days of wandering these lands, and he would be home, enjoying the real thing, even if for one single evening he would dare to take for himself before heading for the lands of the setting sun and into the dubious enterprise he was not about to miss. The trust the War Chief and his family put in him was not to be mistreated or thrown away lightly. Even though he still wasn't sure how to reconcile all this with his true roots, and Father's secret mission. Whom did he owe his allegiance to now? A difficult question he had managed to avoid so far.

Forcing his thoughts back to the present, he looked at the hovering man, a person of about his own age or maybe older, his hair gathered carelessly behind his back, not shaved or tended to in the warriors' fashion, unlike the majority of their most eager audience.

"Why not?" Shrugging easily, Ogteah gathered the painted pits, retrieving one that managed to roll away from the last of the players, the man who had lost but didn't seem to take it hard.

The newcomer dropped down on the other side of the folded blanket, squatting there comfortably, his gaze on the bowl.

"What are you betting?"

Ogteah hesitated. The peach stone game was not his favorite, but he still knew how to manipulate the bowl to get better results.

"A pair of arrows."

Now it was the man's turn to shrug. "Make it something more

interesting."

"What do you offer?"

"A quiver with some arrows in it, all in good shape, if you offer your necklace."

"I'm not betting *this* thing," said Ogteah firmly, his sense of well-being beginning to evaporate once again. She had worked on this ornament long and hard, stringing an intricate pattern of shells, making it perfect for him to wear and be proud of. She said that the strange pattern had something to do with her family history, and that it would keep him safe. "A few arrows or small things like that, if you wish to play. This is not a ceremonial game."

Yet, all the while, the small voice in his head was nudging. A new quiver, in good shape and accompanied by more arrows; oh, but he could do with such an addition to his weaponry, couldn't he?

"Why spend one's time playing over silly arrows?" The man's voice didn't change, ringing calmly, disinterested. "You've been conducting this game like someone who played games of luck in his life. Don't tell me you never bet more than an arrowhead or a wooden spoon. I thought you had more guts than this."

The familiar stiffening in his stomach was back. "It doesn't matter what I bet in my life, or on what or when. For now, I offer the arrows and nothing else."

Luckily, the people around them seemed to be enthralled with the story of another man from their group, not paying their exchange much attention other than a wandering glance or two.

"Oh well, let's bet your precious few arrows." The pair of wide palms came up, in a mocking, surrendering gesture. "I start."

Not wishing to argue over yet another point—there was an appropriate way to determine who was going to play first— Ogteah counted the pits with his gaze, before offering the bowl, noting that their Flint spokesman was still missing along with the his girl, his tale of heroic deeds temporarily forgotten. It wasn't the first time the glorious hero did not deign to miss the opportunity.

"So, what is your destination?" inquired Ogteah's fellow

player, shaking the bowl hard. Too hard. This one didn't know how to do it. Maybe he should have bet the necklace, after all. "Where are you people heading?"

"Back home. Some of us."

"Where are you from?"

The pits were all over the flat-bottomed vessel, displaying their painted and unpainted sides. A bad throw.

"I live in a village near Onondaga Town," he explained, taking the bowl, making it tilt imperceptibly while bringing it to his side. This often helped the pits organize in a favorable manner, even before the actual shaking took place. "My mother was a Flint woman, though, so that is why I traveled to their lands this time."

"My grandmother was a full-blooded Flint woman," the man said with a nod, listening to the rustling pits as they rolled over the flat bottom, not jumping or scattering like his own had. "And so was my aunt from my father's side. They changed families often in their days, didn't they?"

"Yes, they did," agreed Ogteah, over his initial resentment at the attempt of drawing him into the old-time habit of gambling and actually liking the man. "It was different before the Great Peacemaker."

"Oh, yes, it was. They were kidnapping each other right and left. So many adoptees. I wonder what we would have to replace fallen warriors and dead family members with now that you and your friends seem so determined to drag our people into yet another war."

Peeking at the contents of the bowl, he offered it to the man's inspection, careful to keep it perfectly still.

"One point."

The man examined the pits, shrugging with surprising indifference. "So you went to visit your mother's people," he went on, watching Ogteah shaking the bowl lightly, preparing for the next round, warranted by his successful toss. "Why alone? Doesn't the old woman miss her people? Didn't she wish to come along?"

It took him a heartbeat to understand. "My mother long since resides in the Sky World."

"Oh." A thoughtful nod showed nothing but good-natured condolence.

For a while, they fell silent, listening to another outburst of storytelling coming from one of the guests.

"So your friends are her former clan's members, I suppose." A less successful throw had Ogteah handing the bowl over. "Why are they traveling with you back to the Onondagas?"

Even though seemingly light and good-natured, the interrogation began wearing on Ogteah's nerves. Where was this man going with his questions? What was he up to?

"They have their reasons to travel. I haven't inquired after their destination."

Shrugging, he leaned to examine the contents of the vessel, again dismally colorful, no more than three pits lying on the same side. The accursed quiver. It could be rightfully his, couldn't it?

Receiving the bowl back, he concentrated on matters that were more important than meaningless betting. "Most of my companions are on their way to the Mountain People's lands. The Keepers of the Western Door, you know. I will be heading there soon as well. By the end of the Hot Moons their main river will be boiling all over."

"Or so you people keep saying." The man's eyes flickered with challenge, their amusement open, yet their bottom remained sealed, difficult to read. "But I'm not a youth excited by pretty words. Like you, I have seen more summers than this. So now, tell me, why should I consider joining your expedition? Why follow you into the lands of the setting sun and do my best in trying to help them against some savages I have hardly heard anything about?"

In the background, people were still drifting, some going away, others coming back. Their conversations and quiet laughter filled the night, as did the soft cracking of chipped ground nuts and sucked-on pipes.

"Tales of fighting and daring deeds are good only for hotheaded youngsters, eh?" said Ogteah easily, playing for time.

The real reason? Oh, but he wasn't sure he wanted to face this one himself. Why was it so important to make as many young men as possible learn true warriors' skills and not only from storytelling? Why now, and just as his own Wyandot People's union might be getting out of hand with Father's passing? Again, he pushed his uneasiness away.

"Yes, they are," agreed his converser placidly, holding the bowl but not bothering to shake it, his eyes on Ogteah, boring into him, not about to let him get away with platitudes or meaningless talk.

Ogteah shrugged. "Men should know how to war for real and not from mere storytelling." There was no harm in admitting that. It was a logical conclusion every thinking person should arrive at. Little to do with his former people. "Nothing beats the real thing. That's what I'm after, brother, to explore possibilities, to see where I can join the real fighting." Leaning forward, he held his converser's gaze, raising his eyebrows in what he hoped looked like a conspiratorial manner. "They say those Long Tails are fierce people, worse than the savages one hears about here, pretty stories of our brave Flint notwithstanding. Real enemy, real fighting. Maybe some good spoils too, eh?" The wink came easily now, as his companion's expression lost some of its challenging glint. "Makes one's woman happy, those rare things you bring home, to present her with. I heard the western foe has pretty decorations aplenty."

A healthy chortle was his answer. "A sure way to make your woman forgive you that pleasant trip, away from home, away from responsibilities."

"The only one."

He gazed at the forgotten game accessory, willing his opponent to move on without the need to remind him. It would be a glaring impoliteness to hurry a player, but he was tired, and Akweks' absence worried him. If the high-spirited Flint went away to enjoy some of the local foxes' warm welcome, he was taking his time about it, clearly not paying attention to the possibly angry locals, or not even noticing it. It took rich experience and some summers of wandering to learn all about certain if unspoken rules, and that sweet, adoring thing did have her following, if the furious looks of some locals were to be taken into account. A visitor to a new place had to be careful about those things. He, Ogteah, knew all about it.

"Not a bad way of thinking," the man said, shaking the bowl again. The pits in it rustled softly, unhurriedly. "But why now? With so many hotheaded youths willing to follow in the footsteps of you and your friends our Western Door Keepers will end up with too many warriors on their hands. Won't they?"

"I'm sure they'll manage."

The bowl landed with a dull thud. "Something is telling me there is more to it than a mere openness about your plans on your part."

He leaned to watch the pits, difficult to see their painted or unpainted sides in the gathering darkness.

"There is nothing to it, but a mere good thinking. I want to get somewhere in my life, somewhere higher that an average man feeding his family and doing what he is told." The urge to laugh at his own words welled. Was it he who was saying those things? Such ambitious words. Ridiculous. However, if it helped to advance their mission, then why not? Maybe this nosy local would come to fight in the west too, bringing other like-minded friends along. The wolf man would welcome more than mere youths joining their enterprise. "And if my ambition helps our brothers in the west, then what could be better than that? Your union is worth our investment, you know?"

"*Your* union?" repeated the man, staring at Ogteah, one eyebrow climbing high, the other making its way toward the bridge of his eagle-like nose. "And who are you in all this? An onlooker?"

Ogteah snatched the bowl back, the variety of its painted and unpainted contents allowing him to have his next throw. "I didn't mean it to sound that way."

"Then what *did* you mean?" The narrowed gaze was not about to leave his face.

"Nothing!" Exhaling loudly, he dumped the bowl onto the ground, getting no better results than his opponent before. It was getting annoying, this interrogation. Was he to watch every word coming out of his mouth? "What I'm saying is simple. People need to disperse with their boredom, and there is a war about to break in the Mountain People's lands. Among brother-nations, there is nothing to stop a person from joining, from traveling to the neighboring lands and being of help while enjoying himself, carrying home rare spoils. Everyone gains, no one loses; no one but the Great League's enemies. A simple solution, unless one chooses to think in a twisted way." He pushed the bowl back toward his rival. "That is all there is to it."

"As simple as that, eh?" Now the man sounded openly amused. "But you are something, Onondaga man." A quick glance brushed past him as the bowl came into motion again. "You are Onondaga, aren't you?"

"I am Onondaga, yes. Now I am."

"Oh, so you weren't always one of us." Another toss of the flat-bottomed vessel ended with no worthwhile results. "That should account for your way of speaking. You do have a peculiar accent, come to think of it."

Ogteah just shrugged, wishing to end the game and fast.

"A word to the wise." Two rounds of tossing the bowl saw them both arriving at nothing. What happened to his usual way with stones? "Your Flint friend should not be messing around with that Wolf Clan's pretty thing. She gets excited easily, that girl, but her brothers get excited as easily, and there were a few bad incidents, one involving another foreigner, a visitor of the town. It took the man a long time to recover his walking ability in order to leave."

Determined to make the pits slant in the favorable way before starting his next toss, Ogteah almost had the bowl overthrown. Struggling not to let it fall, he glanced at the rest of the gathering, trying to see if the others of their group were still present. They were.

He felt the knot in his stomach tightening. Echoes of Arontaen? Anea and her brother? Back then, the results of his fooling around were disastrous, even though it wasn't he who couldn't walk for a long time after what happened. Yet, now, it was even worse. They could not afford any brawling, any bad rumors clinging to them. The Flint was strong and evidently violent; yet, even if he could take care of himself without getting injured too badly, a fight with local people was not their objective or goal, not even near it. *That* was not the fighting experience that they wished to entice their people into. Also, the man said "brothers," which meant more than one. How many local hotheads were after the careless Akweks?

"Do you know where she might like taking her strolls?" he asked, deciding that the direct approach might work the best with the man who seemed to air aloud everything that went through his head anyway.

His companion's grin was wide. "Certainly not. I'm a respectable man with a family of my own. I don't stroll around with young fowls of dubious inclinations." The amusement was spilling out of the crinkling eyes. "Especially if their brothers have a hard time keeping their eyes on those foxes, until their tempers burst with an indecent ease for anyone's peace of mind."

Ogteah rolled his eyes. "Do you mind if we finish the game later?"

"With the pitiful pair of arrows you consented to bet? No, I don't." The crinkling gaze followed Ogteah as he sprang to his feet, tucking the folded blanket into the bowl to cover its contents. "Maybe I'll come with you. To make sure you don't get lost wandering the town or its surroundings."

"Didn't you say you had a watchful wife to keep an eye on you and your movements?" asked Ogteah, pleased by the offer. How could he know where to start looking? "She might not like you strolling in the dubious company of foreigners, even if not complete intruders."

A good-natured guffawing was his answer. "She won't mind as long as my company involves something as unappealing as male guests."

Ogteah raised his eyebrows. "Good for you. So where do we start looking?"

"Not outside the town, I would say." Their steps rustled lightly, disturbing no leaves and no pebbles that dotted the ground, which wasn't swept as thoroughly as it would have been for ceremonies and rites. "That girl is nothing but a tease. She wouldn't go out of her way to please your eager friend, not her. So no sites outside the town's fence."

"He is a stupid buck in heat, without a reasonable thought in his empty head," muttered Ogteah, not amused.

Oh, but they didn't need this sort of a complication. And what could he do if he ran into a fight? Join it to help his friend? Try to stop it, somehow? Wasn't the embarrassment he had gotten himself into back in the Onondaga valley and in front of everyone enough?

"The spring!" exclaimed his companion triumphantly. "The spring where our women draw drinking water."

"What about it?"

"You may start looking there."

"Aren't you coming along? You said you don't mind."

"We'll see. If your company proves worthwhile."

Ogteah snorted. "It won't."

"What? No more preaching on our Great Union and the need to help each other?" The taunting challenge was back. "No more elaborating on how everyone gains from fighting alongside one another?"

"You heard it all already." Against his will, Ogteah grinned, shaking his head as their steps began tracing their way uphill. "Also, something is telling me that you had it all formed in your head beforehand. You just wanted someone else to say it aloud." Kicking a pinecone out of his way, he chuckled. "And anyway, I'll be busy killing that stupid buck, and it won't be funny or pretty. Nothing entertaining. Unless the filthy fox's brothers do it for me before I can."

"They may do that, yes," confirmed his converser mildly, as though talking about the weather. "They are a violent lot, those second Wolf Clan's longhouse brothers. They have been known for their troublemaking disposition for summers."

Ogteah fought the urge to hasten his step. "Aren't they used to their sister's silliness by now?"

"It's not only her. They are restless, those bucks and their various friends and cousins. They pick fights whenever they can. With locals, too. But foreigners are the best targets, always.

Especially your delegation, coming out of nowhere, with no respectable elders in sight." A shrug. "You should have brought the rest of your friends along."

"Now you are telling me that?"

This time, a pile of branches and swept-away leaves were the victim of his kick. But it was getting worse and worse, wasn't it?

The rasping voices coming from the top of the incline confirmed this conclusion, the hiss of a female tirade interrupted by several angry male outbursts.

He tried to decipher their meaning, but the dragging of his companion's feet interfered. As did the trickling of the stream somewhere up there among the voices.

"Think you found your destination, mysterious foreigner." The man beside him slowed his step. "I wish you well dealing with this."

Pursing his lips, Ogteah hastened his own step, disappointed with the disappearance of his short-time company, if ever so slightly. But of course. Why would the curious local wish to entangle himself in something that fishy, helping the foreigner he only just met?

He listened intently. Again, the girl was talking, not yelling at the top of her voice but close to it, overriding the male voice, then another one. They were talking all at once, shouting. Weren't they afraid to draw attention? This town seemed to be large, spreading on both sides of the hill, with much space between clusters of longhouses. Still, it was no woods.

He counted them without thinking. Three. No, four. Not good. One of the brawlers spoke with familiar accent. The Flint! So he was still well and in strong fighting spirit. Good. Or maybe not so. He sounded as angry as the rest of them, spoiling for a fight. Exhaling loudly, Ogteah covered the rest of the distance with a few hurried leaps.

They were crowding the open space between the dark mass of the fence and the trees adorning the edge, quite a few silhouettes. In the helpful illumination of the moon, he counted them quickly, perturbed. Five men, excluding the culprit and the girl. Not promising. The way Akweks was pressing against the dark poles, defensively aggressive, his knife out, flickering in the silvery light, bode no good to their situation, either. The others were forming a half-circle, some of their knives out as well.

As all eyes leapt at him, Ogteah made sure his own dagger was within an easy reach, his nerves stretched, but not to their limits. Such a situation warranted calm and control, something he wasn't famous for. And yet, it all depended on him now.

"What is going on?" he asked, marveling at the authoritative ring to his voice. So placid, unemotional, maybe even mildly bored.

"Nothing." The Flint's voice rang lowly, somewhat strident, but also not as though about to panic or break into mindlessness. From closer inspection, the side of his face looked darker, with one eye significantly smaller, peering through swollen skin. Yet, his spirit seemed to remain unbroken.

"Nothing, indeed." This came from one of the attackers, a slightly built fellow of an average height but quite an aggressive bearing. Someone who might have been carrying his unimpressive complexion as a perpetual challenge, decided Ogteah, knowing this type. "To treat decent girls with indecent means might be nothing for filthy rats full of excrement, eh?"

"Take your cowardly stupid talk elsewhere," growled the Flint, pushing himself away from the darkness of the fence, his knife out and ready. A motion that caused the speaker to shift backwards, in a defensive manner. "Coward, indeed!"

The murmur among the rest of the attackers rose, their attention back on their victim, their poses strained, ready to pounce.

"Shut up, you stinking rat!" hissed one of them, clearly the leader of the group. More impressively built than his peer or relative, his shoulders broader even if his height was not surpassing the other, this one seemed to be spoiling for a real fight. "Want to be cut up and fed to the wolves out there? That will teach you to mess with decent women."

The girl, now quite a sight, her pretty braids disheveled and her crumbled dress rustling with leaves, gasped, bringing her palm to her mouth. "Please," she whispered, her fighting spirit evidently gone.

"Try to do that!" Spat Akweks back, clearly welcoming the chance to get back at the people who managed to give him a swollen eye.

Speaking of tempers, reflected Ogteah, in the far corner of his mind slightly pleased to see someone else acting stupidly, losing his temper where it would have been wiser to back away. Usually it was his specialty, just witness what happened at the spear-throwing contest. The Flint was in the wrong, and he knew it; yet, he didn't try to smooth matters, preferring to lose his temper instead.

"Wait!"

As one of the knives flashed, he forgot his musings, leaping ahead without giving his actions much thought. The Flint attacked deftly, surprising not only Ogteah but his assailants as well. But for the quick reaction of the leading local, whose body twisted out of the razor-sharp edge's reach with an easy familiarity of someone who wasn't new to knife fights, the man might have been done for, stabbed or at least cut badly enough to be counted out, presenting no threat. As it was, the undaunted attacker lashed back with the same enviable speed and determination, putting as much viciousness into his counter assault. His knife longer, glittering darkly, it cut the night, heading toward its victim's side, following an intricate path.

An onslaught the attacked Flint blocked by a quick thrust of his elbow, deflecting the blow rather than avoiding it. It made his attacker waver, something the experienced warrior didn't miss out on acting upon. A vicious kick at the lower legs sent the man crashing down, unharmed but out of the brawl, if only for a little while.

Turning abruptly, to evidently check if the rest of his opponents gained their fighting spirit in the meanwhile, the undaunted Flint bumped into the girl, who didn't have enough sense to retreat as the others did, or better yet, to run away and be gone.

That gave his fallen rival enough time to spring back into action, his fighting spirit clearly intact. Still struggling not to lose his balance, his curses shaking the air, the Flint lashed out without aiming, twisting his body from the readily poised dagger, avoiding its lethal touch by nearly throwing himself away. Springing back to his feet with an admirable swiftness, he stumbled, evidently having used his bad leg, but his rival didn't exploit the brief opportunity. Instead, he waited, leaning forward, as tense as an overstretched bowstring, ready to attack.

Not thinking it through, Ogteah seized the chance. "Wait!" Keeping an eye on both panting rivals, their undivided attention on nothing but each other and the possible paths of the poised knives, he stepped forward, holding his hands up, palms forward, showing his harmless intentions. "Listen." He didn't bother to keep his voice low, the authoritative ring to it still there, puzzling but very much welcomed. He just hoped it wouldn't abandon him for the duration of this crisis at least. "Just stop this stupid fight and listen!"

Their breaths tore the darkness, the only sound. The rest of the noises melted away, froze, disappeared. No one seemed to dare to blink, and even the night insects stopped their perpetual buzzing.

"Lower your knives, both of you," he ordered firmly, sliding into this new role, quite easily at that. It would have amused him under different circumstances, to hear himself telling someone what to do, had his nerves not been stretched as badly as those of the fighting rivals. "Lower your knives and listen."

Another spell of undecided silence. He tried to find something to say. *It's not the time nor the place to fight your differences out?* And whyever not? The offended brother was rude, and spoiling for a fight, bringing an indecent amount of friends to back him up. They had already given the visitor a swollen eye. He himself wouldn't be stopped from fighting now under similar circumstances. Back in Arontaen he had snapped under much less provocation. And yet, they couldn't have their mission harmed, not in this way.

"It's not the time—" he began, but a sudden movement to his left took his attention away, made him catch the glimpse of a figure that rushed toward them. A girl? What, for the sake of the great and small spirits, did this one want?

His mind registered a genuine surprise, even though the main part of it was still on the frozen rivals and their poised knives. With a good reason, apparently. They sprang back to life at the same time, just as the silly fox stumbled to his side, her arms stretched, palms up, imploring. To push her away from there seemed like a good idea, because the knives were on the move again, seeking their targets, their owners panting, oblivious of reason.

Another heartbeat saw the others gasping as the girl went sprawling into the dust, the thrust of Ogteah's shoulder making her fall faster. Not entirely out of the way, she was still not in the lethal blades' reach, though chancing the danger of being trampled upon. He considered kicking her away from there, like a stupid cornhusk doll. Her whimpering and rolling under everyone's feet was annoying.

Then his mind snapped back into attention as he himself was now struggling to stay on his feet, to hold against the pressure of someone's body that crashed against him. Or maybe it was a hard-rock fist, or a limb. It was difficult to judge by the pain it brought, the tearing quality of it.

He pushed back using his entire weight, or so it felt, deflecting an additional assault with the thrust of his elbow, even though that made him nearly lose his balance. Successful at ridding himself of the worst of the pressure, he caught something to steady himself, a branch of a tree as it seemed, then spent a heartbeat groping for his own knife before his mind cleared again.

Both rivals were back at it, paying little attention to their weaponry now but just going for a kill by all means, wavering there, clutching each other tightly, in a sort of brotherly embrace.

Unable not to, he snorted before pushing in again, inserting his shoulder between the two antagonists, grinding his teeth against the tearing pain it released somewhere there in his arm or his side, where it was only a mere throbbing before.

"Stop it!"

This time, it came as quite a roar, or maybe just a loud growling. He couldn't tell, as all his strength was dedicated to the attempt to push them away from himself if not from each other, heavy, fat bears that they were.

Stupid skunks! His rage kept mounting, giving him more power, against their pressure and against the pain in his side. Stupid, mindless bucks!

"Get away from each other *now!*"

This time, it worked. They pulled away. Or maybe it was something else that made them come apart. He didn't know, busy trying to catch his breath, suddenly worried. The attempt to push the two brawlers away from each other should not have sapped his strength that badly, should not have left him dizzy and in pain. He groped for the source of it with his free palm, the other clinging to his previous support, yes a branch of a tree, how helpful.

"Get away from each other," he repeated loudly, feeling too many eyes upon him, the expectancy of their silence. His palm was holding something warm, unpromisingly wet, but he forced his thoughts off of it, not ready to deal with a worrisome suspicion. "For starters, do that. Then we'll talk."

The moon was pouring its light with more generosity now. In its silvery illumination, their faces looked grotesque, dark masks with gaping mouths and eyes. Somehow it was easy to recognize his fellow player of the last Peach Stone game's round, standing next to the local attacker, his grip on the man's shoulder firm, uncompromising. The others were crowding the brawlers now too, disheveled Akweks among them, standing as still as the rest of them, as though belonging in this crowd.

For a heartbeat, no one said a word, but as he made the effort to straighten up, acutely aware that it was time to say something, to attempt that talk he was threatening them with, they snapped back to life all at once.

"You're hurt!" cried out the Flint, rushing to Ogteah's side with his usual forcefulness, almost pushing him off his feet. The grip of the fingers that tightened around his shoulder was reassuringly supportive but bone-crushing.

"Get off me," he said. "I'm good. Just need a moment…"

"Wait, let me see."

He struggled against the prying hands, even though it made

the pain and the dizziness worse.

"Get away from me. Just stop that stupid fight. It's not the time—"

But the others were crowding him now as well, pushing in, talking at once. He let them take him away from the tree and toward the better lit ground, not liking the way he was forced to lean on his friend in order to do something as simple as walk.

"Stop fussing around. It's nothing." Wriggling into a better position, he glimpsed the uneven line that wound its way along his ribs, glittering darkly but not viciously, trickling blood rather than pumping it. Good. He wanted to groan with relief. "It's nothing. Some of you can't handle a knife, that's all."

But their hands kept pressing, forcing him back when he tried to push himself up, discouraged with the way his limbs refused to cooperate, making it easy for his pushy companions to keep him where he was.

"That thing is not what should worry you, foreigner." The voice of one of the aggressive locals overcame the general murmuring, ringing with no enmity or challenge, curt and matter-of-fact. "Your arm is not in such a good shape, so stop trying to make it fall off for good. You!" As abruptly, the man straightened up, "run to the Turtles' longhouse. Find our uncle and beg him to come here, with his tools and herbs and whatever. Don't let him refuse you, Sister, or make a fuss over it. Tell him the matter is urgent but needs to be kept quiet."

Amidst another brief pause and the rapid scurrying of the girl's feet, Ogteah gave up, allowing them to lay him down, leaning on the massive Flint's hands, relishing their support. *Damn stupid bucks*, he thought, resisting the dizziness no more, letting it take him and lull him into its blissful calm. *To get him cut somehow. How clumsy could those two would-be fighters get?*

CHAPTER 13

Unlike his predecessor, the Head of the Great Council was not a foreboding person. An impressively tall, broadly built man in his mid-fifties, the important leader generated power, but in a calm, reassuring way. Still, this time the prominent face was set in a less than friendly mask, and the eyes boring into Ganayeda related a fair measure of sternness.

"What is the meaning of this?" the man asked again, wasting no time on preliminary pleasantries or small talk. "Our young men pouring westwards like a river inundated by the melting snow of the Cold Moons."

To pretend lack of understanding was tempting, but unwise. Ganayeda made sure his face reflected confidence he didn't feel. Reinforced by a suitable amount of deference, perhaps—not too much, yet not too little.

"Our young men, as always, are eager to join wars and warring, Honorable Elder." Standing the penetrating gaze, he tried to keep his own firm. "There is no law or custom that says a man cannot travel in order to join this or that projected raid."

The gaze resting on him deepened with displeasure. "Indeed, it is not against our tradition to have our men traveling freely, joining in wars if they wish to do so." The dignified head moved slowly, disapprovingly. "And yet, when it's done in a suspiciously organized fashion, when an unheard-of number of people is suddenly traveling as though they were a warriors' force on a raid, when they, incidentally, are heading toward the lands our elders and leaders were already asked to consider sending reinforcements to; well, when something like that is happening, one can't help but to start wondering."

Halting at the top of the trail, the older man turned away, linking his arms across his chest, his gaze traveling the valley below their feet, now nothing but an abandoned plain, a trampled upon field, teeming with people until only a few dawns ago, but not anymore. The meeting of the Great Council was over for good. Unless the need to convene the next gathering should arise, that is. *Oh, all the great and small spirits, make Okwaho be correct in his farfetched predictions and speculations!* But for his brother's forcefulness, his persuasive beliefs and convictions, his strange, unheard-of net of shady informants from the other side…

"What is happening in the lands of the Western Door Keepers?" The voice of the Great Council's leader interrupted his thoughts, forcing him to concentrate once again. It was not the time to regret anything, let alone something he had walked into wholeheartedly, something he believed in, but for those rare moments of doubt.

"As you know, Honorable Elder, there is unrest in the colder lands of the setting sun, among the people we call Erielhonan, The Long Tails People. They aren't pleased with our Great League of Five Nations, and they seem to wish to war on us."

The older man's nod was slow and thoughtful, yet the ice-cold gaze didn't thaw. "We've heard of the possible trouble our neighbors to the west might wish to give us. The reports concerning these Long Tail People and their growing presumption have been reaching the members of the Great Council's ears. Our highly esteemed and greatly admired War Chief keeps a keen eye on all such developments, far away as they may be occurring." One of the bushy eyebrows was arching, reflecting the mirthless amusement of the lurking question. "Why didn't you approach this dignitary first? It is a correct procedure, and given your close connection to the mentioned leader, I would have expected you to do just that."

He groaned inside.

"I have spoken to the War Chief and shared my concerns regarding this matter. And so did my brother, who spent many moons among the Mountain People, participating in their warfare." The wish to pause if for no other reason than to draw a deep breath and thus gain a little time was overwhelming. Instead, he went on with no visible hesitation, or so he hoped. "The War Chief correctly pointed out that should my concerns grow, it was my place to talk to our town's representative in the Great Council, to ask for this respectable person's guidance and advice."

"Did you talk to the High Springs' representative, then?" Again the decidedly cold tone.

Ganayeda pressed his lips together, suddenly annoyed. He was not a youth to be questioned, or even reprimanded in such a patronizing way. "I have not considered my concerns to be worrisome to the extent of bothering our distinguished representative, Honorable Elder."

The slightly raised eyebrows were his answer. "Instead, you decided to act on your own."

Tired of the incessant needling, Ganayeda drew a deep breath. "I regret to hear that any of my actions displeased you, Honorable Elder. Every action I have taken has been done within the limits of our laws and customs, and with the best interest of our people in heart."

"In other words, you made certain to pursue your goals by bypassing our laws but not by breaking them."

The man sighed, then shook his head and turned away, gazing again at the abandoned valley as though admiring the view.

"You are a promising man, War Chief's son," he said finally, his voice calm and holding no trace of its previous bitterness. "Not unlike your father in that you have much courage to act upon your conviction, even if sometimes the others take their time to appreciate your views, if at all." The heavily lidded eyes rested on Ganayeda again, scrutinizing him openly, their curiosity unconcealed. "You are a good man. In your own right, and not only as a son of your distinguished father, even though one can see that he has brought you up well." Another brief pause. "Well, Organizer of the last meeting of our Great Council, apprise me of this situation again. Share with me those concerns you didn't find important enough to approach your town's representative with. If you convince me, I may agree to turn a blind eye to some of your, and your brother's, activities, unless neither of you have managed to prove your claims. And then even my respect for your great father will not keep you from a severe reprimand." The sternness returned, to be replaced with the earnest, matter-of-fact nod again. "Tell me about the unrest among our young men and warriors, and how it is all connected to the Western Door Keeper's wars. Your honesty may very well decide your future involvement in our Great League's affairs."

Iheks and some of the others still loitered by the abandoned campsite, messing with their packs and weaponry, doing nothing in particular. The tramped-upon ground was already swept clean, though still dotted by dozens of extinguished fires, a clear testimony to the presence of too many people for a long period of time.

"What are you still doing here?" Emerging from the depths of his thoughts, he eyed them, grinning, pleased to see his ever-loyal friend around and waiting. "Not in a hurry to return to High Springs, eh? All this fields' cleaning activity... Hot Moons or not, our clans mothers will find enough forested ground that still needs attention, won't they?"

Their grins matched his.

"Can't enjoy any of this without our glorious leader and organizer, can we?" Iheks' eyes twinkled with their usual readiness. "Unless you find more excuses to linger around here, nagging on the Great Council's members."

"Not quite."

The lightness of his mood evaporating, he recalled the conversation with the Head of the Great Council, a long, wearisome interview, an interrogation, really. Looking agreeable, and probably genuinely meaning well, the powerful elder did not hesitate to ask the most probing questions, not bothering to mask them under even a mere coating of politeness. No way of eluding or getting away with half-truths. Not with such a man. Well, of course one doesn't become the leading person of the powerful union by being naive and easy to deceive.

Still, all in all, he had not done so badly, Ganayeda decided, recounting the conversation in his head while heading down the hill and toward the extinguished fires of their side of the valley. Father was left completely out of it, a bit too easily come to think of it. There was no doubt the Head of the Great Council did suspect the War Leader's involvement, with both men having known each other, working together for many winters and summers. However, suspecting or not, his interrogator didn't push in this direction, clearly wishing to leave the powerful War Chief out of it, to Ganayeda's endless relief.

However, he himself didn't fare as well as that. Finding it beneath his dignity to shift the blame to his brother, the real culprit and the originator of this entire mess, Ganayeda saw no other option than to take the credit for it all, the idea and the execution. What else could he do? Okwaho was a fearsome warrior and a force to reckon with, impossible to ignore, especially these days. Still, it was unseemly to have the young buck of little over twenty summers answerable for such planning and execution, so here he was, taking the credit, and the blame in case it went wrong, or worse yet, came to nothing. Oh Mighty Spirits!

"I won't be heading for High Springs, not yet," he said, ruffling the grayish ashes with the tip of his moccasin. "This span of seasons, the new fields will have to get cleared without me." The grin came back easier than he expected. "To the infinite depth of my regret."

"Where will you be spending your time, then?" Iheks' widening eyes made a funny sight. It wasn't often that one managed to catch this particular friend of his off guard.

"Out there in the west." He waved his hand in the general direction of the relevant side belonging to Onondaga Lake. "Only bad spirits know where exactly, or doing what, so don't ask for details."

"Your brother and his wild schemes." The heavyset man shook

his head. "I knew nothing good would come out of it."

His grin still in place, Ganayeda shrugged then led their way toward the place where their tents were erected not long ago, unwilling to discuss any of it within people's earshot. "The Head of the Great Council was quite understanding, considering the circumstances."

"Understanding in what way?" Keeping his voice satisfactorily low, Iheks stared at the bushes adorning the edge of the clearing before following Ganayeda up the small trail, his usual lighthearted attitude and bearing gone.

"He was upset but not too badly, considering the way we forced this issue. He should have reacted more strongly, if you ask me." The trail beckoned, but he slowed his step, not wishing to wander too far away, not with the journey he had yet to begin planning. "That old Onondaga Town's leader is not a person to palm off with our ready-made excuses about warriors going wherever they want to, joining whatever wars they fancy. Well, he is not the Head of the Great Council for nothing, after all." To talk it over helped, as under his perpetual jokes and pretended lightness, Iheks was loyal and smart. And he wasn't involved, not directly. Another good turn. "I had to be honest with him, to a degree; had to make sure I told him some of the truth and not only ready excuses."

A grim shake of the head was his answer. "I take it he received it well enough if you are still here, preparing to head spirits know where. I expected you to be back packing, kicked home to High Springs, not allowed to show your face anywhere near Onondaga Town again."

He heard his own chuckle rolling between the trees. "Yes, I was aware of the possibility it might come to something like that. But he was quite patient. Let me talk until my throat hurt. Didn't mind my attempt at oratory in the least." He fought the temptation to head back toward their people, the hum of their conversations reaching them, joined by what sounded like a female voice. "He is a very wise man, very patient. Let me go through Okwaho's reasoning, all of it, point by point."

"But you didn't let him know it was Okwaho's doing, did

you?" These words held an open accusation. "If something goes wrong, you will be the one to take the blame. Not your brother." A defiant spark made his friend's eyes look unusually dark. "And not your father."

In the relative privacy of the woods, it felt safe to exhale loudly, his exhaustion welling together with his doubts.

"It is the only way to do it," he said tiredly, rubbing his eyes to make the budding headache go away. "Okwaho is not important enough as yet to have him taking the blame, while Father is too important to have him involved." He forced a smile. "I can handle it, Old Friend. I believe in what they foresee out there on the western edge of the Great Lake, and I believe in my own doubts regarding our people's lack of battle readiness. I saw it when Okwaho came back and we ran into those annoying Crooked Tongues. You see, I didn't act cowardly, and I put everything I had into our fight with those people. Still, what Okwaho did was incomparable to what I managed to achieve. He was the warrior, while I was the hunter. Do you see what I mean? To handle various weapons and talk war is not enough. One needs to fight the human foe to learn proper behavior, and if there is a way of achieving that while helping our brothers and members of our union, then what's the better way?" Turning to go, he rested his palm on his friend's back, which was still sagging, as though dubious of what had been said. "They are not wrong about the trouble in the west. It is imminent, and it will need our Great League's attention. So when we come back, having proven our case, I will get the credit and not the blame, leaving poor Okwaho with nothing but more fighting experience."

That brought the anticipated outburst of chuckling. "As though you would do something like that." Now it was Iheks' turn to exhale loudly, in a pointed manner. "So you are heading out there now, following the request of our Great Council's leader?"

"Something of the sort, yes. He wants me to keep an eye on the happenings, to observe, to make sure not too many laws were broken or bent, I suppose." Straining his ears, he listened to the footsteps that headed up the trail they were following. Hurried, light-footed sounds. "We bent enough customs with our unauthorized gathering of warriors. With all that Okwaho was doing out there among the Onondaga settlements and the People of the Swamp's towns as well. Not to mention his Flint friends and our Crooked Tongues troublesome element in the east. I am honestly afraid to learn what they were up to."

But Iheks' grin was back in place. "Our Crooked Tongue will manage. In fact, if enough Standing Stone People get off their behinds in order to join your innovative warring, I bet you would have this man to thank rather than your brother's Flint friends. He has a way with people, that one. And he is a good man, even if sometimes his temper gets the better of him. Enough Standing Stone hotheads would follow him into the lands of the setting sun. I am prepared to put the best of my birds' traps against that claim."

"Speaking of gambling and gamblers," grunted Ganayeda, more amused than put out. Hadn't he liked that man, almost against his will in the beginning? And yes, Iheks was right. The intriguing foreigner was good with people, getting along with unfamiliar strangers better than anyone he knew might have, not sacrificing even a bit of his dignity along the way and giving no ground in the process.

Unless pushed into violence, like the last time, in that spear-throwing contest. A regretful business he still felt bad about. He should have predicted it, should have been there to help the man out. The annoying Onondaga Town's brawler had pushed with all he had, and of course the Crooked Tongue could not go on fending off the offense like an impeccably local man might have. Of course he had lost his temper, and thus almost ruined the game. But for his own timely intervention… And yet, it was his fault he did not intervene earlier, did not prevent the entire scandal.

"He is a good man," he said, sighing. "Very able and capable when choosing to direct his drive into good paths. But the thing is, he isn't one of us, not yet. And until then, I would rather leave him out of our Great League's politics and inner dealings."

Iheks' pointed eyebrows climbed up again. "Why did you let him join, then?"

He flailed his hands in the air, defeated. "I didn't! My brother and his spear-throwing Flint took a shine to that man, got him involved without asking for my advice. And that after Father told him the same thing."

His friend's eyebrows were threatening to meet his somewhat receding hairline by now. "I thought the War Chief did everything short of adopting this man to be his son."

"Yes, yes. Father likes him and appreciates him, and not only because he is the offspring of some beloved cousin from his childhood. He likes him for what he is. But Father is not the War Chief of our entire nation for nothing. He puts the well-being of our people before anything else, and a foreigner who came to live with us of his own free will, and only a mere span of seasons ago, can't be trusted, not wholeheartedly. Not unless some summers have passed and some proof of his unconditional loyalty has been provided." Shaking his head, he snorted. "But what does my brother do? He goes out and enlists this man all the same, sending him with his Flint hotheaded friends to prowl around the east. Sharing all our planning with him along the way and all the secrets, I bet. Stupid buck!"

"You are taking it too far, Old Friend." Iheks' palm landed on his back, warm, reassuring. "I wouldn't worry about our Crooked Tongues friend. Your destination is what makes me curious. What did the Head of the Great Council send you to do, and in what capacity, exactly?"

Turning to head back down the trail, Ganayeda made a face. "I'm to travel to the Mountain People's main town for now, see what's happening, make sure it is not getting too wild or unlawful, I suppose. To represent our Great League, to a degree. But in an unofficial manner."

"Of course unofficial! Like I said, if everything goes wrong, you will be the one to take the blame, to receive accusations from every direction possible."

"It won't." He narrowed his eyes against the strengthening light, having emerged back from the woods, trying to see who their visitors were. People were still milling around, more than the amount they had left behind.

"There is some mighty pretty fox anxious to see you, brother."
One of their men came forward, beaming. "She insisted on
waiting for you, even though her escort wasn't excited about it.
Luckily, it didn't take too long for you two to come back."

"The Onondaga Town people?" asked Ganayeda, not greatly
pleased. What would the locals want from him now that he
needed to be on his way? He had just left their town, and the time
of the day was not on his side. If wishing to detour through High
Springs, stopping there for more than a quick halt, he would have
to start moving soon. It was still more than a day of traveling,
even if one chose to walk very fast.

"Lone Hill. The son of their representative, I think."

"Oh." He remembered the man but vaguely, about his own
age, a quiet, dedicated person who was around and helpful
through this last meeting, with only one strange incident
connected to the spear-throwing contest. Did this man refuse to
participate after the trouble with the Onondaga Town's team and
the brawl that followed? Or was it someone else from the Lone
Hill's players who got all purple with anger at the conduct of the
organizer, one of their own men?

Then the irrelevant thoughts trickled out all at once, as his eyes
took in the familiar pliant silhouette rushing toward him, moving
with this typical unconscious grace he could not quite forget, even
though more than two summers had passed. Two and a half to be
precise. So much had happened, such major upheavals and
changes, and most of it because of her.

"Oh, I'm so glad you didn't leave yet," she said breathlessly,
stopping a hairbreadth too close, pleading with those exquisite
bottomless eyes of hers, such a familiar if quite forgotten sight.

Was she in a trouble, again? he wondered numbly, fighting the
urge to take a step back, or better yet, to turn around and flee. But
for her changing, even a little bit, losing some of her beauty, some
of her irresistible allure. He hadn't seen her for more than an
entire span of seasons, and she was married to a good man. He
forced his mind into working.

"What are you doing here?" It came out clumsily, with such
awkwardness that he wanted to curse himself. "I thought the

people of Lone Hill were long since gone home." More stupid awkwardness. She wasn't present at the gathering. He would have known if she were, being a person who organized the entire event, and having spent enough time in the company of her husband.

The smoothness of her forehead creased. "Oh, I arrived only this morning. My brother," a light nod indicated the rest of their company, with everyone watching them of course, covertly but with an obvious curiosity. "He traveled back here, and I took the opportunity to accompany him."

As though that explained it all. He struggled against the dazzling sensation, feeling back on the ill-fated journey two summers ago, when she never made sense with her presence out there in the woods, but just kept gazing at him out of those huge, tearful, or later, adoring eyes, her expression making him forget prudence and common sense, making him crave to help and protect her. Even back in the Crooked Tongues lands, after the first shock of their initial encounter and her venomous accusations, didn't she run to him later on, making him help her again despite it all, against her adoptive clan mothers and later on with her lover in trouble?

He took a deep breath. "Tell me what is happening, why were you looking for me now?"

Her eyes were turning more pleading, causing his stomach to tighten in painful knots, but the footsteps and the broad figure bearing down on them helped. It allowed him to transfer his attention elsewhere, to the decisiveness of the newcomer's approach, and the barely concealed anger in it.

"Greetings, Honorable Brother." Her sibling's stiff bearing— now he clearly recognized the man, yes, the same person from the spear-throwing contest—made a sharp contrast to the soft expectancy of her demeanor. The hard eyes, not unlike hers but only in their shape, looked at Ganayeda rigidly, cold and distant, giving nothing away. "I apologize for my sister's appearance here. It was not my wish to let her accompany me."

That made even less sense than her unhelpful explanation. If he didn't wish her to come with him, then why was she here?

"There is no harm in this young woman approaching me," he said politely, wishing to finish it fast, whatever it was. "We are old acquaintances, and she knows she can trust me to help her if it is in my power to do so."

That made her eyes, if not her entire being, shine, while her brother's clouded some more.

"I thank you," she said, this time speaking more slowly, choosing her words. "I know I should not interrupt your important work. You do so much for our people! When Ogteah told me you were entrusted with the organization of the Great Council's gathering, I was so proud, so pleased to learn that. He thinks highly of you."

The radiance of her smile was infectious. It made his lips twist with no regard to his will. "You are too kind. And so is your husband."

"Her husband is too everything." There was no mistaking her companion's words and their meaning. Some people, apparently, were proofed against certain foreigner's charm, sharing none of her excitement or ardor.

The reproachful glance she gave her brother showed Ganayeda that it was not their first disagreement on the subject. Again, he remembered the incident of the game and this man's demonstrative refusal to participate. So not all was well in the Crooked Tongue's new family. No wonder, really.

"Her husband is a good man," he said mildly, not wishing to get into troubled family matters, but not about to let anyone talk bad about the people he liked. "He was of a great help in the organization of this event."

A bleak gaze accompanied by a fleeting shrug was his answer.

"Will you let us talk in a bit of privacy, Brother?" she asked briskly, bestowing on Ganayeda another glorious smile of thanks. It warmed his insides quite against his will.

The man rolled his eyes. "Yes, *Sister*. You can ask about your wandering husband in private, if you wish to do so. Just do it quickly. I have matters of importance to attend to. And so does the honorable man you are about to ply with a swarm of silly questions."

This time, the look he received could burn holes in his skin. The poisonous snake, he remembered. This girl could turn very nasty, if provoked. The sweet little thing in need of protection was not always what she was.

He watched her as her eyes shot thunderbolts, following her sibling's retreating back, whose exaggeratedly straight shoulders related his own defiant displeasure quite as well.

"He is such a bad-tempered skunk at times," she muttered, making Ganayeda's wish to laugh grow.

"He isn't happy at your choice of a husband, is he?"

Her showily rolled eyes were his answer.

"Well, it shouldn't matter to you. He is not your clan mother, or real mother or father, or anything of the sort. You are not even living in the same longhouse."

"Yes." She sighed, her gaze still on the defiant back of her sibling. "He isn't that bad. He keeps his opinions to himself, like in all other matters. It's just that since the gathering..." Suddenly, her face fell, and her gaze darted back to him, fully concentrated, again pleading in some strange, indecipherable way. "What happened through this gathering? Why didn't Ogteah come home?"

He drew a deep breath, aware of the gazes, especially that of Iheks, his wish to escape the uncomfortable conversation overwhelming. It wasn't his place to make excuses, to explain the other man's behavior and possible faults. It was not he who was guilty of violent exchanges and maybe even a brief affair. The rumors were circulating, and this man's trouble with certain elements of Onondaga Town did not start with the game and its outcome.

"He didn't come home because he was asked to join an important mission," he said carefully, addressing the easiest of the issues. "I can't tell you much about it yet, but it is something of importance. People who asked him to join hold your husband in great esteem. They believe he can contribute to their mission. Only a few were invited."

Her face lit like a fire splashed with a jar of oil. A beautiful sight that took his breath away, despite his resolution not to feel any such thing.

"Important people asked him to join a serious mission?" Her eyes grew so bright with excitement, he was afraid they would ignite for real. "Who asked him? Where?"

Pleased with the effect, he hid his smile. "I can't tell you more about it, not now. When he comes back, he'll share some of it with you, I'm sure. Actually..."

He hesitated, as the thought hit him. She must know this man better than anyone, mustn't she? And she was a smart woman, suitably perceptive. There was more to her sweet, pretty facade, much more than she was willing to show. A poisonous snake, an industrious fox, a mountain lioness, even a quivering forest mouse, all those epithets the Crooked Tongue had used, oh, but they were more than simple endearments of a man enthralled. Another one who was much deeper than she cared to display. Such a strange couple.

"Tell me." Holding his gaze, he narrowed his own, determined but wary, afraid to make a mistake. Her loyalty to her man might make her refrain from sharing her thoughts or even suspicions, might it not? "After all this time, almost a whole span of seasons, does he feel truly at home here? Has it happened that he regretted his decision to come?" Her frown was deepening with each uttered word, but before she could burst into loud protestations, he held his hand out, palm forward. "I'm not asking out of idle curiosity, or in an attempt to catch him on something he isn't telling us. I trust him, and so do many people I know. Even your brother's resentment is not originating in your husband's dubious origins. I'm certain of that. If it was, he would have to mistrust many people around here, my mother included." That was no comparison and he knew it, but it seemed to put her at ease, her frown smoothing, eyes turning thoughtful. "What I want to know is that. Ogteah arrived here not very long ago, and he is not what clan mothers would call the most desirable community member, is he?" A reassuring smile drew the desired half-grin. "I bet this is what makes your brother unhappy toward your choice of a man. Isn't it?" One side of her mouth was climbing up, faster than the other. As did the knowing flicker of her eyes. "Well, you know him from his Crooked Tongues days, so what I want you to tell me is if you notice that he behaves differently here, on our side of the Sparkling Water. If he feels better or worse here." A shrug came easily this time. "I need to know this in order to find how to help him to become one of us, truly one of us and not just a likable guest."

She was nodding vigorously, her neatly woven braids jumping, lips pursed, eyebrows knitted, wholly immersed.

"Yes, I see what you mean, and I thank you for thinking in this way, for making such an effort." Her smile again warmed his insides, the prettiest sight, wonderfully open, genuine, like back then. He pushed the memories away with an effort. "Well, yes, compared to Arontaen, he is now the example of perfect behavior." The smile widened, turned disturbingly mischievous. "And from what I gathered listening to his father and the Ossossane woman talking, he has been no better back home, among his own Bear People." Her hands came up, fingers interwoven, the smile gone again, replaced by the thoughtful frown. "So in this regard, one may assume that he actually feels better here among our people, more belonging than back among his own countryfolk. Otherwise, he would have no reason to behave, would he?"

What a little orator. Slightly amused, he listened, not analyzing her words but storing them for a future inspection. What she said made sense, oh yes it did, but still, a doubt was nagging. Such a change could indicate what she claimed it did, but it could be something deeper as well, an underlying motive. The Bear People's leader was a great man, an admirable person and a true ally; and yet, like Father, he put his people's interests before anything else, even his private desires. And given their history of hostility and wars, he must have been preparing for the worst while pushing his plans to achieve the best. But how and in what way? And how was his son connected to any of this, he and his sudden deflection to the enemy's side, his sudden change of behavior?

"Yes, I suppose it could indicate a sense of belonging," he said easily, putting his doubts away. For the time being. "So you think he feels completely at home here? Doesn't he miss his countryfolk? He must miss at least the members of his immediate family."

Again her braids jumped with much vigor. "He doesn't miss his family members, because he left them long before he came here. He has a nasty stepmother, and a bunch of stupid half siblings he has no connection with. Even his father, admirable person as he is… was…" The frown was back, replaced by the previous thoughtfulness quickly. "Even this man was never close to Ogteah, was never a real father to him. So no, he misses no one. He loves his new life, and his new family here." Again, the smile caught him unprepared, its openness and its wonderful warmth. "Your family, your father and you, oh you've been like a true family to him, and he does appreciate it, I know he does. I can see it most clearly. You gave him a sense of family that he has never had before."

Almost against his will, her words touched him. Did they mean so much to this strange man, a curious foreigner with unpredictable ways? Did he truly know no family before?

"Where did he go?" she was asking, peering at him with that typical wide-open gaze of hers. "When might he be coming back?"

He concentrated again. "I can't answer either of your questions. He may detour by your village on his way back, which should not be too long from now. But then he would probably be off again. It's a serious enterprise he chose to become a part of, but it's nothing that would not make you proud." Shrugging, he grinned back at her, still not completely at ease, but feeling better for some reason, not as unsettled by her looks as before. It's not that he was envying her to the Crooked Tongues man, he reasoned. Nothing of the sort! It's just that something in him didn't wish to let that first memory of her go, not entirely. "If he does well, it will make your grumpy brother shut his mouth for good, trust me on that."

That made her laugh in a delightfully uninhibited manner. "But for such a chance!" Then the frown was back, clouding the loveliness of a smile. "Will you tell me what happened to him through the days of the gathering? I heard so many rumors, all sorts of nasty stories, each more colorful than the other. He was involved in a violent fight again, yes? Was it bad?" The large eyes were pleading anew, looking at him searchingly, begging for reassurance.

He sighed. "It wasn't bad, and not entirely his fault. The man he attacked was rude and provoking; he was asking for that fight, ready for it. It was not as though he attacked an innocent man."

"You were there? You saw it all?" Her gaze was clinging to him, hanging on his every word now.

"Yes, I was. It happened during the spear-throwing contest, the event he suggested and managed to organize all by himself." It felt good to reassure her in this way. He didn't try to hold his smile back. "My father was impressed. He helped him all along, gave him advice and support. And so did some others. Many people volunteered to clear the field and help around with teams." He shrugged. "As an organizer, he was among the judges of course. It was his event, and people accepted that. All but that Onondaga Town's man. He didn't like to have a foreigner for a judge, so when his throw wasn't declared better than this of his rival, he took it in a nasty way, made rude remarks, persisted with this. And the Crooked Ton—, and your man, well, you know him. He can be pushed only up to a certain limit. Just a little push is enough in his case."

Her face fell, along with her gaze that dropped to the ground, to study the generous carpet of pinecones and brilliantly green needles when it wasn't marred by the gray of the old fires. "Yes. He tries very hard. He makes great efforts to control his temper, but sometimes, when people push... which they do, readily at that," she added bitterly, looking up resolutely, mouth pressed again, eyes dark. "So many are seeking to pick on someone who might be in a weaker position, foreigners being such a good target. Why can't people just be happy with themselves and their positions, or at least, mind their own business?"

He found nothing better to do than to shrug. Of course there were always people who needed to prove something, looking, indeed, for someone less protected to harass. Yet, it was mainly those weaklings' fault, or so he used to reason. Why allow someone to pick on you? It was just a matter of inner strength, of conviction, of self-confidence, the traits and virtues everyone should be striving to have, shouldn't they? No one ever played with the idea of picking on him or his brother, and no, it had nothing to do with their father's position. Or so he chose to believe.

Foreigners? But why would they feel differently, unless they were weak inside? Mother was a foreigner once upon a time. She still spoke with a trace of an accent, and look how far she had come, an important Clan Mother and one of the leading members of their entire town's Clans Council. While Gayeri's Crooked Tongue was always a violent thing, never fitting, not even among his own people. No, it was his fault he was still getting in trouble, time after time.

"This is how it works," he said finally, her gaze persistent, not letting him get away with a shrug alone. "Some people need to prove stupid things, and it is up to a person not to let them get under one's skin while still not allowing them to tread on you. Foreigners have it no worse than anyone else."

Her eyes held no more openness or adoration. Instead, they gazed at him with surprising animosity, as her lips twisted into an openly derisive smile. "One can see that you never lived outside the comfort of your town and your powerful family."

"That's an undeserved slur—" he began hotly, but she turned her head away so abruptly her braids jumped, in no playful way, not this time.

"Don't talk to me about any of this. Just don't."

A heartbeat of heavy silence had him biting the cutting words back. With what happened two summers ago, the kidnapping and other terrible things, and her living out there with the strangers for enough moons, oh yes, she might have the knowledge she was claiming he didn't have. Still, it meant nothing. One didn't need to experience everything to have an opinion on the matter, which was not possible anyway. Why, Father was captured as a youth too, living some time among those same Crooked Tongues, and there was no stronger, more confident, more powerful man in the entire League of Five Nations. No, foreigners couldn't plead their state to excuse weaknesses and flaws.

"I thank you for reassuring me," she was saying, mouth still pressed uncompromisingly, eyes distant, impossible to read, shuttered. "Thank you for telling me the truth and making me feel better. All those stupid rumors..." Her smile seemed to be forced, even though it had warmer quality to it again. "I... I'm grateful, truly. You are a good man. I'm sorry if I said something harsh now, or on other occasions. You don't deserve it. It's just..." Another attempt at a smile. "Thank you for your kind words about Ogteah. He deserves that, a good treatment without prejudice. He is a good man." The question was there, in the painfully squinting eyes. "The rumors were so nasty, so unjust. They even said he was involved with a woman. My brother kept repeating that. But he didn't know who it was or what happened. Just that the brawl had something to do with that. How nasty can people become?"

Ill at ease, Ganayeda motioned with his head, bringing his hands forward, palms up, telling it all with this noncommittal gesture. Yes, people were nasty. Unless the rumor was true. Not involved as closely as she was, blinded with no strong feelings, he believed that particular tale, which might have explained that Onondaga Town man's inappropriately pushy behavior. If it was his women involved with an unscrupulous foreigner, oh that would have made perfect sense.

"I listen to no such rumors," he said, feeling obliged to respond, as she was still hesitating, not doing the only sensible thing, namely turning to go away. She got her answers, didn't she? Wasn't it time to leave now and let him attend to his duties? Her brother was right about some things, grim and annoying presence that he offered on this particular occasion. She *was* interfering with their duties. "Such rumors are, indeed, nasty and usually have no basis or sense. I wouldn't listen to any of this."

Her smile was again free of shadows, openly grateful, the prettiest of sights. He nodded curtly, his own twist of lips brief.

"Just go back and make his homecoming welcome and warm."

Turning to leave, he shook his head, preparing to withstand the inevitable onslaught of jokes and teasing questioning. Iheks would not be him if he didn't make the most out of the witnessed encounter, surely remembering her from the old times. He contemplated sneaking away, to seek less prominent roads leading back home.

CHAPTER 14

The amount of canoes that swayed in the shallow waters or lined the shorelines up to the steeper inclines was staggering. He tried to count them with his eyes, blinking against the glow of the high noon sun. So many boats! Most of them warriors' vessels, long, sturdy dugouts built to contain up to six men, sometimes more.

How many warriors had this multitude of vessels brought? Must be many hundreds, when originally he counted on no more than a few, ten hundred at the most. Oh, but his people were eager to fight!

The prideful smile threatened to sneak out. He had been right all along. The shameful neutrality was not what his people wanted, despite what the leading elements of Tushuway had claimed before. His people were no cowards, no conformists to lower their heads and accept everything their powerful neighbors chose to throw their way.

Determined to leap out of his canoe as gracefully as he could, Aingahon pushed the unsteady support its sides offered with both hands, struggling to stay upright, swaying together with the boat's vibrating. A challenge for a person poised on only one leg, but he didn't care. As one of the leaders, the initiator of this entire enterprise, he could not be seen crawling out of his vessel, not when so many people were waiting to greet him, ask questions, report, or just to talk and be near.

Was he the official leader of this entire enterprise? He didn't know. Having spent nearly half a moon in the Attiwandaronk north, he felt out of touch, unaware of the political developments in his parts of the land, but the previously uncooperative northern neighbors looked up to him in an unmistakable fashion. They did take him to be the warriors' leader of a prominent rank. Otherwise, they would not consent sending their warriors, not in such staggering numbers. It was a wonder they agreed to listen in the first place.

The twitch in his stomach was back, a strange longing. But for her, or rather her miraculous return, they would not have listened. Their leading settlement made itself clear. Those people were not interested in wars their southern neighbors were eager to pursue against the old-time foe. They had their own problematic neighbors to watch, the suddenly united Wyandot. His claim that as brother-nations with more similar traits in common than not, the unification of the others might warrant their own joining together impressed no one. The stubborn elders had eyed him and his followers coldly then hurried to see them off, politely but firmly. At least that.

He shook his head, remembering that strange afternoon. In no position to insist, having nothing to offer but the plain good sense of his words, he was about to leave as the agitated crowd of women fell upon them, speaking all at once, shouting about ghosts and spirits. When he heard her name, he didn't want to use it as an excuse to stay. The urge to protect her was the one that made him get involved. He had brought her there hoping to find her people and her former settlement, yes, but she was his responsibility. No locals would be allowed to harass her, to scare her off or accuse her of being a ghost. Well, little did he know!

Relieved to be out of the boat and on firm land, he paid no attention to the shallow water that splashed around his ankles, soaking his moccasins, happy to be out with no stumbling incidents involved. She was better off back home, among her family and her people. And if her miraculous return made the elders of her town, influential clan mothers in particular, listen to what he had to say while they hosted him and his men for quite a few days because she wouldn't let him out of her sight in the beginning, then that was that. Two more days and here they were, sending messengers to the surrounding towns and villages, to the north and to the west, apparently having many settlements under this town's influence. The gathering that was subsequently held was satisfactorily large, its result unexpected. In the end, he had headed back home, leading over eight hundred warriors spoiling for a fight. What an achievement! And all thanks to her.

He suppressed a smile, the warmth in his stomach spreading, accompanied with a morsel of longing. The strange girl turned out to be the lucky talisman, just as he had suspected her to be all along. Since the moment she had come to him back there in the woods, playing with her knife, stalking him with her eerie, somehow vacant stare, his life had changed drastically, and only for the best. First the War Chief's removal, and being listened to, and now this, the reinforcement from the neighbors he barely expected to let him enter their towns. What a surprise. And all thanks to her.

Another knot in his stomach was pushed away firmly. She was better off left behind, living normal life of a normal girl. He had nothing to offer her, nothing to give, and they had promised to treat her well. Would they summon enough patience to treat her in the way she needed? He wasn't all that sure, yet there was no other way but to trust them. They were her family. He wasn't.

"For how long had they been camping here?" he asked one of the men who had come to greet them, raising his voice to overcome the roaring of the river, its madly rushing current doubling its efforts not far away from here, as though in a hurry to reach its ultimate destination, the Thundering Water, the most dreadful falls anyone had ever seen.

"The newcomers? For two, three dawns. Those who came first had been spending some time here."

He glanced at the people congregating at the wide strip of land, many men, idling, bubbling with life.

"How did you feed everyone and keep them away from trouble without driving the people of that village into dumping you all into their famous falls?"

Onguiahra was a settlement of a medium size, not an influential town, but not an insignificant village as well. Sitting on the lively, feisty river that connected both great bodies of water, it enjoyed a prominent enough position, hosting many travelers, parties of people set on trading their goods, or even warriors. The thundering falls, called by the same name, Onguiahra or Niagara Falls, demanded that any sailing be done under guidance in this stretch of the watershed, stopped before it was too late for the canoes to opt for detouring by foot.

The man shrugged, rolling his eyes as he did. The rest of his followers smirked, quailing under Aingahon's stern look.

"You should have sent me word. I would have arrived here faster." Pressing his lips, he resumed walking, wishing to reach the settlement and its leading men with little delays. There was no need to anger the locals any more than they had already, even if it was just a village, in no position to voice displeasure, not in the face of such encompassing war enterprise, surely. "We will head out tomorrow with dawn. Find another place to camp. On the enemy lands maybe, eh?"

"The warriors' leaders said people should be organized first, before we head out," ventured one of the men after a long pause.

"And chance the enemy hearing all about our warriors' forces in advance?" He tried not to snort. "Who was supervising this affair until now?"

"Thenaintonto. The elders appointed him, and the Clans Council approved."

Aingahon nodded stiffly, expecting no better from Tushuway's authorities. Still, to hear that he wasn't appointed to lead the force he had managed to gather almost single-handedly hurt.

"They mentioned you many times," added one of the men hurriedly, placating. "They said you are to be one of the leaders as well. There are many who were appointed to help. Such a large force! Twelve hundred warriors, and the others still coming. Not to mention the hordes of the northerners you brought."

"Over a thousand men surely, judging by the amount of the canoes," he muttered, determined not to let this news spoil his mood. "Where are the leaders camping? In the comforts of the village itself, I suppose." It came out bitterly. He moderated his tone. "I will detour by the encampment first, see that this multitude of warriors is settled and well, in good spirits. Was someone attending to that, have people talked to, explained?"

"Oh, well, those who led their own people here are camping out there with their warriors."

Those who led the people here, minor leaders such as himself, all this appointed help. He held his grunt back, seeing more people bearing down on them, their hands raised in a greeting, many of their faces familiar from this or that meeting.

Then the strange sensation was back, and his eyes darted toward the bushes adorning the shore, and the more distant trees of the valley ahead. Could it be? No, it couldn't, he reasoned, incensed by the way his heartbeat raced, with this old mix of warmth and expectation permeating his being. She was back among her people, safe and well set, or as well as she could be. It took many talks and reassurances to make her stay. But it was for the best. It was! For her, and for him as well. He could not continue maintaining this strange relationship, coming out to meet her every now and then, stealing cookies to spoil her, having her killing people who displeased him. Even though he could use her skills now that yet another wrong man had been made leader in his, Aingahon's, stead.

The thought made him grin fleetingly then push the silly musings away. Many eyes were upon him now, naturally, all those hundreds of warriors that he had brought here, even if he wasn't entrusted with leading them, and she was safe with her old family, all those fussing around mothers and aunts.

However, the sensation persisted, and walking the narrow alleys of the village later on, trying to pay no attention to the desperate protests of his knee after so much brisk strolling, he found himself glancing around again and again. What if she didn't stay as he told her to do? What if she followed him despite his persuasion? She could do this easily, make the three, no more than four days' journey, as well as to run away from the people she didn't trust, her family or not. Did he wish her to do so? The thought made him uneasy.

"If we start moving tomorrow, it will be good for the people's mood," one of the leading northerners was saying, walking beside Aingahon briskly, too briskly for his taste. "People are getting restless, camping in this place for so long. The spirits that reside in these terrible falls must be powerful and angry. It is not a good place to stay."

Another of the newcomers, a heavyset man of spectacular appearance made by tattoos and scars aplenty, nodded grimly. "If we don't step on the warpath soon, people will start asking themselves why they bothered to make their journey in the first place."

Rightfully so, reflected Aingahon, trying not to let his impatience show. If it was up to him, the entire force would be moving out and into the enemy lands with the first light, instead of loitering here, doing nothing but wondering. It wouldn't be long before people started picking fights and getting into trouble.

"I will talk to our leaders about it," he said, not looking forward to this particular conversation. Or any other. Was his brief leadership over for good? "I will make sure to relate your words along with my own observations."

Easier said than done. He wanted to shake his head, listening to the commotion that was developing somewhere ahead, behind one of the longhouses. Female voices, therefore nothing to do with his responsibilities. Still, he tried to listen to their shouts.

"There might be a meeting of the war leaders," said one of the men helpfully. "The War Chief would be attending that. I'll send someone to find out where and when."

Why didn't you until now? thought Aingahon, making an effort to conceal his bitterness. What was he doing here in the town if the man he came to meet here wasn't around at all?

"Do that."

The voices were drawing nearer, and he couldn't help but try to decipher their words. Agitated females. Last time he heard those, it was about Tsutahi. He strained his ears in an effort to hear.

"I saw her this morning, I'm sure I did. Near the fields of our family, just behind the Porcupine Clan's mounds."

His stomach tightened some more as his legs took him toward the shouts. Not again! Was everyone who glimpsed her thought her to be a ghost? How stupid! But this was not her town, not her family. These people might hurt her if they thought her to be something outside of their world, maybe.

"Well, it's well into the end of the day now, sister, and she is nowhere to be found." Another voice, more agitated than the first, followed by more exclamations. "Not in the fields she was supposed to be, nor anywhere around the town."

The group of women was large and colorful, with quite a few young birds and not only elderly matrons among them. His companions slowed their paces as well.

"Maybe she is strolling the riverside, enjoying the view," ventured one of the younger girls, to the open giggling of the others. "Her husband is dead for too long to be of—"

The elder women's gazes made the uncalled-for outburst of mirth subdue quickly. Aingahon made a face, his relief welling. Nothing to do with Tsutahi, surely now.

He looked at his companions, relaying a message. This was not the time to listen to gossip or enjoy certain sights, even though the younger women were studying the ground now, demurely at that. All of them but one, a pretty little thing, busy stealing glances at him. He looked her over briefly, not about to be distracted by anything of this sort, not before the possible confrontation with the newly appointed war leader.

"Since caught skulking around the War Leaders' meeting last night, no one saw her, just no one," one of the women went on, her eyes gleaming with a certain amount of excitement, lightening the troubled frown.

"But it was on the day before, sister, and she did sleep in her longhouse, or so her family tells us."

"What happened?" asked one of Aingahon's companions, clearly a local man. "Who is missing?"

"The Porcupine Clan's sister," answered one of the women readily. "The one who was married to Yakwe."

"Her again?" The man's voice piqued with keen interest. "She was sneaking around our War Council's gathering yesterday. I remember the uproar it created." His smirk turned into a puzzled frown. "So where is she now?"

"That's the thing, no one knows." One of the younger women positively glowed with excitement. "She disappeared after doing the unspeakable last night. Even though she was a foreigner, she should have known better, shouldn't she?"

"The foreigner?" Now it was Aingahon's turn to burst into the conversation, his interest piquing. "What sort of a foreigner?"

"Well, she was adopted," one of the elder women informed him importantly. "Long time ago. She is a member of our Porcupine Clan, and a good member at that. It was not like her to eavesdrop on our War Council. There must be another explanation to this incident."

"And her disappearance," added the first woman pointedly. "It does sound fishy, sister. You must admit that."

Aingahon paid their exchange no attention. "Who were her former people?"

Their answer had him turning around abruptly, forgetting about his knee. Stifling a groan, he put most of his weight on his good leg, before beginning to walk away briskly, aware of the gazes.

"Send for me the moment one of you manages to locate the War Chief," he tossed over his shoulder, not bothering to look back.

The Mountain People! But of course. He should have expected that. And if the treacherous former adoptee indeed hadn't been seen since the early morning, then she might be well away by now, running as fast as she could, or worse yet, speeding in some small boat, the filthy fox that she was. Two, three days and she would be telling her dirty former countryfolk, not only the size of their warriors' forces, but some of their possible planning as well, just witness her alleged skulking around the War Council meeting. Something their new leader should have made sure to keep a secret, the location of the meeting. But then…

He ground his teeth, making his way down the incline, longing for the walking stick he didn't dare to use, not since Tushuway. To limp was ugly but more honorable. Walking device proclaimed of disability.

Be fair, he admonished himself, diving into the blissful shadow of the small grove that separated the settlement from the river. Everyone knew the custom, and no one would think of displaying such bad manners as trying to pry into the leading warriors' affairs. Even small children knew better than that, so of course there was no need to keep the actual meeting place a real secret. No war council bothered with this. And yet...

And yet, now here it was, a nosy snake that went homesick all of a sudden, after summers of being a perfect member of the community, according to the local woman who must have known her well. A respectable matron at that, not a person to like someone without a good case. So maybe it would still come to nothing; maybe this formerly captive woman was just lost in the woods, eaten by forest predators, fallen off the dreadful falls. But for such a chance!

The bushes in front of him didn't rustle, but something made him snap back to the present at once, his muscles going rigid, senses probing, reaching out, trying to locate the intruder. People's voices were coming from many directions, the calm hum of the huge gathering and the town he had left behind. Yet, in this small enclosure between the thick lines of trees and the bushes, it was only him and the eyes, that familiar cozy sensation.

Hand still on the hilt of his knife, just in case, he leaned forward, then motioned with his head. *Come out.*

There was no need to say those words aloud, even had she been able to hear them. Reinforced with a grin, he knew it would work better than words.

Indeed, she materialized in front of him, as she always did, slipping from behind the cover of the trees like a forest creature— not an *uki*, not her!—with those quick no-nonsense movements of hers. Familiar and different at the same time.

Puzzled, he studied her. The nice-looking dress, wrinkled and splattered with mud, but not a worn out rag like she used to wear, with some of its decorations still intact; the nicely combed hair, braided and not just pulled together with a semblance of a band. Her face looked different too, rounder than he remembered, pleasantly bright. No more unhealthy pallor, even though her cheeks did not shine with a purplish glow only the sun could give. Oh, yes, she had already been losing her previously wild look when he had left, but not to this extent. The girl who was gazing at him seemed older, more womanly. Only her eyes remained the same, studying him with wariness, gauging his reactions, ready to flee. The old Tsutahi of the first summer moon.

"Are you well?" he asked, somewhat at a loss, not knowing what to say, her wariness throwing him off balance. She hadn't looked at him like that since the very beginning, since he had spoken to her for the first time and made her come with him to the town of his people.

No reaction. Like the good old times. He felt like flopping his arms in helplessness. But such gesture might scare her into fleeing. Oh, yes, back to the first days of their acquaintance, before the warriors' forces, before the War Chief. He shuddered.

"Why are you afraid of me?" Carefully, he brought one arm forward, palm up, displaying his harmless intentions.

She winced, and for a heartbeat, it seemed as though she was going to flee after all. Then she froze again, eyes on his eyes. Not his lips.

"Talk to me. Tell me what's wrong, what made you run away from your people." He made sure his gaze reflected the forcefulness of his tone. Oh, yes, it was back to the old days. "Tell me!"

She shuddered so visibly, his heart went out to her. If he dared, he would have pressed her shoulders between his palms, would have reassured her with this simple gesture as he used to do such a short time ago. Had it been only a moon since they left for her people's lands?

"Come," he said, when she kept peering at him, a hint of expectation creeping into the bottomless darkness of her eyes. Now, with her face having filled out and her skin taking a healthy, soft glow, her eyes turned into something quite beautiful, he noticed, unsettled by the thought. She was still just a child, a wild girl, wasn't she?

"Let us find a quieter spot than this one, shall we?"

Unless you are not afraid of people anymore, he wanted to add, knowing better than to do that. To make jokes at her expense wasn't an admirable thing to do.

Beckoning her to follow, he began retracing his steps uphill, slowing down in the hope that she would understand. It was her chance to take the lead now, to find the place that felt safe enough for her. A part of their old routine, but he wasn't sure of any of that anymore.

"Where were you hiding until now?" he asked, when she didn't proceed as expected but just hovered next to him, quiet in her old, somewhat disturbing way.

Out of habit, he glanced at her hands, surprised to see no familiar form of a bundle that was always wrapped around her bow, concealing. His stomach twisted violently. Did they put their filthy paws on her bow? Had they taken it from her, by force maybe? Oh, but if they didn't treat her well...

She stiffened under his gaze, and her eyes grew rounder, filling with fright. Desperately, he tried to push the welling wave of rage away. If he burst out in angry questioning, she wouldn't talk to him at all. It was back to their first days, when he didn't know how to treat her, how to handle the unpredictable sort of creature she was. But back then, he didn't care.

"Tell me what happened, Tsutahi. You must talk to me now, tell me everything." The use of her name seemed to shake the frozen quality of her stare. Just a little, but he could see it. There was no mistaking the familiar flicker. She *was* listening. "Tell me, little one. When did you leave that town of yours? How long has it taken you to travel here?"

Now her eyes slid down toward his lips. He wanted to let out a breath of relief, or maybe even did. His ears were focused on her sounds, not the ones he was making.

"Six dawns." Again that strident, unmelodious, too-loudly-pitched voice. Oh, but he missed that sound.

"Six dawns?" He felt his grin spreading, not the forced thing to make her feel better, but a real one. "But you became slow, girl. Six dawns to travel here? We covered it in less than four and we were sailing in a hundred canoes, coordinating our movements and all."

Her eyes widened with unmistakable fire, sparkling under the suddenly furrowed brow. The gaping mouth completed the familiar picture. He didn't try to hold his laughter back. Which only deepened her indignation.

"I traveled by foot!" she cried out, when finding her tongue in the end. "I didn't sail in a canoe. It's more difficult by foot, and I wasn't always sure of the way."

"You never traveled between there and here before?"

The negative sway of her head was so vigorous it made her disheveled braids fly.

"Why did you run away?" he asked, losing his briefly gained sense of amusement.

Her shrug was like that of a pouting child.

"They didn't treat you well?"

Another shrug, accompanied by pressed lips this time.

"Tell me," he insisted, needing to know. "Why did you leave?" Surer of himself now that their old communication was back, he stepped forward, taking her shoulders between his palms, pressing them lightly but firmly, like back near her town, when forcing her into facing her people. He clenched his teeth. "Tell me what happened. How long did you stay after we left?"

She didn't look up, but like back then, she relaxed in his grip so visibly it tore at him, her obvious trust, and that after he had managed to let her down already.

"I couldn't stay," she said quietly, her voice unusually low, like the breath of a soft breeze. "I just couldn't. I had to go and find you. I don't want to, don't want to be away. Please?" Now the huge eyes were upon him, sparkling unshed tears. "Please. Don't take me back. I don't want to live there. I can't."

The knot in his throat was forming too rapidly, interfering with his ability to breathe. "I won't make you go back. You can stay, of course you can."

How? He didn't know the answer to that. There was none. But maybe he'd be able to settle her in Tushuway, somehow? Make the women of his longhouse care for her until he returned? But then what?

She was pressing against his chest, trembling lightly. "I can do things for you," she was muttering, as though thinking aloud. "I can be of use. Like with those men. I have my bow. I never brought it into the town, so no one took it. No one even tried.

They could not; they didn't know. It was only my knife, but I didn't let them take it. Even though they tried."

More trembling. He felt like shivering himself. Not so much at the careless mention of the killings—he would have to make sure she didn't talk about any of it anymore, most firmly at that—as at the vividness of the images his mind was painting; of her, frightened and alone, haunted, afraid, yet still strong, determined not to let them touch her precious weaponry—such an inappropriate thing for a good girl to have, let alone carry around wherever she went—standing up to the forceful women of her clan, and men, and everyone really. How could he have let her down so? And yet, what would happen in Tushuway and among the women of his clan, should he ask them to take her in? The same thing but worse, with total strangers...

"It's good, good that you didn't let them have your weapons," he muttered, not caring that while pressed against his chest she could not possibly hear any of his words. "It was a mistake. I shouldn't have made you stay."

"Can I stay?" she asked, peeking up carefully, snuggled in his embrace, not showing signs of willingness to leave.

He shifted uncomfortably. There were many people around here, too many for his peace of mind, all looking up to him, trusting him to solve the problems. The briefly gained privacy wouldn't last, and what would he say if caught hugging an underage girl of dubious origins.

Steering her away gently, he tried to achieve as light of an expression as he could.

"You don't have to ask for my permission to stay." Her face fell, and he felt the wave of compassion returning. "But it's good to have you around. I wondered about you and planned to visit after all this was over." Casually, he waved at the river and the hum of so many voices emanating from there. "After we have shown our filthy neighbors from the lands of the rising sun."

Her smile was back, flashing readily, free of shadows again. "You have so many people here, so many warriors. I looked, and I couldn't believe my eyes! I never saw so many people in one place. In all my life. Even back in that town! Even in yours." Her beam faded a little. "Back in that town, you see, there were many people inside their fence, scary how many. They were running all over, and talking, and pushing, and, well..." The painfulness of her frown squeezed his heart, as did her obvious fight for control reflecting in it. "They are not crowding in one place, you see? But here, oh my, I kept trying to count these warriors. On the day before the last one, when I came here, oh, but it was such a sight. I kept trying to count them, and I failed!"

He felt his grin spreading again, remembering the sight of so many canoes covering the shoreline up to the forested hills.

"I know how you felt. I had the same startle today, when I arrived. The amount of boats that are piled upon the shore made the ground underneath it invisible." Shaking his head, he listened to the nearing voices, knowing that he had no time for idle talk, not even with her. Still, she had been here for a few days, as always, an observant little thing. "Have you spent a few dawns here, then?"

She nodded readily, making her nicely thick braids jump. "I came here after I learned that you are not in your town. I thought you would be coming straight here, where your warriors are."

"Good thinking." As always. But this girl could have made such a good warrior. "Do you sleep somewhere around here? With so many people everywhere, how did you manage to find a quiet corner, unless under the dreadful falls themselves?"

"I managed," she said, looking very smug indeed. "I always manage."

"That you do." Still, he didn't like the idea of her sleeping out there, unprotected, despite her fierceness and her way with the weapons. People who came to join his war were no villagers of different sexes and ages. Hardened, or even just aspiring, warriors wouldn't find it difficult to sneak up on her undetected, to disarm her and maybe do her some harm.

"Why are you looking at me like that?" she demanded, her forehead furrowing again. "You are still angry?"

"No," he said, shaking his head slowly, thinking hard. "But I don't want you to sneak around the way you did before. If I let you stay, it would be on my terms." Holding her gaze, he made his voice ring stonily, even though the sound itself would be wasted on her. "Do you understand? If you don't listen to me and do what you want instead, I won't let you stay."

The huge eyes were filling with fear again. What happened to the unruly forest creature who did exactly as she pleased, concerned with nothing and no one? Did she change together with her clothes?

"I don't want you to sleep outside anymore, Tsutahi," he went on, determined. "Or sneak everywhere with no purpose. For now, you will sleep where I sleep, here in the valley. Then, later on, we'll see how we go about it. You will have to stay in Tushuway until I come back."

Now her eyes widened with horror. As she began shaking her head vigorously, he kept holding her gaze, afraid that he had taken it too far. If she bolted away or just dove into the bushes, he wouldn't be able to catch her, not even a glimpse of her. And what if she didn't come back anymore?

She hesitated, actually taking a step back, holding the other foot in the air, ready to run.

"Don't," he said tiredly. "If you came all the way here, you may stick around as well."

"I won't stay in your town," she muttered, her frown as petulant as that of a stubborn child. "I will stay with you."

He exhaled loudly, relieved on one count. She was not going to bolt for the woods. "With me where? In the lands of the rising sun they can use a good shooter, can't they?"

Her scowl could rival that of the thundercloud. "I can be of use. Like before." Another loaded pause. "I *do* shoot well."

Shaking his head, he motioned her to come. "It's different in wars, girl. Shooters like you have nothing to do out there, not with so many warriors attacking. I haven't fought with such numbers myself, let alone led them. We will have to feel our way in this raid, you see?" Suddenly, the ridiculousness of continuing to talk like that dawned. "Just come with me now, and we'll see how to settle you later on. I won't force you into anything you don't want to do. Good? Does this promise satisfy you?" Her adamantly pursed mouth was his answer, her eyes avoiding his. Likely he was just wasting his words now. "I'll try to think of a better solution, but it will be something that won't involve sleeping in the woods while skulking around towns, hunting occasional rabbits. It's not a life for a girl, and you are not such a child anymore. You need a home, family, friends, you know?"

Still no response, even though she was walking beside him obediently, stealing glances. At least that.

"Tell me what happened here since the days of your arrival," he said when the clamor of the shore was back upon them, not welcoming the looming necessity to explain her presence or mere existence to the people. They all would be wondering, asking questions or just staring. "Were there many warriors here already when you came?"

She nodded readily, disclosing that her glances were just to relay her displeasure. So not all what he said was wasted. Good.

"Were there any troubles? People shouting or fighting things out?"

A vigorous jump of both braids insisted on a no.

"But there was that woman from the village," she said, again shouting in an irritating manner. "They were talking about it all over the place yesterday. Yelling and screaming."

"How do you know they were doing all this?" he asked absently, his mind on the meeting with the leaders. "Do you hear better now?"

Her grin held nothing but smugness. "One can see that. Easily. All those waving hands and faces the color of the storm cloud or purple like decorations." Her giggle was surprisingly soft and rolling. "Also, I can hear people's lips, remember? So I know what they are saying, even from far away. Better than you if you try to listen from afar."

Little bragger. He suppressed a chuckle.

"So what happened with this woman? What did she do?"

"Oh, the stupid fowl ran away."

That stopped his progress. "Why do you say that?" he asked, turning to face her, now anxious not to miss a word. "They are still looking for her. They think she might have gotten lost in the woods or something. No one said a thing about running away.

Why would she do that? It would make no sense."

Some of the previous scowl was back, laced with a generous amount of smugness as yet. "Because I know. They don't. They just run around and fume. And do nothing."

He brought his hands up. "Just tell me. Tell me what you know, and do it quickly." Curbing his impatience, he tried not to think of the implications, not until he heard her tale. "Tell me quickly and with no bragging, Tsutahi. It's important. Exactly what did you see or hear?" Oh, Mighty Spirits, but if the treacherous fox indeed managed to reach her former people, and with such news...

For a heartbeat she looked undecided, the scowl and the serenity fighting each other across her lively features.

"I saw this woman sailing away," she said finally, peering at him from under her brow. "I saw her taking a canoe and starting down that creek that flows toward their other river." Her lips twisted with contempt. "She took a small boat. Stupid fowl, she was so clumsy. I would have taken a midsize canoe if I was her." The smugness was back, more pronounced than before. "Even though I can maneuver the smallest vessel ever. Grandfather taught me all about it. We had this tiny slick boat, and could it move with great speed!"

As expected, her face darkened visibly, and the flow of complacent words stopped, like always at the mention of the old man. His heart twisted, but his mind was too busy for spells of compassion.

"When did it happen? When exactly?"

Her forehead wrinkled. "Some time after dawn. No, a lot of time. The sun was not very high as yet, you see. But it was out there for some time." A guilty shrug. "I slept late. It was not a quiet night, you see? Even on this other side of the hill where I slept, because so many people were sniffing around, warriors and the others."

Half a day, he thought frantically, his mind racing. Maybe more. With the easily guessable destination of the treacherous rat, a group of warriors may try to catch up with her. If they headed out immediately, this very evening, with no delay.

"Come with me," he said urgently, resuming his walk. The sun was already too low, promising little daylight. Not good. A whole day of traveling ahead of the traitor. But for his knee he would have plunged into a boat himself, this very evening, night traveling or not. It was imperative to stop that woman. Or maybe not so much. The others might not see the destructive potential, might think it was not that unthinkable that the enemy hear about their plans, or the size of their forces this time. What could they do against thousands of warriors?

"Where are you going?" she was asking, peering at him anxiously, her eyebrows creating a single line.

"I want you to tell our leaders all about it, everything you saw." Her protests were forming again, rapidly at that. He touched her shoulder lightly. "I will be with you all the way, won't let you out of my sight. You have nothing to be afraid of." Slowing his step, he peered at her, holding the stormy gaze again. "I won't leave you alone, not this time. You trust me, don't you? Back in your town, you agreed to stay behind, but I should have known better. Now I do. I won't let you be taken anywhere. You will stay with me until we start moving."

As soon as they are ready, he thought uneasily. Tomorrow if he could help it. Did the deflection of the filthy fowl change things?

"You want to go after her."

He paid her words no attention, too busy thinking, the briskness of their walk taking some of his concentration away. The damn knee! But for this thing he would be sailing himself now. She was right about that.

"It's important to stop her, isn't it? Not to let her reach her people." Her voice came as a welcome distraction.

He rolled his eyes. "It is, but I'm not certain others will see it this way."

"Why?"

"She is heading for her former people, about to warn them, you see." To talk about it helped. As always. Oh, but he forgot how good it was to air his thoughts with her, even though they did not enjoy their usual privacy here. "They can do nothing against such a huge force. Still, a surprise would be a welcome addition, would give us more freedom to act. To split our forces for one. Think about it. A timely warning would give them the opportunity to fortify their towns, to take their villages in. Not the end of our plans, but it is still an unnecessary complication." He flipped his hands in the air. "Who would have thought that a treacherous adoptee would go for such low means?"

"She was a widow," she related, herself deep in thought. "The women said her husband was dead and she has no children." A shrug. "Maybe she has nothing to stay for."

As always, the spell of surprisingly deep wisdom, and just as one would expect nothing of the sort. He gave her a doubtful look. "Her status has nothing to do with it. She betrayed her people, people who had adopted her and put their trust at her. She has no right to live, not after that."

"You would have gone after her?" Her eyes were narrow with concentration.

"If I could, yes. But it won't be possible, unless our leaders agree to send a warriors party." Then the suspicion surfaced. "Don't play with wild ideas."

No response. She was looking at the ground that was sweeping under their feet. He studied her thoroughly. But no, she wouldn't contemplate doing something like that. It was too wild, even for her. And yet...

He touched her shoulder lightly. "Tsutahi, what are you thinking about?"

Her face beamed at him, alight with excitement. "Nothing. Let us go and talk to your leaders, the ones you wanted me to meet. I promise to tell them all I know. I won't be acting wild. I promise." The mischievous glint flickered, impossible to miss. Oh, but she had changed. Again, the thought that it was inappropriate for her to run all over the woods, sneaking around and eavesdropping on people, surfaced. He would have to do something about it, convince her somehow. How?

CHAPTER 15

"I say, that's quite a sight!"

Balancing himself with a certain effort while standing full length in the narrow dugout they were sailing, Ogteah shielded his eyes with his good hand, staring at the long strip of land that lay before him, packed to the brim with vessels of many colors and sizes. It was as though the sand were not there at all, as though the entire shoreline was made out of wooden mounds.

His companions to the traveling smirked, but didn't ask him to sit back, even though their rowing was interrupted by his spontaneous exercise of jumping in the unsteady vessel.

"We haven't been working for nothing, have we?" Akweks' sweaty face beamed at him, the streaks of mud standing out in surprisingly intricate lines, like war paint. "Sit down, man of vigor. We don't have time to watch you thrashing in the water, fighting for your life." Dipping his paddle in the creek with more spirit than before, he caused the boat lurch, waver slightly to one side. "Don't count on me diving to fish you out. I've been rowing since sunrise."

Leaning his body toward the other side, trying to make it look like an easy thing—which it wasn't, not with the strip of cloth soaked with a generous amount of ointment that was still tied around the stupid wound he had acquired in the Standing Stone People's lands—Ogteah heard their third companion muttering under his breath.

"That's the most you can do?" he asked when sure of his stance once again. "You'll have to work harder to get rid of me."

"Gladly!"

This time, the Flint's paddle landed in the water with such force their canoe careened to one side, making even the sitting men fight for balance.

"Stop playing games, you two!" The other rower wasn't amused in the least, nor was Ogteah himself, now clutching the polished wood of the boat's side with his good arm, struggling to stop the rest of his fall with one of his knees.

Successful, even if only partly, he straightened up. "You wildest piece of rotten meat, I'll kill you when I have a chance. The moment I'm rid of this stupid sling."

Not really a sling, the annoying piece of cloth was a hindrance, with its need to be replaced every now and then, to be soaked in a revolting-smelling brew the healer insisted was good to make the wound dry. Back in the lands of the Standing Stone, after the silly brawl, his cuts had been tended to, the one on his arm stitched and its bleeding stanched. Still, for some reason, it wasn't healing as fast as it should, now close to fifteen dawns later, still wet at places, its crust peeling off with no proper scar tissue underneath. Later on, the Lone Hill's healer claimed that it happened due to the delay in treatment, which indeed had been long in coming. None of those involved wanted the silly brawl to become public knowledge, Ogteah more than anyone, even though he wasn't a guilty party, not this time. So they had gone about it in silence, which resulted in his arm not being treated properly, not right away.

Well, at this point, it didn't matter, he knew, making himself comfortable in the middle of their boat, at his originally designated place. It wasn't rotting, his village's and several other healers assured him, just taking longer to recover, and it was actually good that the injury gave him a perfect excuse and an opportunity to detour through home.

Gayeri was ecstatic to have him back, not bringing up any troublesome matters from Onondaga Town's gathering. Instead, she had set about making him feel like an important dignitary returning home, fussing around his wounds, making the most renowned healer inspect him, then, reassured, setting out to cook the richest meal their storage room could provide in this time of the seasons, packing it up and dragging him out and into the woods, to spend the most pleasant half a day he had ever remembered. Plenty of lovemaking, good food, happy chatter, with her shining brighter than the high noon summer sun, oh, but it did make him feel the happiest of men, more alive than ever.

Even her brief confession about visiting Onondaga Town and talking to the High Springs man did not dampen his spirits. She said she had been told only good things and that the dirty loser who couldn't throw his spear straight had no right to make him, Ogteah, so mad with anger. It was all this man's fault, and as far as she had heard, he hadn't been held responsible for any of it.

An encouraging development that cheered him up, even though he knew she might have been choosing to listen to only certain opinions. Oh, yes, that was her, fiercely loyal, a mountain lioness all right, a quality that had been more and more prominent in her with the passing of moons and in the safety of her hometown. A pleasing development. She was a partner worth having, a woman worthy of love, something he had never believed existed before her. A welcome surprise.

"Here we are!"

The canoe jerked, pulling him out of his reverie and straight into the reality of the bright sand and so many vessels and people his head reeled. Like both gatherings he had witnessed but worse, more crowded, more agitated.

A good bit of organization could be of benefit here, he reflected, leaping out of the boat, helping to drag it onto the shore, searching for a vacant space, not a readily available commodity here. The High Springs man, didn't this one arrive here yet? According to the gossip inundating Lone Hill, the organizer of the Great Council's last meeting had been forced to absorb quite a few frowns and maybe even an open reprimand regarding the dubious recruiting activity that made the entire lands of the Five Nations boil. Some said he had been admonished severely; others claimed that, on the contrary, the authorities gave the man the command of the entire enterprise, made him the leader of the huge force.

Gayeri said that neither was true. Connected to a good source of information, having the most direct link to the Great Council itself, she of course would know, even though she protested that her father said nothing, that he would never share anything important that shouldn't be shared. Her brother was the one to sniff this story out while visiting Onondaga Town after the Great Gathering, she related, giggling as they loitered on the banks of the prettiest spring, enjoying its coolness and the wonderful privacy it provided.

He tried to tuck his smile away, aware of the sharp twinge of longing. Oh, but without the old fears she had turned out to be an insatiable beast, forcing him to beg for mercy. Not that he was at his best on that day, after the tiring journey and with his wound still wet and hurting, sapping his strength. One might wish to prepare better for a day-long picnic with a young wife full of love and desires, the beautiful fox who was getting "hungrier" as the moons passed. Weren't women supposed to cool after settling with a man? Apparently, his first attempt at a settled life back in his hometown was no indication. Or maybe it was her, Gayeri, a wonder beyond comprehension, to behold and cherish and love, and enjoy as much as the wild thing wanted and more. What a woman! So radiant, so full of love and secrets. Or rather, one secret she refused to share, hinting that it was a big thing and that she would tell him all about it, but later, after he returned, weathered and battle-initiated but unharmed. That was her condition, that he had to come back unharmed. Otherwise, no secret, she pouted, and he knew that under the childish play she was worried, anxious, troubled for real by his first foray into fighting and wars.

As though there was something to worry about, he had told her, teasing her with kisses that went nowhere. He had been to his share of violent things, and how much different could warriors encounters be? He wasn't the one required to lead and organize. Just wave his club, or rather a spear, run around, and make frightening noises. No sweat, and not much more danger than an evening of a bowl game with hotheads who didn't know how to lose.

"Are you sleeping with your eyes open?" Akweks' elbow made

its way into his ribs, unobstructed this time. "Oh, you *are* sleeping, brother. Well, wake up. Time to have some action, now that we've arrived."

"Where is Okwaho, and the others?"

The wide palm swept in a wide half-circle, indicating an indefinite "out there."

"Somewhere." The young man's forehead furrowed. "Either here, in the thickest of it, or up there in the town. Considering the great leader that this boy has become, it can be excused to assume that he is enjoying a comfortable, pampered life now."

"I doubt that." Not bothering to hide his amusement, Ogteah shook his head. "He would be busy ensuring no mess came out of his grand enterprise before puffing up and starting to live high. If it goes wrong, the already-irritated authorities would make sure to push him so low the bottom of the darkest caves would look like Sky World to him."

"He won't make a mess out of it!" protested the ever-loyal Akweks, losing some of his perpetual good humor. "He knows what he is doing, and he is right about it, too."

"I didn't say he wasn't." Now it was Ogteah's turn to smirk into his companion's darkening face. "But that's not what the authorities back home might be thinking, and for that reason, if for no other, he would have to work hard now, proving himself and his claims after going out of his way in twisting the Great Council's arm." A shrug proved a helpful gesture in straightening his bag on his shoulder more comfortably. "So no high living for our wolf man. Not for a while."

"Oh, you and your spells of deep thinking, *foreigner*." As always, the spectacular Flint was regaining his good spirits fast. "You are more likable when you are playing betting games, displaying no interest in politics and big affairs."

"I like myself better this way, oh yes," admitted Ogteah, unperturbed. Which set the rest of their company smirking as well. "So what do we do now that this huge flock of warriors is herded in, all rounded and trapped on this strip of a shore?"

"We go and look for Okwaho, see what's in the plans." Stretching, the showy Flint flexed his formidable muscles, eyes traveling the forested hill, sliding toward the narrow strip of water and the shores of the other side, not far away from where they stood. This lake was narrow but long. "Some of our newly gathered forces must be camping up there in the countryside. Maybe near that main town of theirs. What was it called?"

"Tsonontowan." This came from a group of men who were passing by, emerging from a nearby trail, the speaker's accent pronounced, leaving nothing to wonder about. The locals.

The nearest man's narrowing eyes measured them fleetingly, matter-of-fact, not missing the signs of their recent traveling. "Where did you come from?"

"From all over the place." The fierce Flint clearly didn't like to be dismissed like a simple visitor. "Do you know where we find the leaders?"

"Which leaders are you looking for?" The raised eyebrows of the local showed that the man wasn't impressed. "There are plenty of those around here, newcomer. Look for your people out there in the valley, behind that hill." A casual wave of the weathered hand indicated the forested area they had been observing. "Most of the eastern arrivals are camping there."

Akweks' chest thrust forward in no promising manner. "We aren't just wandering warriors, local man," he said, ominously quiet. "We've been working hard to make this gathering happen, and you better tell us how we find the leading men of this entire enterprise and not just heads of warriors' groups."

The local man's jaw protruded stubbornly, and he didn't take a step back under the Flint's sudden advance. If anything, he seemed as though deliberating the advisability of stepping forward himself. The rest of the locals were scrutinizing them with their gazes, also not overly welcoming.

Ogteah tried not to roll his eyes. "Look, people," he said reasonably, or so he hoped, stepping forward as well, ready to insert himself between the two would-be rivals, who were still glaring at each other, neither about to give in. He wasted no time on observing them. Instead, his eyes focused on the rest of the group. "We've been traveling long and hard to get here in time, after being busy for more than a moon with this whole thing. We are to report to the Onondaga leading warriors, preferably the man with the wolf tattoo. Is there any chance you can tell us where this man or some of his following can be located?"

That took the others' attention off the intensifying staring contest.

"The man with the wolf tattoo?" One of the locals wrinkled his forehead, as though thinking hard. "He must be out there in the valley now. Or maybe he went back to the town. There was supposed to be a meeting of the leaders this afternoon, wasn't there?" The questioning gaze went back to his peers. "Or were they going to hold it out there in the woods?"

The rest shrugged in perfect unison, all but their first speaker, who was still busy glaring at Akweks. Gauging the dangerous Flint's reactions, was Ogteah's conclusion; afraid of a possible attack, wishing to be ready.

"I thank you for your help," he said gravely, wishing to chuckle inside. With the short-tempered Flint around and ready to pick fights, his role of conciliator, the one to solve conflicts by words and not deeds was starting to look permanent. Him, of all people. He hid his smirk. "Let us go and find Okwaho."

Placing his palm on his friend's back, he felt it flinching under his touch. Was this one truly ready to pick a fight right there on the shore, before they even had time to land properly? But this young buck was worse than himself in some things, something he still found hard to believe at times.

"Do you know the man with the wolf tattoo personally?" asked the first local, startled. With the immediate threat of violence gone, he was recovering faster than his Flint opponent, who was still staring, stiff with rage.

"Yes, we do. We've been working on his behalf among our people in the lands of the rising sun."

"But you are an Onondaga." The narrowed eyes were appraising him closely, with calm interest and not a hint of hostility. "Aren't you?"

"Yes, I am," he said firmly, not about to dive into his own twisted history. "But we are one people now. Five families, one longhouse. So what does it matter at what family's hearth I choose to spend my time or for what family I may wish to fight?"

A light shrug was his answer. "True, brother. Well, let us show you where you find our mutual leader. The wolf man is a good man."

"He is. A true leader too!" Akweks burst into the conversation, relatively calm now and, evidently, deeming it a high time to regain his prominence. "Okwaho was the man who made it all possible."

"Well, it's not like our people had been idling, waiting for you mighty rescuers to paddle in," observed the spiky local, this time only mildly irritated. "We've been warring against our filthy neighbors with much success, and the idea of teaching them a valuable lesson while using our Great League's combined warriors' power has been circulating here since before the Cold Moons."

"With this same Okwaho in the lead!" cried out Akweks, getting angry again.

Why was he so touchy? wondered Ogteah briefly, focusing his attention on the local man. "So you think he might be out there, behind that hill? With the arriving warriors?"

This time, another man nodded his affirmation. The first local was again busy with a new contest of burning glares.

Ogteah felt like groaning aloud. Where did the vital, teasing, easygoing Akweks of the Onondaga Town's valley and their earlier days in the east go? What had happened to this one since the brawl out there in the Standing Stone People's town? He had been hurt on the account of this silly incident, the innocent party; yet, he had managed to forget all about it by now, even though the stupid wound refused to heal well. While the spectacular Flint remained agitated like a wild bear with a splinter stuck in its paw, or a prickly fruit tucked under its tail, ready to explode at the slightest provocation of this or that foreign company, which so often crossed their paths now. Was he to keep an eye on this hothead for the duration of the entire war?

"Come," he said curtly, surprising himself with the uncompromising sternness of his own tone, the cold order in it. "We need to hurry."

Astonishingly, they all turned to follow, even the local toughs. He wanted to shrug.

"See this trail? It will bring you to the other side of the hill quickly. There, you will find anyone you are looking for."

He nodded his thanks, as did the others. Even Akweks managed to move his head in a gesture that might have resembled an expression of gratitude. Without the locals, the rest of their ascent occurred in relative silence, interrupted by the lively chatter of several passersby as they followed the twists of the trail.

"Quite a sight!"

Pausing on the top of the hill, they stared at the colorful hubbub of people and tents and clothes completed with headdresses below.

"More impressive than the canoes on the shore."

Indeed, reflected Ogteah, hard put not to gape. How many warriors were milling down there? He couldn't even begin to count them all, even if the people had stood there without moving. Which they didn't of course. Like swarms of ants, the dwellers of the valley rushed to and fro, moving in groups, or in pairs, busy above a multitude of fires or just strolling about.

"Like an ant nest," muttered Akweks, echoing Ogteah's thoughts, his previous irritation seemingly forgotten. "How many are down there?"

"Hundreds upon hundreds. Worse than the gathering of the Great Council." Over his own previous foreboding, Ogteah shook his head. "I didn't expect it would come down to something like this. Who could oppose such a horde of warriors? The Long Tails won't even know what hit them."

"They will. We'll let them know that, won't we?" A wink of the impressive Flint held much affection. "Thank you for stopping me from attacking that stupid good-for-nothing. He was strutting around, so full of himself, trying to make us look like humble visitors, so he'd feel better. I hate his type."

Ogteah grinned back, rolling his eyes as he did. "You are too touchy. He just didn't notice straightaway what important dignitaries we are, and it got you going. As though he should have. You are getting offended too easily these days."

"No, I'm not." Making a face, Akweks turned away, surveying the spectacular view one more time. Then his eyes rested on the backs of their companions, already disappearing in the shade of the trail. "Well, instead of musing on my alleged touchiness, let us storm this commotion, man of wisdom. See what they are up to down there."

Quite a lot, it turned out. Even though there was no sight of either the wolf man or his influential brother, they were met by many familiar faces, hundreds of young men from all over the Flint and the Standing Stone and the Onondaga lands in whose company they had spent an evening or two each, speaking of battles and heroic deeds. Apparently, everyone who had listened came. A flattering realization.

Held in the highest of respects, they were fussed about, made comfortable, fed. An attitude that pleased the now-affable Flint greatly, but left Ogteah strangely restless. Where was the wolf man and the other organizers?

Not a youngster like those who surrounded him, he took no pleasure in discussing what should be done to the despicable enemy when they got to the fighting and later on, after the victory. For obvious reasons, such talk made him uneasy. These people were lethal when provoked. And provoked they were now. Brilliantly organized, too. A worrisome realization.

When the shadows began lengthening and his stomach could not take one additional morsel of meat or bread, he had slipped away undetected, wishing to clear his head. The High Springs brothers were due to come back soon, people had promised, after the gathering of the War Council was over, and until then, he had nothing in particular to do anyway.

Following a narrow trail that wound its way up the forested hillside in the direction opposite the lake, he made sure that his bow was balanced easily on his shoulder, not wishing to be caught unprepared by either forest predators or confused locals. Not much chance of people missing the presence of the great assembly that had been fussed over so much, not to mention the clamor it created; still, in foreign lands, one could never be too careful.

The quiet of the woods in the near dusk enveloped him, soothing his nerves. If only Father had been alive. Oh, but would the Great Man have welcomed the tale of thousands of "savages" gathered in one place, ably managed by none other than the sons of his old-time ally among the enemy. What would Father have thought or done? What could he? Was there any way his people, *his former people*, could organize themselves as efficiently to oppose a possible invasion of such magnitude? Somehow he didn't see it happening. Maybe if Deer and Rock People had joined Father's union, maybe then. But with Father gone, what were the chances of that?

Keeping close to the narrowing trail because of the increasingly marshy ground, the last of the sun sparkling off the frequent puddles, pouring its light over the flocks of water fowl that waddled between low vegetation, he heard the growling of the river and hastened his step. Whether it was a mighty flow or just a lively creek, he didn't care. The openness of the shore was a welcome diversion, to sit and relax and think of nothing, while the forest would sometimes seem to close in on him, especially when troubled by problems with no solution, a familiar state of affairs.

To what lengths would this huge horde of warriors go after showing the Long Tails what the Great League was capable of? Would they turn around and go home? Or would they go on, burning villages and towns, unstoppable in their new might, dazzled with their victories, reaching the Rock People's lands on the western side of the Sparkling Water, and then what?

The stony fist squeezed his entrails. Echoed by a high-pitched cry that vibrated the dusky air, it sent his heart leaping straight into his throat. So much desperation!

Rushing along the widening trail, he tried to think fast. The river, was it the cause of all this distress? Was someone's canoe overturned?

Oh, yes, it was. Perching on the edge of a low cliff the trail ended with, he saw it straight away, drifting on its side, a scratched, half-broken boat, with some of its parts missing, sporting holes. How did it manage to float in the first place?

The passenger was missing as well, but that mystery was

solved quickly. The frantic splashing not far away pointed at the possible location of the boat's owner. And her misfortune. She was thrashing about, beating the water, flailing her arms with not much to show for all this struggle, clearly beyond any reasonable way of reacting.

"Grab the boat," he shouted, cupping his palms around his mouth, to make himself heard better. "It's right there. Wait for it to reach you."

In the mild swirling of the current, the half-broken canoe indeed was floating on its side, making its way in the direction of its owner. Briefly, he wondered how the woman had managed to actually find herself ahead of her floating vessel. It should have been the other way around, the way she thrashed about instead of swimming.

No response.

Sighing, he tossed his bow aside. In for a swim. Grimly, he kicked away his moccasins. Even though a thorough wash up was not an entirely unwelcome possibility, jumping off unfamiliar cliffs into unfamiliar waters was not his idea of reasonably prudent behavior, not since that dive the last spring on their way to Ossossane.

There was no time to check on his bandage, or bother to remove it at all, as by that time, the woman's head had disappeared in the foam her thrashing about created, to reappear a few heartbeats later, then disappear again.

Jumping legs first, unwilling to strain his bad arm more than necessary as much as to chance an encounter of possible underwater rocks with the bones of his skull should this part of the river prove shallower than it looked, he glimpsed another fast-moving object appearing from behind the bend, where the sounds of the more agitated current came from. Oh, curse it all. Too late to reverse any of his actions, he held his breath but kept his eyes open as his feet cut the surface, exchanging lively afternoon sounds for the eerie world of distorted nothingness.

Not fond of underwater swimming, he clenched his teeth against the stinging pain in his eyes, forcing them to remain open, waiting for the disturbance his jump created to retreat and let him see properly.

No movement reached him other than that of his own limbs. Did the woman drown for good? And what was that other canoe he glimpsed doing up there in the meanwhile?

Just as he intended to kick for the surface, mainly to check on the possible whereabouts of the other boat, not pressed for air as yet, he saw the dark form hovering to his right, jerking with her limbs, struggling weakly. Good!

Disregarding the urge to swim up and toward the light, he pounced on the figure, grabbing her with his good arm, something, a handful of clothing. A wild pull and the sounds were back, along with the wind and the afternoon glimmer. As weak as it was, it assaulted his eyes, made him blink savagely, desperate to scan the surface, to see where her broken canoe was. Did it manage to drift far away in the meanwhile? He hoped it didn't. And what about that other boat?

Bettering his grip on the woman, he made sure her head was floating above the surface as well, hoping that she would remain stunned for enough time, until he found something to hold onto. Drowning people could be a nuisance, panic-stricken and therefore absolutely unreasonable, he knew, likely to make their rescuers drown as well.

Well, his charge seemed to be too weak for that, her struggle mainly done with her mouth, all this gasping and gurgling, her limbs moving feebly, not trying to grab him at all. Grateful for that, he put his attention back on the river, scanning the side where according to his estimation the moving boat might be by now.

Indeed, it was there, a few tens of paces away as far as he could tell, turning around already, sharply at that, expertly. The figure with the paddle knew what it was doing, keeping the vessel relatively steady against the mild current, stabilizing it with a visible effort. Puzzled, he watched the small silhouette of a girl half-standing in the wavering boat, working with her paddle, striking the rippling surface on either side, her arms thin and surprisingly fragile-looking as opposed to the adept surety of their movements, the confidence shown in her rowing.

In just a few strokes she was already near, her face bruised and closed, concentrated on her task, as though not aware of its surroundings at all. So very young! Just a girl.

He tried to slam his mind into working, his body tired of supporting its burden, the woman by his side beginning to struggle with more spirit. The previous gurgling was forming into words, something that sounded like weak protests.

The girl's canoe was very near now, another boat that had clearly seen better days.

"Just let her grab the front of it," he shouted, hearing his voice hoarse and trembling. "I'll bring her to the front of your boat."

His half-drowned charge was pushing with her hands, her voice ringing with better clarity. "No, no!" That made him think of home for some reason. The words of his former tongue!

"Hold the boat steady," he shouted again, doing his best to propel himself and his protesting burden to their left, toward the boat's prow.

The stupid girl stopped her rowing and was fiddling with her sash, paying no attention to his shouts, as though he hadn't said a word.

"Are you listening? Don't let her grab the side of your boat. It will flip over!"

This time, the girl straightened up, her face a study of concentration, looking at him as though he weren't there at all. A few more strikes of the paddle and her vessel was very near, facing them in the way he had told her to avoid, presenting its side. Did she intend to try pulling the drowning woman in? But it was not possible, not with such a small boat and such a small owner of it.

"What are you doing?" he yelled, exasperated. Then saw the light flashing off the polished flint.

Straightening with an impressive speed, keeping her balance as though by a miracle in the slowly rotating vessel, her hand was the only thing to move, as it seemed. He saw it with exaggerated clarity, coming up, shooting forward and downwards like a bird of prey, his mind registering the confidence with which her entire arm moved, the natural sharpness of its motion, the unerring efficiency of it, the realization of who its prey was.

Another spark flashed off the flying flint as it cut the air, and he jerked away, desperately slow, hindered by the unsupportive fluidness of his surroundings and the weight of the body his own still supported.

The shelter of the darkness below beckoned, and he dove for its safety, still painfully slow, his panicked mind registering the sway of the boat, and the image of the girl bent on trying to stabilize it again. Or was she hunting after something among its contents?

The last thing he glimpsed was a bow, a large warriors' affair, balanced easily in her arms, held as expertly as the paddle or the knife before, but by then he was already down, enveloped by the eerie silence once again, this time a bliss, kicking desperately, dragging his unresisting burden along. If the woman had drowned for good now, it was too bad. There was no time to warn her, or do something to help her besides not letting her go for good here under the water, a temptation.

His own chest wasn't doing so well this time, not having the proper time to fill it with enough air to last him until putting considerable distance between them and the insane fox in the boat. Not that there were good chances of that, with her sporting a bow now. What would she bring up next? A harpoon? To impale him in order to fish them out of the water more easily?

Kicking for the darker mass that must be the shoreline rocks, he struggled not to let his charge go, not yet. When it turned desperate, maybe then.

His free swimming arm reacted strangely, not pushing the water with the expected forcefulness, so he let the current take them, surfacing for only a brief moment, when his chest threatened to burst.

No time to scan the surface, not with the possibility of the crazy skunk rowing around, looking to dispose of the spluttering swimmers. Why did she try to kill him?

For the first time, he wondered about it, but then the underwater rocks of the shore he was trying to reach began assaulting his limbs, and he dared to surface again, counting on the cover they might be providing. Indeed, it was much darker here, nothing but shadows. He muttered his thanks to every listening spirit.

The woman was still there, hanging listlessly, as though she was a bag he carried. Still, he made sure her face was fluttering above the water. At least that. When the tiny strip of clear ground presented itself, he dragged her upon it carefully, by now aware of the pain rolling up and down his upper arm. Or maybe it was his shoulder. In any case, it was the wrong arm, not the one that still sported a bandage. Not good. He remembered the push that helped him dive.

Clenching his teeth, he dragged the woman up with as much care as he could, then, rolling her on her side, to let the water flow out of her mouth should it decide to do that—an occurrence that could happen with recently drowned, or so people said—he inspected the arm in question, swallowing a curse. The cut was gaping and bleeding, trickling rather than pumping—at least that!—hurting now.

Craning his neck, he tried to examine it more thoroughly, but the wound seemed to be located too high, crossing his shoulder, hopefully only the fleshy part of it. A bit higher and it would have been his neck, or the side of his throat. He shivered then stifled another curse. What if the crazy fox was still prowling around, looking for her lost prey?

A sudden movement by his side made him jump, his hand tearing at his girdle, desperate to locate the knife. Swaying, he gasped with pain, then realized that it was the woman who had moved, in panted, jerking convulsions. The retching sounds her mouth produced filled the damp air, ugly and frightening, the pinkish foam it spat.

Sinking down beside her, he tried to help her roll onto her stomach, supporting her straining body as well as he could, his own strength nowhere near satisfactory now.

Then the sight of her back took the last of his power away. It looked almost natural, the broken stick that protruded from between her shoulder blades, a little to the right, as though planted by hand, the remnants of the feathering soaked and faded. An arrow! A broken one.

For a heartbeat, he just stared, beyond comprehension. The wild fox had grabbed the bow, oh yes, but she didn't have time to use it, not according to his memory. Even if shooting through water, he would have felt the impact, holding his unasked-for ward as closely as he did. No, there was no shooting, not as far as he could tell. Just flying knives.

He twisted his head to look at his throbbing shoulder then scanned their unsatisfactory hideaway before putting his attention back to the suffering woman. Should the girl with the bow appear, he could dart for the cover of the rocks, but what about the wounded?

She was still coughing, straining desperately, with not much to show for all the efforts besides the pinkish trickle down her chin. He studied the arrow once again. No chance of pulling it out, not without preparations and help; better yet, a whole bunch of healers with ointments and tools. He didn't need to be one such to recognize the sturdiness with which it sat in the slender back, so deep, so permanent. What to do now? Again, he listened intently. The crazy fox. Could it be...

The woman was trying to turn over, or maybe just move into a better position, which wasn't a wonder, with him not being much help. He tried to lean her upper body against the nearest rock.

"Help... you have to help..." She was gurgling, her lips bringing up more pinkish foam. "You have to tell... tell them... you have to—"

Another bout of coughing took her. He watched her helplessly, not knowing what to do. Should he try to pull that arrow out after all? But then what? With or without that fluttering shaft he would need to haul her upon his back, his own wounds notwithstanding, and carry her all the way up to the valley, a prospect he didn't relish, not in his current condition. And she was making so much noise, sure to bring the prowling little skunk here.

"Tell them," she insisted in the same agonized whispering, when able to speak again. "You must find them and tell them." Her eyes clung to him, bloodshot and swollen, wild with fright. "You must tell..."

"Tell them what?" he asked, frightened himself. Dying women

were a sight he could do without, and his own pitiful condition along with the receding light and the strengthening wind didn't help. It was freezing cold in their improvised shelter. It also brought memories of his journey to Ossossane, with Gayeri and her dying wounded. But for her being here, even if as argumentative and feisty as she was back then.

"They are coming… they are coming here!" The harrowed tirade went on, more intense than before, the words pouring out like blood gushing from a wound, draining its owner, unable to stop. "They are so many, thousands, so many. They are coming here."

"Who?" The fear was creeping higher, gripping his chest now, as though he was hosting an arrow somewhere in there as well. "Who are coming?" Her eyes were glazing over, and he fought the urge to shake her back into consciousness. "Tell me!"

As though sensing his agitation, she blinked, and her gaze regained its previous painful intensity. "They brought warriors from the west and from the north, hordes of warriors. So many! Many, many hundreds. Like clouds of mosquitoes, like a swarm of lethal bees…" The foam was seeping again, oozing through the torn lips, fighting the outpour of the words, muffling them. "They are so many. The entire valley of the Thundering Waters, of Onguiahra Falls. They are filling the forests between both Great Waters. So many!"

"Great Waters?" He held his breath, making sure not to let his own voice rise. At least one of them had to keep quiet. "Who are those people? Where are those Great Waters?"

But the retching was back, racking her tormented body. That frightful coughing, the pinkish dribble. Not a young woman, and fairly small and thin, she was still not an easy burden to support, not with his own injuries and exhaustion.

"The Thundering Waters," she croaked, her lips just an invisible line, with no color and no shape, not anymore. "The Great Falls… near our Sparkling Water… and their, their other Great Lake."

He settled her back, as comfortably as he could, his mind racing now, the grip on his stomach as tight as before.

"You are talking about the Long Tails, the people who live on the western side of the Sparkling Water?" Peering into the pastiness of her fading features, he tried to hold her gaze before it went away for good. "Tell me. You asked me to help, didn't you? I will, but you will have to tell it all to me. All of it! Then I will tell them what you want me to."

Them? Whoever they are, he thought, remembering her pleading with him in the beginning, when coming back to her senses. Whoever the ones she wanted to inform were, it was important to know the message she carried. The location of the troublesome place she mentioned told him that. The same direction their warriors' forces were heading. A coincidence? Probably not.

He felt his stomach beginning to churn, interrupting with his ability to listen to the possible noises coming from behind the rocks.

"Tell me. Don't go away without doing it. You came a long way to bring this message."

A wild guess, but now it all suddenly started to make sense. Her lonely traveling, the half-broken canoe, her starved, desperate looks. Not to mention the arrow.

The thought hit him all of a sudden, and he gasped. That other fox, the insane girl who was acting wildly, the one who had tried to kill him with not a heartbeat of hesitation, not the tiniest attempt to communicate beforehand, to tell him what she wanted from him, no possible motive—was she chasing this woman?

No, it made no slightest sense. And yet, the wild fox behaved like someone who was set on her course, someone who knew what she was doing. Oh, Mighty Spirits, but that arrow, was this woman shot before the accident? That would explain it all, the overturned canoe where there was no racing waters or bad currents, the mindless thrashing in the water. Before his intervention this woman was drowning, and now he knew why. She had already been wounded, already dying!

Speechless, he found himself supporting the convulsing body again, without giving it much thought. When she slumped against the damp stone, he leaned forward, drained of strength almost as badly as she was. Her chest was barely moving, but it did, still did. Not for long now, he knew.

"Tell me." His voice was ringing stridently, a high-pitched, ugly sound. He clenched his teeth tight, afraid that his whispering won't achieve better results. "Tell me what you need to tell. We haven't much time." Taking a deep breath, he put his arms on her shoulders, pressing them lightly, reassuringly, or so he hoped. "You have to prepare for your Sky Journey, sister. We will do it together. I'll be with you, and we will make sure you find your path easily. See this sky?" In the flickering dimness of their hideaway, there was not much of a sky to be seen, but he pressed on, hoping she would see what she wanted to see. "They are ready and waiting for you, Grandmother Moon and any star you would wish to pick, to guide you on your journey."

She was listening. He could see that in her visibly smoothing face that was not filling with color, yet seemed less of an agonized mask than before; in the touch of her arms under his palm, no more terrible strain. Could he chance the ruin of the achieved tranquility in order to ask his questions, to bring earthly matters back into her mind?

Her breath was getting faster and shallower, her chest laboring, straining, bringing more foam to her tormented lips. He took a deep breath. "Before you put your mind on your new journey, tell me what you want me to tell your people, what you want to warn them against."

Her expression didn't change. Same struggle for breath, same tranquility of features. The half-shut eyes closed some more, concentrated on something, something he couldn't see or hear. Was she seeing her Sky Path already?

"They gathered many hundreds of warriors. They are camping between the two Great Waters, near Onguiahra Falls. They are ready to come here. To burn our towns and villages."

The voice could not belong to her, so clear and sharp, so measured. Not a muscle in the chiseled face shuddered, not an eyelid moved. The half-closed eyes didn't open. Mesmerized, he held his breath.

"The   Long   Tails   People   I   lived   with   united   with

Attiwandaronk from the north. The man who limps did it. He will lead them, and they will listen to what he says. He is bringing more, hundreds of Attiwandaronk warriors. He won't rest until the Great League is made to suffer."

The ethereal tranquility was shattered by a terrible convulsion that made her entire body stiffen, lurch with a wild force. He didn't try to hold her in place, just cradled her head, whether to support and let her know that he was still there, or just making sure it didn't bash against the rock, her temporary support until now.

Her back arched in an unnatural manner as the gagging grew worse, the terrible rasping, the desperate struggle for one more breath, one more gulp of air. He clenched his teeth until they screeched, himself near panic, ready to jump to his feet, to break into a mad run. Away from this terrible suffering, to be anywhere but here.

In the end, he just held her tight, murmuring customary words, helpless against her agony and her fear. Still part of his mind was on the less immediate surroundings, the river's monotonous dribble, the moaning of the wind, the possible creaking of wet stones, maybe, or other suspicious less natural sounds.

The crazy fox, was she still stalking her prey? He knew she was.

CHAPTER 16

Making sure her canoe was tucked safely in the gap between the two cliffs, camouflaged by rotting logs and some grass thrown around hastily, she made her way up the incline, her anxiety overwhelming. The brief scan of the shallow water by the nearest strip of rocks produced nothing. No bodies. Not even one.

It should have been thrown there, she knew, at least the filthy traitor's body. Judging by the amount of erosion the various semi-hidden coves kept accumulating, it should have been swept here as well, carried along with other things that the current kept bringing from behind the bend. Even the damaged, partly broken canoe of the filthy rat was there, lying on its side, looking pitiful. Just like its owner should be looking now.

Where did her body go?

And what if the treacherous fox was still alive, splashing somewhere, helped by that man, the annoying would-be rescuer who appeared out of nowhere and just as she, Tsutahi, was about to complete her task?

Oh, but these had been such difficult days, rowing against different currents, unable to progress as swiftly as she needed, the foreign woods looming, signaling their warning, urging her to slow her progress. A good warning she didn't dare to take to heed. The stupid fox she had been following left so many glaring marks, so many prints of her headlong flight. Such a clear trail! No danger of losing it, even had she had to follow with her eyes shut and one hand tied behind her back. But for the ability to hear properly, if only for the chance of completing her mission, and when so much was at stake!

The word of their warriors' forces should not reach the enemy ahead of time, he had said back there near the shores of the gushing river that was spilling into the most dreadful falls she had ever seen. He deemed it important, even though the others didn't seem to worry about the treacherous snake sneaking away like that. When she had probed, he admitted that yes, for the best results their advance should be kept secret. A surprise was always the best of allies, to be made much out of it, to squeeze the opportunity dry, something the foreign woman was threatening to spoil.

Following his words with an utmost concentration, afraid to miss even a single one, every sound that came off his lips precious, she immediately knew what to do, yet was wiser than to share her solution with him. The woman had left barely a day before, sneaking away in a stolen canoe. Oh, yes, that small vessel some enraged locals were looking for later on, which pointed at her being an inexperienced traveler. Smaller canoes were difficult to manage, even if easier to make them move. She, Tsutahi, was careful to pick a mid-sized dugout when creeping among the rows of scattered vessels in the dead of night later on. A lead of one single day was nothing to an experienced traveler like herself, as opposed to the silly fox who probably couldn't navigate her way inside her own longhouse from one hearth to another.

However, the mission didn't turn out to be as easy as she mused it would be, even though her own disappearance drew barely any attention, if at all. Even he would not begin wondering, she assumed, not until the second part of the day, when he might notice that she wasn't around his campfire as promised. He would be too busy, and by the time he started wondering she would be back, with good news to report and to make him proud. Two, three days at the most, she surmised, the naive thing that she was.

Biting her lips, she scanned the mighty flow anew, thinking about the mild rapids she had chosen to brave by sailing instead of detouring on foot when the panicked fox would plunge into the gushing flow as well, her own vessel barely floating at this point, floundering and leaking from numerous cracks, the result of too many unnecessary bumps and collisions the light wood had to withstand. This woman was so useless! A clumsy fowl.

Still, useless or not, the treacherous snake had made it so far, and it was only here, in these faraway foreign woods, that Tsutahi had finally managed to catch up with her prey, speeding against better judgment, knowing neither the currents of these foreign rivers and creeks nor the people who inhabited them. Only that these might be the worst of the enemies, the people he wanted to fight badly enough to work himself into exhaustion, gathering together an unheard-of amount of men.

Oh, but he was so strong and efficient, so brisk. So sure of himself and the rightness of his cause. It was good that people listened to him now. Everyone, even her people. He said they didn't want to listen until she came. He said it was all thanks to her that the Attiwandaronk warriors began flocking in by the hundreds, after the elders of her town gave their consent and even their blessing. Somehow, her reappearance back from the realm of the dead made the elders and, most importantly, the clan mothers open their ears to his words. And how proud it made her when he had told her that, how satisfied. She had helped him, even if unintentionally, and she would go on helping him, doing everything she could. He would be pleased to know that the traitor did not reach her people to reveal their secret to them. Unless...

Clenching her teeth, she pushed her way up the cliff, determined. Unless the terrible man who had fallen on her from the sky, jumping off this same bluff probably, and in the worst of timings, managed to save the drowning fox, somehow.

How? Was it possible? And did she manage to hurt him as well? Enough to make him drown?

He had gone down quickly once the realization dawned. It was almost funny to see the expression of utter surprise spreading over his face, before that all busy talking and shouting, blubbering in his foreign tongue. The proof that she *was* in the enemy lands. Oh Mighty Spirits!

Reaching the last of the rocks, she shivered, wet and dreadfully cold, her arms clutching the bow trembling, gripping it with too much force, the arrow already in, ready to shoot, to dart, to defend her against anything terrible that might come out of these woods, like that man...

Clenching her teeth, she forced her mind into more lucid thinking, surveying the uneven surface, noting the trail that led back into the swampy grove, the marks of someone running there recently clear, leaving no doubts. As were the carelessly thrown moccasins, and a bow with quiver, some of its arrows scattering. Was he alone here? Good! Neglecting to retrieve his possessions, too. Oh, but it was a good sign, wasn't it?

Perching upon the slippery edge with the utmost care, ready to duck should her senses alert her to anything suspicious, she scanned the river most thoroughly, again with no results. Oh Mighty Spirits, where were they both, the man and the dying woman? The traitorous snake could not last, not with her, Tsutahi's, arrow buried deeply in the traitor's upper back. But the man, what was he up to?

The closer inspection of his bow and shoes told her nothing. A regular weapon, with an undecorated quiver of arrows. Nothing personal about any of it. Like the moccasins. Just a pair of worn leather shoes, bearing witness to previously attached colorful shells, mere remnants of those by now. Witness to much walking? Long traveling, maybe. Was this man not a local at all?

Angrily, she snatched one of the low-edged shoes, tossing it over the edge with much vengeance. The next one followed suit. The damn stupid man. Why did he have to be here in the first place? What if he managed to save the damn fox, or at least hear her news?

Shutting her eyes against the intensity of her rage, she forced herself to pick up his bow carefully, not doing what her anger urged her to do, namely cracking it in two and hoping that it would make her feel better. It might have, but a good bow was a good bow. One didn't dispose of useful weapons in order to get back at their owners. It was childish of her to become that angry. The thrown moccasins were more than enough. Another stupid impulse that might cost her a possible discovery. What if they made noise while falling into the river?

Carefully, she made her way down, still hesitating. To sail back with no further delays was a sensible thing to do. Whether she failed to stop the word from reaching the enemy or not, there was nothing more she could do but go back and let him know of her efforts. To follow the footsteps of the annoying local was tempting, but dangerous. She might learn something useful while doing this, but she might just as easily come to harm, get captured or killed. These woods were not her woods, and there was no telling how many locals, hunters or warriors, were prowling all around the way this man did. Wretched enemies that they were.

The dusk was settling in. She could feel the coolness of the evening breeze cutting into her limbs, freezing, the shadows lengthening, preparing to swallow their surroundings. The hum of the river reached her ears, breaking the perpetual wall of silence. It must be roaring strongly enough, even though the rapids behind did not warrant so much noise. Relatively easy to negotiate, but for the silly wounded woman who didn't know how to navigate in the first place.

She suppressed a snort then tensed for no apparent reason. Holding her breath, she turned hurriedly, scanning the rocky shore once again, her gaze lingering on the next cluster of cliffs, sliding toward the darkening water. Nothing untoward there, yet she knew she had been watched. The prickle of her skin told her that, sensing the foreign eyes almost physically, burning holes in the places they bore into.

Darting toward the cover of the nearest rocks, she straightened her bow, tossing the foreigner's aside with little consideration. It was of no use now, because only *her* bow was capable of keeping her safe.

The wave of panic was near, but she pushed it away, concentrating on her movements instead, trying not to slip, fighting for balance, not about to let the thought of these eyes overwhelm her. Not now. Later, after she was safe, either by killing her stalker, whether a man or an animal, or by getting away, somehow.

Still, when he pounced on her from behind the same rocks she was trying to reach, surprising her on that score, she was almost ready, the first arrow making its way into her bow, pressing against the pulled string, *reassuring*. She released it without aiming, to deter rather than hit, to gain a heartbeat of respite, a chance to regroup.

Indeed, her missile made him dart away swiftly, stumbling upon the jagged surface, his bare feet not dealing well with the multitude of needle-sharp stones and shells scattered over the slippery ground.

Still, as she fitted another arrow in, desperate to use the unexpected advantage to its fullest, she glimpsed him rolling away, struggling back onto his feet, using every limb to do that, lurching from the possible course of her next missile. Which she didn't release as readily as the first one, taking her time, wishing to make no mistakes, relishing her superior position, with him being so clumsy and weaponless, with nothing but the strength of his arms, with not even a knife out and ready. Oh, but maybe it turned out for the best. With him dead, she could go home secure in the knowledge that she managed, even had the wounded fox told something she shouldn't have.

Her hand pulling at the bowstring with final decisiveness, she saw him straightening into a better position, whirling around, his eyes huge and wide-open, lips nothing but a thin line, arm shooting up and forward.

The dark form that cut the air drew her attention against her will, her mind following numbly. A fraction of a heartbeat saw her still hesitating, her hand itching to release the bowstring, her eyes refusing to leave the approaching object.

When it smashed into the side of her forehead, pushing her backwards and into the damp stones, she felt nothing but surprise. How could it be?

Disoriented, she blinked to make her eyes focus, clenching her bow with both hands now, the arrow not there anymore. Did she shoot this man after all?

The answer presented itself readily. Pouncing in the speed of a forest predator, he was already there, landing beside her, or so her senses told her, desperate to focus, urging her body to lurch away, so hopelessly slow. The nauseating buzz inside her head rising higher and higher, overwhelming, she squirmed and kicked, biting his arm as it brushed against her face in a tempting proximity to her mouth, while he seemed to be putting it all into an attempt to pin her to the ground.

The last thing she felt was a powerful push at the unharmed side of her head, then it became smothering dark.

CHAPTER 17

The wind was blowing strongly, atypically generous for this part of the seasons. It should have been scorching hot now back in High Springs or around the Great Lake's shore, with nothing to move the laden with moisture air, reflected Ganayeda, making himself more comfortable on his perch of an old stump, his preferred form of a seat as opposed to mere squatting.

The meeting of local and newly arrived war leaders was long and heavy-going, a hastily organized affair of many important warriors, with no usual comforts and flowery speeches of the civil authorities' meetings.

"We have too many warriors camping along this side of the lake's shores these days."

This came from one of the visiting elders. Not their generous hosts, war leaders of Tsonontowan, but someone close enough to them. A hint at the overused hospitality could be construed as a terrible impoliteness.

The nods of the local leaders held a clear measure of relief.

"I must agree with our greatly esteemed War Leader of Cayanoghe," contributed one of the Swamp People's veterans. "The site we are using is not suitable for our purposes, not anymore."

Which was true enough, reflected Ganayeda, tired after running around the vast enclosure and all the adjacent clearings and hills. There was simply not enough space. Their hordes of new arrivals were spilling everywhere, with more trickling in every day, hundreds of men, mostly young, eager hotheads but laced with a fair amount of people nearing his age and more.

Whatever Okwaho and his bands of unofficial recruiters did, it was working, with more success than the originators of the idea had counted upon.

He glanced at his brother, a spectacular presence, as always, not a sight people would overlook in a hurry, squatting easily in the forefront, among the deliberating leaders, not awed by such high-ranking company, and not deterred from speaking his mind when he felt his opinions needed to be voiced. The forceful beast.

Oh, but his brother was something rare, a man living by his own standards, a force to be reckoned with. No surprises there of course. Arriving here some dawns ago, Ganayeda had expected to find nothing else but the young beast conducting the grand enterprise of his own making, not about to step into the shadows now that the deed was done. Not Okwaho.

What he didn't expect was to run into the state of turmoil their huge spilling encampment, more of a cluster of camps, was in. No attempts to sort the arrivals properly had been made, to guide and direct, no efforts to make them feel at ease or understand the simplest ground rules. Everything was bubbling with life and energy, not always a peaceful one, with the warriors left to their own devices, to do whatever they liked to dispense with boredom, to alleviate the temporary state of confusion and uncertainty. The local leaders seemed to be at a loss, watching with their eyebrows raised high, and the more mature element among their guests joining the puzzled observation.

Devising his grand future strategy, buried in thousands of discussions of different plans and schemes, worried about the enemy's possible moves, while sending out scouts by the dozens, Okwaho was too busy to deal with mundane matters of making people feel good and at home.

Yes, their monster of a camp was not in the best of shapes, he admitted, but they would be out and moving in a short time, and then all would be well, the warriors would get busy either walking or sailing, or better yet, fighting. The unrest beyond the Ce-nis-seu or Genesee River reported by his army of scouts was a promising indication. The enemy was up to no good, spilling over their own gushing river and the dreadful Thundering Waters in greater and greater numbers over the last half a moon, roaming around in no orderly fashion, harassing villages or sometimes larger, more fortified settlements, persisting with their attacks sometimes, drawing away in other cases. A strange behavior that screamed of general trouble. And this is what Okwaho wanted to verify before moving out, leading their considerable forces to punish the enemy, as the majority of other leading elements demanded to do. The filthy invaders were ripe for a counter attack, not knowing that this time they would be faced with the might of the entire Great League, an awe-inspiring force.

To hold their own most eager warriors from rushing out and toward the west was the biggest of challenges so far, admitted Okwaho, himself eager to fight but for the weight of responsibility. It wasn't wise to just rush out, not knowing what the enemy had in store. Even when entrusted with a few tens of warriors, the leader who didn't check the enemy dispositions was a reckless no-good unfitting to lead children's plays. Back in the lands of the River People, he had learned all about how one should *not* lead and campaign, claimed Okwaho, and he was not about to make any such mistake with the impressive amount of warriors he was now entrusted with.

For how long was he planning to stay where they were? Ganayeda had inquired upon his arrival, walking beside his brother, bypassing old and new fires scattered all around in decided disarray, his experienced gaze seeing a multitude of flaws, thousands of ways to make this huge camp function in a more orderly manner.

At least a third of a moon, was his answer, the smile flashed at him holding it all, a challenging admittance, an amused plea for help. So Ganayeda got to work without delay, not even pausing to put away his bags and see where he and some of his friends and fellow travelers were to be placed. This huge enterprise needed an urgent reorganization before it exploded into something no one wanted to happen. A fight among their own people would be the worst scenario, but the trickling out of more impatient elements would be as bad, whether fed up with idleness and boredom. Such hotheads would be either heading back where they came from, or perhaps rushing forward to fight the enemy on their own. None of the options were acceptable, not when they had gotten so far in their grand enterprise.

So he had rushed all over their monster of a camp, using his semi-official status of an observer on behalf of the Great Council as a means to enhance his authority, to have people listen and follow his brisk but politely phrased instructions.

Impressed, the local leaders insisted on inviting him to every War Council that had been held, and even though it interfered with his organizational efforts, he felt greatly pleased, knowing that his traveling here might have helped in more than putting the Head of the Great Council's worries to rest, because now the monstrous camp and its outlets were in a more temperate mood, with people fairly well-fed and calm, not about to burst like a thunderstorm in the summer, with no deserters or overzealous fighters trickling out.

"I suggest we move our forces west, toward the eastern banks of your Great River." Okwaho's voice brought Ganayeda out of his reverie, back to the wind-swept clearing that was wide and comfortably large to hold local gatherings of the War Council probably, but not nearly spacious enough to host the amount of people attending such meetings these days. "It should not take us longer than a day of walking, if we move our forces in an orderly manner, which would also ensure the safety of our people while on the move against any possible enemy presence."

Suitably deferential, the young man shifted to make himself more comfortable, seemingly at ease in such high-ranking company but for the exaggerated straightness of his back.

"No enemy should be present on our side of the Genesee River," said Tsonontowan's war leader tersely, his bushy eyebrows creating a single line under the direfully furrowed forehead. "Our people have been everywhere, watching our forests and hills with the eyes of an eagle. You should know that better than anyone, Warrior."

An open reprimand. Ganayeda hid his frown, even though it was entertaining to watch his brother deal with this grand assembly of dignified leaders, with a satisfactory amount of dutifully respectful attitude, but still not about to let any of his opinions and ideas go unvoiced or unnoticed, gaining frowns and raised eyebrows among more traditional elements of the local leadership.

"I'm aware of the considerable amount of scouts that have been keeping these forests safe, Honorable Leader," he admitted with a light nod, unperturbed but for the tightening of the generous lips. "I didn't mean to imply to the contrary or underestimate our glorious warriors' hard work and dedication."

Tsonontowan's elder nodded, seemingly pacified, but one of the minor leaders from among the arriving guests drew a deep breath.

"You advocated staying here until we hear more news of the enemy and their possible moves," he said slowly, choosing his words. "What changed?"

Okwaho's lips were nothing but a thin line now. "Yes, I've been of an opinion that we should not make a move before we hear more news from the other side. Yet, I now believe that we cannot wait any longer. The amount of men that have arrived here is staggering. And unprecedented. A few dawns ago, when we discussed the situation, we had over a thousand warriors. But now? Now we count almost twice as many. Over two thousand men who need to be fed daily, divided into suitable groups, coordinated in order to move them around in any semblance of order, an amount of people we cannot keep in one place without eating it out, and so harming the local settlements and their forests." Raising his hands, palms up, he encircled his listeners with his gaze, sincere in his openness. "I believe we have enough people to cross into the enemy lands regardless of their state of war-readiness now. Even if no news of their preparation has reached us so far."

"How do you propose to divide our people?" asked one of the guests, an impressive-looking Flint of considerable age, clearly an unofficially commissioned leader. "According to what measures? In how many groups and of what size?"

As the discussion drifted toward more actual details of the organization, Ganayeda let his eyes wander, assessing the men present. So many hardened, imposingly weathered warriors! He counted more than thirty men, mainly various local leaders, but with enough veteran guests thrown in, all of them of his own age and older other than his brother, who as expected didn't seem to be perturbed by such an irrelevant factor.

Leaning forward, his eyes bright with concentration, the young man devoured every question and answer avidly, unless asked to answer himself, a frequent occurrence. Oh, but the young buck was respected here, despite the frowns against his forcefully straightforward ways. Or maybe it was exactly what those hardened veterans needed, a young, able man to air aloud things experienced leaders did not wish to talk about for the sake of politeness and customary ways. Like the matter of feeding people while ruining the surroundings of the town that hosted them. The local leaders could not bring this matter up, while the guests weren't sure of their stance to suggest changes. Only Okwaho, the real force behind this enterprise, combined enough clout with his fresh, still somewhat youthful thinking to come out with what preyed on everyone's mind.

Oh, but his brother had carved himself a place of his own in this first serious war of the Great Union. The wave of his swelling pride threatened to spill out in an inappropriately wide smile.

"What are your thoughts on the matter, Honorable Representative?"

After the hectic days around their monster of a camp and his frequent conferences with local authorities, it didn't take him a heartbeat to realize that he had been spoken to, the title of representative coming naturally now, warranted officially or not.

"I agree with the assertion that the amount of warriors we have should not occupy the same spot for many days." The feeling of all gazes upon him was familiar, but still unnerving. Translating for dignitaries in foreign lands or organizing the gathering of the Great Council was not like sharing his actual thoughts in an important war council, advising veterans on matters he understood, but only in theory. "With more volunteers trickling in every dawn and evening, we cannot have our forces staying in one place. However, I believe that as long as we are staying in the heart of our own lands, we can split our forces safely, have them camping at different locations until the decision to move is reached. Spread evenly, they won't be such a burden to the settlements that would share the honor of hosting them."

He made an effort to keep his expression as impartial as he could, leaning back, returning their gazes with every hint of calm affability he could muster. To have a pipe or something else to busy himself with would have helped. He should have kept his thoughts to himself, shouldn't he? Did his stating the obvious put him in a silly light? They all must have thought of the temporary solution like spreading their forces already, must have dismissed this idea as unfitting for this or that reason.

Some of the men were frowning, while the others' expressionless features colored with a hint of reserved appreciation reinforced by slightly raised eyebrows.

"As long as we camp in the heart of our own forests and need to wait for a little longer..." drawled Tsonontowan's War Chief, nodding as though to himself. "This can be a solution, however temporary."

"There is a good camping site near one of the smaller lakes to the west," said one of the local leaders, the man whose words Okwaho had supported earlier. "A fairly wide local stream is starting there, near the northern shores of the lake, creating a good enclosure that is easy to watch and defend."

"Honeoye Lake," Okwaho cried out, nodding vigorously. "I remember this outlet. I noticed it last the Awakening Season while passing there. This site can host our entire force if need be. I would feel safe to camp any amount of our people there, with or without an enemy in sight."

"With the enemy in sight, we won't be camping," someone muttered. "Still, splitting our forces in the way the Honorable Representative suggested sounds like the most sensible solution to the problem of thousands of warriors eating out Tsonontowan and the Canandaigua Lake population."

"We could split into four, even five groups." Acknowledging the words with a thoughtful nod, clearly striving to be polite if for no other reason, Okwaho seemed to be busy thinking. "The largest group will camp out there at the foot of Honeoye Lake. It is such an easily defended place. If there was a way to tempt the enemy here, I would have loved to conduct a battle there, with equal or even inferior forces." The dreamy expression was gone. "I suppose it's time to start organizing our men, to ready them for the move."

"Do you think the enemy is unaware of our own battle preparations?" asked Ganayeda, when the meeting broke with the resolution to sort people out tomorrow and maybe the day after that, to be reconvened again before the final decision as to the actual move and its precise destination was made.

Slowing his step, he was pleased to feel his brother halting as well, the view of this part of the lake with its shores packed with so many people it looked alive, the mere ground if not the surrounding forests. It made his chest swell with excitement. So many warriors! The best of the five nations. No, not five nations but one, one longhouse representing the might of the Great League. Oh, but this was the Great Peacemaker's vision, one longhouse, one clan, made of five families.

"They shouldn't know unless they send an impressive amount of scouts, which might prove difficult, don't you think? How would the average Long Tail wander around here, with their dreadful accents and the filthiness of their ways?" Suddenly furious, Okwaho spat. "Lowlifes all and every one of them!"

Ganayeda shook his head, needing no explanation. "It was only one lowlife, and he was assisted if not directed by a perfectly local High Springs' dignitary."

"Still," insisted Okwaho, his face retaining the color of the cloudy afternoon. "One lowlife or not, this accursed delegation should have known better than to bring unsuitable people to talk before our assembly. If something would have happened to Father back then..."

Ganayeda just shrugged, eyes on the swampy piece of land that separated the hill they were descending from the lake that hosted them. The river that gushed beyond it would be the one to take them on, he knew, having toured their surroundings upon many occasions by now. But those were busy days!

"I have plenty of scouts sneaking everywhere around the Genesee River and beyond it, but I wish I had suitable people to send into the actual enemy lands."

"They must have enough former captives around here."

"Can't trust them. Never to the fullest."

The thought hit. "I heard your Flint friend and his party arrived here this noon. If our Crooked Tongues is with him— which must be the case—I would say he would be your perfect candidate for spying on the enemy in their own heartlands. He speaks their tongue, or something close to it, and he is wild enough to warm up to such an insane idea."

Okwaho's eyes lit. "I wish I thought of it earlier!" Then a proud grin flickered. "He proved himself nicely in the places I sent him to, you and your lack of trust in this man. I had word coming from their quarters often, and but for our easygoing betting-games player we might have ended up with half the amount of volunteers coming from the east. Akweks said he was invaluable at putting people at ease, making them gather in one place and mill around, tossing stones and listening to our storytellers. The best of companions to travel along as well, Akweks says, and this Flint boy is picky and not always easy to handle. He has a temper, that one. Sometimes." A conspiratorial smirk flashed more openly now. "He got into a fight in one of the Standing Stone People's towns, I gather. A piece of information I received from others, not him. They say the Crooked Tongue was the one to stop that fight and make everyone go about their business. How about that, eh?"

Amused, Ganayeda did not attempt to hide the crooked quality of his own grin. "Good for him. I never said he was a bad man or not fitting for the mission you were so eager to charge him with. He is a good man. But I still think he should not be involved in our political games. Not for a while, before more summers have passed, before he has proved his loyalty to our people beyond doubt."

An impatient shrug was his answer. "I like this man, and I trust him. For me, he has proven his worth."

"Stubborn buck." Feeling no real chagrin, not anymore—his brother did as he pleased, as always, but so far he had proven himself too many times not to trust his actions and probably his judgment of people—Ganayeda looked at the farther side of the camp that was spreading before them, where the forested area was taking over, separating it from the swampy land. A commotion seemed to be developing there. "When do you plan on moving the people to that other location you favored? How many?"

Okwaho narrowed his eyes, his experienced gaze spotting the potential trouble as well. "All of them," he said absently, hastening his step. "I won't be splitting our people, even though you were right to suggest that. We forgot that we did not move into the enemy forests yet."

"Then why won't you do that?"

"I will, but not in the way they agreed to. I will move all our people out there into that valley between two lakes, the one I was stupid enough to forget about. We should have spread our camp there in the first place." A shrug. "Then I'll make sure I hear from our scouts first, before I decide."

"*You* decide, eh? I wonder how all those warriors' leaders would like hearing that."

Hastening his steps in order not to fall behind, Ganayeda tried to see what was amiss out there near the swamps, with apparently too many people congregated around something, looking agitated if their wide gesturing was to judge by. The Swamp People, he remembered, it was their side of the camp. He had spent some time there the previous night, loitering about, striking up conversations, as though spending an idle evening, but in fact looking for a suitable person to entrust with the general leadership of this group. There were some Onondaga campfires around there as well, and he had talked to Okwaho about it later, pointing out that if some of their people were inclined to mix with their neighbors while camping, it might be a good idea to encourage them to do so, to fight together and alongside each other later on.

"They'll take it just fine," was Okwaho's nonchalant response. "When the deed is done it's too late to argue about, isn't it?"

"Oh, yes, it is. I learned your methods well enough by now."

Indeed, Okwaho's way of doing things then asking for permission later on had proven itself surprisingly agreeable in this particular enterprise so far. It was amazing how many unauthorized undertakings one could get away with, if one was able to work it all out and bring results. Just witness their massive recruiting to begin with. Unless something went wrong on a larger scale, things were happening nicely. Again, he reminded himself to make his own private offerings, just in case.

"It's difficult to hold some of the most hotheaded volunteers of ours in check," Okwaho was saying, eyes narrowed against the agitated talk that was reaching their ears now as the view of the crowding people disappeared with the sharp descent their trail was taking. "Too many of those who rushed here, eager to do glorious deeds, have been sitting on their behinds for quite a few days, having nothing to do but fume." A shrug. "I had to come down hard on a whole group of hotheads only this morning. The stupid skunks sneaked away on a private side-mission, wandering as far as Tonawanda Swift Waters Creek. Luckily, after reaching that point, they had enough sense to turn back, or they might have ended up in the very heart of the enemy land, spilling straight into the Long Tails' river with dreadful falls. So stupid!" His brother's teeth made a grinding sound. "I could have killed the whole bunch of them. Mindless skunks! If they had fallen into the enemy hands while trying to glorify themselves, our entire enterprise would become common knowledge. Then I would be the one trying to liberate them before their ceremony of execution, in order to take pleasure in killing them with my own hands."

"How many were they?" asked Ganayeda, fascinated by the problem he had already been pondering earlier, while spending his time trying to better the functioning of this unusual war gathering. The unrest he had noted among a certain type of younger warriors, who were forced to curb their impatience until their leaders led them into actual fighting seemed to be a rather common occurrence but for their numbers. In such a large force the amount of discontents was of course higher than usual, as was to be expected. And yet, he had been wondering about the local leaders' ability to make so many people obey and do as they are told when it became crucial to coordinate their actions.

"The ones who actually had the temerity to move into the enemy's lands?" Okwaho's voice had a growling quality to it. "About ten, all of them from the same town, led by one presumptuous skunk who thought the world of his leadership qualities. Until this morning, that is."

"In such a strange, extraordinary force as ours, there are bound to be many such restless spirits. But what can you do to make them remain patient and obey? It would be their warriors' leaders' duty to discipline them but for them coming here independently, with no official guidance and no permissions." Momentarily distracted, he listened to the noise of too many people talking at once. "Even war chiefs are not always having an easy time making certain hotheads do as they are told instead of plunging into their boredom-induced private quests to prove their valor and courage."

A loud snort was his answer. "After *my* telling off, they would think twice before plunging into anything independent. And the others will stop and think too."

Even though they had emerged from behind the trees and onto the clear space bordering the beginning of the marshy land, the commotion that brought them here spreading before their eyes— indeed a serious hubbub of too many people congregating around one spot—Ganayeda turned to look at his brother. "What did you do?"

Okwaho's lips twisted into an unpleasantly thin grin, even though his eyes were scanning the milling people, narrow with attention. "I told them to leave. Pack their things and be gone. Not to enter my sight ever again."

He thought about it, not overly impressed. "It must be disappointing for them, yes, to miss the glory of our war here."

The mean-spirited smile widened. "I also told them that I will make sure they would not be able to volunteer into any warriors' forces, neither in their native lands, nor anywhere around the nations of our Great League." The edges of the stretched lips climbed downwards, adding to the quality of the ominous smirk. "They know I can do it. At this point, it would be easy enough to spread their bad names even among their own villages' leaders, let alone among the war leadership of our entire union. By now, I have enough influence to do that."

That made Ganayeda slow his step. "I see." Oh, yes, this was no empty threat, not when it came from Okwaho, his newly gained status and rapidly growing clout, officially sanctioned or not, notwithstanding. "What was their reaction?"

A self-satisfied smirk banished the menacing glow. "They pleaded and pleaded, until I agreed to give them another chance. But only if they behaved as obediently as women preparing the ceremonial meal under the eyes of the sternest of clan mothers and if they distinguished themselves in the upcoming raid like none of their peers." The contentment was spilling. "I predict they will do just that, while the word gets around, discouraging other potentially independent raiders from thinking that they may know better when do we have to move or where to."

This time impressed most thoroughly, Ganayeda grinned. "I daresay you helped the rumors of what happened to spread."

"Of course. Akweks and his men just arrived, eager to plunge into action. I'll set him to work of spreading the word in an unobtrusive manner. He and some of his friends know so many people after all this recruiting. They'll be able to make this incident known."

"Good thinking," muttered Ganayeda, following his brother as Okwaho began pushing his way into the thickest of the commotion, not bothering to stop and ask questions. "What is happening?"

The man closest to him moved away slightly, then shrugged, shooting Ganayeda an affable glance, clearly recognizing him. "Some fellow wandered in not long ago, all cut and bleeding, they say. He brought a captive."

"What captive?"

"Who knows? He doesn't seem to be perfectly local himself. Your Onondaga or maybe a Flint, they say."

Pursing his mouth, Ganayeda hastened his step, anxious to catch up with his brother. An Onondaga man or a Flint? But this wasn't their side of the encampment.

In the small space next to a huge pine with sprawling branches, the agitation was at its worst, with people gesturing wildly, talking all at once, overrunning each other's words. Okwaho was spearheading his way into the heart of it, where a squatting figure was sagging against the wide trunk, in dire need of its support.

Oh, but he should have known!

One look at the familiar, pleasant-looking face, again full of bruises alternated with streaks of dried mud, creating an interesting pattern, transferred Ganayeda back to the Crooked Tongues gathering near that town called Ossossane. Only the ties to secure the man to the tree were missing. And the crowds. Much friendlier, full of puzzled attention, pushing in from all over, some extending bowls with water or similar treats, others offering plenty of verbal advice.

All the while, the Crooked Tongue was doing his best, nodding or answering people, his efforts to do so obvious, expressed in the pasty sweat-coated face and the colorless, thinly clasped mouth, completed by clenched teeth and somewhat clouded eyes. The latter was explained by the presence of an elderly man, clearly a healer, busy messing with the reddish mess on his patient's shoulder, the unmistakable kit of razor-sharp tiny bones and rolls of sinew spread upon a blanket, leaving nothing to wonder about but to pity the recipient of the treatment.

Hot on Okwaho's heals, Ganayeda reached their destination at almost the same time, nodding at people who moved away helpfully, clearing their way. The healer was threading another needle, thus giving his patient a heartbeat of respite, making it easy to catch the fatigued gaze. Pleased, he saw the smile stretching the generous lips, a familiar mischievous grin reflecting in the depths of the heavily ringed eyes.

"That was fast, I say. Have you run all the way?" Shifting as though about to rise to his feet, the foreigner's smile widened, now unmistakably his, but the healer's palm fastened around the grazed shoulder, causing his patient to drop back into his previous position, losing the most beaming quality of the grin.

"In a little while," said the old man, acknowledging the influential visitors' presence with a quick glance and a thoughtful nod. "This wound needs to be closed."

"What happened?" asked Okwaho, dropping next to the squatting men, careful not to block the last of the light for the laboring elder.

"A few strange developments that I thought you should hear about," said the Crooked Tongue quite nonchalantly, but his eyes lost their spark, and his body tensed as the healer's fingers reached for the wound once again, preparing to resume their work. "I asked people to send you word" — a painful pause — "but I didn't think they would find you that quickly... or that you would be able to come just like that." Another quiver of thinly clasped lips, an attempted grin. "Such an important dignitary that you are these days."

"Shut up and let the Honorable Elder patch you up first," said Okwaho, atypically patient, squatting to make his position more comfortable.

Curious, Ganayeda remained on his feet, pleased to see the man in spite of himself. The foreigner was such a mess of good and bad. Even now, when it was more appropriate to get into violent troubles than ever, how did one manage to look this way, as though straight from a battle, or better yet, captivity, wearing a loincloth and nothing else, not even moccasins to cover his cut, battered feet, bare but for the coat of mud and pine needles. Who would be running around the woods barefoot?

"If you think we came here following this or that invitation," he said, grinning lightly, "then you are in for a surprise. We were just passing by on our way to the valley."

"Yes," concurred Okwaho. "We received no word from you or yours. In fact, I learned that you arrived here this morning only a short time ago, when I had word from Akweks."

"Oh, you didn't?" The open puzzlement softened the strained features, breaking some of the stark expression. The healer finished tying another piece of sinew, and was washing the closed-up cut rather vigorously, with no regard to his patient's endurance or the limits of his fortitude.

"Drink, brother." One of the warriors knelt beside the wounded, offering a vessel full to the brim.

A grateful nod was his answer, but as the Crooked Tongue drank thirstily, emptying the cup in almost one gulp, some of the water trickling down his chin, Ganayeda caught the sight of a small figure huddled awkwardly next to the nearest stump, her muddied legs pulled up, face buried in the space the folded knees created, hands tucked behind her back in an obvious manner. A young girl, nothing but a child by the look of her. What was she doing here, and why bloodied and tied?

Puzzled, he put his attention back to the possible answer to it all. "What's with the girl?"

The healer, clearly done with his work, was collecting his belongings with utmost care, assisted by quite a few pairs of helpful hands.

"Don't ask!" Leaning heavily against the supportive trunk again, the Crooked Tongue uttered a sigh of relief, his face haggard and sallow, but the colorless lips were already twisting into his usual lopsided grin. "I suppose we better talk somewhere that offers a bit more privacy, don't you think?"

As he pushed himself up with the help of his good arm, many supportive hands shot forward, but Ganayeda was first, offering his own shoulder to lean against.

"Thank you, brother." Panting, the wounded struggled for some time before managing to remain upright on his own. "Just have someone watch that filthy fox closely, in case she tries to do something stupid. She is a wild thing, and my shirt made a lousy rope."

Okwaho, back on his feet already, nodded curtly, indicating the open space near the next cluster of trees. "We can talk over there," he said, after a brief exchange with a group of the nearest men. His gaze lingered upon their dubious prisoner for only a heartbeat, not registering any visible surprise. "If you can make it as far as there, that is. You look as though you could use some rest."

The man's smile flashed as readily as ever, warm, appreciative, enlivening the grayish pastiness of his face. "My news won't take long to tell, but it might prove important."

Taking the lead as unceremoniously as expected—oh, but the

wild man had not changed during his last moon of traveling—the Crooked Tongue hobbled toward the indicated spot, nodding at those who moved out of their way, grinning easily, his gait bordering on ridiculousness.

Unable not to, Ganayeda made a face. "What happened to your moccasins?"

"Don't ask!" Reaching the wide-branched tree, his projected destination, the wounded leaned against the rough trunk, clearly exhausted. "The filthy fox. She threw my moccasins away. Just tossed them into the river, would you believe that?"

"When it comes to you, I would believe anything." Shaking his head, Ganayeda chuckled. Oh no, it was not the same without this man around. "So this is why you took her captive? To compensate yourself against the lost shoes?"

The man rolled his eyes. "She can throw more than a pair of shoes. Her knife-tossing skills might make you wish to enlist her among our warriors. And she seemed to be able to shoot fairly accurate too."

"That thing?" A glance back at the girl confirmed nothing but his first impression. A folded-up, frightened little creature, terrified out of her wits. Poor thing. "Are you sure you didn't hit your head before running into her?"

"Oh please! You have no—"

"Tell us exactly what happened." Catching up with them, Okwaho's voice rang with a fair amount of authority now, uncompromising, not sharing in their brief spell of amusement. "Where did you run into this thing, and why did you bring her here?"

The Crooked Tongue sobered at once. "Out there on the banks of that local river, beyond the marshy lands. I went there when we arrived, to clear—" His eyes focused and he shook his head, as though trying to clear it once again. "But it doesn't matter. The main thing is, there was a woman there. She came all the way from some dreadful falls of the Long Tails, between our Sparkling Water and their other Great Lake." The bruised face screwed into a direful frown. "She seemed to be a local woman, from somewhere around. She spoke like the Mountain People do. But whatever she did out there among the Long Tails, she said they have gathered a huge force as well, many hundreds of warriors that are camping between the Great Lakes, near some falls or the others." This time, the heavily ringed eyes shut in an obvious attempt to remember. "It was something about the thunder, Oniagu-something."

"Onguiahra Falls?" offered Okwaho promptly, all eyes now, leaning with his entire body, afraid to miss a word.

"Yes!" The wounded's eyes lit. "Yes, this thing."

"How many?"

"She said hundreds of warriors, in the beginning. Then she went on to *many* hundreds. She kept insisting that the entire valley of those strange-sounding thundering waters is swarming with warriors."

"Where is she?"

"Back there on the shore. She is dead."

In the process of beginning to turn away, ready to spring into action, Okwaho whirled back, his eyes widening to exaggerated proportions. "Dead how?"

"The filthy fox shot her!" The Crooked Tongue's eyes flickered darkly. "She must have shot her before I reached her, as when I got to her she was already drowning, out of her canoe and spluttering about. I didn't notice the arrow in her back; there was too much to deal with, but it must have been there already, as the dirty little rat didn't shoot anything that I saw. She was throwing knives, instead." His eyes now as dark as the stormy sky, the man peered at the object of his fury, as did the rest of them, all those who had not enough courtesy to step away, or many others, a plethora of eyes peering from all around. The girl, Ganayeda noticed, didn't react, pressing into the trunk she was curling against with too much force, as though trying to disappear there, her face still in hiding. Yet, she must have felt all those stares, *the enemy eyes*, whether she understood their words or not. Poor little thing.

Bewildered, he looked back at the man he never managed to understand. "The girl did all this?"

"Yes, she did," growled the Crooked Tongue, not amused in

the least. "You can choose not to believe me, but it will change nothing. She shot that woman before I got to her, and she threw a knife at me when I tried to bring the drowning woman to her canoe. I didn't know the filthy rat was after her at the time."

Fascinated, Ganayeda studied the viciously glowing cut, covered with ointment now but still glaringly red, nasty-looking, it's location as well as its depth. A little higher and the Crooked Tongue wouldn't be here, telling his implausible tales, he reflected, his skin crawling in spite of his misgivings.

"We'll deal with your girl in a little while," said Okwaho crisply, as always too practical to dwell on irrelevant matters like the improbability of the possible shooter's identity. "Just tell me what this woman told you exactly, word for word." He frowned. "Where did you leave her body?"

"Out there on the shore," muttered their source of information, somewhat reluctantly. "I thought of carrying her here, but then the girl came back, trying to hunt me down, the cheeky little skunk." The glow in the dark eyes was unsettling in its intensity, reminding Ganayeda how carelessly violent this man could become when pushed. "Must have been thinking the world of herself, that one, with her fancy bow, to go after a grown man as though he were a stupid deer."

"Did you try to question her as well?"

"No, and I won't be going anywhere near that stinking rat. Enough that I had to drag her all the way here, with this bleeding shoulder and no shoes. If not for the things the woman before said, I would have dumped the nasty little fox in the river the moment she lost her senses. But for her killing that woman, we might have learned so much more. And to think of the risk she was taking, escaping the Long Tails like that. Only to die by the arrow of the stinking little rat!"

"Tell me what the woman said before she died," Okwaho repeated impatiently. "Then you can rant and rave all you like."

The Crooked Tongue pressed his lips tight, his scowl rivaling the fierceness of the storm upon the Great Lake. "I told you already. That woman, she was still alive when I managed to bring her to the dry land. She stayed around for long enough to tell me her warning." The loudness of his drawn breath shook the thickening dusk. "According to her words, they gathered a huge amount of warriors, as huge as ours maybe. Oh well, she didn't know about our war preparations. Or so I hope." The one-sided shrug held less resentment than before. "She just managed to tell me that they have many hundreds of warriors somewhere there between their Great Waters, near those falls with the thundering name. They are united with Attiwandaronk now, she said. I think she meant the villages of the people who live closer to our side of the Sparkling Lake, next to the Rock People. We call them Long Tails as you do, but they may be different people. I remember my countryfolk saying something to that effect." Another one-sided shrug ensued. "This might account for the unheard-of size of their forces. Your Long Tails alone could never gather so many warriors, even had they made small boys come out with their sharpened sticks for arrows and spears."

"I have heard of Attiwandaronk," said Okwaho, nodding thoughtfully. "They might be different people from the Long Tails we know, yes. They live at the north, you say? Closer to your former people?"

"Not mine, as mine are Bear People from an entirely different place, but yes, those other Long Tails live near the Wyandot who call themselves People of the Rock. I'm not sure they are different Long Tails or not Long Tails at all, but I heard something to that effect, more than one time, especially while traveling toward the Cord People, who are located not that far away from these places themselves."

Okwaho made a face. "You made my head ache with too many of your crooked-sounding names in one tirade." Then his face lost the briefly gained spark of amusement. "Anything else you remember her saying?"

The stark, fatigued face twisted. "No, nothing much. She was most concerned with the amount of warriors and their intentions to come here. Her mind was wandering all over at this point." The strained features softened. "She didn't die easily. But I think it made her feel better that she wasn't alone, less frightened maybe…"

For a heartbeat they fell silent, respecting the dead.

"Let me know where you left her body. I'll send some of the men to bring her here. In Tsonontowan, they'll give her a worthwhile ceremony, make sure to help her spirit reach the good place it deserves."

The foreigner's eyes focused. "I'll take them to that shore."

"No, you stay where you are. I'll send Akweks to fetch you in a little while, escort you to the tents of our people."

The heated protests were forming, too obvious to miss. Ganayeda chuckled, not liking the commanding tone of his brother any better than the foreigner did, even though the young rascal's orders were not directed at him.

"You need to gather your strength back," he said, putting his palm on the wideness of the unhurt shoulder. "Your news may require a quick reaction, and if you are all exhausted and weak from your wounds by dawn tomorrow, you won't be able to keep up if we move." He felt the crookedness of his own grin spreading, one side of his mouth climbing up faster than the other. "Unless you prefer to loiter up there in Tsonontowan, waiting for us to finish your Long Tails off all by ourselves."

An equally twisted smirk was his answer. "Sounds like not such a bad possibility."

Silent, they watched Okwaho strolling toward their captive, kneeling beside her miserable form, still curled up like a ball, more so now, as she evidently sensed her prospective interrogator's advance.

"Are you sure that it was the girl who shot at the woman?"

"Oh, yes, I am. She shot at me too when she managed to spot me." Rolling his eyes, the Crooked Tongue shook his head. "Luckily, she made more noise than a hungry winter bear, skipping all over those cliffs, looking for me. Still, I didn't expect to be faced by a bow, and of such quality. Oh, but you must see this thing!" A casual wave of the grazed hand invited Ganayeda to follow. "I hope no one tried to touch it while the healer was busy making me suffer."

Ganayeda just followed, not interested in the weaponry of strange warrior-girls. His brother's repeated attempts to catch their prisoner's attention were more fascinating by far. Evidently, Okwaho tried hard to use words only, not to resort to shaking the miserable thing into any sort of response, but the stubbornly hidden face refused to come up from the safety of its hideaway, the thin legs folded with a force he could sense from far away. It was a wonder her limbs still had any feeling in them, if at all.

"I wonder if she understands our tongue," he muttered.

"If she came all the way from beyond that Genesee River, then maybe she speaks more like my people do."

"In that case, he is wasting his time."

The pointed eyebrows were climbing up again. "Didn't your mother teach him her former people's tongue as well?"

"She did, yes. Or rather, tried to do that." Turning to head toward the ongoing interrogation, Ganayeda shrugged. "Okwaho is a brilliant warrior and a promising leader, but speeches and different tongues are not his strong suit."

"I didn't think tongues were my strong suit until I moved to your lands." To his surprise and a certain sense of relief, his companion followed, disregarding his previous promises to keep as far away from the treacherous fox as he could. Okwaho was right about this man; his resilience was a great asset. "Our Wyandot tongues are as close to each other as your five nations' ones. No need to crack your skull trying to understand your neighbors' speeches. But your and my people's tongues, oh, those are two different things," he went on, as chatty as ever. But the man was recovering fast! "And it still puzzles me how smoothly it went for me, the attempt to speak any of these."

It makes me wonder as well, thought Ganayeda, shrugging inside. *Did you truly know not a word of my Onondaga People's way of speaking before?*

Storing the same nagging questions for later consideration, he glanced at the kneeling Okwaho and the circle of people surrounding him, everyone's eyes wide with curiosity. Advice came from many directions, but the hum of their voices, if not their towering presence, was probably only adding to their prisoner's terror, if her desperately coiled pose was of any indication.

"Let me try to talk to her alone, without everyone pressing and shouting," he said quietly, kneeling beside his brother. "She might not understand our tongue. And even if she does, she must be scared out of her wits to communicate, no matter what words we use. One can see that easily, Brother."

Okwaho's frown rivaled that of the sky in the winter blizzard. "I have no time to fuss around her, trying to put her at ease."

"And that's why I suggest leaving her to me. While you are running around, organizing our next move, I'll try to make her talk."

"What she tells us might influence my decisions."

Shrugging, Ganayeda looked up, catching the sight of the Crooked Tongue speaking animatedly to a group of people, still gray with exhaustion but full of bubbling energy again.

"Use the information you have. We might get nothing from this girl anyway." Again, he wondered if she was too terrified to listen and understand. Still, he had to try to make it sound as though they had heard it all already. He raised his voice accordingly. "We heard it all by now, so it's not like we are dependent on what she says. There is not much left to tell, neither about their forces, nor about their movements and plans."

Just in case, he thought, peering at her. Her lack of reaction was a disappointment. But maybe she truly did not understand their words.

Okwaho's shrug held a fair measure of freely expressed doubt. "Well, let me know with no delays," he muttered, barely moving his lips, his gaze telling it all, pregnant with meaning.

In another heartbeat he was already up and away, speaking rapidly as he went, giving directions in a tone that brooked no argument. Like Father, this one seemed to know how to make people listen, whether bearing an official title of leadership or not. His purposeful efficiency did this, the natural forcefulness the young beast had in abundance.

In a few more heartbeats, the space around him and the girl cleared as though by a magic wind. Only the Crooked Tongue remained.

"Do you want me to stay or let you have your talk with the

filthy thing all by yourself?" the foreigner asked, not attempting to squat beside them.

"Let us see how it goes," Ganayeda muttered, his stomach tightening with pity at the sight of the skinny heap of limbs in front of him. So young, so vulnerable. Not much older than his firstborn daughter, maybe. How old was she?

"Don't be afraid, little one," he said, using his mother's tongue, the Crooked Tongues words coming easily, as they always did. "You will not come to any more harm."

No reaction.

He took a deep breath. "How old are you?"

More silence.

"Do you understand what I say?"

He glanced at his companion, defeated.

"She may be less terrified if addressed by a woman rather than a man," suggested the Crooked Tongue, shrugging. "She might be afraid of men for a reason."

He recoiled at the very thought. "She is too young for *that*!" It came out sharply, more loudly than he intended. Quite a bark. The girl shuddered, but ever so slightly.

"Some lowlifes out there may not agree with that assertion of yours." His companion's glare was direful, full of unconcealed fury.

He remembered Gayeri and their meeting at the Cord People's lands. Focusing back on the object of their speculations, he caught a glimpse of the muddied face, peeking out from its hiding place for a fraction of a heartbeat, diving back into its safety as quickly, the bump on her forehead swelling, impossible to miss.

"Don't be afraid," he repeated, pronouncing his words carefully, in the way the Mountain People did. "No one will hurt you. We just want to ask questions, to hear why you came here."

Again, the impenetrable wall of silence.

"Why did you come here?"

Several repetitions of the same, in different tongues. He fought the urge to grab her shoulders and shake her hard. To make her face him, at least that.

"What in the name—" The sudden noise of a fairly large stone bouncing off another flat surface exploded, making him jump.

The Crooked Tongue's eyes were focused on the inanimate figure of their prisoner.

"She can't hear," he said flatly. "Come to think of it, she did behave strangely while trying to hunt me down as well."

"Strangely how?" asked Ganayeda, watching her as closely now, looking for signs. Indeed, she might be too terrified to react to the spoken words, no matter what tongues he used, but the sudden noise of a fallen stone should have registered a reaction, shouldn't it?

"I don't know, small things that one doesn't pay attention to until it all comes together. She threw my moccasins off this cliff without care, then proceeded to try and hunt me down. Even though it gave me a clear sign as to her whereabouts." His eyes, narrow with concentration, were boring into the subject of his musings, their thoughtfulness out of place. "I thought she was just a stupid girl back then, a silly little skunk with too much confidence in her skills. But now it seems that she wasn't stupid or disdainful. Just unable to take some of the noise she made into account."

"If she can't hear, that renders your story of her hunting you down less credible than before. Why would such a young vulnerable thing, who could not even hear properly, run around the enemy countryside, shooting at people?"

"No reason," agreed his converser readily. "And yet, she did all I said she did." A shrug. "Those Long Tails might turn out to be very strange people. Have you met one of theirs, ever?"

Ganayeda rolled his eyes. "There was a delegation coming to High Springs some summers ago. The lowlife beasts, they brought nothing but trouble. It was good to encounter none of them anymore. Until now." Glancing at their uncooperative prisoner, he sighed. "What do we do with her?"

"Keep trying. She must know things we need to know. More so in the light of her strange skills and unlikely behavior."

"Easier said than done. If only she were a warrior." The thought of the means to make a captive warrior talk made him uncomfortable. Who would relish the idea of torturing people?

Still, warriors came to expect such treatment if fallen into captivity and not chosen for adoption. The ceremony of execution was not a pretty sight. Or so they said. There were no such ceremonies held in High Springs, only the stories about old times, when those were the main settlements' entertainment. "I suppose we better give her some space, time to recover her spirit, to understand her situation. Then maybe it will be possible to make her talk."

His companion shrugged tiredly, lifting only his good shoulder but still wincing with pain. "Just keep an eye on her, make sure she never gets out of someone's sight." The fatigued eyes narrowed, measuring the curled-up figure with suspicious appreciation. "She is a fierce little thing. One can see it, even without the knowledge of her afternoon exploits. I wonder what she is hiding."

"Probably much." Getting up, Ganayeda shook his head, his own tiredness welling. "I'll talk to Okwaho, see if he comes up with better ideas. We can't drag her along when we move, but we can't leave her back in that town up there, either. They won't be able to keep an eye on her."

"No, they won't. And we don't want her running back to her people as fast as her legs could carry her. Or racing in that annoying canoe of hers, helped by the current this time. I wonder where she hid her boat. Must be somewhere around." Shaking his head, the man snorted. "She would be telling them stories we don't want them hear yet, do we?"

"That she would." Spotting the unmistakably prominent figure of Okwaho's Flint friend, Ganayeda grinned. "Here comes your escort. Go and get some rest, you wounded adventurer. Try to keep low for a dawn or two, until we move into the enemy lands, at least. No point it getting yourself killed or wounded seriously before we have even gotten to the warring part of this enterprise, eh?"

The man's chuckle held the familiar mischief. "You may be right about that. But all I wanted was to clear my head, to stroll about and enjoy a moment of solitude. Who would have imagined that the local rivers would be full of fighting females, set on killing each other? Some warring experience!" The unwounded arm came up, flopped in the air, relaying it all, the wonder, the indignation, the amusement. "I'm telling you, your side of the Sparkling Water is anything but a boring place." Then the amusement fled. "Let me know what your brother does with the girl, would you? I'm dying to know what she knows."

"I will." Nodding as affably as he could, Ganayeda kept his real thoughts off his face.

Okwaho would probably spill it all to the foreigner anyway, seeing how his brother had grown to appreciate this man with the passing of the last moon and the score of his mounting achievements out there in the east. Indeed, the Crooked Tongue did surprisingly well, contributing mightily to their warrior-gathering activities, in an irreplaceable manner sometimes, if his Flint friends were to be believed.

Still, it was too early to trust the strange man wholeheartedly. Like in this instance. What was he seeking while wandering the surroundings of a foreign land troubled by looming war, wishing to clear his head, allegedly, on the same morning of his arrival? And just as the mysterious informer was racing toward their forces, fighting to bring her news that would be lost but for this man. What if there was more to the shooting incident than some deaf little girl, the most unlikely candidate for the role of the vicious, cold-blooded killer this foreigner was making her out to be? What if it was this very man who had silenced the witness, bringing only selective, maybe unimportant news, leaving the more relevant pieces of information out?

Hiding his frown, he stored those thoughts for later consideration. Later tonight that is, when not in this man's vicinity. If he thought them now, the perceptive foreigner might notice, and grow alerted, whether he was the incredibly lucky and brilliantly resourceful person that he appeared to be or someone with more to his activities and underlying motives than he cared to declare.

"I hope he carries a pair of spare moccasins with him," his companion was muttering, eyes on the nearing Flint, flickering with a slightly amused challenge already. "Don't fancy any more barefoot hobbling over these pinecones and pieces of bark."

CHAPTER 18

Aingahon glared at the group of men, finding it difficult to keep his irritation at bay.

"Who gave you permission to wander into the enemy territory as though it were the fields of your native town back home?"

The objects of his fury stood their ground, glaring back, wary but defiant, not grasping fully what they had done, or not caring for the consequences.

"We did damage that settlement," said one of the men finally, eyes narrowed into slits, as thin as his lips were. "We made them leave their fields and run inside the fence, and two men were killed and a few women wounded." The scowl was deepening, together with the growing defiance of the sparkling eyes. "We kept them locked inside for two dawns, didn't let them come out to work their fields, and Tsutare here shot one of the defenders clean. We didn't do so badly. You have no cause to be angry with us."

Oh, Mighty Spirits, but what was he to do with such simple thinking?

"It is not about the success or the lack of it in the improvised raid you took upon yourself to lead, asking no permission and thinking about nothing but your personal glory," he said through his clenched teeth, pushing aside the urge to strike the man down then kill his stupid friends and followers as well. "You thought about no one but yourselves, acting like impatient children eager to alleviate their boredom and not men who care for the future of their people and their well-being."

Another attempt to curb his anger, not to say harsher words

that were hovering on the tip of his tongue. He needed these
people and the rest of their countryfolk, those who came from the
same village or town. If they left in anger, offended beyond repair,
other discontents may follow their example, reducing his
painfully gathered forces, decimating them maybe.

"You have no excuse for your behavior!"

"Your accusations are harsh, brother." The leading man of the
disobedient group stared back, his gaze steady, unblinking. "You
take it upon yourself to lead us, to tell us what to do, but you are a
man of Tushuway, while we are coming all the way from
Honniasont, following our own leaders, who found it advisable to
travel to this gathering."

He had found it more and more difficult to keep his temper in
check.

"Then maybe you should have listened to your leaders more
carefully, warrior." Aware of many attentive ears and observing
eyes, he let his voice rise. "While willing to come here, bringing
your people along, your leading men agreed to place their forces
under mutual leadership of those of us who are responsible for
the conduct of this raid. Our people are united now. In war and in
peace, our people are not living or fighting alone, not anymore."
His eyes left the sullen, scowling face, traveled to rest on the other
culprits, thirty men in all, the would-be independent raiders.
Burning them mercilessly, his gaze made many of them drop
theirs. Many, but not all. How to discipline those? "We are here to
do it properly, to fight the enemy united and strong, like one
devastating wave as opposed to many angry ripples. Our enemy
is powerful, and he will not bend but under the fiercest of
pressure, something we can accomplish, but only as the unified
force of proud Long Tails and Attiwandaronk People together."

Wearily, he looked his growing audience over, trying to keep
his impatience down. How many such speeches had he delivered
through the last half a moon? Hundreds and more. It was exciting
in the beginning, but now it was wearing on his nerves.

More than five dawns since leaving Onguiahra, the
Thundering Water Falls, sailing along Tonawanda, Swift Waters
Creek, heading toward the enemy lands, everyone bubbling, in

high spirits, as though victorious already, while all he felt was uncertainty of the future, a mounting frustration, a flicker of disappointment, maybe even fear. No sense of achievement, no satisfaction. He was heading into the enemy lands, leading an unheard-of amount of warriors, his dreams of unification seeming as though about to become a reality, and in such a glorious way, through the revenge against the Great League. Not a personal revenge, he had reassured himself. It was for the common good of his people, for the future of their proud existence and ever-growing might. And yet ...

And yet, there was no satisfaction. Just the all-encompassing exhaustion, the loneliness, the nagging thoughts that it was going to turn out wrong, somehow. They were just too many. A ridiculous complaint, and of course he didn't share those particular misgivings with anyone.

Still, what looked like a great achievement, an unexpectedly promising beginning—so many warriors eager to fight, to go out and punish the enemy!—started to become a hurdle as they progressed. One day of traveling down the gushing river of his native town in order to turn eastward along one of its tributaries, and he was hard put not to flare up at people or do something violent. Few did as they were told, namely progress in an orderly manner, listening to their leaders or those he had appointed to lead various groups and parties.

It was difficult enough to sort them all out and divide them, a necessity the importance of which only he seemed to grasp. How could one lead many hundreds of men as one body, just an unorganized crowd that they were? Back near the Thundering Falls, he had spent days trying to devise a simple strategy of moving them around, of establishing ways to communicate messages and pass directions among so many different groups, of battling the impediment their numbers was becoming.

Still, close to ten dawns since first laying his eyes on his unheard-of force and well on their way toward the enemy's main river, the lack of confidence didn't recede, nagging, harassing, making him snap up at people and lose his patience worse than before. Like in the days when he wasn't listened to by any other than a handful of like-minded followers, shunned by the authorities and the leading elements of his town, looked upon askance.

He was still not the appointed leader of this monumental venture, but somehow, they all came to him for directions and advice. A development he welcomed of course, but for the amount of dilemmas, problems, and disagreements he had been called upon to resolve while dedicating all his time and energies to an attempt of putting it all in a semblance of order. How were they to succeed in making the most out of their advantage if the people weren't ready to listen to each other and coordinate their actions?

Back when they had started, it was only half a day into their initial progress, and he had known that even when on the move, their horde of excited warriors had to be divided, at least in two. So upon reaching the first of the great river's tributaries, he had instructed some of the Attiwandaronk leaders he came to trust to take their men, about eight hundred, and follow this smaller river's course until reaching the agreed upon spot near the ridges of the great watershed the enemy called Genesee River. Less than two days of travel away, but he gave them twice as long, insisting on the extensive use of scouts and messengers being sent back and forth all the time. He himself was to proceed along Tonawanda Creek, leading the rest of their men, well over a thousand warriors. Anticipating no enemy forces of a worthwhile size, he felt it safe to split theirs, if for no other reason than to be able to manage their human wave more easily. When reunited with their allies again and at the edges of the enemy forests they would cross the accursed river and begin warring for real. There would be plenty of time to formulate and reformulate their plans before that.

But for all the disobedience, but for the repetitiously independent sorties!

He glared at the men in front of him, frustrated by the fact that they weren't the first nor the last to pursue their private little wars as they progressed along their original creek, turning southward when it was replaced by another flowing stream, then another.

Five dawns of clamor and disorder, of unsatisfactory progress, of the same lack of reassurance from the other part of their forces and no knowledge of their whereabouts. Had the Attiwandaronk already reached the projected meeting place? Not likely, he knew, especially if their own warriors were sneaking away on the slightest of provocations, seeking personal glory, attacking unimportant villages or traveling people. The situation must be no different among their northern allies. He would be naive to assume otherwise.

Attiwandaronk!

He pushed another nagging worry away. Tsutahi! Where was she? It had been near ten dawns—these same accursed ten dawns!—since she disappeared, and just as he had told her to stick around, to stop sneaking all over the woods full of so many warriors, hers and his people or not. He didn't have a clear plan as to what to do with her, besides the only sensible solution she rejected. To be placed in Tushuway until his return was not her idea of being helpful. To stick around for as little time as it took him to send her to the tents of his people and then disappear must have been a better way, at least to the wild thing's judgment.

He didn't have time to worry about it back then, but as the night had worn off and the next day passed, he knew something was wrong. He knew it in his bones. Her disappearance had to do with his warring efforts. It was as clear as a cloudless day of midsummer. She had gone off to do something useful. But what? And why without a word? *And why did it make him so worried?*

When they had left, he went as far as leaving instructions to send him a message when she reappeared. The dwellers of Onguiahra Falls didn't know her at all, unlike some of his Tushuway countryfolk, but he still did his best to convey the importance of her being found and treated well. His stomach tightened in hundreds painful knots at the thought of what could have happened to her.

"I will not tolerate any more independent side-raids," he said, concentrating back on the men he had no means to discipline, no matter how necessary and essential it was. The attempt to sound less stern than he felt came with difficulty. "Be patient until we cross their main river. Then you will have plenty of opportunities to show your courage and valor."

They muttered words that sounded like apologies, with no real remorse or appreciation for his tolerance and forbearance. Filthy skunks!

He turned back toward the others, some leading warriors and just men who liked being around and helpful. Always plenty of these, thank the great and small spirits for that.

"Our scouts should return before dusk. If their reports are favorable, we will camp as near the enemy river as we dare and send word to our allies upstream."

"We should be crossing together with them," offered one of the elder warriors.

"Of course. The moment we hear from our scouts, we reunite." He thought about all the walking around that was still expected of him this afternoon, even without the necessity to move their camp, his knee tied in a close-fitting cloth, helped by its firm support, but still hurting, still crying for a rest. It was a pain to wear leggings at all times, a strange way of dressing while on the warpath, with the somewhat cumbersome wear being reserved for ceremonies and rites, or much colder weather than warm summer moons.

Well, to have people staring at his strange outfit was better than to have them wondering about his disabilities if they saw what means he used to improve his way of walking.

He shrugged. "Let the warriors' leaders, especially the Honorable War Chief of Tushuway, know that we should be holding a meeting tonight."

That should do, he decided. The touchy old warrior liked knowing things in advance. If it wasn't required of him to wander additional distance in order to find the man, he might have talked to their official leader himself, made him feel as though they were following his ideas. A wise course of action that let him have his way more easily these days. If nothing else, his sudden elevation made him hone his diplomatic skills, he reflected, not amused in the least. No more repetitions of the open clashes, of outright confrontations like with the previous War Chief and other leading people of his influential town. No need to remove enemies from his path by violent means, either. He felt his mood spiraling down again. *Where was she?*

A question that was to be answered in the most unexpected fashion just as he became immersed in listening to one of the returning scouts.

"The river can be crossed comfortably not far away from here." A hardened warrior of no little summers, the scout did not spend his time on idle pleasantries, his northerner's way of speaking pronounced, disclosing his Attiwandaronk origins. "There are relatively low falls where the current slows and then widens considerably. They say we can cross there comfortably, without spreading in every direction."

"How far is this place?" He nodded solemnly, trying not to let his excitement show. A good crossing point, and found so soon. Their scouts *were* good!

"Less than half a day's sail along two more creeks." The scout frowned. "With not much forging to do between the two," he added, as an afterthought. Good!

"Tomorrow, we will start with dawn." He glanced at the helpfully hovering men, those who had made it their business to shadow him, knowing who the real leader of this enterprise was. "Send another pair of messengers, to let our allies know. I want them to be there no later than tomorrow midmorning. Their entire force."

One of the men made a movement as though about to rush away just as the figure of a running warrior appeared from behind the bluff, racing down the invisible trail, in a great hurry. They all turned to stare.

"Word from our men, Honorable Leader." Until the man reached them, Aingahon had had a hard time restraining himself from rushing to meet him halfway. This one carried an important message, that much was clear. Something that couldn't wait even one additional heartbeat, his gut feeling told him.

"What is it?"

"The enemy, they are camping, they are..." The man panted, almost doubled over in an attempt to catch his breath. "The enemy was spotted in huge numbers!"

"Where?" he breathed when the pause stretched too long, with the man again gasping for air, still bent, supporting himself with his hands propped against this knees. "Tell me exactly what you've been told. Who sent you?"

"Our people, they received word. The girl came from the heart of the enemy lands, where the water bodies they call Finger Lakes are. The moment they heard, they sent me here."

"Finger Lakes?" He turned toward his scout, his mind running amok, desperate not to succumb to a panicked urge to do something, clinging to the parts of the information he could deal with. "Where is it?"

His own scout swallowed. "I'm not certain what they mean by that name, but about a little more than a day of walk from here there are several longish lakes spreading one after another, at least three or four water bodies." Frowning, the man licked his lips. "If you watch from uphill they may look like fingers, yes. Some of these lakes."

He whirled back to face the panting informant. "On what lake is the enemy camping?"

"They say," the man wavered, as though deliberating between taking a step back or maybe just leaping away. "They said, the girl said..." Another painful pause. "She said it's called Ho-ne-o-yah Lake. Yes, she used that name!" A triumphant note enlivening the man's voice didn't amuse Aingahon in the least.

The girl! What girl? Could it be—Later, not now!

Back to his scout and the others. "Are you familiar with this place? Any of you?"

Their frowns could rival the depth of the moonless night. "Honey-oy means Lying Finger," said one of the men. "In their tongue. Yes, it might be the name of one of those lakes."

"Pick a group of the men you trust the most and head there now."

His scout straightened up, displaying no hesitation. The others followed as readily. "One of us will have to stay, to guide our men toward the crossing point."

As they argued between them as to who would be staying

behind, he felt his heart squeezing with pride. Oh, but his men were the bravest, every one of them.

"Be careful. If they have warriors concentrating around those lakes, there would be plenty of local scouts prowling the surrounding woods. Don't endanger yourselves by coming too near. A general look from somewhere far away to verify their location and possibly the size of their forces would be enough."

A steady look was his answer. "You will know all about it tomorrow, before Father Sun leaves our world."

They were gone before he could as much as nod in response. He put his attention back to the messenger, in a hurry to question the man before other leaders arrived.

"Tell me again what you've been told and by whom? Did your people strike their camp when you left? Are they on their way here?"

The man's face was regaining its coloring, his breathing becoming even enough to allow coherent speech.

"I have been told to find you, Honorable Leader, to give you the news," he said weakly, eyes darting between Aingahon's face and the pine needle-covered ground, undecided as to where to stay. "The girl said she saw hundreds of enemy warriors on the move. She said they were camping between the two lakes. She didn't know those places, but some of our scouts recognized them by her description."

His stomach felt like a wooden ball, knotted in a way that didn't let him draw a deep breath in. "Who is this girl?"

The young man's eyes went up, clinging to his face, eager to say the right thing. "They don't know, but she sounds like one of us, the way she speaks. Must be a former captive." Another imploring gaze. "She didn't say much. She was all battered from the journey, beat up too. No one knows how she found our people. She couldn't hear well, or something. Wouldn't talk to people until our leaders insisted." A nervous chuckle interrupted the hectic flow of words. "She insisted on speaking to you, repeated your name. Had a hard time accepting that you and your warriors were camping elsewhere."

The little air that had managed to sneak through the barrier inside his chest stopped as well.

"Where is she now?" It was difficult to recognize his own voice. So gritting, so strident. *Like the way she talked.*

"Back in the camp, taken care of," muttered the man, gaping at Aingahon, nervous again. "She wanted to go, but they couldn't let her, not in the shape she was in. So they sent me... to bring the news..."

As the man's voice trailed off, Aingahon became aware of the breeze coming from the creek side again, the receding intensity of the heat. The evening was nearing.

"Go back to our camp and get yourself something to eat." This time, his voice sounded almost normal, low and strained, but with no jarring quality to it.

Satisfied, he waved the young man away. It was calming to refer to the mundane tasks of simple organizing, deciding who were the best runners with enough clout among his forces to reach their stubbornly independent allies and force them into meeting up at the crossing point, the strategy of striking their own camp and moving close to a thousand people with no delays and no milling around. So much to do, besides putting his mind to the enemy who had miraculously gathered a huge amount of warriors as well and was waiting for them, seemingly confident, or maybe just unaware.

Oh, all the great and small spirits, please make them wander unaware, thinking they were about to invade, not knowing that they had already been invaded. But for such a chance! Did the treacherous adoptee from Onguiahra village manage to reach these people? Was Tsutahi involved in any of this?

The cold wave was back, washing his insides, freezing them. Could it be that she had been to the enemy lands already? Oh, but why didn't the stupid messenger bring her along? She would have told him so much more about it, and he would have been able to reassure her, to soothe her fears, to make her feel better. To think about her out there, alone and exposed to so much danger, or even back among their allies, her own people, yes, but not the people she needed to reach, hurt almost physically. But for the chance to jump into a canoe or rush off on foot, to reach the camp of the Attiwandaronk by midday tomorrow! Impossible, and not only because of the damn knee. He had much responsibility, an obligation to over a thousand people. His time was not his to decide upon. And yet …

"Find Andauk and send him to me in a hurry," he said, spotting a group of Tushuway warriors who were busy roasting juicy cuts of a hunted deer above a lustily roaring fire, spreading wonderfully tempting aroma. He pressed his lips tight. "And put this fire out. I said small smokeless fires. Wasn't I clear about that?"

They shifted uneasily, not daring to meet his gaze, knowing that they were in the wrong. So close to the enemy's main river, he had forbidden any grand-style cooking, a sure way of spreading evidence of their presence and their looming advance far and wide. A sensible measure he expected the people to appreciate, to take heed of, if not out of respect for his authority then at least as the demand of simple good reason. How naive.

"But this deer is so fresh, and we were going to be quick about it," muttered one of the men, his hands restless, dripping meat juices, obvious in his eagerness to get back to his cooking before their prospective meal got burned. "You'll enjoy the fruits of our meal, Honorable Leader. The best cut of this thing is yours."

He wanted to scream at their hopeful faces, and maybe strike them as well. Were they irresponsible children or warriors? Grinding his teeth, he forced his mounting fury away.

"It doesn't take long for cooking smells to spread far and wide. Not to mention the smoke," he said in the clipped, cold tone, marveling at the calm his words radiated. "We are already in the enemy forests and about to cross into their heartlands. I expect you to behave like grown warriors and not small children. Put this thing out!"

They stood his murderous gaze, but only for another heartbeat.

Turning around, he made sure to put all his weight on his good leg. "Send Andauk and some of his people to me in a hurry. I expect them to find me before the sun disappears."

Oh, yes, Andauk would manage to put some fire under their allies' behinds, to get them moving toward that Genesee River and the meeting point. The big, roaring fire that they needed as motivation; not a careful, smokeless affair. He grinned without humor. How to make people listen, follow direction or simple common sense?

Also, how to reach her or help her reach him before they attempted the crossing? How stupid it was of those people not to send her along with their messenger, or better yet, instead of him. She would have reached him faster, not panting or looking as though about to faint, and her account would have been better, richer in details. She would have had all the answers, and he would have the opportunity to comfort her, to make her feel better.

Had she truly been to the enemy lands? But how and why?

He knew the answer to that. Oh, but he had known it all along, refusing to face the reality since the day of her disappearance, helpless to do anything about it, worried sick. But it changed nothing. Of course she hadn't just wandered off, deciding to keep away from his war. To think that was childish, and cowardly. A reluctance to face the reality wasn't him.

Still, he chose to busy himself, to turn his face away from the suspicion that she had gone after the woman from Onguiahra Falls, trying to stop the traitor from letting the enemy know. Such a dangerous mission, to enter the enemy's heartland in an attempt to catch the deserter, to bring information back. Not every warrior would have summoned enough courage to do that, not every scout. But she did. Alone, consulting no one, asking for no help or assistance. Did she get hurt in the process? The damn man said she was battered from the journey, but beaten too. Beaten by whom?

He ground his teeth. Oh, but if the vile enemy hurt her...

CHAPTER 19

The creek was flowing somewhere there, encouraging with its constant trickling, the sense of permanency and tranquility it relayed. At least that!

Ogteah stretched his shoulders, trying not to groan at the sharp twinge of pain the careless movement caused. The damn wound was still giving him trouble, and just as the other one, the remainder of that stupid Standing Stone adventure, or rather debacle, finally seemed to dry up and close for good. A small mercy. Was he to collect an impressive amount of crudely stitched cuts before his first venture into the warriors' life even began?

Squinting, he peered at the brilliant green of the trail ahead, trying to see through it. Or at least to hear something, to probe with his senses like when on a hunt. But this wasn't a hunting expedition, this was the real thing. Warriors were no deer set on fleeing, not a dangerous predator to tail, one who could turn on the hunter if cornered yet otherwise preferred to avoid the confrontation. Oh no! The warriors were there to fight, to attack or surprise or ambush, in the same way he and the others he was with were trying to ambush the enemy as well now. Their ultimate goal, a killing. A mutual target. He had been there to do the same.

A careful hoot shook the air, then another. They froze, listening. When the third cry tore the early afternoon, he motioned the people who were following him to proceed. The top of the hill must be their final destination. Or maybe not, but they would know more when they reached the rest of his men.

Fifty-odd warriors, he thought, creeping along the rustling

green, careful to make no sound. Warriors of suspiciously similar disposition, hand-picked by Akweks and the wolf man, people with an independent streak and different thinking, troublesome elements, most of them. Like those violent Standing Stone brothers from that town of the brawl, two of whom were now making their way alongside him, following his lead. Not bad men at all, surprisingly easy to get along with once one managed to gain their respect, fiercely loyal, ready to follow. An interesting combination. It was surprising how readily these two volunteered for such an unordinary, clearly dangerous mission, not minding having a person like him, a foreigner with no worthwhile list of heroic deeds to recount, in the lead.

"They must have spotted something." The words brushed past his ear, so faint they seemed to barely move the air.

Ogteah nodded at the man, hastening his step. Three hoots warranted developments. Good. It had been tiring to wander about with no certainty or clear destination, progressing silently, careful to leave no marks, perpetually on guard, bursting with tension, seeking the enemy like scouts, but not quite.

Their numbers were too large to be a group of prowling scouts, but too small to challenge hundreds of enemies. They were there to distract, to unsettle, to cause damage, with their real forces camping back near the northern edge of Honeoye Lake, the site the wolf man had in mind for some time, a good place to contain the enemy, unless the invaders chose not to come. And this is what Ogteah's group of troublesome elements was to ensure. The arrival of the enemy, the timely arrival. The wolf man was quite precise about it, the place and the timing; and in his warning not to fall in captivity, at any price. Anything but that.

Since hearing about the possible size of the approaching enemy, all their young charismatic leader could think of was a battle of unheard-of proportions, an enormous clash of huge forces, the united might of the Great League pitted against its historical foe, to be remembered for many summers, to be repeated by storytellers by winter fires.

It had taken them no time to move their camp, enormous as it was. Two days after the eventful evening through which Ogteah had delivered his news along with his unusual captive saw the shores of Canandaigua Lake clearing of the invading guests' overbearing presence, lapsing back into its relative tranquility. A village between the two smaller lakes, less than half a day's walk toward the west, had the honor of hosting the huge force now, offering a spacious valley surrounded by sloping hills. A perfect place for a thought-out, well-prepared battle, claimed the wolf man, now listened to by even the hardened veterans and warriors' leaders. Such a perfect lay of the land!

With the ambush their young leader was planning, claimed Akweks, while sharing what he had heard about those plans with Ogteah, the enemy would be brought down decisively and for good, in a spectacular fashion. The only aspect was left to be ensured was the enemy's arrival at the right spot. There were many tributaries to the Mountain People's main river, many routes to take while traveling eastwards. What could they do to make the invaders arrive where expected?

One of the ways occurred to none other than the High Springs man, now an important dignitary, the delegate of the Great Council itself. Observant, as always, in the habit of listening to the people while keeping his own council, the man came up with an interesting idea while trying for the great spirits knew what time to make their outlandish captive talk. Or at least listen, as the strange girl refused to do both, either talk or listen. Or to do anything else, really. Less than two days of hosting this thing in their custody and they had despaired of having any reaction at all, good or bad. Was she also dumb, in addition to being obviously deaf, or maybe just unable to speak?

Her refusal to their food offerings pointed at the first possibility; still, before their camp got into a real turmoil, preparing to move, the High Springs man sank deep into his thoughts whenever the girl was concerned, making it his business to speak clearly in her vicinity, disclosing curious bits of inaccurate information while speaking to other people, usually him, Ogteah, sometimes in his native tongue, pretending not to notice her covert glances or the painful concentration in her eyes.

The wolf man must have approved of the ploy, as while their

forces were on the move, and having disclosed every possible landmark of their prospective destination, to leave no mistakes, the girl had managed to slip away, watched quite sloppily for some time.

Having the entire ruse worked out long before it was attempted to be executed—for some reason, the High Springs' man was not as open with him as his brother was—Ogteah would have smirked but for the annoying fox's audacity in stealing the wondrous bow he had appropriated for himself, considering it a rightful spoil.

Such an outstanding weapon, larger and sturdier than any shooting device he had ever seen, but as flexible as any, maybe even more so, with long, robust arrows to match. He had practiced with it already, growing fond of it while earning murderous looks from their captive when the girl saw him sporting his new weaponry. Who would have thought that he needed to guard it as closely against the treacherous skunk who apparently was crazy enough to endanger her desperate attempt at escape in order to recover her lost weaponry?

Shaking his head to get rid of the annoying memory, he slipped through the generous green, sensing one of their scouts ahead before the man materialized next to him, out of thin air as it seemed.

Are they? he gestured, not daring to open his mouth.

The man motioned with his head, indicating the end of the incline.

Nodding his understanding, Ogteah slipped on, his heart beating fast. The enemy, at long last. They must have received word, after all; still, at this crucial point, when one tributary of the mighty river was joining its forces with another lively stream, they needed to make sure the invaders were taking the correct route, not wandering up the wrong creek. A task he and his men were entrusted with. He felt another twinge of suspicious tightening crawling up his stomach, making his limbs light, uncomfortably weightless. An unsettling feeling.

With the others pressing close behind, he made his way toward the indicated cluster of bushes, burrowing his way in, paying little attention to their prickly resistance. What lay ahead was more important.

Crouching behind slippery, moss-covered stones, he glimpsed the view of the watershed below, then wished he hadn't. Such an alarming vision. The current they had been following was clearly visible, dark in the afternoon shadows, running strongly, as though in a hurry to arrive at its destination, narrowing considerably before entering the larger body of water. This one seemed calmer, quite wide, a peaceful look to it but for the swarms of people that filled every gap in the greenery, every bit of the open ground.

Generously lit by the declining sun, enhanced by the alternating shadows, the busily moving groups of warriors looked especially menacing, ominously businesslike, ant-like and determined. So many, and those must be only a part of the invading force, with great spirits knew how many others sniffing around the thickness of the groves, using its coverage where the generous foliage did not let his eyes reach. Not to mention the multitude of those still busy with their vessels, fussing around so many boats one couldn't see the water of the river clearly.

He motioned his followers to fall back.

"How long has it been since they've arrived here?" he whispered, catching one of his scout's eyes, the man he had come to admire, such a dauntless spirit.

The man narrowed his eyes, then held out one finger, bending it in a half. Half a day. Mid-morning.

Ogteah hesitated. To start making trouble or to wait? he asked himself, willing the enemy to take the right course, up the smaller creek that had wound its way here starting at the base of Honeoye Lake, their desired location.

"Time to see some fighting, at long last." The older of the Standing Stone brothers was grinning happily, caressing the club he insisted on bringing along, even though it was an unnecessary cargo to carry than more practical bows. Their mission was to harass the enemy, to lead them on and ensure their progress in the correct direction. Not to engage in outright fighting, not if they could help it.

"Let us wait until they start transferring their boats."

Quite a few faces clouded. He paid them no heed, returning his attention back to the view of the emerging river and the teeming activity around it.

"We will miss the best of the light," breathed someone, coming closer, evidently to have a good look as well.

"And by that time, they will be gone." Another irritated whisper.

Not that fast, thought Ogteah, paying them no attention, himself torn between different courses. To creep down the incline and try to sneak up on the enemy undetected was tempting, a real possibility now that they might be preoccupied with the difficulties of pouring their massive body of boats into the smaller stream. Their pausing at the mouth of the "correct" water body was already promising. Did the strange girl truly manage to reach them with her spells of useful information? What a wild thing!

"We wait for them to start moving, then we decide," he whispered again, his voice firm. The thickness of the grove on the opposite side of the creek beckoned, offering possibilities. "Any signs of them sniffing around here as well?"

Their lead scout shrugged, then shook his head, eyes on the same scenery. "Maybe over there."

"Time to check if the rest of our men arrived there as yet." Straightening up with decision, Ogteah gave the rest of his party a stern look. "Watch them until one of us comes back. Do nothing. Nothing at all! If you spot their scouts or just wandering warriors, kill them quietly if you can. If not, retreat without giving your presence away." Another round of stony staring. "No independent sorties, not until I come back or send word!"

They stared back, some with an open defiance. The Standing Stone leading brother's eyes were as narrow as knife cuts on bark. Ogteah's eyes locked with his, held the mutinous stare until its intensity lessened.

"You are in charge," he said, pleased with asserting his dominance, but not willing to antagonize the man more than necessary. "Make sure nothing goes wrong until I send word back."

The man nodded stiffly, mollified, to a degree.

Diving back into the cool dampness of the grove, he felt his taut nerves relaxing. So far, they had done not so badly. The enemy was found, and they seemed to be heading in the right direction. And if they didn't, he and his men were there, poised on the move, in the position to direct those forces. No failure, not so far. Oh, but how he feared it would come to that. The wolf man put great trust in him, giving a man with no warring experience a leading position, and over such a daring group.

Granted, the bulk of their party was in the same boat, brawlers like the Standing Stone brothers, good at personal fights. Perfect candidates for unordinary missions, like going out, harassing the enemy while luring it straightaway into the trap, maintained the wolf man, grinning widely. They were all notorious troublemakers, those men, and why test their patience, chancing them getting bored and starting to make trouble? Better horde them together and make them do something useful, he had said, his grin shamelessly open. Under the management of a man who knew all about the troublesome behavior or thinking, what could possibly go wrong?

"What do you have in mind?" The unexpected question pulled Ogteah from his half-amused, half-indignant musings. The wolf man should have led this wild party himself, clearly knowing all about stirring trouble as well.

"We have close to fifty men. Enough to try a nice ambush should they head up the Honeoye Creek without our prompting."

The man slowed down, falling into Ogteah's step easily. "It's narrow enough in the beginning, yes. Indeed a creek and not a river in this place."

"Exactly. They would have to spread thin with their boats, in a long, slender line. Do you know of the best place to surprise them?"

"Maybe."

Not willing to interrupt the closemouthed scout's thoughts, Ogteah fell silent in his turn, his elation welling. It might work, whyever not? No matter how numerous the enemy was, no matter how determined. Fifty reckless hotheads with the element of surprise on their side, oh, but they stood a fair chance of disrupting some of the invading forces' movement, of bringing those warriors to their destination as instructed but already ruffled, taught the first lesson of raiding the wrong people in the wrong woods.

"If they didn't choose to follow our tributary on foot, we may lay out a nice greeting up there, where the flow takes the first sharp turn." His companion's voice had a purring quality to it.

"And if they did?" asked Ogteah, his mind racing, eager to execute his ambush no matter what now. "With so many boats and people, they would be better off walking, not struggling against the silly stream that is barely as wide as ten canoes in this time of the seasons."

"They will have to sail, some of them, even if the bulk of their warriors might be choosing to forge. The supplies need to be carried, and the wounded on their way back or forth. This is not a raid of ten men." The scout was walking briskly, staring ahead.

For which Ogteah was grateful, ashamed of his silly musings and the way he kept airing them aloud. Like a boy trailing after a party of warriors. At his age, he should have known, or at least assumed, that a war expedition was more than running around in a battle frenzy, waving one's club. All this planning and elaborate preparations, endless supplies to organize and carry, to distribute several times a day, all this additional ware, tools, war accessories to bear, hadn't he seen enough of such hectic activity for the past few days, since reaching Tsonontowan and their sprawling camp?

He forced his thoughts back to the present dilemmas. They were here to ensure the enemy's advance in the right direction, to disturb some of their progress, if possible, to make trouble. Well, harassing the boats carrying supplies and maybe some occasional wounded or sick should add to their contribution, shouldn't it?

"When we find the rest of our men, take me to that bend you were talking about."

Another placid nod was his answer. Did this man have to pay something for every word coming out of his mouth that he was so stingy with them?

Ogteah forced his senses to concentrate as well, still able to hear the faint hum of the enemy down by the river. So many warriors! Not as many as their people, maybe, but still an unexpectedly impressive amount. The Long Tails were apparently full of surprises. What would Father's union have thought about their war readiness if they heard? Or was it his former people's doing? Did they entice their western neighbors into an outright war against the Great League, somehow? Maybe reinforced them with their warriors as well. Oh, Mighty Spirits, but was he to fight his own people now?

The tightening in his stomach was back, the unsettling squeeze. *What to do?*

He pushed the stupid question away. What was there to do but to go on, doing what he has always been best at—going with the flow, letting life sort itself out. One might go mad thinking of impossible situations sometimes, and he did owe his new people every effort to do well. They trusted him, the High Springs brothers and the rest. They even thought he was capable of leading people, the first to think something like that.

The rustling of hushed voices disclosed the proximity of the group they were looking for. Sure enough of themselves to whisper and laugh. While his guide's frown deepened, Ogtaeh just shrugged. They were in good spirits, evidently, their confidence unruffled by the sight of the enemy. Good! Another group of men he knew he would put to good use. But for bringing more men here! No matter how restless or sometimes outright disobedient they were back in the camp, no matter what misgivings he had in the beginning, after traveling with these people for two dawns, he knew he could handle them.

"Have you had a good look at the enemy?" he asked, spending no time on greetings, knowing that they were aware of his approach, forewarned by these same careful hoots his scout seemed to use more readily than he used regular words.

They nodded eagerly, fifteen hard, able men, some fierce-looking, some ordinary, sporting scars but no more than the regular people did. No glaring difference about them. Still, those were the troublesome elements the wolf man was anxious to use, if for no other reason than to keep them preoccupied and busy.

"Then come," he went on, his impatience welling now that the decision was made. They had not dragged all over these woods just to report the enemy progress and be done with it.

"Where to?" asked a broadly built man, his speech disclosing his Onondaga origins.

"Back to our creek." Not waiting for them to burst into more questioning, Ogteah turned to his guide. "How far is that bend in the river?"

"Not far." An impassive half-shrug had him wishing to roll his eyes.

"Are you sure it's a suitable place to have so many of us huddling there without giving our presence away?"

Another laconic nod.

He turned back to his people. "We'll be off now. Back up the stream, to reach the perfect place for an ambush, to do what we can to hurt the enemy, then back to our forces."

Their frowns matched that of their scout now. Where was their fighting eagerness? With the other group, he had to hold them nearly physically from rushing down the hill, attacking many hundreds of warriors with their bows and an odd club.

"What kind of an ambush?"

"The simplest of them all." He turned away resolutely. "I'll be able to elaborate when we reach the place." A nod toward the unimpressed scout. "Take us there."

He suppressed the urge to push himself past the man. The uncooperative skunks, all of them. He should have brought the Standing Stone brothers along.

"Shouldn't some of us stay and watch the enemy?"

Judging by the rustle of their footstep, they were following. Some of them, or maybe most. He didn't turn his head to verify that. No need to demonstrate his misgivings, to acknowledge his lack of confidence in their obedience, their acceptance of his leadership, confirmed by the higher authorities or not. Watching the wolf man and his way with warriors of all ranks and ages, he had noted what effect an unshaken self-assurance had on some doubters. The man never turned his head to make sure he was being followed or obeyed. Not this one.

"The other group is watching them," he tossed over his shoulder, hastening his step after their guide began walking briskly, at long last. "When we examine the place, I'll bring them over as well," he added, mollified by the lack of further protests.

Their walk, indeed, turned out to be a brief affair, with the light breeze greeting them near the open space of the rocky shores.

"Are there any more scouts here or deeper westward?" he asked, judging that it was permissible to break the silence, which was wearing on his nerves worse than ever, irritated by too many twists and turns of the invisible trail his guide was outlining with his steps. "Our people who are sniffing around here independently?"

A curt, openly impolite wave was his answer. He stared at the broad palm that demanded his silence, wishing to grind his teeth. But they were not—

Suddenly, he knew that something was wrong. The murmurs of their followers' footsteps interfering with his ability to listen, he felt rather than heard a foreign presence. Or maybe it was their guide's stance, the man's slightly derisive indifference gone, replaced by an animal-like pose of a predator about to pounce or a deer about to dart.

Holding his breath, Ogteah strained his ears, but only the hum of the invisible stream and the rustling of the foliage managed to reach him. This and the blurring silhouette of their scout ahead, melting in the surrounding green, gone before noticed.

"What..."

He held his hand out in an unconscious imitation of their guide's previous gesture, ordering silence. But of course they didn't listen.

"What is going on?"

The next moment, the forest ahead exploded with loud rustling, then the muffled sound of running feet, or maybe something being dragged over the damp ground.

Frantic, his senses urging him to act, run, attack before being attacked, *to do something*, Ogteah tore his knife from its sheath, darting toward the source of the noise, crashing through the nearby bushes, oblivious of their prickly touch. The vague memory of their scout disappearing through the same seemingly solid wall surfaced. Oh, but where did this one go?

The thundering of the breaking branches behind his back reassured him, let him know that his men were following, at a close range. As an arrow swished by, he ducked, feeling his foot slipping, twisting on an entanglement of roots.

Fighting for balance, he glimpsed a silhouette darting toward him, and his instincts took over, throwing his body to roll over the muddy ground. A club crashed into the mud where his head had momentarily been propped, making a dull, plopping sound.

More feet flew by in a blur of swift movement, as he scrambled back to his feet, desperate to catch his balance, to see where the next blow was coming from. His left, apparently.

As he struggled to locate his knife again—such a useless thing against a club, but he had no better option—he felt the movement rather than saw it, this feeling of something bad, lethally heavy approaching.

Twirling to get away from it, he knew he wouldn't make it in time, but his senses kept deciding for him, making his body twist as if in a dance, keeping his balance miraculously, absorbing no blow. Just the feel of the movement where the heavy tip swished by, a ripple of air brushing against this sweaty skin.

Surprisingly calm, he watched his attacker wavering, pulled by the drive of the powerful movement, struggling to stop the club from completing its half-circle, something the deadly weapon seemed determined to do. A perfect opportunity.

As though in a dream, seeing everything in a slower motion, he let his hand holding the knife shoot forward, completing the thrust of his body, reaching its target first, the temptingly exposed side offering no resistance, no defensive moves, still busy with whirling around.

Unable to hold on, he let it drag him along, back into the dampness of the ground, finding it astonishingly easy to pin the jerking limbs with his weight, to twist the knife as though knowing what he was doing, as though having done it before.

By the time the body underneath him went still, he was back in a semblance of control, not thinking what happened through but knowing that they must make sure no other intruders were nearby, to attack them or worse yet, to try to get away and warn the rest of their forces.

"Spread around!" he ordered, annoyed by the sight of their faces, encircling him from above, gawking. "Make sure there are no more of the filthy skunks sniffing around here, running to bring reinforcements."

Some of the faces melted away.

"Where is the scout?" To get back to his feet turned out to be more difficult than expected, with his limbs slippery with mud and blood, strangely light, refusing to offer any real support.

They shook their heads, still staring.

"There were people milling around here, certainly," said one of the men, coming back from behind the thickest of trees. "Two different pairs of footprints."

Ogteah tried to make his head work. The clubs pounding inside it were annoying, interfering with his ability to concentrate, this stupid light buzz. "Find the second one before he can get away."

"He is not going anywhere." The scout was back, dragging another body by its queue of decorated hair. "I see you took care of the other one."

"Are you sure there were no more than these two?"

"In this part of the woods, yes." The man shrugged, but with less demonstrated disinterest than before. His gaze resting on Ogteah held a measure of grudging appreciation. "Shall we inspect your ambush's location now?"

Bending to retrieve his knife that, to his endless embarrassment, had somehow slipped away while he was getting up, he felt the others coming back to life, beginning to move. The club of his victim made it into his hands next, a welcome addition.

"What do we do with the bodies?" someone asked, a hesitant voice.

In the prevailing silence, Ogteah straightened up, wishing nothing more than to be left alone, if only for a little while, until his limbs stopped trembling. It was unnerving, the way they all peered at him, waiting for instructions. Were those the same people who had questioned each and every one of his decisions before?

"Leave them here until we are done with the ambush," he said sharply, marveling at the firmness of his own voice. No trembling there, thank all the great and small spirits. The memory of the journey to Ossossane surfaced. "We'll see them off with the customary words for now. That will do."

"No, it won't." The scout scowled, glancing at his own victim, a man whose chest had been pierced most accurately, even though the arrow that did this wasn't there anymore. "You can't leave them here for other possible enemy scouts to discover before your ambush is implemented. Drag them into the thickest of the bushes."

Pursing his lips, Ogteah nodded, busy kneeling beside his own victim, muttering the customary words, knowing that they were of no use if said with no appropriate solemnity. Yet, he could not summon the right thoughts and feelings, not now, when so much was at stake and with the annoying scout being right again while contradicting him in front of his men. Not to mention that judging by the angle of the light that managed to sneak through the thick greenery, they were close to running out of time.

CHAPTER 20

The arrows pounced out of nowhere, so suddenly she found it difficult to comprehend them at first. One moment it was the relative tranquility, the controlled clamor of too many people moving along the narrow stream, disappearing in the afternoon heat behind the bend of the creek she had traveled such a short time ago, hurt, alone, and in a panic, scared out of her wits by the thought that she wouldn't find him in time to give him her terrible news.

The shivers were back, the uncontrollable trembling. Who would have thought that the enemy could be so devious, so ready and unafraid? So fierce and so violent, attacking with everything he had, refusing to succumb, to admit defeat. *That man by the river.* Oh, but he should have died or given up, in the water itself or later on. He was battered enough, wounded, bleeding, hobbling without his stupid moccasins—that must have hurt! Still, he didn't give up, didn't die or go away. He had attacked her with such fierceness, such spirit, throwing stones, of all things. Who would have expected something like that, a stone as opposed to her bow? How stupid. But it worked!

When she had come back to her senses in the enemy's camp, she had almost died herself, her fright choking her, not letting even a little air in. But for the blessed opportunity to hide in the soundlessness, to cower behind the protective walls of the silence. Just like back after her illness, no need to face the terror, to deal with longing or fear. And yet, it was different now. Back then, Grandfather was there, to take care of her and make her strong, while now, oh now she had no one to rely upon but herself, with no luxury of hiding, waiting for the danger to pass or go away. It wouldn't. Just like these terrible hordes of warriors would not, swarming about those valleys and hills like flocks of predatory birds. So many! Evil, impossible to predict. With such vile creatures, it wouldn't help to curl around oneself and disappear inside.

So she had forced herself to think and look around, paying little attention to their questioning. It was impossible to read their lips anyway, had she tried to do that. Which she actually did, for a brief moment, when the man who had knelt next to her seemed to be surprisingly reasonable. He was attempting to talk to her, evidently, trying again and again, patiently at that. Unlike her captor who just hovered close by, shooting murderous glances, looking the worst with his mess of a shoulder and his cut, bruised feet, the sight of which gave her immense satisfaction. Oh, but it was a good decision to throw his shoes into the water! The best decision she had made upon this accursed shore. All the rest was a terrible mistake.

She shivered again, then pushed the memories away, concentrating her gaze on the broadness of *his* back, the muscles crisscrossing it, straining, moving along with their owner's motions, glistening in the afternoon sun. He had insisted on rowing, even though it was more difficult for him, with his bad leg providing no support against the boat's edge, forcing one side of his body to work harder than the other. Still, it was better than walking great distances, so he would sail whenever he could.

If only there was a way to make his leg right, she thought, her chest squeezing hard, the bad memories forgotten. Easy to forget anything bad when in his vicinity. He was so strong, so powerful, an unfaltering leader, with so much conviction, so much vigor and energy and determination, working himself into exhaustion, not giving up or giving in to infirmity or restriction. Too proud to admit to a weakness, any weakness, his knee being a perpetual challenge, to best with every movement, not to let it stand in his way.

Or the terrible enemy. He would not let them best his warriors, or stand in his way. He would show these terrible people; he would destroy them and wouldn't let them harm neither his Long Tails nor her Attiwandaronk people. Nor would he let them harm her.

Still, the doubts would sneak up on her sometimes, the memories of the teeming warriors still fresh. On her headlong flight back to him, when she had managed to escape on their way toward the other lake, the name of which she was careful to memorize, along with the amount of warriors the enemy was silly enough to mention in her vicinity, she had not been able to sleep at all.

Even after running into her people, listened to promptly and taken care of, she never managed to relax enough to close her eyes, fearing the visions her mind was painting too vividly. It was only on the day after that, when their forces were moving to reunite and she couldn't wait, escaping and heading where she overheard his warriors were camping; it was only then, after finding him and crying her heart out in the safety of his embrace that the sleep would come, little by little, gradually, with no nightmares plying her mind. He would know what to do with the swarms of the terrible enemy. He would best them and make them sorry for their brazenness and the foulness of their ways.

As though sensing her gaze, the intensity of it, he turned his head once again, observing the towering wall of green for the tenth time or so it seemed, not liking the way it loomed all around, closing from both sides, hinting at the possibility of an ambush. But for the scouts he had sent ahead, he wouldn't have entered such a narrow pass readily, not in the heart of the enemy land. Still, he was worried, she knew, reading his expression as easily as his lips these days.

Since her return two dawns ago, he had not let her out of his sight. The comforting embrace, a long affair as she needed him too badly by then, breaking down in a way she never had before, was followed by the sternest of reprimands, by the demand of no more independent, self-appointed missions or even a mere wandering about. Or else!

What that "else" was she didn't know, didn't dare to ask or even surmise. Fervently, she had promised to stay by his side, a good compromise, as she still wasn't ready to go back to his native Tushuway as he wished her to do, not without him. So staying by his side she did, quietly and unobtrusively, following him everywhere, watching and listening to his conversations, the endless preparations for the journey and the battle ahead. She had been asked to recount her news again and again, the lay of the land around the rivers she traveled, the smallest details of the enemy warriors and their looks, their attitude, their behavior.

Every little detail mattered, he had told her, and so she made tremendous efforts to remember just everything, even the way the enemy might have been speaking. Oh, yes, some of them were surprisingly easy to understand, talking the same way the Long Tails did. Well, at least when trying to talk to her.

The reassurance that they didn't hurt her but through the capturing she had to repeat again and again, as he had been livid about her injuries, the bruises and the swelling almost gone by now but still a reminder, the cut on her forehead, another on the side of her head that hadn't been taken care of—she didn't allow the enemy to get close enough to see it, but it didn't make his rage at the filthiness of the lowlifes lessen.

Forcing her mind back to the present, she studied the grim lines that ran down the sides of his pressed mouth, his forehead furrowed by so many creases it looked like a wrinkled blanket, his eyes narrowed into slits. The other warrior who sat at the back of their canoe, helping to maintain their speed and their balance, seemed to be worried as well. She could sense his uneasiness, emanating from his hesitant movements when before it was all vigorous rowing.

Glancing at the wall of the brownish green, she felt the twinge of familiar fear. Something wasn't right up on those green-covered cliffs, something... but what? He said they had sent ahead enough scouts, didn't he? And the enemy was still far enough, at least half a day of sailing at the pace their huge wave of people was progressing, with their boats having a hard time navigating the shallow waters of the last summer moon. Oh, but it would be—

The canoe jerked so violently, she cried out, quite against her will. Clutching its side, struggling not to crash against it full-length, her free hand tightening around her precious bow, never out of her reach or sight, she saw the boat's prow lurching wildly, as if attempting to look up into the sky, reeling toward the rocks of the opposite shore.

Incredulous, her eyes took in the sight of the man who was rowing behind her, leaning sideways, as though trying to see something there in the water. When he dropped overboard, headfirst, it created a strange pattern upon the rippling surface, something she wanted to see but for the hand that locked around her upper arm painfully, hauling her backwards and toward the bottom of their boat in the most inconsiderate of manners.

Blinking in confusion, she took a glimpse of him crouching nearby, flailing his paddle from side to side, trying to stabilize the boat that still careened wildly, wavering nauseatingly, leaning toward the opposite site now, not the one their companion disappeared over only a few heartbeats ago. As he jumped to his feet, his position in the middle of the boat with his legs spread wide apart to add to its stability, obviously hurting him, if his tightly clenched teeth were anything to judge by, her numb mind sprang back to life.

The arrows were everywhere, pouncing from behind the greenery of the cliffs or just diving from above, like birds of prey. Thinking nothing of it, she groped her way forward, anxious to reach his side and support him somehow, knowing that this was the main help he needed for now. His bad leg would not let him keep his position for much longer, and he needed to hold on, to straighten the boat up, to bring them back to safety. Them and the others!

A glance at the rest of their boats let her know that they were in the same dire need of help, lurching all around, threatening to collide with each other, their riders hurt or at a loss or struggling, needing him and his reassurance, his words, his directives. And what if he got hurt! The thought alone made her waver with fear.

Clutching the boat's side with one hand, she half-crouched half-stood next to him, propping him with her shoulder in the way she knew he would find useful, taking some of his weight off.

Indeed, he leaned against her readily, making it more difficult to stay upright, but she just pushed harder against her side of the boat, determined. Not to let him down was most important, the only thing that mattered.

"Stay down!" His glance was brief, wild, not overly concentrated.

"Give it to me. I'll row," she shouted, desperate not to lose her stand when the boat lurched again, wilder than before, a blow in its side coming from another vessel, causing it to nearly topple.

He didn't hesitate, not even for a fraction of a heartbeat. Thrusting the oar into her hands, he whirled around, awkwardly but firmly, with no visible effort to spare his bad knee, grabbing his bow as he stumbled toward the back of the boat.

Her teeth clenched, she concentrated on the attempt to straighten them up, disregarding the raining flint with a conscious effort. For now, she needed to keep them from overturning or colliding with other canoes, to make sure he managed to stay upright without collapsing on his bad leg. Without getting hurt otherwise, as well.

A glance in his direction told her that he was still upright, shouting and gesturing, pointing toward the bend of the river, giving direction. With no time to look at the others, she knew they were doing what he said, those who weren't hurt.

The sight of an overturned canoe flowing past, with the limp figure of a man dragging after it, made her shiver. The all-around bedlam must be terrible, the way it was raging, so visible, the shouts and the screams, she could just see them drowning out the natural hum of the river. Sometimes the all-encompassing silence was a blessing.

Another attempt not to let the boat flop over. But for them stopping this mindless milling around, if only for a heartbeat. Or at least the arrows. She tried to pay them no attention, feeling him making his was back toward her side, sensing it most acutely. Proud of her achievement, she made the boat stop for good, holding on against the mild current.

"Take us there." Gesturing widely, he pointed at the thickest of the congregation, where the boats were nothing but a mess of vessels and people.

Why? she thought, not voicing her question aloud. The sight of his face, closed and dark with determination, dripping sweat, his lips nothing but an invisible line, made her heart squeeze. But he would make it all right, not only for them but for everyone. He would.

Nodding firmly, or so she hoped, she turned her attention back to her paddle, wincing as two arrows at once plunged into the water next to it. What if one of these stuck into her? Would she be of use to him if she got hurt?

Clenching her teeth, she manipulated the boat into a full turn, seeing the bend and the inlet shadowed by towering rocks, the place he was pointing at, directing those who were around to dart for its cover. They should be heading there too, she knew, to hide from the arrows as well, to stop and breathe and be safe. Instead, he was making her take them into the chaos, where the canoes were running into each other, colliding, turning over, floating on their sides, their wounded splashing nearby, sputtering in the shallow waters or crawling up the wet stones. But what were they to do in this pitiable mess, besides being overrun as well?

As though wishing to prove her right, one of the nearest vessels lurched like a coyote stung by a bee, whirling wildly, just as he was busy talking to the people in it. Following his gesturing, two of the warriors were just about to jump into the water, while the one with the oar, who was standing full-length until now, rowing as vigorously as she did, waved his hands in the air all of a sudden, in a silly manner, as though greeting the sun, his face twisted hideously, full of pain.

Too busy to follow the strange show unfolding, she put all of her strength into her own attempt to avoid the collision, desperate to escape the staggering vessel's path. The accursed boat! It was too large, not reacting properly like a lighter canoe would.

When the pointed tip of the prow brushed against their side, she pushed it away using her paddle, congratulating herself on the successful maneuver. Or so she thought, until the powerful shove tossed her forward, to slam into the other side, headfirst, and struggle not to fall out of it, her ears ringing, mind numb.

Trying to make sense out of it—but she did avoid the collision with that other boat, she did!—she pushed herself back up using her free hand, the other still clutching the paddle, slick in her sweaty palm. The boat was spinning, slowing its movement, the faint screeching of its sides against another damp wood reaching even into her void.

Not bothering to straighten up fully, she shoved the other vessel away using her paddle again, getting a glimpse of another overturned canoe, their own still vibrating, more vigorously now that her senses absorbed the movement. Whirling around as well, she saw him struggling to get up, palms locked onto the edges of the boat, pulling with desperation. Oh, Mighty Spirits!

Forgetting all about the paddle and the necessity to stabilize their watercraft, she rushed toward him, half-crawling half-throwing herself forward, desperate to help, the sight of his face, stark and frightening in its grayness, making her forget all about the boat and the arrows still falling around, now sparsely, like a late spring's rain.

Blood was seeping from the cut on his cheek, and there were other signs of bruising, but his eyes were what made her stomach heave in fright, the intensity of the pain in them, the obvious struggle to conquer it.

"Are you hurt?" she breathed, dropping beside him, not knowing what to do, whether to pull him up with her own meager strength or to just be there and ready to support him should he succeed getting up on his own. "Were you hit by an arrow?"

He stared at her for a heartbeat, his gaze registering no understanding. Dazed, wandering, clouded with pain, his teeth clutched firmly into his lower lip, cutting into it with no mercy. *Trying to conquer the pain.* Oh, but she knew the signs. His knee, he must have twisted his knee while falling.

Letting her breath out, she reached for him, but he shook her support away, pushing himself up with grim determination, back in control again, his lips, if not his face, coloring. As he leaned against the boat's sides, using the strength of his arms alone, she saw him peering at her briefly, his gaze still wild, still clouded, but more focused now, flickering with familiar concern.

"Are you good? You didn't get hurt?"

Unable to say something, she just shook her head.

"Get overboard and swim toward those rocks. Wait for me there, with the others." He was already up, leaning on his arms, clutching the rough wood with too much force, his palms white-knuckled, bruised and cut too. If he wasn't afraid to overturn the boat, he would be more comfortable, she thought numbly, her mind in a fog, eyes on his legs, one of them bent helpfully, leaning on its knee, but the other limp, useless, twisted unnaturally, in a scary manner.

The melee all around them was as bad as before, with no more than a few heartbeats passing since the massive collision. How could it be?

He was talking to a warrior in one of the upright boats, gesturing with his head. More people swam toward them. Some carried wounded, helping them up into the vessels that fared better than the rest. Those who could swim remained in the water, pushing the jumbled-up boats away from each other, desperate enough to attempt the navigating by mere shoving and pulling. But for the danger of the returned attack.

No more arrows came back as yet, but no one dared to assume it was the end of hostilities, she knew, watching the men working frantically with their oars, separating the vessels, careful not to hurt those who were in the water, working to the same end. All of them following his orders!

Her heart twisting with pride, she watched him leaning heavily against the side of their canoe, one hand still crushing its edge in a desperate grip, the other free now, gesturing along with the flow of his words. He was talking rapidly, shouting instructions, with so many eyes upon him, following his movements and words, doing what he was saying, most clearly, but not attempting to come near, to offer their help in return. Why would they if he was the one to resolve this trouble, to make sure they all got to temporary safety, in good spirits and unharmed.

Oh yes, they relied on him to solve it all, she knew, making her way back toward the prow of their canoe, not about to do as she was told. Namely to flee to safety. He needed her help in taking them both there, to those towering rocks he clearly intended to guide those who didn't reach them yet to, determined to regroup and reunite with the rest of their warriors.

A good plan, but she was not going to leave him behind, to make his way there alone and unaided, with everyone safely there but him. He clearly wasn't about to head there before everyone else did, leader that he was, and who knew what the enemy was up to, why they stopped shooting. Maybe they just paused to get a second wind.

He was glancing at her, she could feel it most clearly, still busy retrieving her oar.

"Where to take the boat now?" she shouted, matter-of-fact, turning to face him in order to see his answer.

His lips twisted in a hint of a grin as he shook his head lightly, his eyes calmer now, the flicker of appreciation in them obvious.

"There, across this mess." Pointing with his free hand, he clenched his teeth tight again, obviously terribly uncomfortable to hover in the way he did. "We make sure everyone understands where they are expected to head then we are going there ourselves." The light flicker was brief, enlivening his stark features. "You do good, warrior-girl."

Warmed by his words, she put all of her efforts into moving them around the splashing commotion, wishing he would just sit there at the bottom of the boat instead of leaning out the way he did, torturing himself with such an uncomfortable pose. Those warriors, they were no children. They should have had better sense than to expect his guidance with every step they took.

Glimpsing him talking to someone, a warrior who swam closer and was holding to the edge of their boat, talking urgently, she held it in place, as motionless as she could, pleased with her skill, knowing he would notice it and appreciate.

"Tell those who were on foot, Andauk's men. They'll get those lowlifes before Father Sun leaves our world tonight," he was saying, causing his converser's face to light with excitement. "I sent them word already, but bring them another one, just in case. They should be on the lookout. Maybe they are the reason the arrows stopped coming."

The encouraged man grinned widely then swam away, to do as he had been told, presumably, to make sure of the retribution the enemy was going to get. But for such a chance! She clutched her paddle tighter then turned to watch him again, waiting for instructions.

CHAPTER 21

"Their reaction was quick and not badly organized, I must admit that. The moment we ran out of arrows and began planning to reunite with our people on the other side, they were upon us, quite indignant and battle hungry."

The Crooked Tongue rolled his eyes, his gaze flickering with mischief, glimmering out of his muddied, scratched, stark-with-exhaustion face. The man evidently did not bother to stop and wash before coming to report the outcome of his mission to the higher authorities. Although there were no more than a few leaders in his brother's vicinity at the moment, reflected Ganayeda, watching the wild man who had fallen upon them so unexpectedly, half a day late and in a battered state.

"Go on," said Okwaho, tight-lipped.

He didn't bother to stop or invite them to find a quieter, more private corner among the bubbling activity of the valley between the spectacularly pretty smallish lakes, his chosen location for the battle he was planning and cherishing every detail of for the past few dawns, since hearing about the size of the enemy forces.

The easy-going, industrious fellow excited by the upcoming adventure was no more, replaced by the tight-lipped, brooding leader with no time to stop in order to eat or sleep, let alone listen patiently to a thousand people who needed to share their troubles or hear words of reassurance. But for his, Ganayeda's, activities all over their monstrous camp, it might have gotten out of hand. At this very moment, they were in a hurry to reach the gathering of the leaders that Okwaho had summoned before his improvised army of troublemakers had fallen upon them out of nowhere, exhausted and wounded, the majority of them, but in great spirits, battle-trained now and eager to get into more action, if nothing else an inspiration and a good example to the rest of their forces.

"Well, it's not like we were unprepared," the Crooked Tongue continued, some of his exploding excitement dimming in the light of such unexpectedly reserved reception. "But having our bows rendered useless, we had to fight with everything that was on hand, even though some of the men did bring their clubs along. The Standing Stone brothers did tremendously well." A grin lit the tired features, reminding Ganayeda why he kept liking this man despite his numerous faults. "The scout you sent with us was a great help. Without him we would not have managed to find that place for an ambush. Or maybe the enemy itself, for that matter." Shrugging with his good shoulder, the man made a face. "As it was, we managed to not only ensure their taking the right course, but also got away with disrupting some of their progress. It was a pleasure to make a mess out of their canoes. They were so sure of themselves, rowing those boats in an unconcealed fashion. Such a leisurely sail. Stupid skunks!"

Okwaho's face was thawing quite visibly. "How many did you manage to kill or wound?"

"Hard to say." The Crooked Tongue shrugged again, his face a study of exhaustion, grayish in color but happy, with a flicker of contentment Ganayeda hadn't seen in the man before. "The first volleys of arrows took many out, a few tens in the very least, if you ask me. But then it became all hectic, with their boats darting here and there, colliding with each other. At this point, it was difficult to say who of those splashing in the water were dead or wounded, and who just jumped over, either fleeing or trying to help sort out the mess of all those overturned vessels." A frown crossed the tired features. "There was this boat that kept darting all around, clearly trying to make order out of all the clutter. It must have carried someone important, but it was hard to hit him from such a distance, as he didn't stand upright like a good leader should."

By this time, Okwaho had slowed his step, his eyes boring at their informer, their attention undivided. "How many came after you? How soon after you ran out of arrows?"

The Crooked Tongue grimaced thoughtfully, his forehead wrinkled like the lake's surface under a strong gust of wind.

"Oh well, there were quite a few of those. We tried to stand up to the first wave, despite our lack of clubs and all that, yet more kept coming up the incline and from behind the trees. At this point, I knew we should make ourselves scarce if we wished to be of use in your upcoming great battle. So I rounded our folk up, and off we scampered. Even managed to carry away our dead." The man's face fell. "They were good men, those two warriors of the Swamp People. We carried their bodies here, to have their people help them on their Sky Journey."

Impressed, Ganayeda watched his brother's eyes narrowing, as did the gazes of the other two leaders, people from Tsonontowan. It didn't surprise him that the Crooked Tongue had done well, managed to handle the situation. Of all people, he knew this man's ability to adjust, to find quick solutions to all sorts of challenging situations. However, what stood out for him in this account was the fact that the man managed to lead a good amount of people, as many as fifty warriors, doing as he had been instructed, yet not missing the opportunity to improvise with an ambush, still thinking as a leader, a person responsible for the others, making sure his charges came back relatively unscathed. A quality he would not suspect the wild foreigner of possessing. And leading notorious troublemakers at that.

"And the other group? You said you split your people, attacked that river bend from both sides." Unconcerned with the delay, Okwaho leaned forward, all ears.

"The others didn't face any surprises. We had no difficulty reuniting with them later on." A one-sided grin flashed. "Your scout was good, kept leading us everywhere, unerring as though we were in the alleys between the longhouses of his hometown."

"He is a local man, you know." In his turn, Ganayeda grinned, feeling obliged to say something when the pause turned too long, with Okwaho sinking deep into his thoughts. "They know their way around their own woods. Naturally, he gave you the best of the scouts."

One of the waiting leaders cleared his throat politely. "The warriors' council awaits us."

Okwaho nodded, still deep in thought. "Yes, Honorable Leaders. Please proceed. We will catch up with you in just a few more heartbeats."

Used to his ways by now, the two older men frowned but turned to go without a comment, not pleased in the least. Okwaho paid them no attention.

"Go and take a rest, brother," he said, addressing the Crooked Tongue. "Make sure your men do the same." The prominent eyes narrowed. "They are still your warriors. Let them know that. Before Father Sun goes to rest, I'll want to talk to you about it. Find me after the evening meal."

The foreigner nodded readily, his own eyes narrow, lips pressed, the picture of thoughtfulness. "I will." A friendly grin at Ganayeda and the man was gone, hurrying down the incline, his paces light as opposed to the tiredness of his previous pose.

"What do you have in mind for this one?" asked Ganayeda, resuming their walk when Okwaho wouldn't. His brother's gaze was still wandering, watching the retreating figure, again not such a presentable view of the torn, muddied shirt and splattered moccasins. "He did very well, better than I would have expected."

"Oh, yes, he did that." Still deep in thought, Okwaho followed, atypically hesitant.

"What are you thinking?"

"Many things." The contemplative eyes focused, rose to meet his. "I want you to be the leading man of the forces that will be hidden behind those two hills. It will be many warriors, as many as six, seven hundred. Maybe more. So of course they would be divided into groups with their own leaders. But I want you to be the man responsible for them all, their organization, their understanding of the mission, their readiness to join our battle and in the precisely right timing at that."

He had expected something like that, but when spoken aloud, it caught him unprepared. "Why these specific forces?"

"Their timing is crucial."

"I see." He exhaled loudly, watching the trail ahead, gaining time. "Did the other leaders agree to your plan?"

As expected, Okwaho shrugged, less concerned with permissions than with the actual details of his projects and plans.

"Not officially, not yet. But I sounded out most of the leading warriors of Tsonontowan and the other two of their main settlements. They asked many questions, but in the end, they seemed to like my idea of surprising the enemy in the middle of the battle." Another shrug. "I expect no difficulties from the other leaders. They'll see the merits of my suggestion."

"They will." Forcing a smile, Ganayeda shook his head, wishing to conceal his inner thoughts, pleased with his brother's readiness to put so much trust in him. "They gave up on the idea of arguing with you at the beginning of this campaign. It's of no use. They won't get anywhere disagreeing with you, and you will still do whatever you think needs to be done, with or without their approval."

A reluctant grin was his answer. "Speaking of being respected by the authorities, they would agree to my proposal more readily if you were to be responsible for this part of the plan."

"Why me? I have no battle experience."

"You'll have plenty after this one." A wink. "But for now, what we need is your organization skills, your way with people, leaders and simple warriors alike, the manner in which you make everyone listen and do precisely as you tell them to do." The powerful arms rose, stretching the broad shoulders, as impressively muscled as ever but barely decorated these days, with no time for showing off efforts. "With you in charge, I can be sure our forces would actually show up and in the right timing. Not when the fighting is practically over or before it has warmed up into anything."

"When do you want these reinforcements to join?"

"That's the thing, I don't know. Not yet. When the time is ripe, I'll send a messenger. Several such." Okwaho's grin had a crooked quality to it. "In such a huge battle, not everyone would manage to reach you, but some will. You would have to be on the lookout constantly, make sure your people are not discovered by wandering scouts before the battle, and of course to watch for my messengers as well." The grin was gone, replaced by a thoughtful frown. "If the enemy learns the real extent of our forces, they might turn away from the battle; try to avoid it, maybe, or go back. Or worse yet, go on, deeper into our forests, forcing me to chase them and thus lose the advantage. It's crucial that nothing of the sort happens. I need them to engage in this battle, and I need them to do so with their spirits high, hopeful of great victory. Only then will we be able to defeat them so soundly they will forget all about making trouble for many summers to come."

Reaching the sunlit clearing, where the shallow stream flowed idly in this part of the late summer, not in a hurry to enter the lake, Ganayeda paused, wishing to delay for just a few more heartbeats before joining the leaders' gathering. What his brother said was another revelation, and just when he thought he had learned it all. Could the enemy try to gain advantage on them in such a way? Attempt to avoid a battle, try to circumvent, maybe? What a terrible possibility. What if they were forced to chase after this destructive warriors' wave, running around pell-mell, with no plan and no advantage?

"I see what you mean," he said slowly, picking his words carefully. "You want to give them a solid hope of victory and make sure it's too late for them to do something about it when you take that hope away from them."

"Yes, that." Okwaho's beam held enough of his old light-hearted self. "Precisely that, Brother. We have enough power and acumen to achieve that, enough brave warriors and good leaders. Gifted people, men like our father's sons, for one." The challenging grin widened. "I have in mind using our Crooked Tongue family member as well. He surprised me, that one. Not only did he seem to manage leading that band of restless spirits I was anxious to send away, to have them doing something, if for no other reason than to keep them from trouble, an achievement in itself. But that additional, hastily concocted plan to ambush the enemy was executed not badly." Another wink. "I told you he is a good man and a valuable addition to our enterprise. I knew I was right about him." The light-heartedness disappeared as suddenly as it blossomed. "He and his band of fearless troublemakers would be holding the communication between our forces. Therefore, make sure to talk to him this evening, get to know some of his people, so you'll have an easier time recognizing our possible messengers of tomorrow."

"Are you sure the battle will happen tomorrow as planned? What if the enemy lingers despite your predictions?"

The large eyes clouded. "The scouts' reports are encouraging, besides the news Ogteah has brought. The enemy has been seen sailing the tributary we wanted, heading toward Honeoye Falls. From there, it's a short sail against the current. Half a day's travel at worst." Resuming his walk toward the grove that was looming ahead, Okwaho tossed his head. "They must be smarting after what our Crooked Tongue did to them, eager to make us pay for his improvised ambush. Well, they better be."

CHAPTER 22

"The enemy is camping on the near side of the lake they called Honeo-ye, a Lying Finger Lake, behind the hills that are spilling many streams into it and another smaller water body called Scanadice, a Long Lake. They are spreading between these lakes in great numbers."

Easing his shoulders, Aingahon eyed the kneeling scout, following the stick that was adding lines to the drawing upon the earth. Such a detailed sketch. The lakes and the creek, even the referred hills were all there, outlined clearly, easy to recognize. But for the ability to squat, to study the drawing more closely, like his other fellow leading warriors did!

"Have you had the opportunity to watch them from close proximity?" he asked instead, pushing yet another wave of impatience away. It was the third scout who had brought him such a generous amount of information since the high noon, as they arrived at the crossroad of two larger creeks and stopped there for a brief conference. "Don't they put any scouts or warriors to guard their own forces?"

"There are signs of warriors wandering these woods, yes." The man looked up, his forehead creasing with a sudden frown, as though wondering too. "But we've encountered none. Neither me nor my associate. We actually managed to find a good vantage point where we could see their camp most clearly. That's when we decided that I should go back and report, while he stayed to keep watch."

The others, two leading warriors from Attiwandaronk pair of larger settlements and more of their peers from his own people of

Tushuway and Honniasont, straightened up, their eyes squinting in unison.

"How long did it take you to come back?" asked the Tushuway man.

"The sun moved barely half a palm." The scout nodded eagerly, anxious to be of help. "If we progress along that other current, either in boats or on foot, we can reach the enemy before Father Sun goes to sleep."

"And fight a night battle?" Displeased but not certain why, Aingahon shook his head, ignoring the slightly raised eyebrows of his companions, the inquiring quality of their glances.

They all wanted to reach the enemy at long last, the warriors and the leaders. But for him they wouldn't have stopped even here, to let their people rest and their scouts to do their work. Oh, but they would have rushed on, on foot or in canoes, rowing hectically, or maybe just running, in a mindless charge like that of an autumn whitetail buck blind with need.

Was he the only one who didn't share in their eager anticipation, in their confident expectancy of a great victory? Was he the only one to smell something rotten here, something wrong, a trouble, a trap?

It had been too easy, too smooth. The journey, the scouting, the locating of the enemy, who were apparently sitting there, doing nothing with these hundreds of warriors. Why?

No, it had been too comfortable since crossing the river into these people's heartlands, besides the debacle of the day before, something he still couldn't think about without grinding his teeth into dust. Such a shame! To be caught so off guard and by a mere band of wandering scouts. The warriors who had managed to catch up with the culprits reported a few tens, no more than twenty or thirty warriors, a pitiful lot who had barely any clubs to fight back. But for the lack of their own organization, the sneaky ambushers would have been dead by now, every single one of them. As it was, by the time he had managed to return a semblance of order among their boats and establish good communication with their other forces that were progressing by land, he had been dizzy with exhaustion, in too much pain to insist on going on organizing the retaliating attempts, letting her navigate their boat toward the shore and into the care of a healer. Too many people had insisted he should do that, and he could barely speak coherently to argue by that time.

Sighing, he glanced at his leg, now wrapped in the tightest of bandages, a wet cloth that clung to his damaged limb like another skin, holding it in place firmly, like a splint would. Such a bad twisting! Usually, when something like that happened, the healers' attempts to put his knee back in place would be the ones to hurt, but shortly after the treatment it would be nothing but a bad memory, with only the regular dull pain to make him remember to be more careful in the future.

However, not this time. Almost a day later and the swelling wouldn't disappear, not completely, the intense, cutting pain still there, still shooting thunderbolts up into his stomach and spine, causing him to limp worse than ever. Without the tight bandage that was soaked in a smelly jelly-like liquid, he might not have been able to walk at all. A terrible possibility that had him clenching his teeth every time anew. What a bad timing! But then, what did he expect? They were on a warpath here, not strolling those pretty woods for pleasure.

"Even if we didn't arrive in time to attack the enemy," said an Attiwandaronk man coldly, his aquiline, strongly beaked nose turning upward, haughtily at that. "There is a merit in reaching our destination before this day has run its course. Tomorrow will see our warriors rested and eager, ready to attack the enemy after appropriate preparations and offerings were made."

The arching eyebrows were challenging him openly, mocking his lesser battle experience. But he should have thought about it, shouldn't he? The appropriate offerings and other spiritual matters concerned with great battles and wars. Not to mention people's condition after long traveling, often on a hungry stomach.

"Those are wise words you are saying, brother." One of their own Long Tails leaders, a man of Honniasont, nodded thoughtfully. "Tomorrow will see our valor and courage in battle. Our warriors will make the spirits of our forefathers proud."

More pretty-sounding, high-flown talk. He felt his stomach tightening in a painful squeeze. "Why are we determined to engage in this particular battle?"

Their eyes turned to him, widening with surprise. A genuine one, he could see that. He swallowed hard.

"They are expecting us. It is as clear as a midday sky of Hot Moons. They know we are coming, and they do nothing but sit on their behinds, waiting patiently. Why? What do they have in store for us? Shouldn't they be concerned with the size of our forces, larger than theirs, according to our scouts? Not to mention our daring and courage in coming here in such a state, ready to fight in a war of unheard-of proportions? They should be worried at least, busy with preparations, plans, strategies. Don't you think it is strange that they do nothing but wait?" He encircled them with his gaze, hoping against hope. "They let our scouts roam free, watch their camping arrangements, learn of their numbers and dispositions. They have known of our approach for at least two dawns by now, probably more, and they don't come to meet us, to battle us closer to our forests, to try to stop us. Why? Why do they let us go deeper and deeper into their forests and woods? Why let our scouts wander around uninterrupted? It doesn't make sense, unless the enemy knows what he is doing, unless he is planning something nasty, a trap we are falling right into. Otherwise, they are foolish and cowardly, and we know they are neither, not them."

Their gazes were stony, full of disapproval, concealing none of their aversion or disdain.

"For a man who worked hard to make this war happen, you are succumbing to much doubt all of a sudden, brother," said the Tushuway man, his lips quivering, twisting in an unpleasant manner. "The enemy appears careless, and maybe weak, yes. Why does it bother you so? We are invading their forests in a great strength, our warriors are as many as swarms of bees and as determined. Like a thunderstorm wind, we cannot be stopped. And if the enemy is cowed by our bravery and resolution, then what is the better course than to fall on them with everything we have, squashing them under the shared power of our strength and courage?"

He felt his face turning into a stone mask under the arrogant reproach of their nods.

"Unless the enemy is not cowed, not intimidated. Unless they are as determined as we are, as resolved in squashing us for good. We cannot assume that they are cowed and frightened only because it suits us to do so. We cannot lead hundreds of brave warriors who have chosen to follow us here into possible traps. Our duty is to consider all possibilities, to be ready for the enemy to turn out not as foolish or as cowardly as we wish them to be." Still impenetrable masks with no flicker of real attention, no glint of understanding, no indication that his words weren't falling on deaf ears. He battled on. "The enemy may know what they are doing by waiting for us to arrive at a certain place they all but invited us to. They may be luring us into a trap by making us fight on the ground of their choosing."

People were drifting closer, listening avidly. At least this. But then, they weren't on his town's ceremonial grounds, to make open speeches and carry people after one's ideas. This was an enemy forest, and no warriors expected to fight bravely and with hope in their hearts should they hear him speaking against other leaders or their plans. Such matters were to be discussed in the privacy of the woods, among warriors' leaders alone.

His companions glanced at their growing audience.

"This is not the time or the place to discuss these matters," said an Attiwandaronk man icily, his disapproval spreading like a predawn mist upon a winter lake, thick, freezing cold. "You should have voiced your doubts in the last leaders' gathering."

Aingahon drew a deep breath. "We should summon another meeting before we move on."

"And let the enemy slip away in the meanwhile," muttered a Honniasont man, his glare scorching.

"Do you have an alternative course of action to propose?" asked Tushuway's leader, his eyes less hostile than those of the others, even if as disapproving. "Something you would have done had it been up to you alone to decide?"

"Yes," he said firmly, the new idea gaining power, growing

rapidly, too good not to give it a thorough consideration, at least that. "I do not propose to change our course, but to follow the river we've been sailing for more than a day now." He paused to let his words sink in, wishing he had time to think it all through before airing his thoughts aloud. "I propose to bypass the enemy's camp, while moving deeper into their lands, attacking the settlements we encounter. There is a large town at the foot of the lake they call Canandaigua, a Chosen Spot, the enemy's main town. I propose we head there." Oh, but he did gain their attention now. Not daring to pause in order to lick his lips, he went on, marveling at the calmness of his voice, as opposed to the storm his thoughts were twirling. "This would drag their warriors from the coziness of their current encampment, would make them chase us and fight on the ground they didn't choose or prepare in advance, places where we would engage them with fierceness and courage, to defeat them once and for all."

They were silent for more than a few heartbeats, his audience and the warriors who didn't have enough manners to draw away, out of hearing range.

"We don't have time to call another leaders' gathering." The second Attiwandaronk man who had been quiet until now frowned, his expression impossible to read.

However, it was this warrior's fellow countryman, the first haughty northerner, such an obtuse adversary until now, who pursed his lips in a deliberating manner. "Maybe we can have a quick meeting with the rest of our peers. Not a gathering, but a brief conferring before we sail." He shrugged, bestowing on Aingahon another of his haughty glances, not much warmer than his previous glares but more thoughtful, somehow. "A worthwhile proposition should be discussed, always, even if its timing is not the best."

He tried not to let his relief show. "Go and find the rest of the leaders," he said, turning to the scout, who was of course still around and listening avidly. Manner-less skunk! "Help him with that." A curt wave of his arm sent the other listeners off as well.

"I won't advocate such a change to our plans," said the Honniasont man, shaking his head. "But I will attend your brief conferring. Let me know where and when."

"Out there, near that grove." The Attiwandaronk man, now all businesslike air and efficiency, waved his hand toward the nearest hill, where some of their warriors had spread out earlier, looking for spirits only knew what. "When the sun has moved half a finger, we should be ready to move, whatever direction we decide upon. So, all of you, please, make sure to arrive up there shortly."

Craving a few heartbeats of privacy, to think his proposals through, Aingahon nodded stiffly then pushed the new wave of tiredness away, retracing his steps back toward the shore. To reach the agreed upon meeting place would mean more walking for him, yes, but he needed this brief moment of privacy without challenging questions and reproachful glares, *with a loyal, helpful, friendly company.*

Involuntarily, his eyes strayed, darted around, seeking among the multitude of milling warriors, those who stayed close to their boats, not scurrying off to do their needs in the woods or to wander about, maybe trying to shoot game, or better yet, setting out on their private side missions. How many of their men had already gone on, progressing toward the reported enemy location, without their leaders' consent to do so? A couple of tens in the very least, he knew, probably more. Another complication. Oh, but he was so tired of arguing over each step, each decision, each suggestion or word. Exhausted really. But for this strange feeling to leave, never to return. He could deal with frustration, with the desperate worry, with the familiar sensation of being curbed and not listened to. Only the weariness was new, the wish to let go, allow them to do whatever they wanted. Bring their glorious wave of warriors straight into the enemy's trap, if they wished it so.

For a trap it was, he knew now, as sure as the cloudless day and the trickle of this creek's waters, so transparent in the early afternoon sun. Some kind of an ambush, a ruse. They had been led here, to those casually spreading hordes of warriors who didn't bother to do anything, not even put a guard around their camps. Such a careless attitude, with no aim and no purpose, and from the formidable enemy that, until this time, fought as well as any warrior nation would, with no fear and no deficit of smart thinking.

Oh, but what were these people up to when they did let her go? A worrisome question with no satisfactory answer, not even in his most inner heart.

Again, he sought with his gaze, pleased to see her crouching next to his boat, where he instructed her to stay before setting out on accosting his fellow leaders yet again earlier, upon their arrival. At least she had been obedient this time. A small comfort.

She must have sensed his approach, or maybe she had just been on the lookout. Her gaze leapt to him, following, the beckoning of his head sending her up and into a hurried run. A shadow of his, a creature out of the wintertime tales, not entirely human. And yet, not a creature at all, not anymore.

He watched her nearing in her springy, light step, his gloom lifting, if only a little. At least she didn't sneak away like some others, another restless spirit who never did as she was told. But no, she wouldn't do that. Not anymore. The old Tsutahi would have gone already, setting to best the enemy all by herself, her and her bow that she managed to save and carry along despite all that had befallen her on this side of the river, the enemy side.

Oh, but she had returned changed, a different person. Quiet, thoughtful, reticent, her old spunk, her childish, immature, smug self-assurance gone, replaced with a serious mask and perpetually narrow, observant gaze. Such a subtle change he would have wondered about had he had time for idle pondering. She had reassured him that the enemy didn't harm her, despite the numerous signs, various scratches and bruises, a result of the wild journey, she had claimed. Just to think of what she had done, a young girl with no ability to hear properly, lunging into the heart of the enemy lands, chasing a traitorous woman, trying to stop her from bringing the news of their advance to the enemy. Almost successful, too! But for the man who had fallen into the river, anxious to save the dying traitor, she would have managed to stop the word of their forces reaching the enemy. Oh, but did she keep fuming about that!

He remembered how her face would twist fiercely, suddenly

ugly in the ferociousness of its wrath. It was her fault, she would hiss, the words coming out with difficulty through her clenched teeth, quiet for a change, with no regular dissonant shouting; her fault she had missed the first shot, wounding but not killing the traitor; her fault the enemy warrior managed to interfere.

"Are you well?" She was peering at him, openly anxious.

He pushed the thought of her being out there, alone and defenseless, and at the enemy's mercy, away. "Come."

The sunlit sand of the nearest shore gleamed quite merrily, encouraging. Behind the bend of the river, he found it easier to walk without too many eyes following him, questioning, expecting, wondering. He wasn't the official leader of this enterprise—no one was, with them being a mix of two nations and plenty of independent settlements—still, they grew used to consulting him before every move, all those minor leaders of warriors. A pleasant development that he felt he greatly deserved but for those spells of uncertainty. Would they listen to his counter suggestion when the rest of the leaders finally deigned to gather in one place? No one would like his advocating of a sudden change in their course, not when so close to the enemy and the opportunity to smash them for good. The word had apparently traveled fast, even among such a huge force as theirs.

"Why are you full of doubts now?" she asked, echoing his thoughts, or maybe listening to them. If she had been his shadowing *uki*, she could do such things, couldn't she?

He suppressed his grin, turning to face her, to let her see his lips. Oh, and what his eyes held as well.

"Tell me again about the time you spent in the enemy's hands."

Her face clouded. "I told you all about it already. I don't want to remember or think about it."

The childish resentment in her voice made the grin come easier. "Well, I need you to remember it now. Not to recall all of it, but details, things I maybe neglected to ask you before."

As expected, a reluctant half-shrug was his answer. He caught her thin shoulders between his palms, turning her with an easy familiarity, making her face him. A gentle but firm push to her chin completed the picture.

Her resistance was minimal, expressed mainly in pouting lips. Such a child sometimes.

"Tell me again how many dawns you spent in the enemy's hands. Try to remember how long was it before they moved to this other lake, where they are located now?" He held her gaze, disregarding the rebellious flicker. "It's important that you remember exactly, and I have no time to spare."

Another heartbeat of glaring from under her brow, then she pursed her lips, concentrating most visibly.

"It was late afternoon when that... when that dreadful man interfered." Her slender throat moved as she swallowed, making him wish to press her to his chest, then take her away, to safety, not anywhere near here. "So I was in their camp that night and maybe another day." The huge eyes were back upon him, glittering with misery. "I can't remember exactly. I was too scared."

He squeezed her shoulders tighter, his heart going out to her. "It's good. Just tell me what you do remember. It's all in the past now. You are away, and I won't let them catch you again." How? he asked himself hopelessly. And just as they were heading back to the wolves' den.

Sighing, he pushed the nagging worry away. If he dealt with the enemy now, somehow, against the stubbornness of his own countryfolk, she would be safe in the end. To send her back was impossible, not from where they were, not alone and unprotected, her spirit and skill notwithstanding.

He had tried to do that when still back on their side of the enemy river, when she came back from her wild adventure, relatively unharmed. Relieved to see her well and spending much time on consoling her and making sure she had came to no serious harm—who knew what the vile enemy could do to a girl, even as young as this one?—he had tried to disregard the danger, ready to offer to every spirit he could think of, begging for a safe journey until she reached Tushuway at the very least.

But of course it would have been easier to make a wandering winter bear go back to sleep. She refused to even listen to such a proposition, wild thing that she was. And he had been too busy to insist, knowing her well enough not to waste his time on something as futile. She wouldn't go, of course she wouldn't. The time spent at the enemy hands evidently did not break her spirit, thank all the small and great *uki* for that!

Still, now, so close to the enemy and the possible trap they were heading into, he felt the pangs of fear returning, groping his insides, crushing them in their deadly grip. She shouldn't be here, she just shouldn't. Even though her help in the last day's debacle was tremendous, the best he could ask for. While everyone panicked or was busy trying to extricate themselves, she was the only one to remain at his side and do whatever was necessary. With no fear, no misgivings, no panicked fits. Such a good companion, a real partner. But still just a girl. How to protect her; how not to let her go down together with them should the other leaders disregard his advice? He clenched his teeth.

She was still peering at him, wide-eyed, full of expectation.

"So you spent a day or two in their old camp, yes?"

An uncertain nod.

"And then?"

"Well, then, as I told you, they began moving to that other lake, to camp between this Honeoye Lake and another one. They called it Honeoye, the long lake. They were talking much about it."

"How did you manage to hear?"

The smugness in her smile was fleeting but unmistakable. "I listened to their lips. The man who had questioned me the most was speaking a lot to the other one." The smugness was gone, replaced by a direful scowl. "To the one who captured me."

"They were speaking in our tongue, then?"

"Well, yes. Sometimes they spoke in a tongue I didn't understand, when talking to others. But with me, this man always talked in our tongue, even though he sometimes twisted his words in a funny way."

"Why did he tell you about their plans?"

She shook her head so vigorously her hastily braided hair jumped. "He talked to the other man about it. The one who captured me. He wasn't talking to me by this point. I refused to talk to him at all!" There could be no mistake in the pride of her voice, ringing again too loudly, in her typical strident half-shouting. "He didn't manage to make me tell him a thing."

He pressed her shoulders lightly again. "Hush. Don't yell at the top of your voice." A deep breath helped to calm the uneven pounding of his heart. Oh, but it was not good, what she was telling him. Why would they talk important matters in front of her and using the only tongue she could understand, not their own native tongue? "How long did it take them to arrive at that other place?"

"Less than a day," she said readily, lowering her voice to a more acceptable level. "We arrived there in the late afternoon, and by nightfall, I was already away. With my bow!" The radiance of her beam could rival the glow of the midday sun. "They didn't even notice me sneaking away. They were busy trying to make it orderly with so many warriors all around. It was such a mess." Another beam. "You do it much better than them, manage so many people and other leaders. They are nothing compared to you!"

He smiled briefly, warmed by her keen adoration, always there and on display these days. Still, the bad feeling welled higher. Why did they bother to keep her at their warriors' camp in the first place, let alone dragging her along while moving to another location? A captive girl like her should have been handed to the town's authorities, offered for adoption probably, or at least kept there for a while. Instead, they had dragged her all around, talking about their plans and the size of their forces in the tongue she could understand, then letting her slip away upon reaching the right location.

The stony fist was back, squeezing his entrails. Why, why didn't he take time to listen to her story more carefully in the first place, when she had just arrived with her news, before he had rushed them all across the river and up the following stream, hot on the heels of the lead that must have been nothing but a bait, a lure, a trick to make them fall into the enemy's trap more easily.

"What?" She was peering at him, anxious again. "What is wrong?"

He rubbed his face tiredly. "Nothing. Or maybe everything. I need to make other leaders listen to what I say. I need them to agree to change our plan, all of it." Even a shrug proved a tiring business. "They won't be pleased with my proposed changes. Neither the leaders nor the warriors. They are all set and eager. They want to reach the enemy and fight, if not today then tomorrow. They won't listen to reason."

Her face was a study of puzzlement, forehead creased into what looked like thousand wrinkles, eyes dark with contemplation, an obvious attempt to understand without asking. "You don't want to fight tomorrow? But..."

He pressed his palms against his eyes, willing the budding headache to go away. As though all the rest was not enough.

"But you wanted that fight. You were working so hard to make it happen!"

Where did he hear it before? Oh, yes, the accusation coming from his own town's war leader. All of a sudden, they did remember who had made it all happen. Good for them.

"Without you, none of my people," she coughed shyly, "my former people, that is, well, none of them would have been here. They came following you, and the others, many among your people, too. They may have their appointed leaders, or all those who appointed themselves, but they all look up to you. You are the one who brought together so many warriors! Why would you wish to avoid the fight now?"

Was she accusing him of cowardice? He glanced at her from behind the protective screen of his fingers, still pressed into his skull, taking some of the pain away. "What are you trying to say?"

Her smile was small, quivering quietly, demurely, in no childish manner this time. "I don't know. I just think that maybe you don't believe in yourself anymore, and I don't understand why. Why now, when you are so close to your goal? Why do you doubt your ability to lead now?"

He shook his head, hearing the air escaping his chest in a loud, explosive sound. The temptation to dive back behind the privacy his palms offered welled.

"I do not doubt my leadership qualities, nor my ability to lead these warriors, even though the shooting of our previous morning was a serious failure on my part." She began saying something, protesting hotly, eyes sparkling, but his palm stopped the torrent of words, demanded silence. "What I do doubt is my ability to convince others, leaders and warriors alike; to make them see what I see." Looking into the stormy darkness of her eyes, still boiling over this last accusation of failure on his part, he grinned without humor. "Even you refuse to see it now, choosing to focus on lauding my leadership abilities, instead. And you are a clever girl, with no selfish causes, no private motives save your loyalty to me. Still, you don't see that they have played you, those clever enemies of ours, that they have spread a trap, sending word through you, an unheeded messenger. I wish I knew what their plans are, so I could counter them, somehow. But I do know that we should not oblige them in doing exactly what they want us to do, following obvious leads, playing into their hands like silly children."

She was staring at him, aghast, her eyes as round as two bowls of corn dough. From the corner of his eye, he saw one of the warriors nearing, making his way toward them, in an obvious hurry.

"Stay by my boat until I come back. Then I will tell you what I want you to do before we head off."

Her eyes sparkled back to life. "No, no, it's not true! I didn't lead them here or carry their messages, concealed or not. They didn't let me go just like that. I ran away, when they didn't look. I did!" Her moccasined foot caused small pebbles to shoot away as it stomped against the wet sand. "I got away, and I brought you word about their forces and their location, with them knowing not a thing about it." Her scowl was deep, defiant. "They might have noticed that I ran away, eventually, but they didn't do anything about it, or maybe they just didn't manage. I was stupid to fall into their hands in the first place, but I wasn't stupid to repeat my mistakes. No one can track me out there in the woods, and no one can catch me. You know it better than anyone. You do!" The tears were glittering, tears of offense at unfounded accusations. He reached for her shoulder, but she recoiled away from his touch. "I didn't tell them a word about our warriors and their location, and

I didn't bring back misleading messages! I did not!"

He drew a deep breath, his heart squeezing. She didn't deserve this sort of accusation, even though he wasn't accusing her, just sharing his thoughts.

Still, of course she did not take well what he implied, and maybe he was wrong about it. Maybe they were all right and he was just tired and overwhelmed, suspecting a trap where there was none, not accepting the simple fact that maybe they were, indeed, handed over an easy victory by the enemy that turned out to be not as dangerous, not as sophisticated as previously thought. But for such a chance!

"Don't get that indignant, little one." Another attempt to touch her shoulder met with success. "Maybe you are right and I'm wrong. Maybe you all are right. Who knows? I might be overly suspicious now. We will see about that." He glanced at the man who had halted at some distance, his pose telling of his impatience. "But regardless of this, when I come back, I will tell you what I want you to do, and you will do as I say. Is that clear to you?" Holding her gaze, he didn't try to hide the warmth he felt inside, this soft glow that had returned only a few days ago, when she had come back. "You trust me, don't you? So whatever I tell you to do, you will. Like with Grandfather, remember? If he had told you to stay here, or even to head back and wait for him at home, you would have done this, wouldn't you? Because you trusted him to know what is good for you, and so you should trust me. I know what is good for you, little one, and you will have to trust me and do what I say."

"I will not leave—" she began hotly, but he raised his hand, silencing her words of protests.

"We'll talk about it when I come back. Think about what I said, and wait for me by my boat." Another fleeting smile and he turned away, suddenly calm and sure of himself.

The tiredness was still there, that deep, frustrating exhaustion, but the indecision was over. No matter what the enemy planned, maybe much or maybe nothing, to engage in this battle would be good, and they still matched the enemy in ferocity, skills, and probably even numbers. What was there to be suspicious of?

CHAPTER 23

The heat was terrible, made worse by the stench of sweat and blood and other discharges Ogteah preferred not to think about, the densely packed people darting between the trees, crowding clearings and trails, seeking to crush or pierce, their clubs and spears hungry, their thirst for blood unquenchable.

There was no pattern to the fighting, no order, no rule. Just the mindless onslaught of clashing clubs and crushing skulls, people being struck down in all sorts of nasty manners, making disgusting, or often ridiculously funny sounds, collapsing like cut-down trees sometimes, but more often pummeled down to twist in terrible pain, with their only hope of mercy in the next blow of their rival, to come quickly and unerringly, to relieve their agony.

Head reeling, sweat rolling down his temples, soaking his hair, making it stand out everywhere—only now did he understand why the experienced warriors arranged their hair in such an elaborate manner, not for appearance but for convenience—he tried not to slip on the wet grass, struggling to see through the mass of the rustling green, seeking out his people with his gaze, all of them preferably, or at least a few.

It was difficult to keep even an eye contact in such a mess, let alone to maintain worthwhile communication. Still, his group of former troublemakers was his responsibility, now a little over forty warriors as opposed to the original fifty, proud men of achievement, bloodied by that first skirmish up the creek, when they had managed to interrupt the enemy's progress, repulse twice as many attackers and then retreat without leaving their dead and wounded behind. An impressive exploit that even hardened warriors like the wolf man and his Flint and Mountain friends lauded genuinely, with true appreciation.

"I knew you had it in you," the unappointed leader of their entire force had said, with Akweks smirking in the background, trying to hide his pride under his usual good-natured baiting. He was the one to suggest Ogteah gather those troublesome elements with whom he got along shamelessly well anyway, to lead them out on an unordinary mission of misleading the enemy. "Good work, brother. Keep an eye on those men of yours. Make sure they do well in the battle. I'll tell you what I want you to do later on, before the night runs its course."

And such a strange night it had been indeed, colored by the expectation of the great battle. Somber and enthusiastic at the same time, intense to the point of upsetting, solemnly cheerful, a strange combination.

No one dreamed of trying to sleep, or even eat for that matter. No cracking of nuts, no smells of roasting meat, no outbursts of laughter disturbed the flickering darkness, no lively chatter. Soberly, people would squat near their glimmering fires, staring ahead, their thoughts wandering the worlds of the spirits, their fingers wrapped around their sacred objects, painting patterns over their faces and bodies, withdrawn into themselves. Others would converse quietly, share plans for the projected fighting, even joke about it.

Thank all the great and small *uki*s for that, reflected Ogteah, remembering how the gravity of the night began wearing on his nerves, making him wish to snap at people, make noise or yell at the sky, and so disperse the suffocating solemnity. But it was tiring, to wait for the day of the battle to be born. The agitated anticipation of the morning's last preparations, the rites and offerings, the War Dance, were a thousandfold more preferable, while scouts came and went, usually on the run, reporting the enemy's whereabouts, their dispositions, their battle readiness. He was all excitement and expectation back then, but now, half a morning later, all he felt was agitation and tiredness. Great battles turned out to be nothing like what he expected. Such an unorderly affair.

Again, he encircled his surroundings with his gaze, darting away from the path of yet another wandering club that seemed to pounce out of nowhere, with no particular purpose. There were quite a few such attacks all around. Not everyone sought a desirable hand-to-hand.

Since the first onslaught of the enemy, it had been nothing but chaos and disarray. Or so it seemed. Even though the wolf man wasn't concerned, wielding his club with notable ease, when not busy running all over, trying to instruct people and make them cooperate with each other. A seemingly futile attempt. No one seemed to think of the general outcome or the fate of the others, their battle frenzy and thirst for killing overcoming their reason and sense, or so it looked to Ogteah.

Spotting the Standing Stone brothers, all three of them, fighting one near another, keeping each other's backs, he made his way toward them.

"Find Okwaho or any of his aides," he shouted, aiming his spear at the enemy warrior who seemed as though contemplating running in his direction, a tall, stringy man of not especially impressive stature. "Ask him if he wants to send another word with any of us."

The shorter of the brothers scowled, raising a skeptical eyebrow as he landed his club on his rival with an impressive force. But for the other man's agility, the enemy warrior would have been done for. As it was, the man stumbled and rolled away, springing back to his feet, unharmed.

"Will do that," said the oldest of the trio cheerfully, wiping the sweat off his brow with the back of his massive hand, smearing a dubious mix of liquids upon it, instead. "Just let us finish with this sorry lot."

"No objections to that," shouted Ogteah, shooting a quick grin at the man. Of the three siblings, this one turned out to be the best of company, and the fiercest. Well, no surprises there. "Just make it quick. He may need to send that word soon, with all the mess that is going on here and down there by the lake."

Since the first onslaught, the enemy had managed to push the Great League's warriors back toward the creek twice, even though each time they had managed to regain their position. But not to push on. So now the battle raged hopelessly balanced between the water edge and the forested incline, remarkably vicious, but as ill-organized as in the beginning. On that score the enemy did surprise them, turning out to be glaringly confident, better coordinated than expected, their fighting spirit soaring.

He whirled to see more people spilling into the cramped clearing, two figures engaged in an already developing combat, their clubs swishing relentlessly, trying to beat one another to their targets.

Darting behind the same tree that had given him its support, Ogteah saw his previous rival rushing to close the distance, his club high and ready, his unprotected torso on full display. One more heartbeat and he would be in the club's range, a true danger against the lesser sturdiness of a good spear. But for the opportunity to switch weapons from time to time!

Not wasting his time on any more musings, he let his instincts guide him, always the best of solutions in violent situations. His javelin had barely left his hand before it buried itself in the charging man's belly, already closing the range, about to land his club.

Twisting away from the descending cudgel—what a nice weighted tip this club had, such an invested thing—he saw his rival's eyes glazing, turning so wide they seemed as though growing in size. The expression of surprised astonishment didn't last. Another heartbeat saw the man gagging, his face twisting terribly, in an inhuman mask.

As the club slipped to roll in the muddy grass, Ogteah blinked, watching his rival topple over and onto his side, his mind strangely numb, noting irrelevant details—the brilliant green of the grass as opposed to the deep brown of the muddy earth, the darkness of the crimson flow spilling upon it in much force, as though in a hurry to cover it all, the gargling howls that shook the air, inhuman in their intensity.

As he went on staring, a movement to his side startled him into an involuntary leap, a familiar swish, as expected, accompanied by a push. Not a vicious one, it sent him forward, to crash on top of his wriggling victim and into those terrible screams, now accompanied by a stench, such a disgusting odor that he had already learned was emanating from the insides of human bodies.

Blind with panic, he rolled away, pushing with both hands, one of which reacted quite clumsily, in a slow and painful manner. Oh Mighty Spirits, but he needed to gain an upright position, to see what was coming, to counter their attack. And the spear! Where was his spear?

Heart pounding madly, trying to burst through his ribs, he spun from yet another assault, seeing pieces of mud or maybe some other nasty substance splattering from under another round tip of a weighty wood, this one adorned by a glassy flint edge. Oh, Mighty Spirits, but he needed his spear back!

With desperation, he kicked at the blurry silhouette that was nearing again, pleased to feel his feet connecting with something, crashing into it, pushing it away. At least that!

Too busy to give it additional thought, he scrambled to his feet, glimpsing the club of his previous rival, lying in tempting proximity. Oh, but he needed *this* thing!

A glance at his current enemy informed him that the man, indeed, must have lost his balance before or was close enough to it, his struggle to get back to his feet obvious. Just what he, Ogteah, needed. A leap toward the fallen club cost him his own only recently gained upright position, but it was worth it.

Rolling away from the possible path of the attacking cudgel, back at its relentless pounding again, he collided with another entanglement of human limbs, two other rivals beyond the stage of accepted weaponry as it seemed, trying to knife or maybe just strangle each other.

Using their bodies as a prop to push himself up with as little consideration as his own situation warranted, he knew that one of his men was in dire trouble and needed help. A Standing Stone younger brother, alone this time, with his siblings nowhere in sight.

"Hold on!" he gasped, hoping that the man would hear him and take heart. The way this one's rival was upon him, clutching his knife, driving it on despite the fierce resistance of the opposing hands was not promising, not for his charge. Yet his own predicament was as dire.

Gripping the slick, well-polished handle with both hands, trying to come to grips with the unfamiliar feeling, having never fought with a club before, Ogteah stumbled, somehow managing to bring his new weapon up, desperate to stop the blow. It was descending rapidly, in a hurry to hurt. Oh, but for the previous support of a tree; or at least a heartbeat of respite, to spread his legs and steady himself. He wouldn't hold against that blow, his senses were screaming, not such a fierce, well-directed hit. And yet, it was too late to try to avoid it now, and he had had enough rolling around in the revolting mud.

Sweat rolling into his eyes, he didn't dare to blink it away, his arms absorbing the impact, straining to remain where they were, trembling with the effort, betrayed by the rest of his body that hadn't managed to achieve a stable enough position to offer a worthwhile support.

In desperation, he twisted away while giving in, the polished tip reinforced by the cutting edge brushing against his side, pushing him on with shaming ease.

Back on the ground again—oh, but it was hopeless!—he squirmed in order to reach at least a semblance of a position that might allow him some means of defense. Nowhere to roll away to, not with the other pair still struggling next to him, their knives contesting, rushing for a kill. So the Standing Stone man was still alive and kicking. Good!

His own rival towered above, preparing his next blow—the final one, surely—taking his time. A glimpse of the decorated moccasin moving to root in the grass told him so. Oh, yes, the man was readying to hit his hardest, anxious to finish his victim off, fed up with chasing someone who didn't know how to handle a club.

He didn't think, not for a fraction of a heartbeat even. Giving up on the useless piece of polished wood, he hurled himself at the widespread feet instead, grabbing the nearest moccasin with all the power he could muster, pulling hard.

A deafening thud was the next sound his mind registered, as

his body lunged forward, taking control of the situation, doing what it always did best, letting its instincts decide. No more panicked thrashing about. His fists made a fast work out of it, landing with practiced ease. Echoes of Anea's brother? The man didn't even move when Ogteah paused, out of breath.

Blinking, he looked up, to encounter a stare accompanied by a faintly taunting grin of none other than the Standing Stone man, crouching next to him, barely recognizable under the coating of too much mud and blood, some of it obviously his.

"They say people fight wars with weapons, you know?"

Ogteah blinked again. "Are you all right?"

The broad face twisted, as the man pushed himself into a more upright position. "Not sure about that."

Climbing down from of his own former rival, Ogteah glanced at the crumbled heap of limbs, the bloodied face contorted, mouth gaping, dripping saliva, not dead surely, but harmlessly unconscious to pay him any further attention for now, then crouched down next to his man.

"Where are your brothers and the others?"

"Back by the river... running your messages." The man's muddied palms were pressed against his stomach, blood seeping from between his fingers, in a distressingly eager manner.

"We'll take you back there too. Plenty of healers must be around there somewhere."

A glance shot at Ogteah made him shiver. Briefly unguarded, it allowed him a glimpse of the man's fear mixed with a childlike hope.

"Just let me get my spear."

The man impaled on his favorite javelin was already dead. Thank all the great and small *ukis* for that! He shivered again, remembering the inhuman screams, the wild twists of the pierced body. But for the clubman, he would have had to do what? Kill his rival off? Hasten his Sky Journey to make it easier for him?

He pushed the disturbing thoughts away, then rushed to pick up the spiked club as well. Such a worthwhile spoil, and he should be starting to practice with clubs sooner or later.

"We'll bring you down there, find a good healer, have you rest and recover," he said, kneeling back next to his charge.

But with such a nasty wound, it might be wiser to bring the healer to this man and not the other way around, wouldn't it? Still, one couldn't leave the injured to sprawl just like that until help arrived. The noises all around told him that the battle was raging at the foot of this hill as much as back near the creek and along the lake's shores. So many warriors on both sides!

"We'll bring you back, then send more of our people up there." Hauling the groaning man up, himself grinding his teeth in frustration—this buck was heavy, and suffering—he went on talking, helpless against his growing concern. "I was on my way up there too, as all you people just spread around, unruly skunks that you are."

"Doesn't he want to bring... to bring the rest of our people in already?" It came out as another groan.

Ogteah did his best in propping his charge as comfortably as he could against his own wounded shoulder. That old cut from the stupid girl, still held by the crud sinew the healer didn't have time to take out. Also, he needed to check his own side, which was hot and pulsating with pain, nowhere near unbearable, but still. The damn spiked flint.

"Maybe he does. Or maybe he just wants them to be alert and ready."

The wolf man, indeed, deemed it important earlier throughout the morning battle to send word to their hidden reinforcements, not to summon them, but just to let them know that they might be needed sooner than expected. He was worried, Ogteah knew, sharing a brief word with their young leader while fighting near the shore along with Akweks, where the hostilities were at its thickest. The enemy turned out to be more numerous, better prepared than expected, battle hungry and not afraid. They had already pushed some of the defenders' forces to retreat into the creek, then shoved their way up again. Such a fierce onslaught!

His stomach twisted, with hunger, or so he hoped. If no one thought of sleeping at night, none dreamed of stuffing their bellies either.

"You don't gorge yourself silly before the battle," Akweks had said back when the darkness was at its thickest, his face broad and young, glimmering softly in the faint light, full of its usual spunk. "If struck down or wounded badly, you want to go on your Sky Journey prettily, with no ugly vomit covering you from head to toe. And no feces, either. Think about it."

A thought Ogteah actually preferred to avoid. "But if you are hungry and sleepy," he had asked instead, inspecting his weaponry for the thousandth time since the scouts reported the enemy's arrival last afternoon. "Won't you find it difficult running all over, screaming and waving your club?"

"Will I?" The young warrior's laughter rolled inappropriately loud, drawing reproachful glances from the people offering by the nearby fire. "Believe me, you won't be thinking about any of it tomorrow, running around, as you so eloquently put, waving that silly spear of yours. You will be too busy, and also too wound up, to think of matters like sleeping or food." Dropping his voice, he reached for Ogteah's former spear, touching the base of the polished flint, running his fingers alongside the leather strips that were tying it to the sturdy base together with the sap-glue. "Speaking of waving spears, I have plenty of better weaponry than that sharpened stick of yours. May let you use that pretty thing. Lend it to you, temporary, eh? That's one good win I will always cherish."

"Shut up. I like my new spear well enough. But for your constant bragging, I wouldn't remember that other sharpened stick at all." He made sure his snort did not reach anyone's ears but theirs. "Cherish it all you like, I don't care."

"Of course." The young Flint's lips twisted with familiar friendly derision, then the baiting grin was gone. "But I mean what I say. Take your spear back. At least for the duration of this battle." The broad palm came up, imploring. "I mean it. I had a feeling about it, the other day. When we were leaving that other lake, near their main town... Remember that captive girl you bothered to drag to our camp? When I saw Okwaho's brother bringing her food, before they were setting off, well, it was very strange, it was as though I didn't see her before. Or maybe it was that she never looked up until this time. Well, she did on that day, and somehow, well, somehow her eyes made my hair rise. There was something about her gaze, something strangely frightening. She was looking at you, you see? You were busy talking to Okwaho's brother, so maybe you didn't notice, but she was staring at you quite intensely. It was disturbing this gaze, and it brought the image of your spear into my mind."

Studying his friend's atypically troubled frown, Ogteah felt his own hackles rising, the sudden gust of night breeze breathing coldly, making him shiver. Where did the wind come from? Wasn't it humid, so suffocating hot before?

"You are talking nonsense. What does the stupid girl have to do with our battle? She was just that, a silly thing thinking herself a warrior. I'm glad she got away and relieved us of her annoying presence." To grow angry with the stupid would-be warrior girl helped. It made the ripple of superstitious fear go away. Why would his friend, afraid of nothing until now, feel strange about that odd captive of his, now gone for good. Or maybe not. Did the bothersome skunk travel on, after conveying the message the High Springs man wished her to bring to the enemy, the location and presumable size of their forces? Somehow, he knew that she did.

"Got away, eh?" Akweks rolled his eyes, evidently over his spell of disquieting premonition as well. "Don't forget that I'm as close to our leaders and organizers as you are." Then the scowl was back, the direful furrowing of the wide brow. "Just take that spear and use it in the battle." As the sturdy pole swished, flying through the darkness, Ogteah caught it without thinking, his fingers closing around the familiar slickness, enjoying its friendly warmth. "Then you can hand it back to me, you straightforward gambler with too much pride. Take good care of this thing, and make sure it doesn't break over someone's ribs, or better yet, skull."

Well, it hadn't so far, reflected Ogteah, struggling down the hill, supporting the wounded as well as he could, while clenching the contested spear in the same palm he was clutching his newly acquired club as well. Akweks would be happy to hear the tale of the lives that spear had taken, five as far as he could remember, with the last one being a spectacular throw, right through the man's guts. As disgustingly frightening as such death looked in reality, it would make a good tale to tell by the fire, he knew, hastening his step even though the wounded leaned on him heavily now, with his entire weight, dragging his feet with the utmost effort.

"Almost there."

Reeling, he jerked away to avoid a collision with some panting warriors, who burst upon them from behind the bend of the trail, their paint smeared together with their ripped-off decorations.

The enemy! He shoved his charge toward the nearest tree.

They didn't even pause before attacking, all three of them rushing forward, getting in each other's way, yet before he managed to decide what to do with either his spear or the annoying club, both still gripped tightly in his sweaty palm, more people surged up the muddy trail, breaking through the bushes, a mix of different colors and decorations this time.

Relieved, he recognized the oiled, spiked-up patch of adorned hair, the heavy club just an extension of Akweks' broad palm, his powerful shoulders and chest glimmering with remnants of old paint and the coat of newer evidence of the man being in the thickest of the fighting.

A loud whoop came out on its own. Letting the annoying club go, Ogteah threw his spear without aiming, the first of the attacking warriors making an easy target. As it slid against the painted chest, pushing the leaping man off his feet, he lunged forward, anxious to retrieve his weapon as much as to make sure his rival was injured badly or dead, himself still in control, not about to succumb to silly rolling around like back in the woods. In the next heartbeat, it was over.

"Send a few of your wild warriors. Find Okwaho's brother. Tell him, tell him it's time." Akweks was breathing heavily, leaning on his palm propped against his slightly bent knees, his club dangling free, swaying above a headless body. A glance at the skull smashed to a pulp, nothing but a revolting mess of red, brown, and gray told Ogteah that here was another sight he could do without, the non-existent contents of his stomach trying to travel in the wrong direction.

He swallowed forcefully. "Will do that. He thinks it's time?"

"Yes, yes." The grin was spreading, flickering with amused appreciation. "Send two or three groups, a few men each, then gather the rest of your troublemakers quickly. I want you to come with me, you and your men." A wink. "You are supposed to lead them, you know? Not run all over the woods, picking independent fights."

Busy kneeling next to the wounded Standing Stone brother again, who by now slumped at the base of the tree, curled around himself, evidently in great pain, Ogteah didn't give any of his readily spicy responses that would have been on the tip of his tongue under different circumstances. "I need to get him to a healer."

Akweks narrowed his eyes then straightened up. A curt gesture of the bloodied palm summoned one of the newcomers who came alongside with him.

"Take him down to the river, where the other wounded are. Then come back quickly." Another heartbeat of pondering and the broad arm shot up, detaining the man. "No, don't come back here. Head toward the hill that is facing the creek, where the fighting is at its worst. Meet me and the others at its foot, on the waterside." A quick nod at Ogteah. "You too. Round up as many of your man as you find, then hurry there. Don't take your time about it. Be as quick as a buck in heat seeing a fat doe."

"What are you up to?"

But the impatient gesture of his friend's massive arm cut his questioning short. "Just be there, unless you are off to summon our reinforcements yourself."

About to roll his eyes and maybe to tell the pushy Flint to stuff his orders he knew where, Ogteah noticed three of his men crashing onto the trail from behind nearby bushes, all cut and bleeding but in high spirits, clearly victorious, with one of the newcomer's arm cradled in a rude, hastily improvised, sling.

"About time!" He gestured them to come over, not surprised when all three rushed toward him with no visible protests or hesitation. Why would they?

Akweks' eyebrows, he noticed, climbed high, in an open and somewhat grudging appreciation. "Get the rest of them, great leader. Then hurry up to join us around that other hill. Besides the pleasure of greeting our reinforcements personally while seeing that stunned expression on the filthy enemy's faces, they say their leader, the man who limps everywhere around this field and gives everyone orders, is fighting there now, with much spirit they say. Wouldn't it be a pleasure to strike such an important bird down?"

"Yes, maybe. Not a bad mission, you ambitious warrior." Fighting his grin, Ogteah concentrated back on his men, noting that the rest of the Standing Stone brothers were still missing. Oh, but he would have to remember to offer a prayer and maybe something of his for their wounded sibling to get better.

"That man, I saw him," said one of Akweks' newcomers, rubbing the tip of his club against the dry grass absently, evidently trying to get rid of the revolting mixture that stuck to it. "Some people say he enjoys the protection of the Evil Left-Handed Twin himself. They say that sometimes, when he might get struck, an arrow comes out of nowhere, taking his rivals down and into the mourning platform."

"You saw that?"

They were all staring, reflected Ogteah, his and Akweks' men, even the wounded, who was yet to be taken away, despite the clear orders.

"Some of it." The way the man shrugged disclosed his lack of knowledge or an actual eye-witnessing to testify to that matter.

"Well, we'll get a chance to see it for ourselves and soon, won't we?" A wink, a light wave of the weapons-free hand and the impressive Flint was gone, his spiked hair jumping stiffly with the sharp movement.

CHAPTER 24

Tsutahi wanted to vomit. Fighting her nausea down, she leaned forward, resting her stomach on the warm stone, trying to see better.

At least the smell was not as terrible up here, on this relatively high bluff, with the light breeze coming from the lake, bringing a semblance of freshness, too gentle to cool the heat, but still so very welcome. It made the traces of the unbearable stench disperse, the foul odor that came from the valley down below, from the shores of this loathsome lake.

Oh, but did she hate the sight of this lake from the very beginning! Such a vile place. Why did they have to return here? He didn't want to come here, he didn't. He argued that it was wiser to bypass this unimportant place, to foil the enemy's plans by going straight toward the other much bigger lake and the large town that stood upon its shores. So large and important, so unprotected. A perfect target. Still, they all preferred to go and fight the enemy instead, falling into a possible trap he was distrustful of. Oh, but why wouldn't they listen to him? Didn't they know how wise he was, how farsighted and always correct?

Clenching her teeth, she squinted, concentrating on the battle down below. A slaughter, really. It was frightening, the way those warriors went about killing each other, with such determination, such ferocity, such zest. She never imagined that it would be so ghastly, blood everywhere, and bodies—not dignified, prettily laid dead, but cut and slashed and torn open corpses, with their limbs broken, or their heads smashed.

Oh, but how violently sick she had become earlier, while

wandering down there, trying to find him despite his clear orders to stay by their boats, not to move a pace away from the creek. Enveloped by the silent screams and by stench, she had stumbled over a body with nothing but a caved in, messy stump instead of a head, which made her vomit and vomit until able to stagger away and into the grove of the nearest hill. There, in its relative safety, it was easier to return to the lucid thinking, to start observing the battle from this nicely removed, elevated position. Such terrible bedlam, and he was out there, and with his bad leg giving him so much trouble. And what if…

The thought alone had the power to send her running frantically, searching for a good spot. This hill was suitably rocky, full of comfortable bluffs. It let her observe various parts of the valley and the battle raging between its forested parts, to find different vantage points. With his bad knee, such spots proved to be of help, provided he hadn't been made aware of her intervention. Oh, but he was so proud.

A thorough scan of the nearest part of the valley, closest to the hill and the lake's shore—ah, there! Her bow came back to life at once, her grip tensing, tightening on the slick shaft, pulling the string firmer, another arrow sticking from between her fingers, more waiting in her quiver. But she was wise to spend her journey back here preparing as many arrows as she could, more than her quiver could host. She would need them, every one of those.

Proudly, she watched him wielding his club, holding it with both hands, maneuvering it as though it had no weight. He was such a great warrior! Still, his rival was moving too fast, as though dancing all around him, forcing him to turn sharply, to defend himself in clumsier ways. Oh, but the vile man had noticed his infirmity! The tightening in her chest gave way to a new splash of fury. It was easy to aim, easy to pull the bowstring to its limits, easy to replace the flying arrow with the next one. Pleased to see the dancing man down and squirming, she shot another, just in case. That other warrior was close enough too, looking as though about to attack his unprotected back.

Ensconced in a better feeling, she didn't dwell on his movements, knowing that he might not be pleased with her interference. Still, it was better this way. He had killed enough warriors by now, had run around more than he should, coordinating everyone in hearing range. The other leaders didn't do half of what he did, and they had no infirmities like broken knees, no difficulties walking around.

Indeed, done scanning the general view of the valley and the adjacent shores of the lake and the creek, she saw him talking rapidly, surrounded by their warriors as it seemed. Sometimes it was difficult to tell the enemy from their people.

Well, he seemed to be safe for a little while, until his warriors dispersed again, following his directives and orders. The wide gesturing of his hands left no place for doubts. He had been instructing them, and they were all now wise enough to listen to him and not to argue. About time!

Worried, because he began walking away, in the direction of the lake and out of her sight, his following growing with every step, she jumped to her feet, welcoming the opportunity to stretch her cramped legs. If he was leading his people closer to the creek and the fierce fighting that must have been raging there, then she would have to find a new comfortable spot.

Clenching her bow, she hurried back, crushing through the thickest of the bushes, indifferent to their prickly resistance. The wind her headlong run created cooled her sweaty face, such a welcome relief in the terrible heat. She thought about her stash of additional arrows, some of them nothing but polished sticks with sharpened, slightly charred edges she had prepared hurriedly while on the last part of their journey, stored up there too, tucked in another quiver. But first of all she needed to find out where he went.

The breeze was stronger at the top of the hill, with the trees spreading sparser, allowing a better look of the valley and the slopes on the opposite shore of the creek. It took her barely twenty, maybe thirty paces to cross the dry, bumpy ground, to peek at the slanting incline of the other side.

Her heart going absolutely still, she glimpsed it for only a fraction of a heartbeat, unable to draw a breath, her body throwing itself backwards and under the cover of the nearby bushes, acting with no regard to her mind. *Oh, Mighty Spirits, but they were everywhere, those swarms of warriors. So many!*

One heartbeat, then another. Frozen in dread, she peeked out again, her head free of thoughts, the fear splashing higher and higher, rising like a river after the Cold Moons, gripping her chest, threatening to drown her for good. *Where was more enemy coming from?* Spreading between the trees and along the clearings, circumventing the hill mainly, some were making their way up as well. Multitudes of them, as far as her eyes could reach. Maybe hundreds, maybe more. But where were they coming from? Weren't the enemy fighting his warriors?

The next thing she knew, she was crashing through the thickest of foliage, racing down the slope, oblivious of the branches flogging her limbs and her face, her hands clutching the bow, ready to use it, as always. This had nothing to do with the terrible sensation of panic and fear, with the wild tempo her heart was tapping, urging her to run faster.

He needed to know, oh, but he needed to know right away. He would know what to do, how to counter this new menace, but he needed to be warned, to have those few additional heartbeats to prepare, somehow, *to do something*.

Even though the mayhem that spread before his eyes as he ran down the hill was terrible—so much gore, blood, broken bodies strewn everywhere, and the smell, such terrible stench—to finally join the battle was a relief.

Clutching the club tightly with both hands, his bow and quiver of arrows swaying behind his back, Ganayeda tried not to let the clatter all around confuse him, seeking with his eyes. From his elevated position, he could see a whole lake of people splashing, spilling between the trees and back into the open grounds, their clubs rising, their spears flashing, their spirits inflamed, fury unrestrained.

Still, one could see the difference where the fresh forces began pouring in, eager and deadly, spoiling for a fight. The word must have gotten around, as at first, only the places where his men barreled in seemed to lose momentum, the enemy halting abruptly, gaping in disbelief, while the defenders took heart and attacked more fiercely than before, eager to kill their rivals.

Then more agitation seemed to spill all over the valley, with more and more warriors pouring in, those who had a longer way, either circumventing the hill or ascending it to descend again. All over the valley, the enemy was pausing, gaping, to be cut down more easily by their original rivals and by the furious newcomers, eager to have their share of the fight.

Oh, but his men did listen!

The smile of pride threatened to sneak out, difficult to battle. He had made sure to instruct everyone, speaking with each group and almost every warrior in it, and not only the leaders he had appointed to lead clusters of people. Already divided by nations and towns, their fellow warriors everyone arrived with and preferred to stick together, the men didn't argue when he insisted on dividing them into even smaller groups.

This way it would be easier to coordinate their actions, to fight more efficiently, to make the best of their surprise, he had reasoned, explaining it all in a general assembly he had called on the day before the battle, when the enemy's approach had been reported with reassuring finality.

They couldn't hide in one place, couldn't huddle in the same grove behind the hill, not while numbering over eight hundred men. Such a large amount needed to be spread evenly, coordinated by words of messengers, otherwise the enemy might sniff them out and spoil their surprise. So they would have to trust their leaders, the carefully chosen people he had appointed with deep consideration and thought, he had told them, and do what they were asked to, with no questions and no independent actions. Their fortitude and patience, their self-restraint, their ability to follow instructions and not to rush out on their own were of paramount importance, he went on, pleased with their undivided attention, surprised by it.

Were these the same restless spirits not always capable of

listening even to their own appointed leaders? The men were now hanging on his words, their eyes telling him that his message didn't fall on deaf ears. It wouldn't be easy to wait and do nothing, knowing that their brothers were in the thickest of the fight, defending the Great League of the Longhouse People, distinguishing themselves. Still, the outcome of this greatest of battles their union had to face depended on them, their fortitude as much as their valor, to come out at precisely the right time and finish the enemy for good.

"They need more people up there," he said to one of his fellow minor leaders, a man of Tsonontowan, pointing toward the creek's bend, where the enemy seemed to enjoy certain advantage, fighting with ardor, pushing the defenders toward the pebbles of the shoreline, successful despite the fiercest resistance.

"I'll round up my warriors, take them there." In another heartbeat Tsonontowan man was gone, disappearing with the same abrupt eagerness all of his charges displayed, spoiling for a fight.

Ganayeda beckoned one of the passing by warriors. "Find your leader and tell him to take at least fifty or more men to the bend of this creek, where the fight is still undecided." The man nodded eagerly, hurrying away on a run, asking no questions

Another of his fellow leaders swept by. "Yes, let us lend our men worthwhile support."

Ganayeda nodded briefly. "Follow me."

Again, no questions, no arguments, no protests. He gestured to other warriors, grinning at them with his eyes, pleased. "Scan the lakeside and let me know if our people out there need reinforcing as well. I'll be down there, at the mouth of the creek."

At the foot of the hill, the turmoil pounced on them, the mayhem of blood-freezing war cries, of thundering blows and screams, of panted breaths and sweating bodies, of distinct creaking resulting from breaking bones, such a terrible sound.

"We need more people here!" Despite the hubbub enough warriors responded to his gesturing hands, coming closer, listening avidly. "Tell our men who are fighting near the lake or uphill."

A push in his upper back nearly made him fall as he whirled around, his mind still busy calculating the possible whereabouts of reinforcing groups, ringing in confusion. One of his warriors was bringing his club up again, leaping from the path of a falling body, the one who must have hit him, Ganayeda, in the process of falling. In a momentary stupor, he watched it still jerking, lurching upon the mucky ground, as though trying to perform a strange ritual.

"He was about to attack you from behind," shouted the club owner, the wave of the bloody hand light, uninhibited.

Before Ganayeda had a chance to say something, the man was gone, diving into the melee to their left. Concentrating, he shifted his grip on his own club then took his thoughts off the general outcome of the battle altogether, remembering Okwaho's words. *Think of your immediate surroundings, not of what is happening on the larger scale when in the middle of it; only the people next to you, the enemies and your friends, exist at this point.*

Okwaho had repeated this same advice more than once on the previous night, while sneaking to visit their side of the hill under the cover of darkness, chancing giving their surprise away. It was no casual visit, even though his brother claimed it was so, making Ganayeda laugh quietly but mercilessly. Just passing by, indeed.

Still, he did understand Okwaho's concern, knowing that, as a worthwhile leader, his brother was ensuring all was well and prepared, not out of distrust or a lack of belief in his, Ganayeda's, ability to organize his people and do his part—Okwaho knew how good he was, how thorough, how meticulous, that without him this entire enterprise might not have happened at all, disintegrating into a terrible mess instead, like back near Tsonontowan. No, it wasn't lack of faith, not at all. It's just that Okwaho was a true leader, unable to relax and just wait, doing everything in his power to ensure his plans and strategies were going to proceed without a hitch.

Where was the young rascal right now? he asked himself, trying not to worry, the troublesome images sneaking into his head unwelcome and uninvited. Not now!

Attacking the man who leapt into his path, he steadied himself quickly, whirling to face his new rival. Quickly, but not quickly enough. Still, this time he was ready, his club, pleasantly light in his hands, pouncing, flying in a half-circle, connecting with his rival's temple, crushing it with a decisive thud. There was no need to finish the man off even.

Having no time to kneel next to the inanimate form, he muttered a quick address to the man's spirit, while turning back, ready to face new dangers. Remarkably few at this point, he was quick to notice, with the clear majority of their men dominating this side of the valley, his reinforcements mainly.

"We are heading on, toward the creek," he shouted, gesturing at the nearest men and the others, those who were around and listening. "Let the others know."

The breeze was stronger near the waterline, rushing through the sparsely spread vegetation, welcome in its cool freshness. The stench, which seemed unbearable in the beginning, was haunting his nostrils not as badly now, but it was good to have a gulp of fresh air.

The fighting was bad enough near the pebbled shores, hopelessly balanced or maybe even tipped in the enemy's favor. The invaders seemed to put it all in their last attempt to gain an upper hand, refusing to lose their spirits, attacking with daring and fierceness, mindless of their lives anymore, as though the surprising reinforcements fortified their fighting resolve instead of harming it.

Oh, but these people were worthy rivals! Or maybe potential brothers, to take a seat in the shade of the Great Tree of Peace, in the Longhouse of the Great Peacemaker's vision. He pushed the irrelevant thoughts away.

"About time!"

The beaming face of none of other than the Crooked Tongue leapt into his view, barely recognizable under the thick coat of dried blood and dust, the remnants of the paint adding to the grotesque vision. Flint People's coloring, judging by the smeared fragments. Why Flint?

He eyed the funny picture this man's hair made, sticking out in strangest of fashions. "About time, eh?"

Avoiding the swish of a wandering club, a blow that was clearly meant to hit someone else, Ganayeda turned to confront its owner nevertheless, noticing that the Crooked Tongue was still wielding his spear rather than a club, a strange choice of weaponry for a long, strenuous fighting.

"Where is Okwaho?"

Done with his rival, an already wounded, clearly exhausted Long Tail, Ganayeda rushed to catch up with his less ordinary peer, pleased to see the man doing well in the battle, sporting new cuts and bruises but bursting with cheerful vitality akin to what he had displayed back in Onondaga Town, while organizing his spear-throwing contest or since being entrusted with his small army of troublemakers to lead and to do with as he saw fit.

"Oh, he was there." A noncommittal wave of the decorated spear he hadn't seen in the man's possession before indicated the other side of the hilly shoreline. "But he went to gather more of your fresh warriors' forces. Bring them here, you know." The heavily ringed eyes sparkled with familiar light provocation. "No use having the hundreds of you milling out there, where you have to look hard to find any enemy."

"To look hard after we barreled in and cleaned this side of the valley of this same enemy!" cried out Ganayeda, surprised with his own indignant reaction. It wasn't as though they did nothing but hide, he and his men.

Ducking a throw of someone's spear, the Crooked Tongue turned away, to face the challenging enemy, still grinning. "No offense was meant, High Springs' man." The unconcerned words trailed after him, as cheerfully cheeky as their owner was.

Ganayeda shook his head, amused, but only a little. To cut into the melee with the new surge of vengeance helped. He and his men took it upon themselves the harder mission that required much patience and fortitude besides the regular valor and bravery in order to help his brother's intricate plan that, indeed, seemed as though it had worked splendidly. They did not deserve to be accused of having it easy.

Nearer the lakeshore, where the creek was at its widest, the fighting was raging fiercely, with the invaders still organized into more than just sporadic resistance. His reinforcements pouring in, following Ganayeda's and other leaders' efforts, the enemy was pushed back steadily toward the lake rather than the creek, away from their previous night's camp and their multitude of boats as well. A good development. Why let the enemy have an easy way out, those who might like to entertain the idea of getting away? Not many, judging by the ferocious fighting. Oh yes, these people *were* worthy rivals.

Okwaho's spear-throwing friend from Cohoes Falls caught his eye, as he pushed his way toward the row of low cliffs that adorned this side of the lake, atypical for the otherwise relatively flat scenery. A reasonably dense outpour of arrows was cascading from there, forcing people to duck or move away, yet the spectacular Flint was pushing his way up, skipping the wet stones, wielding his massive club as though it was nothing but a walking stick.

Curious, Ganayeda watched him for a brief moment, safe in doing so while being surrounded by so many of his own warriors—there was an advantage of being in the lead, sometimes, a protective screen to enjoy—puzzled by the purposefulness with which the young warrior was determined to ascend the sloping rocks.

The arrows, he surmised, gesturing to the few of the groups' leaders he spotted. Oh yes, there was a need to eliminate the shooters, the lively activity up the cliff boding no good, with too many enemy warriors surging up and down the nearest flat top, spilling in organized groups, the young Flint's obvious destination.

"He is trying to get to that grass-eater who gives everyone orders from up there." The Crooked Tongue was again beside him, shielding his eyes against the glow of the early afternoon sun. "How about we direct some of your warriors and the others there? It would be easier once we dislodge that lowlife who orchestrates the last of their resistance and hopefully get rid of him while going this." A wink. "Akweks might like to have this glory all for himself, though."

"How many are they up there on that cliff?"

"I don't know." The wide shoulders lifted in an indifferent shrug. "I'm taking my men there now. Then we'll know better." A twisted half-grin held less of the previous warm friendliness. "I'll send you word, when we know, I suppose."

Ganayeda pursed his lips. "Do that."

CHAPTER 25

Aingahon leaned against the protruding stone of the rocky wall, unable to fight the temptation. His knee, previously just throbbing then later on pulsating with pain, was now shooting the sharpest twinges up and down his leg. The tight bandage of leather that usually helped, at least to a degree, loosened its grip during the insanity of this day. Which was no wonder of course!

With all the mad rushing up and down the trails, fighting, leaping to crush someone's skull, avoiding being hit in his turn, darting and pouncing, running all over, making sure his men were spread evenly, not warring in large congregations, leaving the others to fend off the enemy undersized—no, of course he'd had no opportunity to try and make it easier for his suffering knee.

How could he, when there was no time even to inspect any of the new injuries, unless those prevented a person from fighting on? An aspiring leader of his caliber could not let his infirmity interfere, could not tell people what to do while sitting comfortably and waiting for them to do his bidding. Enough that the enemy did manage to surprise them, did manage to outsmart, to ambush them into...

Grinding his teeth, he pushed the mounting wave of frustrating fury away. He did suspect, did hesitate, did try to prevent their coming here, into this innocently spread valley between two smaller lakes. Had he only been listened to! Another wrong turn of thought.

With an effort, he pushed himself away from his rocky support.

"Send more men down there to collect the arrows," he tossed toward one of the leaders, a man who was standing by aimlessly, as though waiting for guidance. At this point of the battle, the few remaining leaders had lost their initial forcefulness, become less assertive. Some wandered with no purpose, waiting for his words. Others turned to mindless warring, charging fiercely, paying no attention to their duty of directing the battle. Now it seemed that he was the only one who tried to manage anything, to conduct a semblance of an organized fight, to think of possibilities of retreat. Did they all want to die bravely and be done with it?

"Arrows?" The man was staring at him, annoying in his bewilderment.

"Yes, arrows," he repeated as patiently as he could, hurrying toward the edge of their bluff, paying no attention to his bad limp, not anymore. "Our men up here are doing a good thing by shooting the enemy down. But they are running out of arrows fast."

Shielding his eyes, he looked at the melee that was gushing all around their elevated perch, the enemy so numerous, so determined, inspired to new fits of bravery now, with their fresh forces closing in on his people from behind. There was no way to win this battle. And no way to make the best of it. They were too badly outnumbered to hurt the enemy for real, too dispirited by the terrible surprise. How could he save the men who were still out there and fighting?

"Tell the warriors who are not busy shooting or those who are on their way down to pick up every arrow they find and carry them back here," he repeated tiredly, glancing at their temporary refuge, the flat top hosting many warriors, those who either came to regroup, about to join the fighting at the lake, or those who felt they could be of use up here, defending their obviously last stand, shooting or running messages, quite a few leaders among those. All accepting his ascendancy now. But for them acting the same only a few dawns earlier!

Paying the following man no more attention, he stalked away, seeking out the warriors he trusted the most.

"What now?" This time, it was an Attiwandaronk leader, the

man who had argued with him most venomously back by the mouth of the accursed creek, now his staunchest of supporters. "It is going badly for our people down there, with the lowlifes having their reinforcements to rely on."

"We should bring all our men here." He encircled the spacious plateau with his gaze, tired beyond measure. "Send those who are willing to carry this message. Tell everyone they encounter to gather here."

"Make our last stand, eh?" The man snorted grimly, his nod curt, eyes cold. "Yes, I suppose it's time."

Aingahon said nothing, making do with a mere shrug. Yes, it was time, even though they would surely not all die here. They couldn't. To leave their towns back home undefended, devoid of so many capable men was unspeakable, a thought too scary to let it enter one's mind. But how to make the remaining warriors leave without hurting their pride by implying they might be cowardly enough to just go while the braver of their peers fought and died?

Making his way toward the other side, where another pocket of fighting was developing, with some enterprising enemy trying to storm their cliff in an unsophisticated, outright attack, he nodded encouragingly at the man who crouched upon the steep edge, shooting in even intervals. "I'll have more arrows brought to you soon."

"They are drawing closer."

"Yes, I know. When you run out of arrows, join the fighting over there."

A vigorous nod was his answer, but the man's eyes lingered, narrow, apprehensive, expectant. Seeking reassurance, he knew, having none to offer.

"If you find yourself by the creek, able to grab a boat, sail home," he said, beyond caring how his suggestion would sound. "I would rather have as many of our men returning, to defend our homes, to live, if for no other reason than to fight another battle."

The eyes peering at him widened then narrowed again. With understanding.

He breathed with relief. "Spread the word."

Turning as hurriedly as his suffering knee allowed him to, he went on, his club more alive in his palms now, crying for action. Some people would go back to defend their homes against the victorious enemy, but he wouldn't be among those. That was one thing he knew beyond a shadow of doubt.

The noise at the widest of trails was rising, the fighting there clearly intensifying, with the enemy pressing harder, sensing the victory. Growing more impatient too, having fought for so long, such a hard battle. How could he use this obvious lack of patience for their advantage?

Before hastening his step, he looked around once again. The last matter to take care of. Tsutahi.

She was crouching at the same bluff he had sent her to occupy when she came running here such a very short time ago, pell-mell, out of breath, near panic, to ignite a similar reaction among the others. New enemy forces were rolling down one of the hills and around it, coming in great numbers, was her frantic message, delivered in a hysterical shout. Oh, but how this information hit him back then, him and the others.

Clenching his teeth until his jaw hurt, he drew a deep breath then beckoned her, knowing that she would respond at once, never having taken her eyes off him. His guarding spirit. But not anymore. No more helpfully flying arrows, with their longer, sturdier shafts, coming every time he was having a hard time against this or that rival. How it had angered him during the morning battle. What did she think of him to help him out like that, to pay no attention to the battle or this entire war, the general good of their people, to be concerned only with his own private safety, as though he couldn't take care of himself? Did she think he was a lesser warrior because of his injury?

He grinned without amusement. None of it mattered now. Only her safety.

"Listen to me carefully, little one," he said, as she halted besides him, barely stopping in time not to collide with him full length, running in her usual headlong speed, anxious to be near. He eyed her flushed face, smeared in its customary mixture of mud and sweat, a little of dried blood—he hoped it wasn't hers— scratched and bruised, but not terribly so. Only the paint was missing. A warrior-girl.

His smile threatened to sneak out uninvited. But she was such an out-of-place little thing.

"Go to the other side of that cliff now, out there, where the rocks are facing the lake. Climb down or jump into the water if you must. It should be a safe jump." She was peering at his lips, her forehead creased like a wrinkled blanket, reading his words, anxious to understand. "Swim to our boats at the mouth of the creek. Take possession of one and sail upstream, toward the place we camped yesterday, before heading here." Her eyes were narrowing into slits, but he went on, in a hurry, having no time for arguments, not now. "Just do as I say. Sail there and hide. I will be heading there too, later on, and so will some others. This is what I asked everyone to do. Stay for a day, if you wish it so. Rest, gather your strength. But don't wait more than that. If I don't come, sail home and wait for me there. Do you understand?" Catching her shoulder with one hand, so painfully thin, nearly bare, the sleeves of that new dress from her people's lands torn into near non-existence by now, he held her gaze, willing her to listen. "Head for Tushuway. I'll find you there later on. Not anywhere here in the enemy's lands. I won't be looking for you here, do you understand me? Only if you are waiting in Tushuway. Or in your Attiwandaronk town. Only there, Tsutahi. Do you listen to me? Do you understand?"

The protests were forming rapidly, he could see that. Tightening his grip, he held her closer, trying to give her some of his strength, some of the calmness that permeated his being, making his heart slow its mad racing. She should know it was all good. Otherwise, she wouldn't leave without him.

"Go to the boats and sail home. This is the only way for me to find you after it's all over. Otherwise, if you linger in these lands or do something against my instructions, you will not see me again, ever. I will not be staying here after it'll be over. None of us will."

Oh, yes, anything but that. Even if it meant a more difficult journey toward the Sky World, not straightaway from where his spirit would start it but with a long detour. He felt his stomach tightening in hundreds of painful knots. Not now. Later, when it's time. Not with her frightened, wide-eyed gaze on him, so childish again, so unprotected, the mutinous expression replaced by an open fear. But for the opportunity to press her to his chest and make it all right again, somehow.

"We'll talk about it later, Tsutahi. Not now. Now do as I say. One time, just this once, do as I ask you to do. Will you?" The smile came easier than he thought, not forced at all, even though he felt his own lips trembling a little. "Just go now. They need me out there." The smile gone, he narrowed his eyes again, not sternly but firmly. "Tell me you will do as I say. Tell me you will sail for Tushuway, wait for me there. Tell me!"

She was shaking her head in neither denial nor confirmation. Or maybe it was a yes. He had no time for any more talking. So much to say, or to do for her. No opportunity to do anything, not even to comfort her properly, to instruct her or find someone to care for her. Like her grandfather, he was leaving her all alone, with no company and no protection, just some stupid knowledge a girl shouldn't possess in the first place. More warrior now than after her grandfather, how useless and stupid!

"Go now, little one. Don't linger here, but do as I say. It will all be good, you'll see!"

Will it? People were waiting for him, anxious, impatient. They needed him there by the edge of the cliff, to join the last desperate fighting, to organize the retreat of those who would agree to retreat.

He clenched his teeth fiercely, hating the suffocating wave that was pressing inside his chest. Such bad timing for everything. Another knot in his throat was swallowed.

"Go now, warrior-girl. Go quickly. It's time."

Turning toward the others, quite a large group and growing, he drew a breath through his clenched teeth, his stomach as heavy as the rocks around him, and as stiff. It was all going so badly wrong, but at least she would escape this, would do as he told her. This time, he knew it for certain.

CHAPTER 26

"Bring the damn bows, or anything that shoots. Throw rocks, for all the great and small spirits' sake!"

The wolf man was beyond a regular stage of frustration, gesturing widely, shouting orders and instructions right and left, not bothering to pause for breath.

Hundreds of warriors seemed to mill all around the contested slope, pushing and shoving, eager to brave the steep trail. Or to attempt to do that, as the defenders were as eager not to let them, their fighting spirit unbroken, showering the ascending warriors with all sorts of missiles, from arrows to stones.

Determined to make the most out of that last stand of theirs, reflected Ogteah, pushing his way out of the commotion, beckoning his men to follow, those who were close enough to see him. In such a bedlam, it was easy to lose eye contact.

He had tried to stay close to Akweks earlier, while joining the first storming effort, after talking to the High Springs man, but they lost each other quickly in the growing commotion, especially with the fierce Flint's stubborn determination to be the first atop the accursed hill, craving a dramatic hand-to-hand with the leader who had been holding this last spell of resistance. Akweks had claimed he knew who it was. The same limping lowlife who had been seen giving orders to everyone throughout the entire battle, or so it seemed.

The ambition Ogteah laughed about, not missing the opportunity to needle his friend, himself not as enticed by such aspirations. Let anyone who craved it have this particular glory. For himself, he had been satisfied by the mere outcome of the battle to think of personal achievements beyond the knowledge that he had done seemingly well. It was good to know that he was a warrior now, a true warrior; that he didn't succumb to panic or fear, didn't flee or shame himself in any other way, fighting as bravely as the others, killing his share of the enemy, even if it must have been nothing compared to what Akweks or the wolf man had achieved.

Putting his attention back on the contested slope, he grinned again, amused against his will. Such an inviting target all those eagerly pressing warriors were presenting, insisting on scaling every possible trail, no matter what. No wonder the wolf man was livid, watching how the enemy was not about to miss out on the opportunity to shower his men with arrows, and yes, occasional pebbles and stones. Hurled expertly, those caused no little damage, and there was no need to aim even. Whatever you threw at such a densely packed crowd was sure to hit this or that head. Stupid, indeed, but what other choice did they have? There was no other way to finish the accursed battle.

Not relishing the idea of being pushed and jolted all the way to the top of the contested cliff, Ogteah glanced in the general direction if the lake. "How about we look for another way up?"

Crowding next to him, his men, about half of his original group, looked at him, openly attentive. That encouraged him.

"We go around, climb the harder way," he mused. "They must be too busy with this side of their hill, watching our men trampling each other to enjoy the lake's scenery. Unless it's too difficult of a climb."

He glanced at the scout, whose placid, slightly doubtful expression kept angering him as much as it did back at the mouth of Honeoye Creek two dawns ago. Why did this man keep trailing after them, keeping close and acting as a part of their group ever since they had returned from that sortie, accepting his, Ogteah's, leadership, if he was in constant doubt in regard to him and his decisions?

"Is it?" he prompted.

"No, it's not." An indifferent shrug was his answer. "A doable climb. Unless they try to stop you."

"Then we go there now." Impatiently, Ogteah turned away without thanking the man, waving his hand in order to draw the rest of his warriors' attention. "Over there. Tell the others."

The oldest Standing Stone brother as always was the first to respond. Nodding eagerly, the heavyset man yelled at his peers, reinforcing his words with broad gesticulation, pointing where Ogteah was already heading, enjoying the breeze that was blowing from the lake's side, bringing relief in the heaviness of the afternoon heat. Not to mention the stench.

"They think too simply, those warriors." Pleased to see most of his men following dutifully, now the entire remnants of the original group, over three tens of warriors, more than enough to surprise the enemy from the other side, or at least to take their attention from the main storming points, Ogteah snorted. "We could just sit and wait for the enemy up there to run out of arrows and stones, to come down and let us cut them, or capture or whatever we want to do with them. No need to crowd that stupid cliff the way they do."

"They can't wait for too long. It will get dark in the end." The scout again.

"The way they are huddling down there, getting a few warriors up at a time, it might become dark before we make it to the top anyway." Shrugging, Ogteah bent to pick up a large sharp-edged pebble. "Gather stones as you go. If they notice us climbing up, you start pelting them with those things. With us having no bows, this might help."

"As always, the wildest mission is ours, eh?" One of the men flapped his hands in the air, drawing quite a few laughs from all around.

Only the Standing Stone pair remained quiet, proceeding ahead in grim silence. Sighing, Ogteah stifled his own outburst of brief mirth. Having no time to check on their knifed sibling after delivering the wounded to one of Akweks' warriors' hands, he remembered the blood that had been seeping through the man's fingers, the lifelessness of his face, not daring to hope for a positive outcome; the concern his companions' bleak expressions reflected too well.

He shook his head to clear it of irrelevant thoughts. "Let us hurry."

"Better start going up here." The scout was again talking levelly, looking down his long nose, as though the matter had nothing to do with him. "Further down, there is no shore at all, just water and a more difficult climb."

Ogteah glanced at the man, put out as usual for no apparent reason. There was something about this one's comments, something unbearably haughty. Yet, the scout turned out to be correct again. After a short time of skipping between the rocks, the clamor coming from the top of the cliff was back upon them, with only a few ledges to climb in a precarious way. The water sparkled directly beneath their feet, not far enough to make the thought of a dive into too daunting of a possibility.

He gestured at his men to keep quiet, waiting for the others to catch up. More than his original thirty by now. Good. With little benevolence of this or that guiding spirit, they may surprise the enemy, may have their precious few heartbeats to reach the top of the cliff undetected. Judging by the noise coming from up there, the defenders were still busy repulsing the frontal attack.

Tucking his spear under his arm, pressing it with his elbow, he pondered his options, needing both hands to complete the last part of their journey. No easy solution for that. Was he to clench the accursed spear between his teeth while scaling the remaining part of their climb?

A curt nod invited two of his warriors, those who were nearer the ledge and looked ready, to start moving in the meanwhile.

"Just make sure not to draw their attention until we are all up," he whispered, reaching for the nearing crack in the warm stones. By whatever means, he would have to make it, cumbersome spear or not. The others had it easier, most clubs having a leather thong to tie it to one's wrist comfortably. But for such a device. He removed the spear back into his palm.

A shadow fell across the stones the man above him was reaching for. A small, slender shadow. Incredulous, he lifted his head to stare at none other than the captive girl from Tsonontowan—oh, yes, unmistakably her, with her small, heart-shaped face and the wildness of her gaze, the air of animal-like wariness it radiated. She was balancing on the edge of the cliff and to their right, peering at them from above, obviously aghast. For a heartbeat, or maybe even less than that.

The next thing he knew, her bow was up and ready, another familiar picture, like back in the river, rising with no hesitation, no pause, no uncertainty. In the way of hardened warriors, though she was just a girl.

Aghast in his turn, he tried to grab his spear, struggling to bring it up at the same motion, the narrow ledge he had stood upon hindering his movements, the racing of his heart not helping. The others, those who hadn't started climbing yet, the men who were farther away down the trail and occupied better positions, why weren't they doing something? They had no bows, none of them, but at least they could hurl a stone. She was dangerous, this fragile-looking thing. Despite her looks, she meant death. Still, they all seemed to just stare.

Struggling with his spear, balancing precariously on his narrow ledge, he heard the familiar hiss. Only one. Followed by another. The sound of rasping cry erupted, familiar too, painfully at that. The figure above him, the man he had sent to proceed ahead because of the stupid spear, shuddered then plummeted down at once. Not sliding or falling, but dropping like a hurled stone, to disappear in the water below, generating a loud plop, not to surface again, surely dead. Another plop told him that there were more victims to the girl's archery skill.

Having no other choice but to press on—it was either that or letting go in favor of a dive, something he might have contemplated but for the men he was responsible for—he pushed his way up with a desperate effort, leaping onto the next stone, then another.

The next frantic scan of the surface above let him know that the girl was gone, disappearing back where she came from. To warn her people of course. The only possibility.

"Hurry up!" he cried out, pushing on, oblivious to the danger of falling now. "Just get up there in a hurry."

The remnants of his men didn't need a reminder. In a short

time, the first wave was up, only seven men, but enough to face the enemy and stop them from pelting the rest of the climbers with stones and arrows, such a vulnerable target.

He threw his spear at a nearing warrior, a part of a group bearing on them, maybe ten or more people, those who clearly enjoyed the timely warning. Oh, but he would have to find that girl and kill her for good this time. What a filthy, treacherous snake!

In a hurry to retrieve his weapon, which hit its target nicely, impaling its victim for good, he didn't notice the club until it was too late to avoid the hit but by throwing himself to the ground, to roll away and hope that the enemy would miss the opportunity to make even more out of his attack.

A futile hope. The push his shoulder received made his roll a clumsy matter, and as he scrambled back to his feet, using every limb he could, he knew he was done for. The club was descending again, he could feel it most clearly, heading toward his unprotected back, determined to break it, to smash it into nothingness.

In a panic, he whirled around, hands forward, as though trying to stop the blow, which should have come earlier, but didn't. How so?

Momentarily stunned, he stared at Akweks' grinning face, his beam one of the widest, his club already back up, glistening with fresh gore, Ogteah's attacker at his feet, motionless, not even twitching.

"Get your spear, wild man, and come," the spectacular Flint cried out, face so smeared it was unrecognizable, his shoulder and upper arm bleeding, the wide chest displaying new cuts. "You came just in time."

"How?" It was still difficult to form words. "You... Where did you come from?" He clenched his fists against their trembling, afraid that his feet would buckle under him when he attempted to walk, whether on order to retrieve his weapon or to follow his friend's invitation.

The broad grin widened. "From the regular path, you adventurous warrior. Not by climbing rocky walls." The roaring laughter had a pleased quality to it. "I saw you taking your men out and around that hill. So we doubled our efforts, me and Okwaho, if only to beat you to the top, you pushy Crooked Tongue."

That did it. He felt his own laughter bursting out, too wild and maybe somewhat hysterical, but he didn't care. "You were herding up that slope like stupid deer. Me and my people, we had a better idea of fighting the enemy."

To wrestle his spear from the dead man's torso took him no time, his initial disgust and revulsion not surfacing, not anymore. Neither did the smell that was released along with the smeared weapon make him gag, just wrinkle his nose in brief disgust.

"Better idea, eh? And this is why I had to rush here, stopping that club from smashing your lazy behind." Akweks was turning away, already beginning to walk briskly. "Come, hurry. They are drifting to your side now, and I don't want to miss the opportunity to get to that limping bastard who leads them, now that they are about to be beaten for good. Especially with Okwaho taking the best of our men to clean the creek where they stored their boats."

Indeed, the battle was raging all around the steep rocks, sporadic outbursts of hostilities rather than regular fighting, as though, having been warned of their arrival, the enemy had thrown it all into the last attempt to overthrow at least the cheeky intruders who dared to attack from the unexpected side.

He sought the small figure with his eyes, his grip on the spear tightening. Where had the filthy little fox gone?

Akweks was again pushing into the thickest of it, seeking his glorious hand-to-hand. Now he could see the enemy, indeed an impressive type, as broad-shouldered as he wolf man and as tall, wielding his club fiercely, either very confident or beyond care. His gait was the only thing to ruin the spectacular view he presented. What a bad limp!

Glimpsing the High Springs man talking to a group of warriors, clearly directing them toward the same target, he drifted in the direction Akweks had gone, noticing that the battle was as good as over, with barely a few tens of the enemy warriors still fighting and no arrows flying around at all, not anymore.

He shielded his eyes, seeking again. The damn girl with the damn bow. Not a chance of her dying or going away, not this one.

Akweks was already engaged in the fight he so lusted after, fencing with the enemy leader, prolonging the moment of the actual attack, both of them, sizing each other up. Two worthy rivals.

He noticed some of the others pausing to glance, their people and the remaining enemy, not making a move toward the fighters. A hand-to-hand, oh yes. He grinned, knowing who would win this, pleased for his friend.

"I hope he takes him as his captive," muttered a gloomy voice by his side. One of his men, an Onondaga but from one of the western villages, not a person he had known until receiving his group of hand-picked troublemakers to lead, stared at the fighting with a bleak gaze, not elated by the uplifting sight. "All of them, those who aren't dead yet, I wish to watch their execution ceremonies, one by one."

He didn't comment; just put a comforting hand on the man's back, patting it briefly. The warrior who had been shot as they climbed up came from this man's village.

"Our brother will not be left to seek his Sky Path all alone. We will build his platform and will conduct his ceremonies, even if we don't find his body."

The man just shrugged, shaking the comforting hand off. "I hope the enemy dies suffering, all of them."

Watching the desolate figure stalking off, Ogteah felt his chest tightening. He had liked that other Onondaga man as well, a light-hearted, reliable fellow.

The fight was progressing at full speed now, with both men attacking simultaneously, with great vigor. What the enemy leader lacked in freedom of movement, restricted by his disability—oh, but one could see how difficult it was for him to step on his bad leg, if at all—he made up for with his obvious skill. Such powerful blows. One almost made Akweks fall, as the Flint tried to block it a fraction of a heartbeat too late, the weighty tip of his club trembling, his legs not spread widely enough to support his stance. The enemy, at this point enjoying the advantage of slightly higher ground, as both fighters had pushed it nearly to the edge of the cliff, pressed harder, the cutting tip of his club sparkling darkly, thirsty for blood.

His breath caught, Ogteah watched his friend giving in under the pressure, twisting to avoid the razor-sharp touch, losing his balance in the process, but rolling away quickly to escape the worst of the blow.

A glaring line stretched across his powerful shoulder as Akweks staggered back to his feet, still nimble and strong, but shaken, almost toppling over the cliff's edge. Had his rival not been so busy with his own struggle not to stumble, clearly sparing his bad leg or just not trusting it to hold him while steadying his club once again, it might have gone bad for Akweks. As it was, the Flint was up and ready again, eager to meet the new onslaught, if not to deliver one yet.

Ogteah let out a held breath, realizing that he kept the air in his chest for too long. Just a short moment, a few heartbeats, at the most, but those were so essential, so lethal.

As both rivals resumed their fighting, their movements slower now, either tired or just more careful, having tested each other's strength, he saw the High Springs man drawing closer, standing near the edge, following the hostilities with his eyes narrowed to slits. Some of his men stood nearby as well. Keeping an eye on their leader, was Ogteah's conclusion.

More people pressed closer, their eyes glued to the fighters, mesmerized. He let his gaze stray for a moment, seeking, scanning the rocky surface and the warriors crowding it. No unmistakably small, slender silhouette among those. Still the knot in his stomach refused to loosen. She was here, somewhere, his instincts told him. Watching, prowling, meaning harm.

His nerves stretched, muscles as cramped as though he had been forced to sit in a prolonged ambush, he forced the air through his knotted stomach, taking his attention off his surroundings, unable to not do so, even though no warriors guarded him to make sure he wasn't attacked. Or maybe some of his men did. He felt their presence, the Standing Stone eldest brother and the Onondaga village man, and some others his mind registered but numbly, focused on the battle at the edge of the cliff, seeing Akweks reviving his fighting spirit, pressing the attack as the enemy leader stepped badly, on the wrong leg apparently, wavering precariously, his face twisting with pain.

When Akweks' club descended, so hurriedly it used no accumulated drive, the man had enough presence of mind to twist his body, bringing his club up in an attempt to at least partially block the blow, despite the way he had partly swayed partly thrown himself toward the nearest bluff. The mighty brush of a club's weighty tip against his shoulder came in somewhat helpfully, sending the man faster toward his destination, to crash against the sharpness of the warm rocks, groaning through his clenched teeth but still upright, enjoying the cliff's hurtful support.

Sweat rolling down his face, just a grotesque mask of smeared paint, dust, mud, and blood, hands busy clutching his club, the enemy leader blinked forcefully, his colorless lips pressed into an invisible line. No time to wipe one's face in such a situation, reflected Ogteah, and no point in doing this. Oh, but he did look in a bad shape, this man, yet he didn't seem as though about to give up or give in. Not that one. A tough beast. He felt a twinge of regret clenching his stomach. A pity the man was destined to die.

Suddenly, his eyes caught a movement. Something slunk somewhere near, something dangerous, bad. His senses screaming danger, he forced his eyes off Akweks, who was leaping forward, anxious to deliver the final blow, sensing his rival's exhaustion, knowing it was time.

His club victoriously high, the spectacular Flint pounced like a predator, a mountain lion, leaping high in the air, but Ogteah's gaze didn't follow his progress. Instead, it darted aside, brushing past the enemy leader, taking in the way the man hunched over, still leaning against the rock, not daring to leave its support, one leg thrust forward, the other folded awkwardly, taking no weight, his club high and ready, but not as ominous-looking as before, not now that its owner was going to lose.

Still, Ogteah's gaze kept sliding on, as though being pulled by a force that wasn't his, noting the details—the way the surrounding warriors were staring, leaning forward, their breaths evidently caught; the way the wind swept some branches and dry leaves, as though anxious to clean the place, to take away the reminder of the deadly activities, all this blood and gore; the way, farther down the slope, other people were still waving their clubs or an occasional spear, or others kneeling beside the fallen warriors, theirs and the enemy's, muttering prayers. And then her, the familiar slender figure, rushing ahead, bringing her bow up as she did, in such a well-remembered gesture.

Then the world shook, and the eerie sensation was gone, shattered by the terrible scream. It rang in his ears, jerking him back to life. In the next moment, he was running, still unbearably slow, not moving at all compared to the arrow—*this long, sturdy stick, longer than usual, its feathering different, fluttering in the increasing speed it was creating, unerring*—the arrow that was already reaching its target, burrowing its way in, burying itself in the glistening skin of the leaping Flint.

"No!"

He realized it was him who was yelling, not caring for anything other than to reach the fighters, to warn Akweks, to make the arrow change its course or not to leave its bow at all. Something, he had to do something! There must be a way. It was just a matter of those heartbeats, just a few, two at the most. There must be a way of changing *that*!

The enemy leader was turning, staring at him, Ogteah, eyes wild, not sane anymore, a cornered animal. Oh yes, he had seen it once, back at home, when they surprised a mature wolf, such a magnificent animal even when cornered, resolved to fight to the death. He saw the man's club pouncing from below, darting in a half-circle, the spike upon it sparkling with vicious yearning, thirsty for blood. If not Akweks' then someone else's.

Desperately, he tried to halt, or at least to change his course, stumbling over his friend's body, already slumping there on the ground, lacking in life. The spear, where was his spear? Useless in such close fighting against a club, it was still a weapon. What was he thinking, charging in such a way? Oh, but he wasn't charging, he remembered. He was just trying to warn Akweks.

The blow was so vicious, it took his breath away. One heartbeat, then another. Or maybe much less than that. When the rocky ground crushed into the side of his face, he didn't try to understand what happened. It was more imperative to get a gulp of air, just a little bit of it, really. He needed it badly. To stop the spreading agony, to deal with it, to understand what happened. It was so eerily quiet. Only him and Akweks. Lying there so peacefully, his limbs spread, warm and covered with dust. And the enemy's decorated moccasins, moving closer, one firm, determined, the other dragging. Oh, yes, the man was limping badly, wasn't he?

Somehow, he knew what was coming, an inexperienced warrior though he was. It was too clear not to understand. Pushing with his good arm—the other too numb to even think of using it, sending harrowing pangs of pain up his chest, trying to squeeze it into the inability to breathe again—he turned as much as he could, determined to see the blow, to meet it with his eyes if not his spear.

It was so difficult to see! The light, so blinding. The enemy, just a dark silhouette, not a very stable form, wavering too, or maybe it was just the light.

He blinked to see the club better, descending already, diving like a bird of prey, determined to take life. *His life!*

He tried to draw a deep breath, desperate against the pain. Just this once, only this. The stupid ring that was pressing into his torso, it had to loosen, for only a little while. Why was it there at all?

When the dark silhouette of the club swished by, falling beside him in a deafening thud, he wanted to shut his eyes in frustration, the noise it produced hurting, as though the other pain wasn't enough. The light still shone as badly, pouring on him unrestrained, with the enemy not there anymore to shield it.

The silence, he wanted it back, but it broke with a terrible cacophony of yells and screams and running feet, so many. He shut his eyes, but it didn't help. The pain was splashing everywhere, in colorful waves.

"Bring here a healer. Now!"

The roaring bellow tore into his painfully gained solitude, ringing in too close a proximity to disregard like the rest of the clamor. Strong hands grabbed his shoulder. The good one, thank all the great and small spirits for that!

"Anyone who knows about healing, just anyone," the man went on, his voice familiar, comforting at that. With an effort, he forced his eyes open. "The rest of you spread, comb this cliff, make sure there is no enemy capable of fighting left." A pause. "And Find Okwaho. Tell him I need him here *now*!"

The High Springs man's face looked bizarre, funny in the way it swam, twisting, changing forms, longer, then shorter, drawing away, then coming back.

"Can you hear me?" he kept asking, leaning too close, making it more difficult to breathe again, as though it wasn't enough that he had to fight for every gulp of air as it was. "Tell me you understand what I say."

To blink again and again helped. It made the man's face slow its nauseating movements.

"Yes... yes... can hear. Stop asking that." Was he the one who was talking, in this strange, croaking voice some old people had? "It's... a-annoying." What was with all this stuttering? He clenched his teeth tightly.

The face in front of him broke into the widest of smiles. "Oh yes, you are going to be well. Just hold on until we get the healer to see you. Try to stay awake. Will you?"

He attempted to nod, but it was too painful to do that, so he rolled his eyes instead. "If you stop... stop moving... like this." To close his eyes made him feel better. Less movement, less nausea. With those clutches crushing his ribs with every breath taken, he wasn't sure he would survive the act of vomiting. Not that!

"Just hold on, brother. You are going to be well. I'll see to that."

And that was as good a promise as any, he reflected, relaxing as much as the pain allowed him. If the High Springs man said he was going to be well, then of course he would be. That man didn't give his promises lightly.

He resisted the waves of dizziness that were trying to lull him into letting go. "I… I thank you… grateful— "

"Stop talking." Another firm order. "Just stay with me until the healer comes. Open your eyes, and don't drift anywhere." The grip on his good shoulder tightened. "You had me worried there for a little while, but you will be all right, Crooked Tongue."

He felt his lips stretching into a very crooked sort of a grin. Or maybe he just thought they did.

CHAPTER 27

Watching the cracked, colorless lips twisting, if only a little, made Ganayeda feel better. The man didn't look well, which wasn't a wonder, really. The hit he had seen this one absorbing could have sent anyone straight onto his Sky Journey. Such a powerful blow!

The memory of what happened made him shudder. As did the sight of Okwaho's friend, still lying there, surprisingly peaceful, limbs spread, eyes partly open, lips stretched into a victorious smile. Even his club was there, lying next to him, right where it fell alongside its owner, ready to be picked up again.

They should bury him with his club, he knew, his chest tightening, the air as though reluctant to be drawn in. Okwaho would see to that. Poor Okwaho! He would feel terrible when he learned of his friend's death, the friend he went to such lengths to save once upon a time.

Still, the young Flint had died victorious, about to finish the enemy off; not just an enemy but an important leader, a worthy rival he had challenged to a duel that made even the fighting people stop and watch. Such a spectacular fight, turned into such a terrible debacle.

He beckoned one of the minor leaders. "Comb this cliff once again. Make sure no enemy is left to wander around." Another motion of his head summoned more of his men. "Go down there and scan the lake shores. Take at least forty warriors with you. As many as you can gather."

Who would have thought? he asked himself again, his hands trembling with the effort to support the wounded as well as he could, lips moving, talking, encouraging, uttering promises he didn't know how to keep. The Crooked Tongue was in bad shape, barely here, his spirit determined to stay, yet still undecided, his wounds severe, plenty of broken bones probably and what not. Still, he knew the man needed his presence, his reassurances. He could sense it in his bones.

How did this one know what was coming? he wondered, reliving what had happened such a short time ago. They were all busy watching the duel, such spectacular hand-to-hand, both Okwaho's friend and the enemy good and skillful, the Long Tail's limp hindering him, but his club of a better quality, easier to handle, sporting a cutting edge.

Those two fought so well, and there were times he feared for their Flint representative, but then the enemy's leg failed him, and the young Flint went for the kill, so sure of himself, victorious already. Such an elating moment. Cut short by the Crooked Tongue's warning scream, the mad dash the man made in a desperate attempt to save his friend. Too late of course. The arrows flew faster, especially *those* arrows.

He recalled the brief sight of the girl, yes, this same skinny, wild thing the Crooked Tongue had captured before, their bait in their desperation to bring the enemy to battle on the ground of Okwaho's choosing. It worked perfectly, just as they had planned. Such a decisive victory, but for what happened now. Where did this girl come from again, and why? What was she doing in the thickest of the battle?

He clenched his teeth, the following memory making the knot in his stomach squeeze his ribs. The Crooked Tongue reaching the fighters, too late of course, but oblivious of the reality, crazed with desperation; the enemy leader turning to fight his new attacker, or so the man must have thought, surprised with the interfering arrow as well—what honorable warrior wouldn't be?—striking the Crooked Tongue down with his club.

He shuddered again, remembering his own rising dread, as he ran toward the edge of the cliff, oblivious of his own safety as well, needing to stop what was happening. It wasn't a duel anymore, not since the arrow, but he was too late, just as the Crooked Tongue was too late before, and the club was already poised to deliver the final blow. No way to stop it, unless...

And then his instincts were the ones to decide, and his own club became a missile, to hurl with all his strength, aiming hastily, but knowing that he wouldn't miss, he couldn't, not from such a close distance.

Reliving the moment again, he remembered the vastness of his relief even before the club hit, crashing into the man's temple, sending him reeling sideways and over the edge. The mere feeling of doing something made him feel better, the fact that he did manage.

Shaking the memory off, he concentrated on the warriors who were crowding all around, pressing from every direction, seemingly at a loss for what to do. Waiting to be directed, as always, but he couldn't leave the wounded, not yet. The man needed his presence, his encouragement and support, at least until placed in the healers' hands. In crucial moments it was as essential as the treatment itself, he knew, having not been wounded seriously himself, yet somehow just having this knowledge.

Glimpsing one of his warriors, he beckoned the men.

"Go down there and search after the enemy leader's body." Squinting, he looked around, the glow of the afternoon sun making it difficult to see. "Organize a group of at least twenty warriors, and be careful. There is no telling how many of the enemies got away and are wandering out there with no purpose, desperate enough to fight again. Or to shoot you in the back, for that matter." He frowned, not wishing to think along these lines. "There is that girl with the bow that some of us already encountered. Watch out for her. She is as dangerous as she looks harmless. Remember that, and warn our people."

The man just nodded, face tight, eyes dark with attention.

"I saw her," said another one. "They say it was her arrow that took the Flint warrior down."

Who said that? wondered Ganayeda, nodding at the men to start moving. Who saw her besides the Crooked Tongue?

"If you see any of our leaders, those who were in the ambush with us, send them here as well." Glancing at the men from the Crooked Tongue's group, two of the most notorious troublemakers from the Standing Stone lands, he gestured for them to come nearer. "Take your people and go down there too, join the search."

"What about him?" As expected, the Crooked Tongue's warriors weren't receiving orders without an argument.

"He will be all right. I'll keep an eye on him until the healer comes. He won't be leaving on his Sky Journey, not that one."

A glance at his charge did not reassure him. Neither did the lack of reaction. Holding his breath, he leaned forward as close as his awkward position permitted, fearing the worst, yet unwilling to move his patient in case he was still around and suffering. Was he going to die after all? Had he already?

"He is still around." The grimy fingers of the Standing Stone man were pressing lightly against the wounded's throat, feeling it out. "His heart is still beating."

"Good." Weak with relief, Ganayeda drew a deep breath. "Go down there, to the creek's shore, where the rest of our warriors are. Bring back one of the healers, the first you encounter." He shifted his limbs to relieve the strain, then wished Okwaho was here instead of the crowding warriors, so many of them at a loss, not knowing what to do in the aftermath of a battle, a new experience to them. Frankly, he didn't know what to do now himself. "I can't believe this entire hill is devoid of one single medicine man!"

His suggestion was greeted eagerly, with no words of argument or even a comment. In the next heartbeat, the man was gone, followed by a few others from the same group. Oh, but these people loved their unconventional leader. He looked up, searching their faces.

"Take more of his men and go around," he said, addressing one of them, an Onondaga warrior of easily igniting temper. "Comb this hill, then the creek's shore, where the enemy stored they boats."

"Looking for what?" asked the man dubiously. "More enemy?"

"The girl." This came from another man, a square-shouldered warrior, with no smeared paint added to the usual mixture that covered all of their faces by now. "He will want the filthy fox to be found." A nod toward the sprawling wounded was brief but unmistakable.

Ganayeda frowned. "Who are you?"

The man didn't blink under the pointedly cold scrutiny. "Am I wrong?"

"No, you aren't, warrior." The glaring lack of honorific address irked, but to admonish someone while crouching upon the ground, looking up at the insolent fellow, felt silly. He pressed his lips. "Join them if you know what your mission is anyway."

"I was about to do that, yes." The man nodded placidly, unperturbed. "My scouting skills may come handy. It helped him and his men not a little through the past few dawns." A shrug. "We'll find you the murderous fox. You can trust me on that."

CHAPTER 28

Crouching in the midst of the unfriendly, viciously prickly vegetation, Tsutahi clasped her mouth with her palm, clenching her teeth desperately, afraid that their clattering would give their presence away. She could sense the people prowling the creek down below, walking the shore, painfully slow, scanning it with their eyes, of that she was sure. But for the ability to see them better, or at least to hear, to know what they were up to, when they would be leaving for good.

He shuddered, a weak, agonized movement, and what would have gladdened her enormously before—every sign of life was good, promising—now made her tremble with fear. What if he began vomiting again, like he had when she had first managed to drag him out of the lake and onto the small rocky shore? What if he doubled over and twitched in the most hideous of manners, retching savagely, bringing out everything from water to a dark blackish liquid that smelled like blood but didn't look like it, suffering oh so very badly. He had groaned so loudly she could hear him most clearly, but back then, even if frightened, she was only too glad to see him coming back to life. Earlier, when dragging him out of the water, she wasn't sure that his spirit hadn't already left on its journey for good. Oh, Mighty Spirits!

Reliving the terrible happenings upon the top of the cliff, she went rigid with fear once again, pressing her mouth with force, wishing to groan. Oh, but how close he had come to the beginning of his Sky Journey. How resigned to this reality, too.

He had resolved to die in this battle, she knew, unable to bear the thought of defeat, the possibly disastrous consequences it brought to his people. And maybe hers, too.

As though it mattered. Back upon that hill, all she knew was that he wanted to send her away, to keep her safe, yes, but what did it matter if he wasn't going to come back with her? He had told her to leave and wait for him somewhere there, near his town or wherever, but he was lying about it. His eyes told her that, so calm and accepting, while his lips uttered hollow promises.

Too frightened to argue, with people killing each other all around them and him being so concerned, out of patience, anxious to go back and join the terrible slaughter, she had wandered off toward the side he wished her to leave through, only to run into more invaders climbing it eagerly, anxious to join their victorious countryfolk.

Her first reaction helped, with two of the men going down and into the lake, but there were still too many of them, and no matter how dearly she wanted to shoot her former captor as well—that man again!—there was no time to linger. He needed to know about this new danger. He needed to do something about it. And so, again, her warning came in time, and he appreciated that, he did, not put out with her disobeying him once again. Oh, but she knew that she still could be of use to him, and maybe somehow, in some way…

The hope that was shattered cruelly as the fight progressed, with them being so few against so many, the local warriors pouring in like a swarm of wild bees, relentless and determined, and as cruel. And she was helpless to do anything, to keep him safe in the way she had done before, having no vantage point, no elevated ground to enjoy.

When he was fighting with the warrior who challenged him, another slightly familiar face—was he among the people who had captured her by that other long lake?—she almost died every time he seemed near stumbling or being hit. He fought so skillfully, with such bravery and spirit, but his leg was hindering him badly. It was almost too late when in the end she simply ran toward them, throwing caution to the wind and just shooting, outright, not caring who might see her doing it or what they might do to her. What did it matter? If he died, she didn't want to live. Seeing

Grandfather off was more than enough.

And then, then…

She shuddered again, shutting her eyes against the recollection of the unfolding nightmare. Her arrow flying, hitting its target, like always, but that other man—oh, Mighty Spirits, but was her path to be crossed by this terrible person again and again?—that other man seeing her, knowing what she did, but instead of lashing out at her, going mad, screaming and leaping toward the fighters, with that other enemy warrior already dead, obviously. Still, he rushed on, and before she could release her next arrow, already tucked in the bow, ready to pounce, *to save him again,* people stirred into yells and screams, and mad running, blocking her view, forcing her to resume her run toward the fighters.

Limp with fright, unable to see, she had forced her legs into moving, reaching the rocky edge in time to watch him taking that warrior down before being pushed toward the low cliff, hit by a flying club that smashed into him, tossing him like a cornhusk doll, to crash against the sharp stones and topple over those, dead or alive, she didn't know.

What came next was nothing but an eerie dream, a ghostly nightmare: plunging into the cold water, not aware of her actions at all—how did she get there?—diving into the blurry depths, searching frantically, choking on the muddy water, oblivious of the danger or even the need to breathe; then seeing the movement, just a glimpse of it, but more than enough to give her direction; darting there in a pure frenzy, clutching onto him, blind toward everything but the need to bring him out and away. He was still alive, he was, *he had to be!*

Oh, but how she managed to do that she still didn't know. Somehow. With the help of this or that spirit, or maybe the Right-Handed Twin himself. They surely knew how urgent her predicament was, how desperate.

And now, here they were, on the shore of the creek already, reaching it somehow, by a miracle probably, away from the lake but chased after, pursued by the enemy who evidently took the time to organize that chase. Were they after him only or after them both? She didn't know, didn't spend time thinking about it. If only he were in better condition, not as badly wounded, or at least fully conscious.

She rested her palm on his chest in a warning as he moved again, trying to straighten up, his face a hideous mask, stark, with no coloring, twisted with pain.

Leaning closer, she shook her head, signaling him to keep quiet, not certain he would understand. His gaze was wild, unfocused, eyes torn open, their pupils huge, panicked. Still, her touch made him relax. She could see that. The awareness was flooding in, the colorless lips clasping tighter, conquering the pain.

She signaled him again, pointing toward the thick bushes and the creek behind it with her eyes. These men were still there, she was sure of it. Oh, but she needed to know, to see where they were heading.

Wait here.

Not daring to even whisper, she hoped he could read her lips the way she read his.

His eyes narrowed. *Where? How many?* His lips were barely visible, just a bloodied, cracked line. No way to decipher what they said, but she knew what he wanted to know.

Just wait. I'll be back shortly. This she related with her eyes and hands only. A smile to try to make him feel better, then she slunk away, twisting between the prickly vegetation, caring not for the way it tore at her, making its business to scratch her skin or pull at her hair, like the enemy it was. This wasn't her forest.

A gust of fresh breeze told her that the creek was near again, somewhere below the thorny line. Cooling her sweaty face, it made her feel better, but she gripped her knife tighter, painfully aware that her bow was not with her, not anymore. And just as she needed it the most! How so? She didn't dare to even think about it, let alone try to understand. Did she drop it while plunging into the lake after him, mindless with panic, or did it go down along with her and just drown somewhere there in the murky water? Oh, Mighty Spirits!

The wave of cold dread was back, washing over her sweaty back. The men were farther now, three drawing away silhouettes as opposed to the original four she had counted earlier, when spotting them for the first time, sniffing around, talking and gesturing. But for the ability to understand what they said!

Well, now they were relatively far, treading in the water, heading for the nearest bend, or so it seemed. Good. Just let them walk on without any more pausing, she thought urgently, her heart beating fast.

Then it stopped all of a sudden. One heartbeat, then another. Nothing happened in her chest as her eyes followed the movement, the dark form treading its way up the incline, slightly to her left, slinking among the prickly wall, skirting around the worst of the bushes. *Heading straight toward their hideaway, where he still lay, barely conscious, if at all!*

Her heart sprang back to life together with her limbs that pushed her toward the moving silhouette, regardless of sanity or reason. Just to stop him, not to let him reach—

Breaking through the bushes like a crazed winter bear or a panic-stricken deer, she saw the man whirling, his pose that of a predator ready to pounce, knife flashing, too brightly for the dimness of the thick vegetation. Or maybe it was the polished spike of a club sparkling in such a way. She didn't spend her time pondering this.

As her body twisted to avoid the hit of a twisted branch aiming to flog her face, her arm came up with a readiness that surprised her. It was as though her mind wasn't directing it.

The antler handle slipped from her palm in a slow, confident motion, reassuring, promising. The perfectly polished flint glimmered, cutting the air, hurrying to bury itself in the enemy's body. No nosy man would be finishing him off. Or her, for that matter.

Stumbling on the entanglements of roots, she grabbed another protruding branch to steady herself, seeing her rival twisting away, wavering but not falling, not disappearing from her view. The antler glimmered, sticking out from the flesh of his upper arm, quivering there, doing barely any harm.

Aghast, she darted aside, as the man pounced, his club swishing, hindered by the wounded arm but not enough to stop its attack. It crushed the branch she had held onto only a heartbeat before, flying on as though by the accumulated drive, breaking more bushes in its fall.

Momentarily stunned, she watched it, expecting its owner to go after it, tumbling down too, giving her a moment of respite.

It didn't happen. The man threw himself at her with an astonishing nimbleness, grabbing her shoulder with his good arm, his other palm crashing into her chest, taking her breath away.

Caught under his weight, she wriggled madly, beyond understanding of how they got there, to squirm upon the harsh, rocky ground, with all those splinters, stones, and pinecones eager to stab, her back hurt, chest straining, unable to get enough air. Or maybe it was her throat. It hurt too, where his coarse palms fastened onto it, squeezing, making the last of the light dim.

Her own palms reaching frantically, grabbing and beating, she felt the smoothness of the antler, and it gave her strength, but the trees above swayed with an increasing speed, and the strange peacefulness it brought made her pause, stop her frenzied struggling. It was better to let go and float, it lessened the pain and the worry. What was she so agitated about?

The last of the light swirled in a pretty show of silvery gray. The Sky World! Oh, but it was more beautiful than she thought, not blue but radiant and dusky, shimmering. Grandfather, he would be...

In another heartbeat the good feeling shattered, torn by the suffocating wave, so powerful it threatened to tear her apart. It started in her chest, welling into her throat, ripping it with the agonizing cough, choking it with terrible nausea.

Curling into a ball, unable to see for the dizziness, she gulped the air desperately, getting painfully little for all her efforts, a mere trickling.

When finally able to concentrate on something other than the wonderful sensation of breathing, she felt *him* rather than saw, collapsing in a heap, panting as badly as she did—the flickering mist enabled her to see that much.

His hand gripped her shoulder, feeling it out, trembling with an effort. He was talking, asking her something, she could feel it, his face still a dreadful mask, contorted with agony.

Pushing herself into a straighter position, she peered at him, then at the limp body of the man beside them, sprawling strangely, like a thrown away doll.

Blinking, she forced her mind into working, understanding but slowly, painfully dense, her heart pounding, throbbing in her ears. He was pushing himself up too, one hand still clutching the crooked, rotting log, the other grabbing the air, trying to catch something. A nearby branch?

Without thinking, she rushed to his side, still dizzy and badly nauseated, but paying little attention to it. He needed her help, with all his wounds. The memories flooded back, in a powerful surge—the fighting, the cliff, the desperate diving, the man who was too fast, escaping her knife, attacking with terrible fierceness. The others, those who were searching for them, scanning the creek below.

"We must..." Supporting him as best as she could while he struggled into a sitting position, she forced her voice into whispering. "We must go away... people... there are more..." She swallowed the new bout of coughing, aghast by the amount of noise she must be making. "Down there by the water... must go..."

"Yes." He nodded stiffly, his features stark, rigid with pain. "He was scout... maybe alone..."

She pulled his hand more forcefully, the panic flooding back. "No, no, there are more! I saw... saw them, before that man... the scout..." How did he know it was a scout? It didn't matter. "We must..."

"Yes, yes." Swaying, he clung to her, clutching her shoulder with too much force, his lips bleeding from the fierceness with which his teeth tore into them. "We go up...uphill... into the woods. Then later back, when they stop looking..."

Struggling to stay upright while not letting him fall again, she barely nodded, having nothing to offer in a way of an argument anyway.

CHAPTER 29

The drums were pouring from every direction, filling the valley with their wonderfully calm, monotonous pulsating. Not the type of beat to work people up like in a regular War Dance, this one was a celebration, the warriors' way of expressing their gratitude, their thankfulness to the Great Spirits.

Even though he was in no condition to participate fully, Ogteah felt the magical tempo reaching out, touching his spirit, letting it soar along with the soft beating, making him wish to stomp his feet with true warriors' spirit, an impossible feat, not with his injuries, the pain even the slightest of movements was causing, even mere walking. Nevertheless, he let the music take him. Everyone did. Even the wounded in worse condition than his.

With no poles to hurl their axes at, the warriors just twirled in many circles, filling the valley near Onondaga Town with the wonderful energy of thousands battle-hardened men, those who fought in a cruelest of wars, besting hordes of enemies, coming back, victorious. But not everyone, far from it.

The old pain was back, worse than the one that was gnawing at his ribs or tearing at his broken arm, or throbbing at the upper part of his back, where the enemy's club cut in with its vicious spike, tearing much flesh, even if not his insides. Thank all the great and small spirits for that.

And yet, this other pain was worse, far worse! Here, in the peacefulness of the Onondaga Town's valley, where it all had started, the memories of his friend pounced at him from everywhere, the vital, boisterous, ever-loyal Akweks, with his boyish bravado, his lazy confidence and readiness to needle and bait, his sudden and unexpected spells of deep thinking. He was a thinker, this easygoing, show-off Flint, now far into his Sky Journey, maybe already there, in the Sky World and among the spirits. Yes, he must be. It had been more than ten dawns, hadn't it?

It was difficult to tell, difficult to keep count, as the days following the battle were nothing but a blur, clouding in a haze of agony, hot and cold and hot again, dreaming sometimes, or just floating between the worlds, with no foothold and no grip, afraid, oh terrified really, not knowing if he was still alive or maybe dragged into the Underworld of the Evil Twin, the most likely possibility judging by the pain. Yes, this was the worst of it, the pain, all the time, nothing but torment, whether he moved or stayed still, slept or kept awake. Such a ghastly memory!

Sometimes he would despair, let the agony take him and lull him into its suffocating depths. Mostly, though, he would fight it, with desperation, struggling to get a grip, to understand, to find the answers. Where was he?

In those cases, his efforts would usually pay off, as then he would not be alone anymore. The High Springs man would often be there, as strong and reassuring as always, as reliable as the sky and the forest, offering his strength, keeping him, Ogteah, safe, making sure his spirit did not spiral down or soar up, leaving for good. It was good to know that; it made the pain less unbearable, possible to deal with.

The wolf man would sometimes be there too, restless and busy, but genial, another friendly face, a reliable presence, another one who didn't wish to let his, Ogteah's, spirit go and not come back. Now the undeniable leader of this entire force, the man who had made it all happen, he was greatly occupied of course, surrounded by warriors and leaders, always, even when visiting wounded friends, the heroes of this battle. It still puzzled him that people made much of his involvement in this war and the preparations for it, as though his contribution was truly that important. Of course it wasn't. He was just there, fighting like anyone else, not as bravely as some, certainly not like Akweks.

Akweks!

The pain would return doubled, squeezing his insides worse than the invisible ring around his cracked ribs did. Akweks, dying so bravely, in the middle of the most important duel of this entire war, the glory he craved so! Dying in such an untimely way, cut down by the treacherous arrow, of all things. The realization that would stab him anew every time he would surface from his own dives into the nightmarish depths, the awareness of it fading, then coming back. No more pleasant evenings by the glimmering fire, no idle needling and joking around, no unfailing loyalty and support.

His men were usually by his side too, in pairs or small groups, all those who survived the battle, close to three tens out of the original fifty. When he managed to stay awake permanently, they kept him company, squatting around and making jokes, sneaking him tasty treats despite the healers' instructions, making the medicine men frown. The best of company he was grateful for, needing it badly, still afraid to remain alone, just in case, never fond of solitude anyway.

When it was time to leave, to begin their journey back home, his men padded one of the canoes most thoroughly, with too many blankets, before helping him into it. He was still in no condition to contribute to the rowing, but at least at this point he was able to sit more or less comfortably and even walk around a little.

His ribs would take time to heal, the medicine man had told him, the pain wouldn't go away easily or quickly, but his arm was now on the mend, and it was the main thing. Apparently, the way it had broken, so badly its bone cut its way through while cracking in two or more places—oh, that powerful blow, but did he remember it well—was what caused his spirit such indecision as to whether to leave or stay, what put his life in a real danger. All the rest, cracked ribs and the cut on his back were just something to add to the suffering, no more than that.

He shook his head, now, almost half a moon later and safely back home, amused, even if partly. But it was a bad thing, this battle. So much death and pain and injuries, and for what? To make the Long Tails go home? Oh well, it must be a good reason, as good as any.

The drums were fading, and so did the echo of thousands of stomping feet, the chanting dying away, the hum of many shouting voices. People were shaking their heads, as though awakening from a dream.

Feeling the same, Ogteah looked around, the aroma of cooking food tickling his nostrils, making his stomach growl. Since the ability to keep the food down returned to him, he seemed to never have enough, hungry again after every meal and snack, yearning for more. He was going to eat the entire Onondaga Town out, was Gayeri's conclusion, and it had only been two dawns since his and the other warriors' arrival, to find the place of the Great Council's meetings inundated with visitors, men, women, elders, and children, hundreds of people eager to greet the victorious heroes. The word had traveled around fast, apparently.

The soft glow was back, warming his insides. She would be among the onlookers now, or maybe busy with those meals, vigorous, sparkling, purposeful, as always—an industrious fox. No, not a fox. A mountain lioness, her main facet these days. Strong, loyal, beautiful, her love boundless, her adoration unconcealed. His stomach tightened with anticipation.

"Come." One of the Standing Stone brothers waved his hand, materializing next to Ogteah just as he was busy protecting his battered ribs in the pushing crowds, put out with the necessity to do so, hating his inability to walk straight as yet. As though the cumbersome splint fixing his arm in the most uncomfortable of positions was not enough hindrance to begin with.

"Why hurry?" He forced those words out, trying to sound light, the pain in his side sharper than usual, not helped by the inadvertent push of one of the passersby.

"Their War Chief is about to speak." Another of his men fell into his step, easing himself next to Ogteah easily, naturally, helping with his mere presence, keeping the pressing people away. "The Onondaga leader said to bring you up there, to stand among the rest of the leaders."

"Why?" Grateful for the help what was offered in an

inoffensive way—no actual attempt at supporting him in order to make their progress easier, something Ogteah wouldn't have, his pitiful hobbling or not—he glanced at his companions, curious. "Why would they want me there?"

A grim shrug of the Standing Stone man didn't say much, not surprising Ogteah in the least. Oh, but this one still mourned his brother, regaining none of his formerly aggressive spunk. He and his surviving sibling. Poor family. He remembered the knifed man he had carried partway down that hill. Maybe if he had hurried back then, or managed to interfere in the fighting earlier on.

Another thing to ponder, to come to grips with. Was he guilty of the Standing Stone brother's death? Or that of Akweks? Was there something he could have done but didn't?

"Why wouldn't they? You are one of the leaders," his second companion went on, joined by some others. "Of course you should stand with them when the War Chief is speaking."

"And you are thick with the Onondaga brothers, anyway," contributed another, a Swamp People's man, an easygoing, lighthearted fellow who didn't hesitate to protest against Ogteah's proposed leadership back near Tsonontowan, such forgotten memories. "You should have seen how worried they were when you couldn't decide whether to stay or go." A good-natured wink. "One would have thought that the leaders of their status should be busy with the aftermath of that battle, reorganizing people, chasing the enemy maybe. Not worrying about one hotheaded leader who got his ribs cracked."

Ogteah just snorted in response, busy paying attention to his every step, trying to make it less painful, this Onondaga Town valley being so rocky and uneven.

"The Mountain People would take it from there," he said, when to his endless relief the incline ended, but not the necessity to clear their way through the crowding people. "It was not our purpose to chase the enemy or invade their forests. Just to render them useless, to cut down their aspirations when it comes to crossing that Genesee River again."

"Oh, yes, our Western Door Keepers would be crossing that river themselves, instead." More good-natured chuckling came from all around, with many warriors joining the topic everyone loved to discuss these days.

"Good for them."

"Maybe I'll be traveling there again after the Cold Moons."

"Oh, yes, me too." Several voices took up on that suggestion.

"To make sure they are not forgetting who made their work so much easier, eh?" Grinning, Ogteah winked at his men, feeling better by the moment. Oh, yes, another raid after the Cold Moons, and why not? His ribs would be as good as new by then, and the gained battle experience would come in handy, wouldn't it? For him and his men alike. "Or they might be tempted to forget our part in that great victory of theirs."

The War Chief had not yet started his speech, and it was not clear if they would hear the man's words or not in such a vast crowd. He made the rest of the way by himself, spotting many familiar faces, answering their greetings, even though it made his progress more difficult.

The damn pain! Such a nuisance, and in more ways than a mere walking. He rolled his eyes, remembering the previous afternoon; and the following night as well, unable to suppress his smile.

Like on the day when he had detoured by his village on the way to the Mountain People's lands, Gayeri, over her initial dread at discovering the extent of his injuries and how close to death he had come, had tucked plenty of delicious foodstuff into her basket, all his favorite treats and snacks, and paying no attention to his difficulty in walking, dragged him out and toward the prettiest clearing with a brook, in the location fairly removed from Onondaga Lake, so nicely secluded. A miracle, as there was no privacy to be had anywhere in the crowded valley and the nearby groves. Too many returning warriors were greeted by their loved ones, arriving here from every corner of the Great League, the reunited couples wandering all around, eager to be alone, to manifest their love and their happiness in each other's arms.

But they all were silly, she had said smugly, piling blankets one upon another, tucking them neatly, making it cozy and soft for his battered ribs.

"Silly, or just unfamiliar with these surroundings," she went on, chattering happily, as busy and efficient as ever, beautiful in her open delight at having him back, as though her natural beauty had doubled itself, an impossible feat. "But me? Oh, I'm a local fox, know every hill and spring around these places. Onondaga Lake is not the only spot worthy of wandering, especially at night. All those foreigners just don't know any better." She beamed at him, kneeling beside her basket, fishing out his favorite cookies with berries and nuts. "So they are huddling all together, those lovers, trying to look the other way,"—another giggle—"while we, oh we will be having a better time. In privacy. With no one to interrupt our activities, eh?"

The glimmer of her eyes was enough to set him on fire, the promise it held. He cursed his ribs inwardly, so clumsy with the stupid splint, but she threw herself beside him, her delight and elation undimmed.

"Don't, you wild man," her lips were murmuring, pressing, her body propped helpfully, enticing and supporting at the same time, making it easier for him to recline and hold her tight. "No need to go wild yet. We have enough time to make up for those summer moons of being apart. I won't let you off easily, you know. You will have to make it up for all this waiting. You will pay dearly for this, brave warrior and promising leader that you are."

Her laughter trilled, such an uplifting sound. He shut her up with a fierce kiss.

"Nothing will stop me from making it up to you, woman," he muttered, hands busy with her clothing, refusing to pay attention to the pain. "And then making it up to you some more."

But the lovemaking didn't go well. With one arm being useless and the rest of his battered body protesting fiercely, refusing to lend him support, and the pain spiraling, impossible to ignore, it was hopeless. Still, the wave of acute disappointment shattered against her unwavering happiness, melted in the radiance of her smile.

"We'll wait, and you will just owe me more lovemaking, warrior," she whispered, reclining beside him, face hiding in his chest, hands wandering, leaving a wonderful glow in their wake. "Plenty of debt to return. You will have to work day and night to please me, but we will let you heal properly first." Her giggle tickled his skin. "So you will be able to repay it all properly, a good, thorough lovemaking for each day of worry."

"I will," he had promised, pressing her with his good arm, still terribly uncomfortable, but feeling better by the moment, with the sharpest of the pain gone. But cracked ribs were truly no good for this sort of activity. "I missed you, you wild thing, you know that? I never believed one can miss another person so much. Traveling to all those towns and villages and all I kept thinking of was you. It was easy to remember, your beauty, yes, but mainly the beauty of your spirit. There is truly no one like you, just no one." He grinned, remembering his lands. "I used to wonder about that back in Ossossane. I even asked the High Springs man. When I ran into him for the first time, I asked him about the women of your lands. You were so different, so special, so I kept thinking that it must be your people's thing. But, oh my, now I know that it is not true. You are one of a kind."

She was pressing closer, reviving some of the pain, but he didn't mind. "You think so? Truly? Will you always love me like that?"

As much as such a question might have irritated him coming from someone else, he didn't hesitate. "Yes, I will." Steering back to the safer ground, he grinned again. "I've been to so many people and towns this summer, you know? Flint and Standing Stone People, and some western Onondaga settlements. Not to mention that Mountain People's main town called Tsonontowan. But you know what? They have no beautiful sights like that one," his gaze measured her pointedly, in unmistakable manner, "not even near."

Having peeked from her hiding place at his chest by now, she giggled, eyes mischievous. Yet, there was an inquiry in their depths, a questioning scrutiny. "Not even here in Onondaga Town?"

His sensation of well-being evaporated. "Nothing happened in Onondaga Town."

She pressed into him forcefully when he tried to move away. "I know, I know. I didn't believe rumors." A small pause. "I tried not to listen, but it was hard, sometimes. People are terrible, so nasty and bad, at times."

"This spear-throwing contest was a disaster," he muttered gloomily, the brightness of the afternoon not as warm or as welcoming as before.

"No, it wasn't. They loved this contest, everyone talked about it." She caught his face between her palms when he attempted to turn away. "Everyone who came to our village talked about the last meeting of the Great Council and the largest spear-throwing contest anyone had ever seen or been a part of."

He shrugged lightly, another motion his ribs didn't like. So many gestures to avoid even when simply talking. "The contest was good, until your man lost his temper and tried to make a mess out of it."

"No one talked about this other than some stupid people who didn't like you in the first place. And they are few and growing less with every passing day. They come to know you and then they see what I see, a good man and a wonderful person."

"Yes, a nice man until he loses his temper or his patience and starts doing stupid things," he drawled stubbornly, but not as frustrated as before, the bad feeling receding, like always in the warmth of her adoring smile. Which was twisting suggestively now, her pointed eyebrows climbing up. She was seeing through him, this woman of his. Too easily sometimes. "Oh, you!"

She laughed outright, teasing, then her smile lost its challenging quality, took on a deeper glow. "Remember I promised to tell you something, if you came back unharmed?"

He nodded, not truly remembering.

"Before you went to this war," she prompted, again seeing through his half-hearted pretense. "When we spent this nice afternoon out there."

"Oh, yes, one can't forget *this* welcome home in a hurry."

She peered at him from under her brow, evidently not pleased.

He raised one eyebrow. "I remember you talking about secrets, yes. Stop making faces."

"I'm not making faces. But you clearly are not that curious."
The way she pouted made him wish to laugh, a sure way to bring
the pain back. And make her rage worse.

He grinned widely, admitting his guilt. "I am, I am curious.
Tell me."

She still glared at him, lips pursed stubbornly.

The attempt to remain patient was becoming more difficult.
"Just tell me." Her sulking started to annoy him. "You promised if
I come back unharmed, you will tell me. I remember it now. Most
clearly at that. So here I am, back, alive and demanding to know."

That made her snicker. "Unharmed, I said unharmed. You
came harmed all over."

He rolled his eyes. "Oh well, then keep your secret until I get
better. After I pay you all this lovemaking I owe you, tell me
then."

The smile blossomed again, a deep, feminine smile. "It may be
too late by then to keep it a secret. You may discover it on your
own if you take your time to recover. In a few moons, everyone
will know."

He caught his breath, understanding all of a sudden, feeling so
hopelessly foolish for taking so long to realize what she meant.

"You don't like this news?" Her gaze clung to him, filling with
disappointment.

"Yes, I do. I just didn't expect..." He swallowed, thirsty for a
gulp of water. "I didn't think..." Her eyes were filling with tears,
so he caught her wrist before she could pull away. "Listen, this is
good news. Very good, very important. I didn't think about it,
didn't know you wanted, but if you do, then of course this is good
news." She was struggling mildly, staring at the quilt that
decorated the edge of the blanket, refusing to look up. "Stop
making faces, you stubborn woman. I'm glad, truly I am."
Reassured by her half-shrug, the way she stopped struggling
against his touch, he reached out. "A baby? Right in there?" The
smoothness of her stomach felt different under his seeking palm,
maybe not as flat anymore, yes. Or was it just his imagination, the
knowledge of what was in there? "It's so strange. You look no
different."

She giggled. "Of course I'm not, silly man. But I feel different, and you will see the evidence soon enough. That girl from the Wolf Clan's longhouse next to the fence, she gave birth to her baby at the last new moon, and did her belly look huge. Bursting, really." Snuggling against him, she covered his palm with her own, guiding it along the smoothness of her skin. "Mine will be as huge."

And now, making his way through the crowded incline, he let his mind dwell on this development once again, glad to have time to think about it without her lively, fiercely supportive presence, to come to terms with it on his own.

A child growing in her belly, his son? Or maybe a daughter. Poor thing, with such a man for a father. But maybe not that poor. Could he try that again, to be a father, this time for real?

Well, after that monumental failure back home, when he had left without looking back, missing neither the child's mother nor the baby himself, they all knew what a terrible person he was, himself ahead of everyone. And yet, back then he was a failure on every other count as well, while now, well, maybe now it was different. He did change in so many aspects, and he wasn't doing so badly in these lands of the "savages," was he? Maybe he could be a father too, why not?

On the elevated ground, the leaders stood proudly, watching the splashing lake of faces, their own glimmering contentedly, hiding their satisfaction but not very well. The corners of the War Chief's mouth were turned upward, as though ready to break into the widest of smiles. Still, the man emanated his typically calm, unperturbed, dignified authority, spreading his arms forward, ready to speak.

A nod from none other than the High Springs man directed Ogteah to his designated place, indeed among the prominent dignitaries. Far above his status, even should his brief leadership over his wild band of violent elements be taken into account.

His eyes brushed past the wolf man, standing at the forefront, slightly behind the most prominent leaders, the War Chief and the Head of the Great Council, impressive and proud, belonging there. Oh, but this one had changed profoundly, grown and hardened, lost his youthful eagerness, slipped into his role of a warriors' leader, an undeniable authority, a man whose words were not disputed lightly, if at all. A replica of his powerful father.

The death of Akweks had hit this man hard, Ogteah knew, had killed something in him. A friend from the earlier days, the Flint was the young man's spiritual brother, a part of his youth. But not anymore.

His heart squeezed with compassion. If he felt the loss of this youth so acutely, the man he had just met and grown close to over the last few moons, how must it feel to lose a friend of quite a few summers?

The War Chief was speaking already, addressing the Great Spirits first, thanking them, his voice rolling pleasantly, in a powerful surge. One had to learn to speak in this way, he thought, trying to concentrate and listen, failing to do so. He was so tired, and the spreading smells of the roasted meat didn't help. All he wanted was to eat again, then relax in his woman's caring arms, on that lonely clearing with the brook, away from everyone, for days on end if he could make it happen.

A child by her? Would it be as sweet and as lovely as her? A wild boy or a beautiful girl? And shouldn't she stop working in the fields in her condition?

"Today we have gathered not only to thank our Great Spirits for the wonderful gifts they bestow on us. Today we have come here to laud our glorious warriors, the men who stepped up in defense of our Great Union and our very way of life."

The War Chief was well into his speech now, his voice rolling powerfully, reaching every corner of the valley, or so it seemed, judging by the faces of this enormous crowd, all turned to the orating elder like sunflowers following the progress of Father Sun. Such a great leader, triumphant, proud, content, confident in his people's superiority, their ability to best the enemy, any enemy. Still, on a closer inspection, he could see that there were shadows in the man's eyes, something deep, closed, impossible to decipher. A flicker of sadness? Could it be?

"People of the Longhouse, we are one nation, one house of five families. Five brother-nations, brothers who are ready to stand up for each other, to defend our longhouse against every foe. Because those who come against one of our families are coming against our entire longhouse, our entire union. Whether the enemy is attacking, or even just harassing this or that entrance, or maybe climbing onto the roof to pelt stones on the family that is sitting right in the middle." The brief pause accompanied by the slightest twist of lips brought an outburst of laughter the orator must have been expecting, sobering as quickly, pressing on. "It doesn't matter what family among our five nations is attacked. The moment it happens, our entire union will come to its aid, the way our brave warriors have done in this time of the Green Corn Moon, in an unheard of attack of the hordes who thought they could come and assault our villages and towns, rob their goods and their people, kill and kidnap and hurt, take these forests as their own."

He found himself listening, swept by the man's words. Oh yes, the Long Tails had the gall of doing just that, crossing the Mountain People's river and in such numbers, meaning to do more than just a large-scale raid. Did they mean to take the forests between that Genesee River and those other larger Finger Lakes to become their own hunting grounds? Did they plan to ravage those villages, ruin them and then build their own? What gall. And yet, had he still lived among his Wyandot Bear People, wouldn't he have applauded to this news, eager to learn about such a raid, especially if successful? Wouldn't his former people try to do that one day as well, now that they were united in the union of Father's making? Wouldn't it—

He shook his head, getting rid of these thoughts with determination, not about to dwell on any of it, not anymore. He lived among these people now. He hunted with them and cleared their fields. He fought in their wars and formed true friendships, real brotherhood sometimes. They were his family, Gayeri and the child in her belly, his true family, no matter where he came from. The High Springs man and his brother and his powerful father and the others, all those people he fought alongside, they were his people. They treated him as one of theirs, appreciating him for what he was, accepting him with all his faults and still thinking him to be a good person, a worthy member of their community; someone to be trusted, burdened with responsibility, whether while organizing an unusual event like a spear-throwing contest or leading an atypical segment of undesirable troublemakers bursting with restlessness. They were using him according to his talents and skills, something his people never thought to do, not even Father. Oh, well, maybe Father, yes, in the end, but none of the others.

He hid his grin, forcing his expression to remain serene, sensing another gaze upon him. Gayeri's father. The respectable elder, the representative of their village was of course standing among other elderly dignitaries, in fairly close proximity, his face narrow and lined, sharply angled, a mask carved out of wood. Not an ugly mask or unpleasant. And not freezing cold, not anymore. Since Ogteah's return from the lands of the Mountain People, the dignified elder did not treat his daughter's undesirable husband with chilling frostiness, not anymore. His demeanor did not change, but his eyes did.

Which was a good thing. He didn't grudge the man any of it, not the previous coldness nor the change of behavior. It was understandable, wasn't it? But the acceptance felt good, one more bark square in his private dwelling, a compartment in a permanent longhouse, something he never dreamed to have, not for real.

CHAPTER 30

The lake glimmered peacefully in the late afternoon light, the sun still bright but weakening, preparing for its journey into the other world.

Ganayeda studied the rippling surface, glancing at his father every now and then. Many eyes were upon them, following, but the people kept away, respecting the great leader's wish to stroll in a measure of privacy, accompanied by his son.

Shielding his eyes, Father was peering at the faintly outlined hills of the other side, shadowed by the nearing twilight already.

"Our great victory puts an end to the possibility of these people sharing in the shade of the Great Tree of Peace." The War Leader's voice rang softly, with no grievance or accusation, no grudge, only deep sadness, so out of place, especially after the proud speech he delivered such a short time ago, lauding their victory to the sky. "His dream was of every nation upon our Turtle Island sharing in our union, every one of them. And yet, we didn't manage to make peace with one single nation or union since he left. Not a single one! It is still our five original peoples in the way he had left it. But what does it make us? An accomplishment or a failure?"

The narrowed eyes were upon him, suddenly dark with disappointment, pain, maybe longing. Ganayeda's chest squeezed. Did Father still miss the legendary Peacemaker, the man he was reported to bring here once upon a time, the Messenger of the Great Spirits who had changed their people's lives in the way that made them great and invincible?

"I see what you mean, Father," he said, choosing his words carefully. How to reassure the great man? How to make him feel better? "But it's hard to perceive what we have achieved as a failure, even though I understand your desire to see other nations sharing in our great union, enjoying its wise laws and the dignity of its ways." Licking his lips, he peered at the man, desperate to convince. "But there are many aspects to the peace or war making, many sides. People are stubborn sometimes, or petty, or just don't wish to see. Both sides have wise, farsighted men of your stature, leaders who could see far and wide and who aren't afraid to act upon their conviction, promoting a better future for all of us. Yet," he shrugged helplessly, "there are people who wouldn't look beyond the tip of their noses, beyond what is easy to see. These people, they won't only refuse to work for a better future, but they would obstruct the work of those who are trying, people like you, people like the Wyandot leader, people like the Messenger of the Great Spirits was."

The intensity of Father's gaze was lessening. "Yes, of course." His shrug was accompanied by a mirthless grin. "But I wish they weren't so many, those people, so determined. It would have made our work somewhat easier, wouldn't it?"

He grinned in his turn, relieved. "I wish it too, Father. It is rather difficult to work under such conditions."

The older man's chuckle made him relax for good. Oh yes, Father was back to his strong, unwavering self again.

"The Head of the Great Council spoke highly of you. He attributes much of this war's success to you."

"He does me too much honor." As embarrassed as he was pleased, Ganayeda shook his head. "It was incredible, the size of not only our but the enemy forces. I never imagined how difficult it is to organize such a large amount of warriors, from feeding to moving them around. It is almost impossible to pass on one's directions or even orders without losing some of it in the process. So many groups and minor leaders have to be involved, and in the most intricate pattern, everyone having an opinion, readily offered at that, a comment, a critique."

Father was listening avidly, eyes attentive and free of shadows. "I never expected any of you to gather such a large amount of warriors. Not even half as much."

He knew his smile might look a little too demure. "We did what you told us to do. It worked."

"Your brother distinguished himself mightily in this campaign."

"Okwaho? Oh, yes, this boy is a born warriors' leader. He planned this battle in a brilliant way, and he made it all work, preparing and conducting most of it all by himself." He shook his head, remembering. "He was everywhere, Father, just everywhere. In every place that needed reinforcement, every spot that was about to give in under the pressure. The enemy surprised us, you see? They were larger in numbers than even we expected, not badly organized, fiercely determined. They had fallen into our trap, but after much work, and I still wonder how it happened. That leader of theirs, the man who fought to the very end, he seemed to be a person who should have seen through our ploy. Their captured warriors told us as much." He shrugged. "A pity this man got away."

The War Chief rolled a flat, perfectly polished pebble contemplatively around his palm before tossing it into the water, to leap along the wavy surface, time after time.

"He might have been killed and his body taken away by the current," he suggested, straightening up but not before picking up another pebble. "You were too busy to look for him properly, I gather."

Ganayeda snorted. "No, we weren't. Well, I was, yes, with the Crooked Tongue playing with the ideas of dying right there in my hands. But his people, the wild bunch he had managed to organize and lead—how, I'll never know, they were such unruly warriors, each and every one of them!—well, his violent lot went wild with indignation, spoiling to avenge his injuries. They had rushed down that cliff and into the lake without looking around, caring not about the fact that the other leaders might like to have them doing something else." He grinned. "If that Long Tail was there, dead or alive, they would have found him. He had no chance against such a bloodthirsty force."

"So, you think he might have managed to get away?"

He shrugged, picking a stone in his turn, enjoying its smooth touch.

"To stir trouble for us again?"

"Not any time soon. They can't have so many people at their disposal to gather another force half as huge as their last one. Or so Okwaho says."

Father's eyes grew suddenly cold. "Unless he allies with the Wyandot who live closer to their side. The Rock People, I presume."

"Yes, the Rock People," muttered Ganayeda, busy thinking this possibility over. Not a heartwarming prospect. "But why would the Wyandot wish to ally themselves with the people who already lost?"

"Yes, they wouldn't. Unless seeing a possibility, something that would work to their advantage."

"You think they might do that?" He peered at the man, wishing to see through him now, to know what he knew. Father had various contacts everywhere around the Great Lake, and maybe near the other one as well.

"No, not for now. But you should take this possibility into account in the future. Maybe a distant future, yes, but don't forget to think broadly. In this and many other aspects." A weathered palm landed on his shoulder, wide, reassuring. "You have grown into a remarkable leader, son, and you make me proud. I know that our Great League is safe in your and your brother's hands. You will lead our people into an even greater future." A sigh. "Whether in war or in peace."

He felt the warm wave washing over his face, coloring it in a way he hoped the gathering dusk would conceal. "You are too kind, Father. I will do everything in my power to live up to your high opinion and expectation."

For a while, they kept silent, letting the breeze refresh them, cool their faces and maybe their spirits as well. The sky glimmered dark blue as opposed to the pinkish hue the idly floating clouds were taking. Such a beautiful sight under the rustling green of the foliage all around.

"He visited the Long Tails a short time before he was gone." Again, Father's voice had a dreaming quality to it, soft, low, caressing. "He was late for the Second Gathering of the Great Council because of this visit."

Knowing whom his father was referring to, Ganayeda held his breath, thirsty for every morsel of unofficial information about the Great Peacemaker and those legendary times, a curiosity ignited by the time spent with the Wyandot Bear People's leader and the woman of Ossossane. "He wanted to have them a part of our union?"

The older man nodded, eyes resting on the lake's surface again, not seeing it but wandering the mists of the past.

"He said they were interested, yes, willing to listen. He was excited by this possibility, working day and night, wandering out there, sending delegations. The Crooked Tongues were supposed to arrive for this meeting as well. He had invited them without consulting with anyone. Oh, but were the leading men of our newly born union angered! Especially this snake, the First Head of the Great Council." The reflective smile filled with sadness again. "Then it went out of hand. I tried to hold it all together, but it broke into tiny little pieces, worse than a pottery bowl crashing into the hearth's stones."

Now it was Ganayeda's turn to put his hand on the desolately hunched shoulders, such an unfamiliar pose for the man he had always seen perfectly straight-backed and strong, so determined, so proud, the power that held so many people and towns, the entire Great League, together, keeping it safe from inside and outside upheavals.

"You kept his legacy alive, the union of his creation, his laws, the new ways of our people. Without you, Father, we wouldn't have any of it, neither our Great Peace nor our strength and union to enjoy. Mother keeps talking about it, remembering the times it all might have gone to pieces but for your strength and conviction, your power, your understanding of the Great Law of Peace, your determination not to let it fall." Unable to bear the sadness, the open grief of the man he always knew was as unshakable as the hills and the forests of High Springs, he pressed his palm tighter, wishing to give his father of his strength. "You tried to save the Great Peacemaker, to keep him alive and around—the Crooked

Tongues leader and the woman of Ossossane told me about these events. But it wasn't in your power to do so. He was the Messenger of the Great Spirits. He couldn't stay. And yet, Father," he peered into the familiar face, pleased to see the spark of attentiveness enliven the sad features, bringing the man he knew back, "you did what needed to be done, you kept his creation alive, and you made it grow into something that can't be broken, not even by thousands of united enemies. The Long Tails, they weren't alone in this attempt to make our Great League crumble. I learned all about it in the Mountain People's lands. There are more than one nation of scattered villages between their other Great Lake and the Crooked Tongues to the north. I learned it from several different captives. The man who had led them had these people united, those whom we call Long Tails. But he failed, Father. He failed not because he did it badly—he must have been a talented leader, this man—but because our Great League, your and the Great Peacemaker's creation, is stronger and firmer than all those hastily concocted unions our enemies are trying to put together, the Wyandot included. Don't you see it, Father? It is as clear as a drawing painted in the clearest of skies. So easy to read and to understand."

The blossoming smile made him breathe with relief. It held it all, the familiar calm wisdom, the good-natured appreciation, the slightly amused admittance.

"As I said, you are an outstanding man, Son. The Great Spirits smiled when they bestowed me with you." The smile widened. "Our Great League is in good hands when people like you are caring for it. It reassures me better than words. I know our longhouse of Five Nations is strong and durable, not a structure to fall apart, certainly not at the first shake. No, I have no doubts about it. But I wish," the smile dimmed, even though the sadness didn't return, "I wish we could have extended it, built it longer, added compartments to host more families. Like we do in our actual dwellings, you see? Our Wolf Clan's longhouse has grown since you lived there, with your mother receiving permission to add compartments for two more families last Awakening Season. You see? This is how our Great Union should be. This is how he wished it to be. But, well," the grin was back, stretching the generous lips, lifting the thin lines of scars that were still hiding among the wrinkles. Not a mirthful affair, but holding none of the previous desolation, not anymore. "We should be grateful for what we have. Like you wisely pointed out, our Great League is an exceptional union, and our Great Law of Peace will keep us safe for many summers and winters to come." The large eyes twinkled. "Delivering so many thanksgiving speeches, I probably should listen to them myself from time to time. But now I wish to hear all about those Long Tails who are, apparently, not all are Long Tails as we thought them to be. How many different peoples do they have out there by the other Great Lake? What tongues are they speaking?"

It was already dark when they made their way back up the incline, treading carefully, nearly blind without a torch to light their way. The moon was hiding behind the clouds, hopelessly thin in itself. Ganayeda smiled to himself, knowing that if it was up to him he would have stayed out there by the lake's shore for the entire night, enjoying this exceptional man's company, the wonderful wisdom of his comments and observations. The tale of this campaign, the logistics of managing so many warriors whether while moving or staying in camps, the preparations, their endless arguments and deliberations, having too many leaders, too little organization; their ploy of luring the enemy to fight on the ground of their choosing, the ambush, the nerve-racking waiting, the battle itself, oh but those took time to retell, a pleasure to discuss with a person of Father's grasp and perception. If only there was more time to do that.

"I'm glad you had the chance to save Ogteah's life." Father's voice rang again softly, contemplatively. "He is a good man."

Ganayeda grinned, knowing that Father cherished a soft spot for the strange foreigner, either due to him being the son of some long-lost cousin from the forgotten past, or because he liked the wild man for what he was, probably the latter.

Well, he himself was not in disagreement with this, not anymore. The Crooked Tongue was a good man, and it was good to finally have his measure, to understand him better and put the nagging suspicion to rest. Whatever made this man come to their lands, he was one of them now, his loyalty tested, its results satisfactory.

"Yes. He is a brave man, and he contributed much to our warring. In his own very peculiar way." He grinned. "Like you said once upon a time, this man can be an asset when approached and used correctly, according to his inclinations and talents, unruly, restless, unpredictable spirit that he is." Chuckling, he moved a bunch of prickly branches away. "It was Okwaho who saw this man's strengths first. He was the one to discover how useful he could be, how good and loyal and efficient given certain less regular tasks and missions. I admit, I didn't appreciate Okwaho's reasoning at first, but now I know our future warriors' leader was right. Among other remarkable things, that brother of mine has a knack for choosing the right people, for recognizing their talents and inclinations while using those to the benefit of his plans. He evokes people's loyalty, and he makes them wish to work for him and excel." He sobered. "The death of his friend hit him hard."

"The Flint youth from Cohoes Falls?" This time, the silence was brief, but not as cozy as before. A heavy, uncomfortable silence. "I remember him from the spear-throwing contest. He was one of the few who pierced the hoop's perfect middle, along with you and two others." The flicker of pride in Father's voice was unmistakable. And pleasing. "It pains me to think of this young man dying due to treachery and foul means, rather than the result of a fair hand-to-hand."

Storing the compliment for later consideration, as always, feeling uncomfortable when the conversation dwelled on his strengths and achievements, Ganayeda found it safer to return to the original subject.

"The Crooked Tongue took his death almost as hard. Besides being ready to endanger his own life while trying to save the Flint's, he buried his favorite spear together with this man, giving him the weapon he never separated from through the entire battle. They had been as close as brothers since their warriors-gathering travels." He sighed. "The Flint was a good man."

Not to mention the bow, he reflected, remembering the best of his spoils, now tucked safely back in the camp, to travel home with him and never leave his possession. Such an exceptional weapon, so large and sturdy, yet flexible, made from two different kinds of wood, it's edges tilting more sharply, allowing the shooter to pull the string more forcefully, to shoot at greater distances. Oh, but the Crooked Tongue did act strangely when it came to good weaponry. The bow was his ever since he had captured the girl, even though the filthy little fox did manage to steal it back while being allowed to run away. So, when the wondrous weapon was found shortly after the terrible duel, everyone knew whom it belonged to, unless the wounded died. Which he didn't. Still, just before they had left for home, the Crooked Tongue, by then already able to walk, or at least to hobble unaided, had given this spoil to Ganayeda, refusing to discuss the matter at all. A shooter of his, Ganayeda's, skill could use such a weapon better and more efficiently, the man claimed, his face closed, thin and haggard, eyes sunken, lacking their usual spark. He himself was served well enough with his regular bow.

Reluctant to show how pleased he was, Ganayeda had argued, to no avail, deep down knowing that it was the man's way of thanking him for saving his life. Also, the grieving Crooked Tongue didn't want the accursed weapon, he knew, no matter how wondrous or precious, not the bow that killed his friend.

"Many good men die in wars, so very needlessly at that." Again, Father's voice held a measure of sadness. "But it seems we are unable to rid ourselves of this necessity to war and be ready to defend ourselves." His shrug was barely visible in the darkness. "At least now, thanks to your success, it will be easier to gather warriors, to get the approval of the Great Council to do so." Another warm pause. "Like I said, our Longhouse is in good hands when people like you and your brother and your cousin from across the Great Lake are caring for it."

And that was the truth, thought Ganayeda, not hiding his contentment, feeling safe to smile to himself under the cover of the darkness. They were the good keepers, worthy sons to the great men their fathers were.

CHAPTER 31

Wiping the sweat off his face, Aingahon straightened up, longing for a gust of wind, just a little breath of breeze, really. It was suffocating hot, unusually airless for the end of the Green Corn Moon, the first of the Falling Leaves Season.

Not that they were going to enjoy any of it. There was neither green nor white nor any other corn to be had; no cookies and no porridge, no beans or squash to add to their stew—all the food that he had always taken for granted.

Well, with no women to tend the fields, in their case, the remnants of just a few longish plots adjacent to the cabin behind the clearing, the meat was to be enjoyed as it was, with no flavoring. An unfamiliar diet, but she claimed she knew how to make her plots bear fruit again. The next Awakening Season, she promised.

He grinned to himself, trusting her to get what she wanted, not to let anything stand in her way. If she wished Mother Earth to bestow her with its fruits after neglecting her field for so long, a whole span of seasons if not more, then that was that. She would have her harvest, of course she would. Nothing, not even Mother Earth, would dare to oppose this girl.

However, all this would have to wait for the Cold Moons to pass, with the nearing winter offering nothing but meat, everything they would manage to hunt and prepare, plenty of work, and not enough time or strength to do that.

He shrugged, then wiped his brow and resumed his efforts, slashing the edge of the long pole with more vigor, trying to pay as little attention as he could to the vigorous protests from various parts of his body, his ribs and his head mainly, but his knee of course joining the celebration with an old well-familiar glee. Under regular circumstances, he would have changed his position, tilted his body in a way that would allow his leg to take as little pressure as it could. Yet now, close to half a moon since the battle and the terrible journey back home, he was still in no condition to do that. So his knee had to do with less fussing around than of yore. Oh well.

Pushing his hair off his face, he eyed the chipped edge, not sharpened enough yet, temporary as this beam was intended, to last one single winter, until he would locate, cut, and prepare real durable poles, to extend the storage room, to make it a real room and not just a facade, uncovered and barely supported. Wrong season again, but the collapsed side of the cabin left them with no choice. So a temporary solution it would be, until after the Cold Moons, when the bark was possible to strip off the suitable tree, to prepare the coverage for the walls and the sturdy supportive beams of the frame.

He grinned, pausing again, out of breath. Oh yes, for now their longhouse was ridiculously short, not helped by his slow recovery, so difficult to do the simplest of tasks. He pushed the tiny wave of frustration away, surprised how effortlessly it came to him, with an indecent ease. He, who had had such a hard time coming to grips with failures or difficulties, let alone disabilities. That broken knee! Oh, how it colored his life, back in Tushuway and everywhere he went, how thwarted it made him feel, how angry with himself and the others. And maybe even before, frustrated with his people's relative unimportance, with the growing power of their neighbors, with his inability to change it in the blink of an eye.

Well, now it all was gone, and he had a cracked skull and possibly a fractured rib or two to add to the collection of injuries he wasn't certain were going to leave without a reminder. Not to mention the memory of the monumental failure, the extent of the defeat, the magnitude of it, not a failed raid but a failed war, the end of the dream, no unity, no powerful dominance for his people, not anything but the fear and doomed expectation. The

Great League would dominate, would expand, would set the tone for everyone, even the Wyandot, united or not, even though those northerners might as yet offer a challenge to the growing giant. But not his people, not anymore.

The longing was back, and the desolation. But then...

He shrugged, and resumed his work, chopping at even intervals, disregarding the pain. This pole would be ready today, stuck at its designated place before the sun went down and into another world. But for a good durable axe. He made a mental note to search for good pieces of wood and a large enough flint. The amount of items to make through the cold winter moons was long and growing, especially now that he began feeling better.

Oh, but it was good to be able to move with no pangs of terrible pain tearing at his insides, leaving him dizzy and unable to breathe. Whatever was cracked there inside him, ribs or possibly other things, it had showed him that his knee was not the worst that could happen to a person. What if he didn't regain his ability to move freely? A worse fate than death, worse by far.

Well, he hadn't been sure about any of it back then, in the lake or the mud of the creek's shores, or among the prickly bushes. It might have been the beginning of his Sky Journey, a different travel than he had expected, made bearable only by Tsutahi, a reassuring presence.

Had she died, too? he had wondered back then but briefly, hovering in the ticklish fog, soaring into the painless dizziness, then plummeting down into the worst of agonies. Not a peaceful journey to the Sky World, nothing he would have expected. Still, she had been there, and it was better this way.

If only he had been able to progress on his own. It was terrible that she had to do it for him. Even though being already dead, he could feel what a strain it had been on her, to carry him in this way. It wasn't right, but there was nothing he could do about it with his spirit floating like that.

Or so he thought until she had left. Then the sensation of being safe faded, and the attempt to get up in order to find her had him plummeting back into the worst of ordeals. So much pain! It felt like dying again, the struggle to get up, then reeling and faltering to where she might have been, evidently fighting again, in danger, judging by the sounds of the strife, all those strangled noises and thuds of the falling bodies.

He clenched his teeth again, trying to remember. The fragments were so broken, scattered in disarray, not enough to comprise a picture. She was about to die, he remembered that. Or maybe she had been dead already. Most probably, as the man was upon her and she wasn't struggling—her, who never gave up or gave in. It terrified him, the realization. It gave him strength to do... what? He didn't remember.

The memory went no further than the loudness of the thud the man's body made while crashing into the ground amidst so much pain—his pain!—to lay next to her, in a strangely relaxed pose, as though needing a rest all of a sudden. A scout, judging by his outfit and the lack of painting, he had known, collapsing next to them both, ready to resume his Sky Journey, unpleasant as it was but safe, now that she was back with him again.

Yet, her coughing wouldn't let him, the way she twisted and strained, fighting for breath oh so very desperately. She needed his help, didn't she? So he made his best crawling closer, holding her or maybe just touching, trying to reassure.

Shaking his head at the memories, he bettered his grip on the knife, her best quality dagger, with an antler handle and such a long, sturdy, unusually wide blade, glued to the antler with much sap, fastened with many strings, too many. Not a good throwing missile, not like a regular knife, but such a wonderful tool to work with. Or to contemplate its usefulness. Better than to think about what happened, the battle and the defeat carved in his memory too firmly, not about to break into fragments and fade like the journey back home. But for something like that to happen.

And yet, here, in the peacefulness of her realm, even those memories hurt not as badly as he would have expected. He had lost on all counts, and he had exposed his people to a terrible danger now that they were not only as divided as before but weakened dreadfully, losing so many of their finest men and warriors. So many dead!

He didn't dare to think of these numbers. Surely not everyone who had fought were gone, in the Sky World already, watching and grieving but unable to help. No, there must be enough of those who made it back home, to recover their spirits and their lives, but at what price?

Still, in the soothing serenity of her clearing, the frustration and anger refused to accumulate. He had done his best, everything he could. He had tried, and even though he had failed, there was no shame in what he had done, no guilt or humiliation.

He should have died back there beyond the enemy river, and maybe he did. It certainly felt like dying, and the new world he had woken up into had nothing to do with his previous life. A sky world maybe, yes, whyever not? Her and her grandfather's cabin and their carefully arranged clearing certainly felt like that, and he didn't know how he had arrived here, as after that desperate struggle above the creek, his spirit truly had left, fluttering in a strange place of freezing cold and unbearable heat, or terrible nausea, not helped by the motions of the swaying canoe—oh yes, he had been at its bottom, he remembered that—of fear and pain but peacefulness too, an all-consuming tranquility. If the Star Belt of Gadowaas was made of people's faces, then he had been given the star he needed to guide him on his journey to the Sky World and keep him safe, a star with her features. And if she had guided him to another place by mistake…

He grinned, then put his mind back on his task, determined not to let it wander again. Whatever this place was, he liked it here, and they still needed to have this cabin made ready to withstand the blizzards of the Cold Moons. Not to mention their food supplies that would consist of meat and dried berries, and little else besides those, unless he recovered enough to go out and fish in serious quantities before the first snow storms struck, to enliven their meals of smoked meat and little else.

He could hear her coming back, moving about the clearing, skipping in her new dancing pace. A different, lively, vibrant Tsutahi, cheerful and high-spirited, beaming with brightest of smiles; a confident thing, sure of herself and at home. No more wariness or haunted looks, no restlessness, not even the familiar angularity of limbs. The skinny, unhealthily pale creature was gone. Where to? Did it disappear together with his old haunted self in the stench of the after-battle creek? Maybe.

He didn't dwell on these questions, not yet. It was disturbing to think about her in any other way than as a child, a little creature to protect. She was nothing but a young girl, she was! Even though she claimed to have counted sixteen summers by now, or close to it, insisting that her mother had birthed her on Cold Moons, when the blizzards were at their worst. Or so Grandfather had said.

Oh well, he was not about to argue with the legendary old man, such a powerful presence in her mind and upon this clearing. Still, she was nothing but a child if her behavior was to go by, naive, trusting, often outright adoring, a fiercely loyal companion maybe, but not a woman to love. Not yet. Maybe later. Was it possible? He shrugged at his own silly thoughts.

"Here you are!" Bursting into his cozy hideaway, she beamed, sweaty and out of breath, panting. "I got two fat does. Two! And it took me only four shots! Would you believe that?"

He made no effort to fight his grin. "Yes, I do. Looking at you, I do believe that." To straighten up was still difficult, so he leaned on his pole instead, studying her. But she did look her wildest, disheveled, panting, smeared in wet earth and plenty of meat juices. "I'll come with you, and we'll drag those things here." Not a beckoning prospect. It still was painful to lift himself off the ground, let alone something as heavy as a fat doe.

She waved her dripping palm in dismissal. "No need. I skinned them both. That's what took me so long, the skinning. I spotted them right away, shot them right there on the spot. Could have got more of the herd, maybe another buck, but for them being so many and me all alone. So they ran away and left me with all this work." The little bragger was shouting at the top of her voice, in no melodious manner.

He fought the urge to tell her to lower her voice. But she deserved to brag, didn't she? Doing so much hunting, carving and smoking, ensuring their upcoming winter with great drive and determination. Had she had time to do this, she would have gone fishing as well, the warrior-girl that she was, doing men's work so easily and with joy, but useless in any of the female tasks, her cooking tasteless, her skills at sewing two pieces of leather together nonexistent. The moment he could sit upright unaided and move about, he had insisted on roasting the meat she was bringing, giving up on the idea of enjoying something as complicated as stew. Neither knew what needed to be put in the boiling pot besides the meat to make it taste more inspiring.

"So you brought it all here?"

She nodded vigorously, eyes shining. "It took some walking back and forth, but now it's all here." Then the smile faded, as her eyes scrutinized him, shadowed with worry. "You don't look good. You need to rest. Go back inside until—"

"I'm good!" Abruptly, he returned to his pole, not liking to be fussed over, not in this fashion. Enough that she did all the work, as though she were the man around instead of him. "It'll be ready before the sun goes down, and then that part of the wall won't look so eager to crush in." A brief glance in her direction deepened his resentment. "Don't order me about."

Not surprised with her lack of response, as he had been speaking with his back to her until his last sentence, immersed in his task or the attempts to make it look like an easy work, he went on chopping the wood, feeling her glare almost physically. But she didn't like being dismissed in this way, a willful little thing.

He paid her no attention, hearing the sound of her feet stomping out, kicking something on their way, an old pottery pot by the clanking of it. There were still mounds of work ahead of her, with the richness of her catch. Two fat does, plenty of meat to put for a smoking.

Sighing, he put the pole down, or rather let it drop, not about to strain his uncooperative ribs more than he had to.

"Go and rest yourself," he said, emerging into the sunlit clearing in front of their cabin, where she was busy arranging large logs in the way that allowed her to put a slow fire under the simple construction of beams supporting one vertical plank—their meat-smoking device.

Sensing his presence, she looked up, lips pressed in too obvious of a way, pouting, childish and feminine at the same time;

too feminine for his peace of mind.

"What?" The skulking tone made his grin return. What a spoiled little fox she had been at times, used to getting her way, if for no other reason than because she was the one to take care of herself.

"Finish making that fire, then go and rest. You did enough for today. I'll put the meat up for smoking."

Her scowl deepened. "You wanted to get that pole done before the dusk." An outright complaint.

He shook his head, not fighting his grin anymore. "Get off that fire, hunter-girl. You worked hard today, harder than me." As he pushed himself past her with little ceremony, preparing to drop beside the already carved parts of the deer, all juicy and dripping, its smell delicious, she moved reluctantly, glowering at him from under her brow. "If for no better reason than to go to the spring and wash yourself. One can smell you from a day of walk away."

Her anger was threatening to explode, about to produce smoke, he was sure of that. Enough to treat that meat instead of a fire? he wondered.

"Stop making faces." This time, he held her gaze, smiling in a genuine way. "You work hard while I do nothing. It makes me feel bad. Useless. You may not know that, but men don't like feeling this way. I'm sorry for snapping at you before."

A small half-shrug was his answer. "You were terribly sick. And wounded. And almost dead." The reluctant smile blossomed. "Of course you can't work yet. It's no laziness. You are still not well."

"Well enough to help around. And to go without receiving orders from you, you willful thing." He shook his head, then laughed again, the sensation of well-being prevailing, such an unfamiliar feeling, certainly not in those quantities. "It's my turn to give you orders. Go up there, wash yourself, rest a little, until I roast some meat. After we eat, we'll best this pile of meat together. How about that?"

Another shrug, a much livelier affair. Then she sprang to her feet, her beam returning. "Don't give me orders either. You are not Grandfather." The mischievousness of her tone was unsettling again, unfamiliar, as was the flicker of a smug female challenge, something he glimpsed in her face before she turned to run away in her regular pace of a hunted deer, a sure-footed, confident creature.

He dropped next to the neatly carved chunks, shaking his head, wondering again where this new path was taking him, to what places. What was the purpose in all this?

He didn't know, didn't bother to spend too much time thinking about it; he, who was always so busy planning ahead, preparing, analyzing, needing to have every future possibility under control, faced in advance. So strange. Now he just didn't care. The woods were important, and the spring, this cabin and the owner of it, so innocent and vulnerable, so fragile, yet the strongest, most resilient person he had ever met. The woman who bestowed him with another life.

Yes, there must be a purpose to that, but this time, he would wait patiently for this purpose to reveal itself. No more rushing and pushing, no more frantic struggle to understand and make the events happen. His people would weather this downfall, somehow. They would recover and grow strong again, to fight the Great League another day, maybe. With or without him to push this particular struggle along.

AUTHOR'S AFTERWORD

The first serious military clash between the Great League of the Iroquois and the Erie People (Erielhonan or Long Tails) is relatively well-documented. In his *History of Ashtabula County, Ohio*, written in 1798, Rev. S. D. Peet dedicates more than a whole chapter to the battle that might have shaped the following history of this entire region.

Long Tails/Erie were a prominent nation who, until up to the 16th were reported to occupy the southern and eastern shores of Lake Erie, spreading as far out as Ohio River Valley. Having been an inseparable part of the Great Lakes' demography, they played an important role in local politics and developments, a people that no one made the mistake of overlooking or omitting taking into account. Neither the Great League, not the Wyandot confederacy, nor various smaller nations around both great water bodies made this mistake.

According to the reports, furnished mainly by the Great League and recorded by the wandering French missionaries centuries later—not perfectly reliable sources, the first having no objectivity in the story, obviously, and the second having no understanding of local mentality and cultural traits—the Erie People were powerful and warlike, feared by their immediate neighbors, even the members of the Great League, at least prior to its creation. Or so the story goes.

To the north and west, where the famous Onguiaahra/Niagara Falls are cascading today as spectacularly as they did centuries ago, Attiwandaronk People populated the land, a small confederacy of various sub-nations that were later recorded and known to us today as Neutral People. The Wyandot had mistakenly lumped them together with their Long Tails neighbors, even though those people were no Erie. However, the two powers would unite from time to time, enjoying a complicated relationship, especially in the face of the growing alliances all around—the Wyandot and the Iroquois, in particular. It must have been unsettling, to watch such dominant neighbors uniting into powerful political bodies. Not an occurrence farsighted people would choose to ignore.

In this book of the People of the Longhouse series – or rather the Great Peacemaker's saga – I wanted to explore such a development, a large-scale war that might have defined the Great League's path from those relatively early days, as judging by the later centuries, its political and military dealings and the vastness of its influence, the pattern of its expansion has been set from those earlier times (as far back as the 12th century, maybe).

The Great Peacemaker wished to have more people and nations sharing in the union of his creation; the various clauses and laws of his constitution, the detailed and very minutely documented Great Law of Peace, make it perfectly clear.

However, only five original nations remained the members of the exclusive union up until very late post-contact times. Why? A fair question, as the neighboring people were not so dissimilar to the Five Iroquois Nations, neither culturally nor linguistically. Still, something prevented even the Peacemaker's native Wyandot from joining the Great League. Early military clashes? Well, it is one of the possibilities. The documented oral tradition certainly supplies accounts such as the one I based "The Warpath" on. The detailed report regarding this battle could be found among the chapters of "History of Ashtabula County, Ohio" by Williams, W. W. (publication date 1878, Philadelphia).

Other challenges that the creators of the Great League or those who inherited this responsibility might have been facing were as interesting. At some point, they might have come to realize the possible flaws in their unheard-of political body, long stretches of peace as opposed to the threateningly uniting neighbors, lack of readily available warriors' forces in case of emergency—no standing army, not among the Great Lakes' dwellers—or even a certain lack of discipline and organized way of fighting among those who were used to raiding in small groups and in a sporadic manner.

As always, I made every possible effort to stay as close to the described events as possible, not to change important locations and to try to use the original names of towns and places whenever possible.

Tushuway, indeed, is reported to be the Long Tails/Erie People's main town, located near the modern-day Buffalo.

Up the Niagara River and toward the Lake Ontario, Onguiahra Thundering Waters, or what we know today as Niagara Falls, was located a village that carried the same name, belonging to Attiwandaronk/Neutral People.

Later, Niagara River might have served as a natural border between these people and the Seneca, the Mountain People, the Keepers of the Western Door, but in the earlier days, it must have been Genesee (Ce-nis-seu or Beautiful/Good Valley) River that marked the edge of the Confederacy's reach and influence.

A little to the east, at the foot of Canandaiqua Lake (Ga-nun-da-gwa Lake, the Chosen Spot), among the other beautiful Finger Lakes, Seneca/Mountain People's main town Tsonontowan was most certainly located, documented well enough. But the invading Erie didn't come that far. Met at the foot of Honeoye (Ha-ne-yay-a or Lying Finger) Lake, unusually large forces fought their historical battle, the battle that must have influenced the future of the entire region, placing the Great League at an unarguably dominant stance, the most powerful confederacy of its times. The most powerful, and the most advanced.

In those times, between the 13th and the 17th centuries, no country or federacy or confederacy in the entire world seemed to manage a truly democratic way of government, none but the Five Iroquois Nations who had listened to the Great Peacemaker once upon a time.

What happened next is presented in the fifth book of the People of the Longhouse Series, "**Echoes of the Past**."

The story continues with

ECHOES OF THE PAST

People of the Longhouse, Book 5

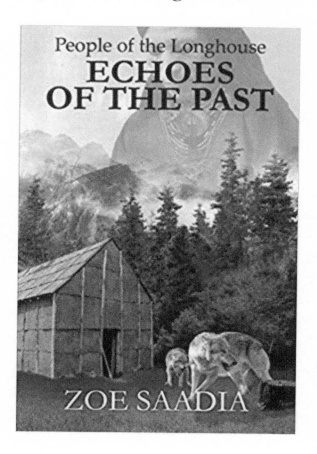

CHAPTER 1

"Come on, you can do it."

The War Chief's outstretched hands shook as he held them up, not touching the balancing figure but ready to catch it should the adventurous climber lose his grip on the ladder's rung and fall. A slim chance, as the child was hanging on to his precarious perch with an obvious desperation, taking no chances by freeing one of his hands in order to reach for the next challenge, opting for staying where he was, gripping it for dear life.

No adventurer, this one, reflected Ogteah, amused. A perfect opposite to the wild thing that was already hopping up there on the upper shelf, forcing his way through the clacking pottery, happy and unconcerned, having scaled this same ladder with an indecent ease before the watching grandfather managed to discern his intentions and rush closer, just in case. A fierce addition to the War Chief's family, unlike his twin brother, a perfect opposite.

"Go ahead," prompted the War Chief. "You won't fall, but I'm here to make sure of that. See how close?"

The older man's voice rang hoarsely in the dimness of the compartment, even though in this part of the day and the season the interior of the longhouse was well aired, with all venting holes opened along the long corridor, and both entrances gaping into the crispiness of the high noon. No stinging smoke to make one fight for breath like in the earlier time in this season. Still, the old man's cough was rocking the air with alarming frequency, the result of a prolonged illness acquired through the Cold Moons, or so Ogteah was told, worried to hear this particular news.

Having arrived in High Springs only this morning, he didn't

fail to notice the prominent leader's pallor and the haggardness of his features, the way the man's bones were protruding sharply, in no encouraging manner. Oh yes, it was easy to see the cough in the thinly pressed lips and the lightly convulsing throat, the way it was held back, with typical stubbornness.

Straightening up, he glanced at the standing man, ready to spring to his feet in case of a need.

"Come on, little one." One of the large palms moved closer, touching the child's back, supporting, giving it of its strength. "You can reach your troublemaking brother, lend him some support, can't you now?" The mischievous glance shot at Ogteah, accompanied with a light wink. "No use trying to get him down now either, once he has made up his mind. A stubborn little thing."

Ogteah grinned then got to his feet anyway. The resumed conversation offered a good pretext. "I would have worried about the other rascal."

A glance at the upper shelf confirmed his claim. The wilder twin was busy plundering, stumbling between baskets and items of wear, spilling some of it as he roamed about, high spirited and unafraid but clumsy, having the restrictions of his still developing walking skills to deal with. They had seen not much more than one or maybe one and a half summers of their lives, remembered Ogteah, not truly interested in babies that weren't his own. The Wolf Man's woman was staggering about with this or that baby tied to her back or snuggled on her breast on his last visit in this town, more than two seasons earlier, way before the Cold Moons. So maybe they didn't see more than one span of seasons, after all.

"What did you find up there, Takoskowa?" called the old leader, shifting on his toes while still maintaining the same pose, keeping the more timid twin safe. "Don't make a mess out of it or your grandmother will have my skin for this."

A tumbling down basket with remnants of dry cookies was his answer. His favorite ones, with nuts and berries, discovered Ogteah, catching the flying object, balancing it so as to not let more of its spilled contents fall on the floor. The perfectly round face peeked from above, puckered in too obvious of a manner.

The flood of tears was imminent.

"You wild thing." The War Chief's voice trembled with laughter, dripping warmth. "Why did you do that?"

"He didn't. I don't think he anticipated the unruly basket jumping off that shelf after a simple tossing and throwing it around," suggested Ogteah, amused yet wishing that someone came already and took the children away. The opportunities to talk to the prominent man alone and undisturbed were few and far between, unless he asked for a private conversation specifically. Which he didn't. There was no need for that. He hadn't come to High Springs on his own initiative, not this time. The invitation of their unofficial warriors' leader was the one to bring him here; word sent through a casual third party, nothing alarming or even formal. Still, it had him started on his journey here at once. The Wolf Man wasn't in a habit of summoning people, especially those he trusted with responsibilities, for simple pleasures of good company or to pass time. Not this man!

Knowing that it was unseemly to demand the talk he was summoned here for immediately upon his arrival, Ogteah had wandered off, greeting many friends he had all around this town, getting filled with food offerings at every place he had visited until his stomach threatened to burst. It was unheard of to see a guest off before he sampled the tastiest of the local treats, and of course no visitor would claim his full belly as an excuse, a terrible impoliteness. So now, a quarter of a day later and enjoying the company of the renowned old leader, he could barely breathe, let alone think of anything edible nearing his mouth for the duration of the next moon at the very least.

He didn't count on the powerful leader to be idle and alone, intending to go out in search of the man's powerful elder son, the Wolf Man's influential brother, a very important dignitary these days, en route to all sorts of positions of power, the representative of his town in the Great Council being one of the proposed speculations. However, the War Chief was at home and alone, visibly aged, thin and haggard, weakened by the winter sickness that he was still recovering from, something no one outside the town had heard about. Why? wondered Ogteah. Was it a matter of pride on the War Chief or his family's part, or were deeper political motivations involved?

"Oh well, intentionally or not," the old man's eyes twinkled, turning back toward the more timid counterpart of the wild whirlwind that was again sweeping through the upper shelf, "we are done for as it is, the three of us, so just go up there and help your brother make the new order out of things, will you? Come on, little one. You can do it for your brother's sake, can't you?" A following outburst of soft laughter ended with what sounded like a suppressed cough, the wrinkled face twisting, losing some of its recently gained color that the activities with the energetic pair of toddlers must have brought. "And it will... will be safer up there... when your grandmother comes back..."

As Ogteah rushed to the older man's side, his eyes scanning the interior of the lower shelves, seeking a bowl of water, or better yet, a container with medicine, the War Chief shook his head, holding the rest of his cough between the tightly pursed lips, his eyes glittering with wetness that the effort must have brought but determined, as forceful as always, ordering him to leave it at that. But of course! What man of pride and dignity would concede to being treated like a sick person unless truly unable to help himself? Still Ogteah fumed at the womenfolk of this family for leaving the old man unattended, with no better company than lively toddlers to watch after.

"There is water in the bin," he said as noncommittally as he could. "I'll get you some."

The nod of the old leader was accompanied by an apologetic smile, while the large hands pushed their charge up gently if firmly, uncompromising now. The boy on the ladder screwed up his face in the exact imitation of his brother's before, amusing and puzzling Ogteah once again at the fact that two human beings could look that much alike, just a replica of each other, one person presented twice. Afraid to retrace his steps back toward the safety of the earthen floor, the little thing evidently opted for the wisest solution of trusting his grandfather, letting the old hands guide him up the treacherous path, keeping him safe until reaching a more stable ground.

"Thank you." The older man accepted Ogteah's water with gratitude, draining its contents quickly, in almost one gulp. "The annoying cough!" Another spasm was conquered more successfully this time. "It will pass eventually, but does it make one's life difficult sometimes, especially when the worried women spot you doing this." A chuckle ended with more alarmingly barking sounds. "I swear I'm tempted to do what sick animals do, crawl away and let the illness pass by itself, in peace and no fussing around."

"I can understand that." Ogteah grinned, not truly relating. When sick or wounded, he liked being attended and kept company with. Well, as far as it was Gayeri who did that, of course. His woman certainly knew how to spoil a person and make him feel better and fast, unlike her fussing aunt or various female friends and relatives. So maybe the War Chief just lacked proper company. Or maybe he was a different person, striving to be at his best, hating being caught in a weakness, the likelier of assumptions. A great leader of countless summers, oh yes, the old man must have been needing to feel powerful and of use.

"Every man would." Breathing with more ease now, even though the colorlessness of his face was still alarming, the old man positioned himself to the left of the ladder, ready to catch falling toddlers should they begin tumbling down the upper shelf. Judging by the noise both boys were now making, not able to converse as yet due to their young ages but communicating by calls and grunts and excited exclamations, it was the most prudent course to pursue. "So, what have the Lone Hill's people been up to? That village of yours *is* busy expending, turning into a large settlement with all their growing population, eh? Something you've been contributing mightily to, or so one hears."

As always it was easy to join in the great man's laughter, the impressive leader's ability to put his conversers at ease remarkable, something to wonder about.

"This sort of news travels fast, doesn't it?" He tried to suppress the familiar glow, knowing that the old man didn't care, not the way he, Ogteah, did. "She doesn't mind having another child. I thought she might wish to avoid that, with her aspirations to join our longhouse's women council, but she says it won't interfere."

He brought his arms forward, palms up, an accepting gesture that reflected none of his real excitement, real elation concerning this particular matter. Oh, but how he had rejoiced when she had told him, the moment she knew, just a few dawns after her blood didn't come. So different from the first time, when she had waited for him to come home from his first war, with him being wounded, exhausted, shaken, not excited in the least by the prospect of turning into a father yet again, the first time back in his lands being such a failure. And yet, how little did he know back then, having no clue, not the slightest.

The girl Gayeri had brought to this world only a few seasons later and after much fear, on his part more than on hers, come to think of it, with the shadow of his missing mother looming in the background, reminding of childbearing dangers, was an enchanting, flawless creature, the most perfect human being, exciting beyond measure, a true fruit of love. Having known his daughter for close to three summers by now, he was still amazed at how his excitement with her never faded, blossoming and growing with every passing day, enhanced by every development, every new skill she had learned so fast and with such eagerness, having a mind of her own on many matters by now, freely expressed, and great deal of cheek into the bargain.

He had spoiled the girl rotten, Gayeri kept complaining, powerless against their daughter's charm as much as he was, something the little beast possessed in abundance, just like her mother before her, he suspected. Gayeri said that many of her problems arose out of her being atrociously spoiled, never disciplined, a claim confirmed by her aged aunt's attitude. Still he would grin and take no notice. His daughter deserved everything she wanted, the prettiest pelts and the shiniest purple shells straight away from the far east. His venturing into the Flint People's lands and their warfare beyond the Great River had both his women looking as decorated as a ceremonial ground before an important ceremony.

"It will interfere, of course it will. Another child will slow her down, but not for good. Women know how to deal with it." The older man moved sideways, following the creaking of the planks above their heads. "How is her father? I heard the Honorable Representative has not been well through the Cold Moons."

"No, he wasn't, but he is well now." Deciding that it was his duty to tell the details the old leader might not learn until fit to travel, Ogteah positioned himself next to the ladder, ready to join the hunt after falling toddlers as well. "The False Face Society healers have found right foods for the Honorable Elder to eat along with the foods he was to avoid. It changed his health for the best ever since." He hesitated. "He will be attending the Great Gathering of the next moon."

"Good." The War Chief nodded thoughtfully. "I should love to meet him there. There are matters I wish to hear his opinion on before those are brought to the august assembly's official consideration."

He hated the knot that was tightening in his stomach, undesirable and unwelcome. It could be anything that the renowned leader might have wished to discuss, anything and everything. It didn't have to be his, Ogteah's, former people or their growing impudence, with the talks of peace abandoned some summers ago, on that same span of seasons when they had received the word of Father's death, the summer the Long Tails were defeated so soundly. Since then, the resumed war was a looming possibility, but it was something he had managed to push out of his mind with a measure of success. There was no need to agonize over possibilities until they happened, no need to toss on his longhouse's bunk sleepless, thinking of what he would do should the war break out. It was a waste of time. When it happened, he would have enough time to feel bad, trapped, torn, undecided. But until then there was no need to lose his inner peace, or his presence of mind for that matter.

Enough that he had gone to fight the Flint People's traditional enemies last summer because of that, to be away in case the Wolf Man decided to start gathering warriors for the raids that were to be sent across the Great Sparkling Water. A plan that worked nicely, his private scheme of getting away, as a few raids were indeed sent across, with some of his former charges from the

Standing Stone People's lands joining in, to tell him all about it later on. There was not much success in those ventures, with the glaring lack of knowledge as to the location of more important towns than a few scattering villages to assault, or even the enemy's actual war readiness. There was not enough information to be had, and the only encouragement was in the fact, or at least the assumption, that the enemy had been facing an equal disadvantage. A small comfort.

"What was wrong with the representative's health, anyway?" The War Chief's voice tore him from his unhappy reverie, brought him back to the dimness of the compartment and the agitated blabbering that was pouring from its upper parts. "The usual winter sickness?"

"No, it wasn't that. The Honorable Elder was losing his strength very rapidly, turning as thin as a stick, wandering into the dream worlds too often. The healers didn't know what to do, until the man of False Face Society from Onondaga Town came. He made the elder cut fat foods out of his eating habits, made him eat only greens and fruit and drink water sweetened with honey. Then the Representative got better and better, until most traces of illness were gone." Moving closer just in case, Ogteah watched the older man taking a hold of the balancing ladder that was pushed from above, in a clear effort to mount it. "He is satisfactorily fit these days, not needing attendance apart from his special foods being prepared." He grinned. "Gayeri took that responsibility upon herself, otherwise her father would have had a harder time to survive, with the rest of his womenfolk being quite an unorganized lot, prone to hysterics and not much usefulness otherwise."

The War Chief's laughter was merry, even though inhibited by a new bout of coughing, as he stretched his arms, trying to reach for one of the descending toddlers. The adventurous one, judging by the deftness and the self-assurance of his movements. No need for help there. "If you are not careful, you'll end up living with a clan mother."

Ogteah didn't try to stifle a chuckle. "I'm careful."

The sound of rapid footsteps made him glance toward the

stretching corridor, his other senses still tuned to the elder man and the growing commotion upon the upper bunk. The remaining twin, left behind, was beginning to howl lustily, with much gusto.

"Father!" The Wolf Man burst upon them, skirting over the glowing embers of the nearest hearth in one forceful leap. "You should be resting. Not running after two wild rascals. You promised!"

"That's not what you think," pleaded the powerful war leader, smirking without shame. "I'm not running after anyone. Those two wild things were running after me. Before deciding to raid the upper bunk, that is." Moving away, he let the indignant father scale the ladder in order to retrieve one of his howling treasures, the other twin already down, exploring the space under the lower pallet with zest. "I'm telling you, this pair is unstoppable."

"You should be resting, Father," insisted the Wolf Man, not amused. "Mother would kill us both if she knew. Have you drunk your medicine?"

"Not yet," admitted the War Chief, giving Ogteah conspiratorial look. "But I will. You can put your worries to rest, honorable clan mother."

The Wolf Man snorted with a flicker of his old mischievousness. "I'm nagging with good reason," he muttered, giving Ogteah a look of his own. "He made us seriously worried through the last of the Cold Moons, you know. And still I keep catching him messing about with the twins." Bending to retrieve the more spirited part of the pair from under the bunk, dragging the culprit out with little consideration to the protesting toddler's will, the timid boy already nestled snugly under his father's free arm, the man shook his head. "I'll dispose of these two and will be back quickly."

His footsteps echoed firmly, typically determined, as though no protesting or howling toddlers hindered his step.

"They are challenging, this pair," said the War Chief, sinking onto the lower bunk with a sigh of relief, his smile wide, holding no shadows, the sunken eyes crinkling. "I never knew how challenging a pair of twins could be."

"I can only imagine," nodded Ogteah, secure in the knowledge that his daughter didn't have to share her parental attention with anyone so far. "And they are so different even though they look exactly the same."

"Twins always are." The older man's smile was surprisingly wistful, holding sadness. "People expect from twins to be as alike inside as they are outside, but they are not one person, such children. Being a pair, they are completing each other, complementing one another's differences, you see? They are one and two different things at the same time."

"Like the celestial pair, the Great Spirits, the Right-Handed and the Left-Handed Twins."

"Oh, yes, something like that. But not in the good as opposed to the evil sense." The eyes peering at Ogteah twinkled, even though the man's face contorted, dealing with a new bout of dry cough. "It would be too easy if people were to be divided in such a way, wouldn't it?"

Ogteah nodded, rushing toward the bowl of water once again.

"I was born to be a part of such pair." The water gulped down to its last, the man reclined back, obviously tired. "We were about the same, my brother and I. And when he might have looked as timid as our little Tsitsho does now and I was as wild as that unstoppable Takoskowa the Mountain Lion, my brother was always the drive, the thinker, the mind behind our adventures. It might have not looked this way on the outside, but it was I who followed him or his ideas and not the other way around." The intensity of the gaze lessened, blurred, wandering through the mists of the past. Not a happy place, reflected Ogteah, surprised, his heart twisting at the sight of the sagging shoulders, at the deep voice that all of a sudden lost its storytelling quality, dropped to mere whisper. "They said I had sapped his strength when still back in our mother's belly, and maybe it was the truth. He was always sickly, not as robust as I was, not as forceful in disposition." The eyes focused, rose, peering at their converser, challenging. "Still he was the drive behind our adventures, the originator, always."

What happened to him? Ogteah wanted to ask, but couldn't bring himself to do this. Whatever made this man's brother go away, it wasn't good, or pleasant, or timely. The War Chief had lost his brother, his other half, and it must have been bad, the anguish of the lined, grief-stricken face told him that. So much sadness! Outside himself, he put a comforting palm on the weathered shoulder, relaying it all in one simple gesture.

It helped. The eyes focused, cleared. The smile that blossomed was brief, showing a measure of gratitude.

"Such long-forgotten memories." Shaking his head as if trying to be rid of those, the man sighed. "How did we get onto this subject, when all I wanted was to quiz you about your recent adventures in the land beyond the Great River of my people? It must have been interesting out there. Aside from my son, I know very few Onondagas who went to fight as far the lands of the River People. What made you join those particular raids?"

"Well, it was an interesting journey, yes." Grinning lightly, Ogteah shrugged. "I suppose I wanted to get to know my mother's people better. To go and fight alongside them seemed like a good start. What with some of my friends from the Standing Stone lands being eager to talk me into it." He felt his grin widening. "Some of these folk can be forcefully convincing, and the stories regarding the lands of the savages your son provided while loitering over this or that campfire didn't help to put any of us off the projected raid to help our Eastern Door Keepers." He smirked. "Not that I would dare to use the word 'savages' in your son's presence."

"You better not, yes." The old man's laughter shook the air, ending with a new outburst of coughing. "Unless you wish to... to end up... being lectured on the River People and their merits and integrity, enemies or not." The old eyes looked him over shrewdly. "Also it kept you away from the developments in our areas; away from encounters with your former people, their raiding parties or our retaliating efforts."

His sense of wellbeing evaporated at once. "That was not my intention at all."

But the older man's smile held no reproach. "I didn't mean it as an accusation." The pale lips stretched in a kinder way. "You are a wise man and I approve of the manner in which you conduct yourself under the strangeness of your circumstances. You proceed wisely along your chosen path, and your loyalty is not doubted, not by the people who matter. Your loyalty to both your former and current people." The wide shoulders lifted in a shrug. "I wish we could help you with that by keeping the peace between both sides of our Great Sparkling Water, the way the Great Peacemaker wanted us to do, the way your father and I strove to achieve."

The warm coziness was returning, banishing the chill. "If only Father had not begun his travels to the Sky World so soon."

"Oh, yes, if only." The older man sighed, fending off another outburst of cough. "But when it comes to this particular undertaking, the peace between our peoples, it seems that the Evil Left-Handed Twin himself takes a special interest, thwarting all our efforts and plans."

"Father was trying so hard—"

The echoing footsteps heralded the return of their forceful company, with the Wolf Man bearing down on them, unhindered by protesting children this time.

"Dumped them on their cousins," he reported, panting. Dropping on the vacant mat near the fire, he let his breath out loudly. "My brother's daughters are old enough to watch after toddling babies, and if they stay in their longhouse while their entire clan went out preparing the fields, then they have only themselves to blame, lazy skunks that they are."

"Hanowa is still recovering from the winter sickness," protested the girls' grandfather, reproachful.

"And her cheeky fox of a sister?"

The older man raised his hands in the air, palms up, defeated. "Yes, this one must have stayed behind to laze around." A wide grin. "So yes, she got what she deserved. But she'll actually deal with your wild pair, you just wait and see. Even with little Takoskowa. She is a match for him. She'll manage."

"We'll hear her carrying on about it for moons, either boasting or complaining." Obviously somewhat less enamored, the girl's uncle rolled his eyes. "Why do they always have to be away and swamped with work just when we need them, those women?" His chuckle rolled down the corridor, deserted but for faint snores coming from one of the farther compartments. Then the lightness evaporated. "I'll be off with the first light."

The War Chief narrowed his eyes, the good-natured expression leaving his taut face as well. "Where to?"

"First Onondaga Town of course."

"Thought so." The older man nodded. "Then a swift stroll westwards?"

"No, it's too soon for that." The younger man hesitated, eyes resting on his father but lacking in focus, wandering through some inner worlds. "Or maybe yes, but not seeking an actual volunteering, not yet. Just preparing the ground. Clearing the field, one might say." The contemplative gaze focused, shifted, came to rest on Ogteah. "That's why I asked you to come here this time. I need to talk to you."

The memory of the unauthorized recruiting three summers ago made Ogteah's stomach flutter with anticipation.

"Will we receive official permission this time?" he asked, pushing the possible destination of those future recruitments aside. One thing at the time, and gathering warriors' forces, officially or less so, was the most pleasing activity, as satisfying as it was rewarding. His mind rushed through possibilities. Okwahli, the oldest Standing Stone brother and his various cousins would be involved, and some other of his former charges, the troublemaking elements of the Long Tails War he had kept close in touch with ever since.

"It depends," drawled the Wolf Man slowly, his smile one of the widest, an openly conspiratorial grin, full with as pleasant memories. "When the time comes to the actual recruitment, I believe we will have the permission to do that." The smile disappeared as quickly as it came. "But for now some of us will just travel around, sound people out. No need to bother the councils with any of that." The dark eyes narrowed, measuring Ogteah quite openly. "However, I would rather have you busy with a different sort of a mission."

"What?" For some reason he didn't like this gaze, the strange glee in it, the excited anticipation. "What would you rather have me doing?"

The man sprang to his feet with a startling suddenness. "How about we go for a walk, breathe some fresh air? This corridor is barely visible from all the smoke." A businesslike gaze leapt toward the older man. "Father? Are you up to a walk out there with us?"

The War Chief's smile flickered weakly. "Your mother would have me thrown out of our longhouse if I left without drinking that medicine she is sure to send here at the high noon. So you two go for a walk, and maybe I will join you later, toward the afternoon."

The younger man nodded thoughtfully, flashing an affectionate smile toward his sire. "We will be back before it happens."

Watching the old man recline on his bunk with obvious relief, Ogteah fought down a bad feeling. Somehow he didn't want to be involved in secret side missions. Not now that he had proven his worth and his ability to lead people. Why did he suspect it was something the Wolf Man wasn't sure about, something shady maybe, worthy of the old Ogteah from the other side and not the new man he had become?

"It would be refreshing to lead a huge force again, but one we were entrusted officially with," he said, as the thatched roof of the façade swept above their heads, giving way to the pleasantly soft rays of sun, satisfactorily strong for this time of the seasons, just before the summer moons hit.

"We won't get there that fast." Absently, his companion kicked at a thrown log, his gaze again wandering, busy with his inner thoughts. "But I do want to be prepared in advance, so when the need arises I'll be there, gathering our formidable force of warriors with no troubles and no delays." Another kick at the hapless log. "It was a near miss back at the Mountain People. Our lack of knowledge about the Long Tails and their war readiness was appalling. We could have been caught napping under the trees, or worse, not there at all, wandering with our monster of a force in the places we weren't even needed. Or not there in the first place, sending no help to our Western Door Keepers at all.

Think about it." The dark gaze focused, flew at Ogteah. "We knew something was going on, but the real extent of it was nowhere near to what I was expecting, and but for a few lucky developments, this first great victory of ours could have turned into our first great defeat. And then even the Great Spirits wouldn't have helped us, because certain elements among our enemies would have pounced on us without a second thought, regardless of their own war readiness. Wouldn't they?" The suggestively arched eyebrows were accompanied by a fleeting, somewhat mischievous grin. A difficult combination to resist. "Our lovely neighbors from across the Great Lake wouldn't think twice before plunging into their war canoes, would they?"

"No, they would not." Somehow, when this forceful warriors' leader dwelled on the subject of his former people, an often enough occurrence these days, Ogteah didn't feel threatened or pressed to be carefully noncommittal as with some others, even the War Chief himself. "But we were prepared and ready, and with a little help from the Great Spirits we did achieve a great victory instead of a sound defeat. So why would you fret about it now?"

His companion made a face. "I'm not fretting. Just not happy with the need to tread in the dark when it comes to our enemies and their dealings. We know painfully little and sometimes it's a real hindrance." Slowing his step in order to skirt around a row of extinguished fires, the man blew the air through his nostrils. "Take that much-lauded Long Tails' adventure of ours. Had we only known in advance that they were gathering warriors and in such numbers, planning to head here in force, we wouldn't have to go around the Great Council to gather our own forces. We would have their keen and eager blessing instead, and more help and encouragement than we would have known what to do with. It would have been easier and more pleasant, and we wouldn't have had to gamble and guess, chancing a great failure instead of a great victory." The man's prettily embroidered moccasins made a screeching sound as he stopped abruptly, facing Ogteah, forcing him to do the same. "Do you see what I mean? The simple knowledge of their intensive warriors gathering would have been enough. I wouldn't have asked for their war plans and exact numbers of their fighting forces, even though it could have been helpful to have those as well. But that would be too much to ask. What I would have settled for happily was the most basic information, the mere knowledge of the fact that they were going around, enlisting unusual amount of people or trying to do so, planning to cross that Ge-ne-see River. That's all." Another snort. "That limping leader of their, the enterprising grass-eater that he was and probably still is, bore watching. But we didn't watch him. We didn't even know of his existence, let alone his enterprising activities."

Agreeing in general with what had been said but at a loss as to where his companion was trying to get, Ogteah found it safer to shrug. It was not like the businesslike Wolf Man to reminisce about the past, glorious or doubtful or anything in between.

"How do you propose we should have gone about it, learning of this man's activities?" he asked, rolling a pebble with the tip of his moccasin, watching the half circle it drew in the dry earth.

"Through you. Or people like you, if there were more of your type around."

"What?" That got his attention off rolling pebbles and back toward his companion's smirking face in an instant. "Me? What's that has to do with me? I'm no Long Tail! I've never been to their lands and my knowledge of their minds or politics is no better than yours."

"No. But you are what you are, the perfect person for just that sort of a mission, and you know it as well as I do." The now-amused gaze flickered, challenging, mocking but in a friendly, genuinely appreciative way. "No one can blend into unfamiliar surroundings the way you do, strike easy friendships and be everyone's acquaintance in one single lousy evening, embraced and admitted by the locals as though you were one of them. I swear I kicked myself hard for not thinking about it back then, when we were milling around Tsonontowan, making its residents angry. I kept complaining about the uselessness of our scouts and the untrustworthiness of former adoptees from among the Long Tails until my brother said that if anyone could have gone into the enemy lands, sniffing around, it should have been you, the restless adventurous spirit that you are. That's when I kicked myself viciously for not thinking of that in time."

He couldn't help the chuckle that threatened to erupt into real laughter, imagining his formidable companion reaching to tear his prettily done warrior's lock out in frustration, spitting muttered curses along the way. He knew the man too well by now.

"I hope it hurt, that kick."

"You would." A hearty laughter was his answer. "But smirk and make jokes as you might, he was right, that brother of mine, the wise person that he is. You are made for such missions, and we should have asked you to do that back then."

"Instead of gathering warriors or fighting? Not sure I would have chosen to do that."

"No, not instead! Before, way before, brother. What use would your information have been to us if you told us about it when we were already milling around the Mountain People's lands? None, none whatsoever." The raised eyebrows made Ogteah feel stupid. "But if you went sniffing around there before, a whole season before or even more, when I had my inkling but nothing else to base my assumptions on, oh, then it would have made a great difference. Then your information would have saved us plenty of headache and unlawful actions. Not to mention that the fighting would have happened on the other side of that Genesee River, the *correct* side of it!"

"I see." Squinting against the sudden gust of wind, Ogteah nodded, unable not to appreciate the wisdom in such an innovative approach. "Yes, it could have been done, I suppose. But well, you didn't even know me back then. We have met much later, if you remember. I could barely speak your tongue in an understandable manner in those times, so I say, you missed nothing by not sending me straight away into your favorite enemy's claws. And you did achieve your great victory later on, so there is no point in kicking yourself about any of it anymore." He winked. "The post-deed wisdom is always the deepest. Didn't you know that?"

"And the most useless, yes, I know." The Wolf Man made a

face, then shrugged. "Unless one learns from it, and this is what I've been doing, Lone Hill's man of wisdom. Not reminiscing about the past for the sake of musing about it. Do you know me so little?"

Ogteah grinned back, unabashed. "Who knows?"

His companion's snort dissolved in the crispy air. "Cheeky grass-eater, that's what you are and always were." Then the grin came back. "It's never too late, they say, and not all our enemies lay as low as the filthy Long Tails do now, licking their wounds. Other people were active as you know, their alliances growing stronger, implacably inimical, set on the warpath since the sad event of four summers ago. The same event that must have pushed the Long Tails into their imprudent adventure."

He stopped listening, his stomach tightening in a hundred little knots. "I won't be spying on my former people!" It surprised him, the way his voice sounded, calm and firm, albeit with a strained tone to it. "Don't even think of suggesting something like that."

His companion's face hardened. "Why ever not?"

"Plenty of reasons and I won't go into any of them."

Their gazes locked and for a while the staring contest professed enough danger to make the air around them thickened.

Then the younger man shrugged and turned away. "Do as you please." The dark gaze retuned to Ogteah, considerably colder, holding just the slightest amount of disdain. "You may find it hard to reconcile your loyalties if that's the way you feel, now that your former countryfolk deem it wise to profess their warlike intentions. You will not be able to escape being involved, one way or another."

Ogteah drew a breath through his nostrils, his lips pursed too tightly to use them in this way. "I'll manage."

"I wish you luck with that." A snort and the wide back was upon him, drawing away resolutely, the decorations on the broad shoulders jumping with every firm step.

Ogteah stared at it until it disappeared behind the next building's wall.

ABOUT THE AUTHOR

Zoe Saadia is the author of several novels on pre-Columbian Americas. From the architects of the Aztec Empire to the founders of the Iroquois Great League, from the towering pyramids of Tenochtitlan to the longhouses of the Great Lakes, her novels bring long-forgotten history, cultures and people to life, tracing pivotal events that brought about the greatness of North and Mesoamerica.

To learn more about Zoe Saadia and her work, please visit
www.zoesaadia.com

Made in United States
North Haven, CT
27 June 2022

20655360R00307